Spring Fling

Also by the Authors

By Julia Kent
Random Acts of Trust
Her Billionaires: Boxed Set

By Sara Fawkes
Breathe Into Me
Anything He Wants

By Cathryn Fox
Silk in Whispering Cove
Cowboy's Way
Pleasure Exchange
Pleasure Prolonged

By Lauren Hawkeye
Pink
Three Little Words
Seduced by the Gladiator
My Wicked Gladiators

Spring Fling

A NEW ADULT ANTHOLOGY

JULIA KENT
SARA FAWKES
CATHRYN FOX
LAUREN HAWKEYE

red
AVON
IMPULSE

An Imprint of HarperCollins Publishers

Excerpt from "Take Me" originally published in *Fling*. Copyright © 2013 by Sara Fawkes.

Excerpt from "Teach Me" originally published in *Fling*. Copyright © 2013 by Cathryn Fox.

Excerpt from "Tame Me" originally published in *Fling*. Copyright © 2013 by Lauren Hawkeye.

"Share Me." Copyright © 2014 by Julia Kent.

"Shake Me." Copyright © 2014 by Sara Fawkes.

"Show Me." Copyright © 2014 by Cathryn Fox.

"Shock Me." Copyright © 2014 by Lauren Hawkeye.

EPub Edition MARCH 2014 ISBN: 9780062328533

Print Edition ISBN: 9780062328557

10 9 8 7 6 5 4 3

Spring Fling

SHARE ME

By Julia Kent

To good girls gone wild. Some of us just take longer than others.

One

"YOU ARE NOT breaking up with me," Emma hissed, twisting the quarter-carat engagement ring her fiancé, Ryan, slipped on her finger seven months ago, the Labor Day before their senior year of college had begun. A light breeze and sunny skies had made the day perfect, with his sun-kissed hair flopping into his eyes—those warm, hazel eyes so puppy-dog in love that her own heart had felt it couldn't contain all her happiness.

"I am, Emma. I am." Those same eyes now turned down with sadness and a kind of pity that scared her more than his words. He was serious. Ryan was shattering her entire world, right here, right now. The painted cinder-block walls of her dorm room suddenly looked like prison walls. Who decided to paint concrete? They should name the paint Soviet Gray. Soul-sucking Gray.

Dementor Gray.

"No." The word came out of her mouth like a bark,

ferocious and insistent. "We booked the church! And paid the deposit for the caterer and blocks of rooms at the hotel next to the stone barn where the reception will be . . ."

"This isn't an argument," he said gently, coming closer but avoiding touching her. Ryan played football for their small liberal arts college, and carried the muscled weight of a linebacker. "You can't reason your way out of this."

"Yes I can! Because you're being unreasonable. Why would you do this?"

"People change." Say it, Ryan. Here it comes.

"Because people change."

"You never change, Ryan! You wear the same concert T-shirts you've worn since we started dating in high school. You've ordered the same meal at every Chinese restaurant we've ever gone to. You sleep in the same position, and you—" *You orgasm the same way. With that screwed-up face and a victory shout like you're an extra in the porny version of* Braveheart.

"You're the one who never changes, Emma. I wear those shirts because you like them. I order that food because you want me to share it with you. I do everything your way, and now, honey, it's time to do one thing my way."

"Breaking up is not the same as ordering lettuce wraps for dinner!" she shouted, incredulous.

"I didn't say it was. It's just—"

"But what about *me*?" Emma's throat began to close. It was the first week of March and they were graduating in ten weeks. A summer of work to save up, and then Harvard Law for her, and whatever law school Ryan got into (but it had to be near Boston, of course). A wedding in August a year later. A honeymoon in the tropics. Kids after she made partner at a big law firm. Everything was laid out like a blueprint in her mind, carefully drawn by a meticulous architect's hand to craft a life that was orderly, predetermined, and destined for success.

But life threw you curveballs. They'd both learned that the hard way, five years ago. A year into dating, during their senior year of high school, Ryan had been diagnosed with testicular cancer. Emma had been by his side every step of the way. Remission had come quickly, but the real hurdle would be the five-year all-clear. Ryan's appointment was next week, and then—Emma hoped—they could both just breathe.

"You'll be fine," he soothed. "Someone will come along one day and appreciate and love you the way you deserve to be loved."

That was supposed to be you.

"Who is she?" Emma rasped.

"She's no one. There is no she."

A cold wave washed over her. "He?" If Ryan had discovered he was gay, at least they could remain friends. Having a gay ex-fiancé held a certain cachet, too. *No, I had no idea. He hid it so well, although the fact that he never . . . you know . . . went down . . . should have been my first clue . . .*

And then none of this would be her fault. Because

otherwise, all the responsibility was about to be thrust on her shoulders. That was the cold reality of how this worked: when you get dumped, it must be *you*.

"He what?"

"Is the she a he?"

"Is the what a what?"

"Are you gay? G-A-Y."

His thick eyebrows shot up, leaving those hazel eyes round, his face comical.

"God, no, I'm no fudgepacker," he insisted. His eyes narrowed. "Where'd you hear that?"

"Fudgepacker? Seriously? C'mon, Ryan, your own brother is gay. Don't use slurs like that."

His face went slack, then red with fury. "That's exactly why I'm ending this."

Words failed her. A tight ball of disbelief bounced in her chest.

Ryan seemed to struggle with the silence, leg jumping up and down, making the bed vibrate. Finally, he added, "It's not you. It's me."

More clichés.

"My heart is breaking in a thousand pieces right now," he added.

What's next? Let me guess. "I'm just not ready for a relationship with anyone right now, but . . ."

"Emma, I'm not really ready to be married right now. But if I were, you'd be my first choice."

"Six years," she finally gasped. "Six years together and you throw it away like . . ."

Ryan pressed his lips together and sat on the edge of her bed, fiddling with his class ring.

"I can't accept this. We can fix whatever's wrong," she begged.

"What's wrong is you."

Shock choked whatever words she wanted to say. And then she found her voice. "Are you sick? Is that why you're so . . . so . . . different?" They'd been dating a year, were seniors in high school, when he was diagnosed with testicular cancer. She'd been by his side every step of the way.

"Not sick."

"Is this about Harvard?" Her early acceptance letter had arrived this week. "Are you jealous?"

"Oh, Emma. Just . . . why would you . . . ?" She'd flustered him. Aha. An angle. As long as she could keep him talking, maybe she could talk him *out* of this.

"It *is* about Harvard, isn't it?" A cold dread filled her as she stood and walked across the room, mercifully escaping his bobbing legs, that nervous twitch of his driving her mad. She wondered what she looked like to him right now. Long black hair in an oily top knot. Pink yoga pants too long, the cuffs tattered from scraping on the floor. A torn college sweatshirt. If you're going to get dumped, you want to at least have brushed your teeth and be attractive enough to make him waver.

"Why now?" she asked. Questions swirled through her mind as her ring dug into the base of her finger, feeling like a handcuff.

And not in a good way.

His hesitation made ice flow through her. "You *are* sick! You said you had an oncologist visit coming up. But that's next week!"

"They had a cancellation and I went yesterday," he said, clearly uncomfortable.

She crossed the room and reached out to touch him, the warmth relaxing her. Whatever was wrong, they could overcome it. He was being gracious, trying to spare her feelings—break up with her so she wouldn't have to go through the cancer with him again. *Oh, Ryan.* This was the man she knew so well.

"What did they say?"

Those big hazel eyes looked right through her as he shifted and twitched. *Oh, please please please please, God, I'll do whatever you say. Don't make us go through the inpatient complications, the puking, missing Homecoming—all of it.*

Please.

"I'm clean. Five year checkup is done and Dr. Miller told me he never wants to see my face again." What should have brought a huge grin and a hug instead left Ryan with a hangdog expression.

"That's wonderful!" she squealed, throwing her arms around him.

It was like hugging a rock.

Confusion coursed through her. She pulled away. "So the worst is over. Did they talk about sperm counts and fertility chances? Because we're on track for kids in nine or ten years, and if there's a chance we can—"

"Emma. *Emma.* Stop!" he barked, putting distance between them. "Just stop."

"You don't have to break up with me now! You're healthy! You don't need to try to spare my feelings and—"

"Where did you get that idea?" The hardness in his eyes made her head spin.

"Then you're still ending this?"

He nodded.

"Why?" She sounded like a wounded animal. Like Nancy Kerrigan after getting the crowbar to the knee.

"Because I've just been thinking, and there's no reason to wait. I'm done."

"Done? Done, like you've blown your load and you're done?"

"No need to get vulgar, Emma." Ryan's eyes registered shock and dismay. She never spoke this way. Always the good girl, always friendly; profanity was a last resort, as if her DNA fought against it.

"Fuck!" she chirped. "Shit! Damn! Cocksucker!"

"I said I'm not gay!" Ryan protested.

"I wasn't using it that way, you asshole."

"Hold on—name-calling really isn't—"

"Jerk." This felt good. A little too good. The anger and resentment and the flood of all the wedding preparations she needed to undo—it washed over her like a tsunami, carrying her sputtering and gasping for air, drowning under a tidal wave she was powerless to stop, much less fight against. She would make call after call, send e-mail after e-mail, endure pitiful look after pitiful back pat— and Ryan would just walk away.

I can do so much better than you.

"You can do so much better than me," Ryan said, as if reading her mind. For all she knew, he had a cheat sheet scribbled on one palm.

Six years. Six years of planning and organizing and coordinating. Six years—much of it worried about him in the shadow of cancer, struggling to remain placid and sweet, knowing that if she were just *good* enough, if she were just *on top* of everything, nothing bad could happen.

Nothing could go wrong if she just gave enough. Tried hard enough.

All the years of planning, orchestrating her way to high school valedictorian, choosing the perfect volunteer opportunities (candy striper) and part-time jobs (animal shelter worker). Straight A's through AP courses and a 4.8 average meant she'd rocketed through undergrad in three years, but took an extra year to earn a master's degree just so she could be here with Ryan.

Gone. All of it gone at the whim of the dull-eyed man in front of her.

Something snapped in her.

"Asshat." The word came out like a bleat, a blurted insult she didn't know she knew.

Ryan pursed his lips and looked away.

"Hosebeast."

"What's a—"

"Twatwaffle."

"Is that even a word? Now you're just randomly shoving words together."

"Premature ejaculator."

"Emma," he growled.

"Nose picker."

He shrugged.

"And eater."

"I never did that."

And she thought that one would send him over the edge, but *noooooo*. It took:

"Pinky dick."

Holding her breath, she caught his eye. What had been wishy-washy and mealy-mouthed in her (ex) fiancé turned into a sharp retaliation as he said his response on the in-breath, giving the words an ethereal rasp.

"You fat, controlling, egotistical bitch."

And there it was.

A slow golf clap was her only response, all the words caught behind a giant lump in her throat that gagged her.

I gave you everything.

Ryan's brow furrowed and he swallowed so hard it sounded like a bullet clicking into a chamber.

Which, in a way, it was.

That sound was the death of her future. The cancer had threatened to steal it. And now? Ryan's freedom from the cancer seemed to be stealing it, too.

She couldn't win.

"I can accept 'controlling,'" she replied, a sort of disgust coating her body, like a force field she hadn't asked for but had just appeared. "'Egotistical' is a bit much, considering the fact that I've tolerated your narcissism for so long. That, and your pinky dick."

He seemed baffled by her calm demeanor, as he reddened.

"But 'fat'? Really? From a linebacker?"

"I'm muscle," he insisted.

"Beer muscle." In five years he'd be that guy, the one who hung out at the local sports bar and waxed rhapsodic about his glory days playing football for a school best known for finally admitting men in the 1990s and for its mascot, Zoinkies, a bizarre mesh of Barney the Dinosaur and Pooh the Bear. Zoinkies had three legs (for no apparent reason), which meant everyone—from sportscasters to freshman—just called him Tripod. "How can you call me fat? So I have the freshman fifteen—"

"Kilos," he muttered.

"You're dumping me because I'm fat?"

"I'm breaking up because I can't stand being with you anymore."

That was blunt. She could handle blunt better than clichéd.

"What happened to the wild girl I met sophomore year of high school? The one who got high in the cooler at the school restaurant, who listened to hard rock while suntanning on the roof of the school?"

A wisp of a nostalgic smile on his face made Emma close her eyes, exhaling deeply.

"She's still here," she insisted, holding her hand over her heart, as if keeping it in place. "But that's not what you needed. Not after . . ." The words weren't necessary. Ryan's diagnosis had changed them both, deeply and irrevocably. How could she drink with her friends under the bleachers at football games on Friday nights when he was recovering from chemo infusions? What kind of girlfriend went out teepeeing the trees and bushes of soccer players when her boyfriend had an infected lymph node?

"You always have to be right, Emma. *Always*. And it's not fair and it certainly isn't attractive." The bite of his words had a resignation. Alarm bells went off inside her. Resignation was worse than anger. Apathy worse than disgust. Once he hardened himself to her, that was it. No convincing him to stay.

And as he said, she always had to be right.

Right?

He spat the words out like broken teeth, sputtering through the last sentence. "I'm reevaluating my entire life and—"

"You get the gold medal of cancer treatment—the five-year all-clear—and you decide it's time to *dump me*?" A metallic taste and a rush of saliva made her mouth hard to move, the words disjointed and dissociated, as if she hovered over them, watching the syllables float out her mouth.

A crack in her voice made Ryan wince. He closed his eyes and nodded slowly. "I decided I need to live a different life."

No. Just . . . no. "I stopped being wild for you. Quit drinking, ditched all my partying friends, became good for you. Ryan," she pleaded, "I have to be right because if I don't micromanage and plan and calculate, the world might stop making sense." And your cancer might come back, she thought.

But he just said it wouldn't.

It was all too much.

"I never asked for all of that," he answered, words slow and even.

Outraged gasps sputtered out of her, one after the other. "You—what? You never asked for that? Of course you never asked for it. When someone loves you, that's what they *do*." Emma pressed the pads of her fingers against her lips, the soft hush of her breath hot as she exhaled, air coming in through her nostrils, down into her lungs, pressing her diaphragm out, sorrow filling her, disbelief exiting. Too numb to cry, all she could do was stare blankly at Ryan.

Pain twisted through his face. "And thank you. Really." He bent down and touched her knee with a kindness she didn't expect. Locking eyes, his were grief-filled and resolute. "But that's not a reason for me to stay in a relationship I just don't want anymore, with a woman who has been taken over by fear."

Fear. Wild. Good. Bad. Always right. His words whipped through her mind like a whirling dervish.

"It should count for *something*." Fury pushed the disbelief out of her and took its place.

"It does," he said, faltering.

She knew, though, that he didn't mean it. Somewhere inside, he'd decided he was done with her. Along the years she'd changed, and he had changed, and while she assumed they would change together, right now Ryan was perfectly clear that he didn't want her as she was.

And that was the only Emma she could be right now.

Brushing his hand off her knee, she stood, a shimmering anger building inside. Ryan was breaking up with her and she had no choice. No words she said would matter. His face was a mask, as emotional as an Easter Island statue. All the years of making sure that the world made sense within tiny little compartments, each designed to hold one part of her shattered heart as she showed a cheerful, good face to Ryan and the world. Far too many comebacks swallowed in restraint, so many wild friends carefully weeded out, her entire adulthood (so far) marked by making Ryan the center of everything, she in his orbit.

And now, just when all that work, all that sacrifice, all that love and focus and determination had paid off, he—

Left her?

Emma crossed the room, slid open the closet door and stared at the crooked stack of scrapbooks that held the equivalent of sixteen credit hours of work, except she would receive no A for what was in them.

These were for her wedding.

Carefully color coded, the books represented more than just hours. They were the embodiment of her future, of overcoming a past that started with shedding her old party-girl self and turning into someone else. Each scrapbook gave her a glimpse into her future self as Ryan's wife. Cutting pictures from magazines, comparing shades of peach and hues of gray, examining the sheen of ribbons in thirteen colors of beige—all that work was less about

the frivolity of appearance and more about the investment of her soul into a future that was a payoff for so
much pain.

Pain. A pink, roiling cloud of fury filled her eyes as she
went numb, then flushed with heat, instinct kicking in as
she reached for the taupe book marked INVITATIONS.

"This is the book with invitation patterns." Heavy and
gravid, the book felt serious. Sedate. Respectable.

She flung it at him, striking him straight in the belly.
It fell to the ground with a satisfying *thwack!*

"What the hell, Emma?" he shouted, rubbing his
navel.

"And this one has shades of fabric for the bridesmaids
dresses." The weight of it in her arm made her triceps
burn as she heaved it, smacking against the wall behind
his head.

Ryan edged toward the door, decidedly uncomfortable with this impromptu game of Wedding Plan Dodge-
ball.

"You're losing it," he mumbled, hand on the door-
knob.

"Here we have the sex toy party I'd planned—"

"Sex toys?" The sudden interest, the lascivious tone,
made her blind with red rage.

"Ugh!" she shouted, heaving a final scrapbook. Her
favorite.

The Honeymoon.

It hit the intended target, catching Ryan below the
eye, sending him backward like a contestant on *Wipeout*,
his legs staying in place until he dropped to his knees, the

crack of bone on linoleum triggering a simple satisfaction in her.

You're terminated, fucker.

"*I* am breaking up with *you!*" she shouted, triumphant. Inside, she shook so badly her heart may have descended into her vagina, but on the outside all she wanted was for Ryan to wipe that stupid, smug, empty look off his face.

And seventy pages of glued-on pictures of tropical honeymoon sites had done what no words could.

"You aren't a fat bitch. You're a crazy bitch!"

"I'm a crazy bitch who stood by your side through *everything*. And this is what I get?" She pushed against his shirt, finding the touch of him repulsive. To think she'd just slept with him last night. That stopped her cold.

"You made love with me last night, knowing you were doing this?"

He took two more steps, into the hall, and turned back. The skin under his eye was red and a thin welt ran from under the corner of his eye to the bridge of his nose. Ouch.

A trickle of compassion started its flow in her, until he said: "No, Emma, I didn't make love to you. I fucked you with the precision you so specifically demand. You received seven deep kisses, five minutes of finger fucking, and about three minutes of pumping. Then you pretended to come."

She clapped a hand over her mouth. *He knew?*

"And then I had to think about anyone but you to finish up. And before you ask: Scarlett Johansson."

"Oh!" Her stomach fell nine thousand floors, like an elevator in free fall.

"You're boring, Emma. You want to know the real reason I'm done? *You're boring.*" His good eye took in her figure. "I can't spend the rest of my life with someone who's too afraid to live."

Two

"I AM SOOOOO glad Casey got food poisoning!"

Emma stared, hard, at her friend Melissa. Some of the stupidest shit came out of her mouth.

A little tact-challenged but still fundamentally good, her friend picked up on Emma's dropped jaw and corrected herself. "I mean, I'm so glad you were able to take her spot on this trip!"

"Me, too." *I think.* The past three weeks had been a complete blur. Ryan's mom had called to apologize for creating a human being who would do this. Emma's dad had told her not to worry—the deposits were all refundable, given Emma's obsessive need to book all the service providers and event locations eighteen months in advance.

"Some lucky bride and groom will grab your spots, dear," he said.

"That's not helpful, Daddy," she told him through gritted teeth.

Karma kicked in on a minor level then when she became the beneficiary of a cancellation: a group of friends going to New Orleans for senior year Spring Break had an opening.

Emma had never gone on a Spring Break trip that didn't involve helping build homes for charity or cleaning exam rooms in Central American vaccination clinics. The girls who went on those crazy, hedonistic trips were just having fun.

Emma was the girl who contributed to society.

You're boring.

Ryan's words had wounded her. Haunted her. Etched themselves in her soul. Even the fat comment didn't hurt as much as being told that the Emma she'd built, extracurricular by extracurricular, grade by grade, résumé entry by résumé entry, just wasn't enough.

Giving up speech team to spend Saturdays with him during chemo that year, skipping Homecoming because he was too nauseated, becoming a candy striper at the hospital after seeing how lonely other patients were—patients who didn't have someone as devoted as Emma by their side—was all tossed aside like an old toy on Christmas morning.

She was tossed aside. She wasn't enough.

So what was?

Plagued by questions Ryan wouldn't answer, and upon learning that he—long ago, without her knowledge—had booked his own Spring Break soiree on South Padre

Island, she decided to indulge in the ultimate service project:

The Unboring of Emma Barton.

"That guy is totally checking us out!" Melissa whispered on the plane. A prettier version of Barbie, Melissa was being kind. The tall, dark, handsome, wide-shouldered, cobra-backed god in a silk Calvin Klein T-shirt and jeans so sculpted to his ass they seemed shrink-wrapped, was most definitely not looking at her, Emma thought.

"Hot guy in D3," announced a voice in front of them. Heather and Jordan, party girls from her dorm and super tight with Melissa, turned around and leered at her. Popping an earbud out of her right ear, Heather pulled the scrunchie out of her brown ponytail and ran her fingers through her hair while Jordan smirked at Emma in a way that always made her feel like she was being judged.

Both were practically pulling out the popcorn to watch this.

"Hi there," he said toward them, twisting while standing, shoving his carry-on into the upper bin.

Emma gave a feeble wave. Swoon. Thick, black, curly hair and olive-toned skin made her want to lick him and taste the ocean. An accent. A hint of something Mediterranean in his baritone, dulcet tones made her wet, the sudden discomfort and throbbing need so disturbing she almost bolted off the plane.

TSA would nab her if she did that, and then she'd be on a No Fly list, and that would mean she couldn't get a good legal internship after her 1L year at Harvard Law, and—

An elbow dug into her ribs. "Say hi back," hissed Melissa through gritted teeth, a fake smile on her face. "He's totally hitting on us."

"Stop saying *us*," Emma replied through her own fake smile. Melissa was slim and willowy, while she was curvy. Stacked. Voluptuous.

Most definitely not fat, though. *Fuck you, Ryan.*

"Maybe if we're lucky it will be us. Ever done a three-some?"

Blink. Choke. A fit of shocked coughs wracked her body, plumes of color exploding behind closed eyelids. What kind of trip was this?

"And I don't mean the kind with you, your boyfriend, and the giant dildo," Melissa added helpfully.

Dildo? Ryan was so vanilla he'd balked at the idea of a flavored condom.

"I can't help but insert . . . myself into a hushed conversation about dildos," Hot Guy said, now seated, leaning across the aisle with a sophisticated elegance that made Emma think of a magazine spread come to life.

You see models in *Vogue* and *Esquire,* and you drool and make "I'd tap that" jokes with your girlfriends. But no one in your life is really like that.

And then one day he's leaning across the aisle of a puddle jumper, smelling like citrus and dirt and musk and making you want to hump an armrest, and you realize that those models aren't all products of Photoshop airbrushing and the best horny imaginations of young twenty-something interns.

By God, they're real.

Talking about dildos with you.

"No, I do not have those kinds of threesomes, either," Emma said furiously, the sentence preprogrammed into her mind, slipping out like a neural impulse in the space of silence right after Hot Guy made his endearing comment.

He leaned in closer, fingers resting on her forearm, the sensual touch like a clit stroke. "What kind of threesomes do you enjoy?"

Beep. Emma's brain rebooted. Out of commission. Her clit, on the other hand, jumped from the backseat into the driver's seat, finally ready to see what this body could really do in fifth gear on an open road.

An open road named . . .

"Miklós Stannos."

Oh, my. "I'm Emma Barton." She smiled with her entire face, eyes wide and interested.

"You're Greek," Melissa gasped.

"Close. Half Greek and half—"

"Hungarian," Emma said with him.

His eyes lit up and one eyebrow rose. "You are Hungarian?"

"My grandmother was. Her name was Erzsébet. And her father was—"

"Miklós." They said it in unison, the way Emma remembered it. MEEK-losh.

"Then you know my nickname."

"Miki." She fluttered her eyelashes.

"You're practically related," Melissa muttered, reaching for the airline magazine. "Could be committing incest," she said under her breath. "That's bad."

Emma's turn to jab her in the ribs. She hit Melissa's boob. "That's for when we land," she joked, winking.

At least she hoped that was a joke.

"What are you doing in New Orleans, Ms. Emma Hungarian?" Was he flirting with her? Unbelievable. From the daggers Melissa was shooting at both of them, Emma assumed the answer was yes.

"It's my final year of college, and in the fall I start law school—"

"Impressive. Where?"

"Harvard." The word rolled off her tongue with a rush. She still couldn't really believe she'd done it. Made it to Harvard. And now she and Ryan would move there and—

Correction. She. Just her. A pang of recognition made her belly ache.

"Doubly impressive. I went there." Miki brought her back to the conversation. Her ears perked up.

"For law?"

"No—to the Kennedy School. I earned a Ph.D. in Public Policy."

Miki looked like he was close in age to her. "How old are you?" she blurted out.

"Twenty-four."

"You just graduated?"

He shook his head, eyes only on her, completely consumed by her words. No casual interest. No games. Just a genuine, focused attention that rattled her.

In the best possible way.

"I graduated two years ago and went to work in international development."

Her turn to frown. "Why New Orleans, then?"

"Hurricane Katrina."

"That was eight years ago."

He shook his head sadly. "It might as well have been last year for some areas. I've been sent to study why some areas are still not repaired."

She could listen to him read the manual for her printer with marbles in his mouth. That accent. So cultured and beautiful.

"You're contributing to the greater good. I love that. I'm that way, too."

"Oh?" he brightened. "Are you on a service trip? Working for Habitat for Humanity?"

"I—" Shit. Any other time she could have said yes, but no. Right now she was just ready to get her drink on and fuck anything with a dick.

A well-wrapped dick. One with an amazing accent . . .

Those eyes. That mouth. Telling him the truth might make him turn away. So she told a half-truth. A three-quarters truth.

A mostly true truth.

"Every year I do a service project for Spring Break," she answered solemnly. *Except this year.*

"That is wonderful. A woman after my own heart." Miki took her hand and stretched it across the tiny aisle, placing it on his own heart.

Hers slammed in her chest, wriggling around with

good effort down her esophagus, into her stomach, biking over her ovaries, and swimming through her juices to land in her pussy.

The Ironclit Triathlon.

She wasn't after his heart. But she'd take other body parts . . .

"We're not fixing houses or saving the whales or giving orphans foot massages," Melissa burbled, pointing to a $499 cuticle remover in the in-flight catalog. "What do you think of that?" she whispered to Emma.

Miki pulled his hand away from Emma's and frowned. "But you just said . . . Did I misunderstand?" he asked.

"Every other year that I've gone on a Spring Break vacation, I've gone on service trips," she explained, stomping on Melissa's foot.

"Ow!"

"Sorry," Emma said with a tight smile. "Tight quarters. These airlines pack us in like sardines."

"Vindictive sardines," Melissa hissed.

"We all need some fun in our lives," Miki mused. Good catch.

"I've spent my entire life following the rules and being the good girl." The words tumbled out before she could stop herself. Those soulful eyes, focused solely on her. His lips were the perfect shade of pink, molded as if they were meant for luscious encounters. Hands manicured and strong, with strong wrists that glinted with a smattering of dark hair. A wristwatch—how quaint. No one her age wore a watch. It added to his allure.

As did the way his shoulders bent as he pulled back,

the tapering of his chest like an inverted triangle, muscle nipping in at the waist to what she imagined was a perfectly seamless stomach, bisected by a beautiful black leather belt with a silver buckle.

If she could just place her flat palm against that belly and sip a shot of tequila from his navel, her life would be complete.

"What is wrong with rules? They keep society in order," Miki said, frowning.

"Nothing's wrong with rules. At all. I wouldn't be a lawyer if I didn't like rules," she said, an airy fake-sounding laugh.

"But you just said . . ."

"Arbitrary rules about what people should and shouldn't do, based on applying a moral standard of their own making to someone else—that's what I am talking about."

"Ah. Morality. So easy to blame when you can't give yourself permission to do what your heart wants."

A slow uncoiling of want began made her pulse pound, her heart speeding to catch her racing mind as the implication of Miki's words tapped into an older part of her, the wild, wanton Emma from six years ago, the young woman she'd been *before*. Before Ryan's cancer, before she'd bargained with God that if she were just good enough, could he please let her boyfriend survive?

She had held up her end of the deal. So had God.

But Ryan . . .

The rush of desire as she locked eyes with Miki threatened to undo years of a constructed self. Who was she without Ryan? Without her bargain?

Without restraint?

She needed air. Space. Time to think without those tempting eyes on her, bewitching and inviting.

The plane was about to take off, though, and she couldn't just leave, so the second best option kicked in. Standing, she smiled as politely as possible and said, "Excuse me," heading toward the back bathroom. Most passengers were settled in now, waiting for the pre-takeoff announcements, and a thin sheen of sweat broke out all over her body. Just a few minutes alone in a bathroom designed to hold human beings the size of one of her thighs should give her the solitude she needed to reset.

As fate would have it, the bathroom was unoccupied. She opened the tiny door, stepped in, and began to close it when a hard obstacle stopped her. Puzzled, she turned back to see a head of dark curls dip in, push gently against her, and then slip around, shut the door, and flip the switch to Occupied.

Hot breath pushed against her neck, along with one hell of a thick bulge against her navel as Miki's hot wall of muscle pressed into her. With nowhere to put her arms, she found herself sliding them around his waist, the T-shirt he wore as soft and yielding as she'd imagined, his torso hard and ribbed under her touch. Inhaling meant taking in his scent, the exotic mix of spice and citrus and arousal sending her into overload.

"What does your heart want, Emma?" he asked, eyes narrowed, staring at the engagement ring on her left hand.

"Oh, God, no!" she whispered. "The engagement ended

three weeks ago." Idiot! She'd forgotten she was still wearing the ring.

But had she really? Was she wearing it out of habit? Or fear?

"Then no other man has your heart?"

"No other man has anything of mine."

The crush of his mouth on hers sent her stumbling backward, but his hands planted firmly on her ass pulled her into him, the wet need growing to a pulsing ache as she did the unthinkable: made out with someone other than Ryan in an airplane bathroom on her way to New Orleans to get her fuck on.

She always was an overachiever. Nothing like starting before the plane even took off.

His hand slid under the waistband of the same yoga pants she'd cursed earlier, gaining easy, fluid access to her bare ass, then sliding over her hips as his tongue danced with hers, lips nipping and sucking, pulling her lower lip between both of his with a motion that made her knees melt. No one had ever kissed her like this. She didn't know you *could* be kissed like this.

And then that hand moved forward, and with the grace of an artisan his finger slid between her newly waxed skin and found the beacon throbbing red and screaming for attention. Miki's mouth, his fingers, the way his arms moved across her body, how his legs held strong and pressed into her—he devoured her like a man who possessed her.

How could someone she'd just met have her pinned

like this, a frenzied vortex in seconds under the sheer force of his desire? As logical Emma clawed her way to the surface, Miki dipped two fingers inside her dripping self and used his thumb to stroke her pleading clitoris. Bucking against his hand, she rode him hard, fingers shoving into her as his thumb stroked her to ecstasy. Logical Emma was ridden out of town, tarred and feathered, as Lusty Emma took over.

"Oh, God," she moaned in his mouth. Nothing she'd experienced with Ryan—her one and only—had prepared her for Miki. Adrenaline and lust pumped through her as his fingers hooked up and stroked some secret spot inside her that made whatever veneer of propriety remained disappear completely. A small mewling noise in the back of her throat turned to a loud scream that came out as a strange hiss, Miki's mouth muting it as his tongue sought to drown it out, the flick of his thumb against her slick skin strumming her to what Ryan had never accomplished.

The orgasm slammed her body, Miki's fingers following her contortions as she writhed in ecstasy, his other arm firmly on her ass, keeping her hips and breasts smashed against him, tight control all his as she moaned into his mouth, her breath impossible to catch.

This frantic energy made her feel like clawing his skin, the releases—now in receding pulses—driving away all thought.

With a shudder, she went limp against him just as a sharp rap on the door jolted her. His half grin, sultry and teasing, made heat shoot to her pussy once more as he began to lick his fingers and answered, "Yes?"

"The plane is about to take off. Please find your seat," said a female flight attendant.

Emma pulled her pants up and realized how wet she was: her hairline was soaked with sweat, and a small spot of moisture poked through her cami where her breasts met.

And then there were the completely soaked panties . . .

"Emma," he whispered.

Rap rap rap.

Miki opened the door and moved with such grace and swiftness she wondered if he was supernatural, if she'd conjured the image of what had just happened in her mind. The line between reality and dreams was tenuous at best, like her sanity these days. On what planet did something like this happen to her?

A quick look in the mirror showed her eyes she didn't know. Her own brown eyes, the deep, earnest chocolate brown that Ryan had told her was so beautiful and "girl next door" now had a wild, untamed look.

More like "hussy next door."

She rather liked that.

Miki. In a few seconds she would open that door, walk back to her seat, and . . . what? Pretend that it never happened? Act as if the first orgasm she'd ever had with a man hadn't just happened with a complete stranger she'd met fifteen minutes ago? Who'd licked his hand to savor her juices?

Ryan wouldn't even go there. Said he didn't like the taste.

Men were out there who did. What other kinds of

men had she missed out on? Squaring her shoulders, she opened the bathroom door, caught the glare of two whispering flight attendants who shot her sidelong, disapproving looks, and made her way back to her seat.

Two knowing eyes greeted her as she sat down in her seat, flustered, sure that everyone on the plane could read the emotions on her face and smell her . . . excitement. Miki motioned to her, then hiked his hips up off the seat and reached into his back pocket. He handed her a white square.

A business card. Miklós Stannos, Ph.D. Program Manager for a major nongovernmental organization anyone who read *People* would recognize.

"Emma, when you have a spare moment in New Orleans, give me a call. We all need to have some more . . . fun, and you've convinced me."

"Convinced you of what?"

"That perhaps I can be of service in helping you to put aside the morality you have engrained in you and help draw out the real you." There was no mistaking what he was offering as his eyes roamed languidly over her body, making her wish she'd chosen something other than a purple cami and yoga pants for the flight. At least she wasn't wearing flip-flops.

The lust in his expression made her body pulse with a craven need to have him in her, to feel the rush of his skin against her cheek, his thighs against hers, the tight thrust of a man wanting her. Now. Mile High Club membership had never appealed to her, but if she was reevaluating her life, this was one area she definitely needed to reconsider.

Would he join her in the bathroom again?

"Thank you," she stammered. "I don't have a card . . ."

"Then write your phone number on me."

On your cock, gladly. "On my hand," he explained, pulling a pen from his pants pocket. Uncapping it with his mouth, he handed her the fine silver pen, the weight of which made her feel more mature. This was no cheap Bic ballpoint. As her hand grasped his and steadied it, a jolt of energy passed between them. This was the hand he had just used on her. She could smell herself. Pressing the pen down to write the letters, she found her core shaking from within, as if a magnetic force were pulling, pulling, where he had just caressed the epicenter.

And Miki was the magnet itself.

A vision of his body above hers, her legs wrapped around him, hips bowed and open for the animal rutting she wanted, invaded by lust, slammed by pure, uncontrollable passion—

"Are you cold?" he whispered.

Hot as fuck. Cheeks blazing and voice uncertain, she started to answer him when a melodic, professional voice interrupted them.

"Dr. Stannos?"

Doctor.

"I am so sorry to interrupt," said the flight attendant, who was eyeing Miki like he was her dinner. She very certainly was not sorry. "Your upgrade to first class has gone through, and you may be seated next to Mr. Collins now."

"Oh," he said quietly, a mixture of disappointment and determination sending Emma into a cotton-headed world of confusion.

Standing slowly, he unfolded those taut legs and opened the overhead bin, retrieving his luggage. The flight attendant shot Emma an impertinent smirk.

Bitch. I'm totally making you give me four bags of chocolate-covered pretzels to make up for this.

Miki turned and bent down to Emma's eye level. "Please call me." He held the hand with her number aloft. "And I will call you. I cannot take a shower until I do." Smile. Eyes. Hotness.

"Yes," she said breathlessly.

And then he was gone, various female heads craning toward the aisle as he passed, watching a butt that even Michelangelo could not have carved.

Only God.

"That was a little too close for comfort," Melissa rasped.

"Huh?"

"You don't want to hook up with some international development dude who whizzed through grad school in record time and who would fulfill every one of your OCD, anal retentive fantasies, Emma."

"What? Of course I do! Are you nuts?" *And I did,* she almost added.

"No. I'm realistic. The whole point of this trip is for you to let your hair down and fuck whatever comes your way that you like. This is New Orleans. Spring Break. It's like a buffet of dicks. Pick the ones you like and leave the rest behind."

"A buffet of dicks?"

"An all-you-can-eat buffet, no less."

"Are you two talking about buffets?" "Heather's voice floated back from the row ahead of them. "I heard there's a midnight dessert one at our hotel."

"I like the buffet of dicks better," muttered Jordan, sitting next to her.

"You heard that?"

"We heard everything," they said in unison.

"Damn, Emma, you got a guy's phone number already and we haven't even taken off!" Heather squealed. "You win for fastest Spring Break hookup ever."

She started to open her mouth to tell them what had just happened in the bathroom. Did that qualify for the Mile High Club? Probably not. You needed to be in the air for that. But still . . .

"Not quite," Jordan argued. "Remember last year when Casey fucked the airport shuttle dude in the back of the little bus?"

"The rug burn from the floor was like a tattoo," Melissa added.

"She what? You guys never told me that!" Emma hissed. Competitive streak kicking in, she realized Casey still had her beat. Not worth it to tell her friends what had just happened.

"What happens in New Orleans stays in New Orleans," the other three chanted.

Emma fingered Miki's card.

Indeed.

Three

THE DESSERT BUFFET was not a myth; here they were, jet-lagged and overexcited, standing in front of enough minitortes to give Martha Stewart multiple orgasms . . . and were those cream puffs on the other table?

Nutella cheesecake? *Ah, God.*

Kudos to the chef for designing a spread of sugar, fat, chocolate, and other delights that would meet the needs of every woman staying at the hotel. Whether you were on your period and needed chocolate to maintain the delicate balance between homicide and weepiness, or had decided that calories don't count on Spring Break, this was way better than some cheesy continental breakfast freebie with stale doughnuts and apples that looked like Johnny Appleseed himself had harvested them.

"Did you know they have miniature tiramisu?" Melissa asked, shoving a piece of cherry cheesecake in her mouth.

"What about water? I'm parched," said Emma. Every time she tried a new treat, Ryan's voice popped into her head. *Fat. Freshman Fifteen. Kilos.* "Asshole," she muttered, stuffing a piece of revenge truffle past her pursed lips.

"What? I thought you liked tiramisu?"

"Not you." Emma laughed, the sound like layers of tightness relenting. "It's just . . . Ryan."

"Again?"

"It's only been a few weeks." She struggled not to cry. "Now I'm just upset about the idea of what I've lost. Not Ryan himself."

"Keep saying that enough times and maybe it will be true," Heather chimed in from behind.

"Hey, I—" Emma's protest was cut short.

"Ready for Madame Ysabeau?" a well-preserved, older woman asked, interrupting them, her voice carrying a cultured New Orleans accent. The hotel had a set of concierge workers milling about the room, and this was a well-coiffed woman around Emma's grandmother's age. Blond, smooth, and a little too tight, she carried herself with an elegance Emma knew she could never match.

"Madame who?" Melissa asked.

"A local legend," the woman replied, eyes wide with a kind of seduction that seemed a little too unctuous for Emma's tastes, but she had Melissa eating out of her hand. Sapphire eyes lined with the perfect balance of eyeliner, mascara, and shadow met hers, the lower lids crinkling up with genuine mirth. "You all need to have your fortunes read before braving the fun of this week!"

Emma snorted. "I'm not the type . . ."

"That's the point!" the concierge urged. "Be different. Live on the edge. What happens here stays here. Don't you want a road map?"

"How much?" Emma asked, certain it was a scam.

"Madame Ysabeau asks only for what you believe her services are worth."

"That would be zero from Emma," Jordan said through a mouth full of chocolate cake.

The concierge shrugged. "It's your choice, of course. But don't leave New Orleans with regrets." And then she was off to talk to another group of giggling women.

"C'mon," urged Melissa. "She's right. YOLO!"

"What's YOLO?" Emma asked.

Her three friends stopped cold and looked at her like she was twerking in a Miley Cyrus costume. "You Only Live Once," Heather choked out.

"You mean that stupid phrase people use to justify the most ridiculous behavior?" Emma sniffed.

"Just shut up and do it," Jordan growled, dragging her to a thick, purple, velvet curtain that looked like something you'd buy in a cheap Halloween costume store.

"This is so stupid," she muttered, but followed Heather, Jordan, and Melissa through the curtain.

A sign read: PLEASE WAIT FOR MADAME YSABEAU TO COME TO YOU. It hung precariously from a gold, braided cord.

"Does the hotel bring her in just for suckers like us?" Emma whispered to Jordan, who looked like her stomach was ready to explode.

"Anyone have some antacids?" was Jordan's response. They all shook their heads. She belched openly.

"I think," said Melissa, answering Emma's question, "she goes to different hotels. She was here last year."

"And did your fortune come true?" Emma asked, snorting derisively.

"She said I would find three joys and one disappointment." Melissa smiled broadly. "And that's about right. I slept with one really nice guy, had another guy fall asleep while going down on me—"

"Ewwwwww!" the other three groaned.

"—found $120 cash sitting on the sidewalk, and got the perfect pair of Jimmy Choos at a consignment shop for twenty dollars."

"Your idea of a joy on Spring Break is so pathetic," Heather said.

"We can't all find seven guys in seven days," Melissa sniffed.

"Seven?" Emma gasped.

"Don't judge," Heather replied, holding up a hand. "What happens here stays here."

"So I can fuck a donkey and go home and act like it didn't happen?"

"Do you *want* to fuck a donkey?" Madame Ysabeau said in a deep woman's voice, the tones like gravel and chocolate liquor; a smoker's voice scratched and broken by time.

"What? No! I—"

"You should be first," the woman commanded, hooking one finger and peering at Emma. Entranced and startled, Emma obeyed, entering a small enclave, usually a restaurant booth, though now decorated.

"You do not believe that I am legitimate," Madame Ysabeau declared.

Emma's cheeks burned. "I—"

"Do not bother with social lies. I do not need them." Her accent was slight, like Miki's, but different. It unnerved Emma.

"Okay." Everyone liked social lies. That was how people functioned. How conflict was avoided. Without social lies, how could you go to a family party and not kill someone, or have a college roommate? What did she mean she didn't want social lies? That was like saying you didn't like chocolate.

"Your hand."

Emma slid it across the table. Madame Ysabeau turned it over in her soft, dry hands, which felt like animated snakeskin as she checked out every square inch of Emma's palm and fingers. Ryan's engagement ring was there, hanging slightly loose. In the last few weeks Emma's appetite had been erratic. Maybe five pounds were gone.

For the next ten minutes that's all Madame Ysabeau did. Touch Emma's hand and look at lines and curves and divots and wrinkles.

Setting it down on the table, she looked at Emma and locked eyes.

"You will be married soon."

Her heart leaped. "To Ryan?" She glanced at her engagement ring. He'd asked for it back and she'd refused. A gift was a gift.

"No."

"Then who?"

"Two men."

"*Two?*"

"Two."

"So I'll have two marriages? The first man I marry won't work out? I don't understand."

Madame Ysabeau spread her arms out on the table and said, "I cannot interpret. Only read."

"That's it?"

Troubled eyes met hers. "No. Who you are is a mirage."

A mirage?

"An old saxophone player is the source of all your joy."

"A what?"

She closed her eyes and took a deep sigh. "I see a life you must unravel in order to live the one you are meant to live."

That meant letting go of Ryan. *Duh.*

"And I see fear in you so full it crowds out all that your heart needs."

Ouch.

Another long sigh, then she opened her eyes. "My fee for the vision is what you believe it is worth."

Pfft.

"But in this case I would like to propose a very different arrangement, Emma."

She hadn't told Madame Ysabeau her name.

"Give me something you possess right now that represents the life you wish to leave behind. It does not need to have great value."

"That's it? That's all you want?"

"That is more than enough."

The glint of candlelight reflected off her ring. In anger, when she had refused to give it back, Ryan confessed that it wasn't a real diamond. All the shopping and comparing and research she'd done to find the perfect marquis cut, the best deal, and the highest value had been complete bullshit, because Ryan just went on the Home Shopping Network and bought an exact replica made of zirconium.

Sliding the ring off her finger, she handed it to Madame Ysabeau, who did not seem surprised.

"Do you believe that what you give me represents the life you wish to leave behind?"

"Yes."

"Then that is good enough." An assistant appeared, Madame Ysabeau fled behind a dark curtain, and Emma found herself in the outer room, surrounded by Melissa and Heather.

"Where's Jordan?"

"In there."

"It's like the McDonald's drive-through of fortunes," Emma cracked.

"What did she say?"

"My life is a mirage, and I'll find joy with an old saxophone player."

"What? That's nothing like the fortunes we get."

Emma shrugged. "And then I gave her my engagement ring."

Two slack jaws greeted her. "Are you out of your fucking mind?" Melissa screeched.

"It was fake," Heather reminded her.

"Yeah, but that . . . that means it's really over between you and Ryan," Melissa said, sliding her arm around Emma's shoulders.

To her surprise, Emma wasn't sad. Instead she felt relieved. Liberated, even. "Well, it *is* over."

"And the ring was a fake?" Melissa asked, eyes wide.

Sighing heavily, Emma twisted the newly-bared skin on her left hand. "More than the ring was fake."

FORTUNES DONE, AND stomachs full of chocolate, the witching hour had hit. With two hours left of bar fun, the four poured out onto the street, the balmy air doing nothing to rouse Emma from her exhaustion.

"I just want to go back to the room and sleep," she whined.

"Okay, grandma," Jordan cracked.

Whatever response was about to pour out of her mouth halted cold, for there stood Miki on the other side of the street, waiting to get into a jazz club.

"Isn't that—" Melissa started.

"Emma?" he shouted, peering into the night. "Is that you? From the plane? Harvard Law?"

Heather rolled her eyes. "Are you capable of uttering a sentence that doesn't include those words?"

"Hey!" Jordan protested. "We're proud of her."

"Sure, sure, but it's not the best pickup line when your goal is to find a hot guy to fuck."

"Depends on the guy." Miki's voice surprised her. How had he crossed the street so quickly?

"Oh, dear," Heather backtracked. The skin on Emma's back, from ass to neck, began to prickle with a slow burn, the sensation like a force field once more.

"Miki," she said, shock evident in her voice. As his arms reached out for her, she realized he was kissing one cheek, then the other, ending with an embrace that was anything but polite. Was that an ass grab with his right hand?

"Emma," he said pleasantly.

"I love how Europeans greet people," Melissa said. *Hint, hint.*

"I love how European guys fuck," Jordan muttered. "Except the Irish guys. Every one of them was terrible in bed."

"Then allow me to make up for the sins of my countrymen by whatever means necessary," said a sultry, lilting voice. The four women turned toward the melodic words.

"Let me introduce my friend, David Collins," Miki said, gesturing to a man on his right.

Oh, holy hell. Six feet of sinew and cheekbones that called out to be kissed. A face that should be ridden. And brown eyes so rich that she could stare and stare and turn to stone.

Or quivering flesh.

Definitely quivering, throbbing flesh.

David wore a very worn leather coat, the kind a guy who rides bikes would wear, and he extended his hand in a friendly shake. "I'm pleased to meet you, Emma. Miki mentioned you on the plane ride here."

Irish. The accent was deep and unmistakable, rolling over her breasts and thighs like a burst of wind and heat. David looked an awful lot like that actor who had just been chosen to play in the new *Fifty Shades* movie.

Bring on the Red Room of Pain.

"But there might be an exception to my experience," Jordan said under her breath. "I need some more data points."

"Mmmm, data points," Heather growled, practically drooling as she took in both men.

"Where are you lovely ladies headed?" Miki asked, eyes burning into Emma.

"Wherever the fun is," Melissa giggled.

In bed, Emma thought.

Five sets of eyes suddenly flicked her way. Shit. Had she said that aloud?

Miki's eyes went wolfish and predatory.

So did David's.

And they only had eyes for her.

"Don't mind me," mumbled Jordan.

"You get the feeling we're gratuitous?" whispered Heather to Melissa.

Emma caught every word, and they'd pay for that later, but right now she was hypnotized by both men.

"Come across the street," beckoned Miki. "David says it's one of the best jazz clubs in N'awlins." His attempt at the local accent was adorable.

David snickered. "Don't even try, Miki. Just shut up and be pretty. Though you don't hold a candle to Emma here."

"Extras. We're just extras and Emma's the star," Heather mused, pretending to check her nails.

"Hot guys!" Jordan shouted.

"Well, thank you!" David said.

"Not you," Jordan retorted. "I meant that group from Tulane over there."

"N-Not that you're not hot," Emma stammered.

"What about our friends inside the club?" David asked, a huge, amused grin making his face even more kissable. Emma's insides warmed, then throbbed, then ached for release as she realized she was hot for both men.

Both.

"Friends?" Jordan's interest was piqued.

"We have a group of guys from work over there. Enjoying a few drinks and some great jazz."

"How many guys?" Melissa inquired. As if the answer mattered; if their friends were anything like Miki and David, Emma knew her friends would be all over them like beads at Mardi Gras.

David and Miki shared a look. "Three." Their voices mingled.

That was the right answer. Jordan didn't even check traffic before stepping off the curb and marching across the street, Melissa and Heather like ducklings following their mother in formation. Miki stepped to Emma's left and David to her right as they made their way to the club.

The line to get in was even longer now. "If we flash our boobs, do you think we can skip the line?" Melissa whispered to Emma.

"Probably not, but flash them anyhow," said someone ahead of them. Jordan perked up. Manwhores were her favorite. She sidled her way through the people ahead of them in search of the cock attached to that voice.

Ironically, it was attached to a guy from . . . Tulane.

Within minutes they were let inside, Miki and David slipping the guy at the door some undisclosed amount of money. "I would have just flashed my boobs," Melissa hissed in Emma's ear, making her laugh.

"What a mirage," David commented. The club was definitely not what Emma expected, more sedate than she'd have thought. This was more her parents' style.

That word. "Mirage?" she asked, her voice rising an octave, remembering Madame Ysabeau's fortune for her.

"You think it's one thing and it turns out to be quite another," he added. Eyes crawling over the large, smoky room, he seemed to share her impression of the night-club.

Her eyes jumped from one man to the other.

"Indeed," she murmured as they entered the club, filled with throngs of patrons around small tables and a few large booths, all speaking in hushed tones, clouds of smoke hovering above tables like ghosts.

"You don't see that back home," Emma mused as they wove through the crowd, Miki in front, David behind her.

"See what?" asked David.

"Smoke." Miki searched the crowd and Emma searched his face, finding the planes of his cheekbones so forbidden, so divine.

"Smoke? Like fags?"

The word made Emma stop cold and turn around to stare at David in disbelief.

"Sorry," he chuckled. "I meant cigarettes." The lilt in his voice curled her toes. "I forget that the word can be offensive here. But . . ." He frowned. " . . . people don't smoke in bars where you live? What good is that?"

"Secondhand smoke is very dangerous," she said reflexively. *You sound like a sixth grade health teacher. Shut up, Emma.*

"But who doesn't love a good fa—uh, smoke, with a drink or after a fabulous romp in bed? Drinking without a cigarette is like making love without coming."

A new set began, the drum line starting softly, just enough to drown out Emma's sharp inhalation. Bed. She hadn't slept with anyone other than Ryan for nearly six years. Before they started dating she'd been a bit of an experimenter. Some would say loose. A virgin in name only when she started dating Ryan, true. But still a virgin. That had been freshman and sophomore year of high school. All grown up with so little experience, the implications of David's words sank in, making her wet and curious.

Miki's warm palm covered the small of her back and more heat blanketed her as he leaned in to the nape of her neck and whispered, "I found our friends. Come sit."

On your face.

"Of course." David's words echoed through her. Ryan's throwaway comment from their breakup looped through her. *Too afraid to live* . . . The mental echo creating a cacophony she needed to silence.

With Miki's hand. Or mouth. Or cock. Or . . . hell, anything.

"A round of tequila?" Melissa asked as Miki steered them toward a group of guys at a half-empty table.

The cocktail waitress overheard her, and Miki added, "Make them doubles."

"You guys here on business or pleasure?" Jordan asked David. The Tulane manwhore must have been a disappointment; she scooched into a chair and said nothing about him.

David threw Miki a mysterious look, one that made Emma's vee heat up. "Something like that."

"Mixing the two?" Emma asked.

"If that's an offer, then yes." His words poured over her in sensual waves as she gulped the first shot of tequila, the liquid hot and shocking, like something else she imagined hitting the back of her throat.

"Why don't you introduce us to your friends," Jordan said, acid in her voice, though none of it was for Emma. "Emma seems to have double the attention."

With a flick of his wrist, Miki signaled to the waitress, who brought over a new round.

"I'm drinking doubles!" The second double shot of tequila was sinking in.

"Double the fun," David said, giving her a serious smile that made promises she hoped he would keep. A glance at Miki, whose smoky gaze pinned her in place, and the fire in her belly grew.

Ryan who?

Miki and David introduced their friends, Mike, Lars, and Luke. Jordan, Heather, and Melissa settled in like vultures finding a dead cow in the road. Or something like that. Emma's thought processes were decidedly diminished as Miki bought her another round.

"No, no, I can't . . ." But she could, and did, the new shot sloshing against the back of her throat, burning her with a power that made all her worries fade. Emboldened, her hands went straight for Miki's lap as she found him hard and whispered in his ear, "It's your turn."

"Actually, it's David's turn," he said, making a deferential gesture toward his friend.

Are you kidding me? Every. Woman's. Dream. A hot man steams up the airplane ride and now he's handing me off to his equally hot friend?

"Ménage is the new anal," Melissa murmured in her ear, reaching across the table as David wrapped one long arm around Emma's shoulders. *Threesome? C'mon. No way.*

And anal? What?

"Why are you worrying your ring finger like that, Emma?" David asked, his voice neutral and curious. Stunned, she looked down and saw her right hand playing with the empty space where the ring she'd worn for half her adulthood used to rest.

"She was engaged until her asshole fiancé dumped her

three weeks ago," Jordan shouted from across the table. *Speaking of assholes* . . .

"Fool," Miki said tightly.

"I know I was," Emma said, rushing to explain.

David's laugh, a booming, rich sound, went straight to her core. "He meant your fiancé, Emma. A fool."

"Was he bad in bed?" Miki ventured.

"How would Emma know?" Melissa giggled, downing a shot.

"Of course Emma would— Oh." David interrupted himself and made a strangled noise in the back of his throat, turning to Emma with eyes that clearly found her even more alluring. "You," he added, "could use some basis for comparison."

"She could use a wild time," Melissa added, sucking down yet another double shot. "Hey, how about blowjobs?"

All of the men turned as one unit, in such perfect synchronicity Emma wondered if they were sitting at a table with robots.

"She means the drink," Jordan added dryly, Lars's hand sliding up her thigh.

"The drink?" Miki choked. "Someone named a drink a 'blowjob'?"

"If you can buy a Screaming Orgasm or Sex on the Beach, why not buy a Blowjob?" Emma asked.

"Why not?"

Six shots in and Emma's new resolve to get laid without strings was strengthening. The only question was: Miki or David?

Or both?

The cocktail waitress delivered four perfect little shot glasses, but stopped herself before putting them on the table. "Table or floor?"

"Floor?" David's voice held a smoky tone of intrigue.

"FLOOR!" Melissa shouted. At that exact moment the band finished its song and took a break. The bar was mobbed, but the room quieter than Emma expected.

She knew what was coming next, but was this a tradition in New Orleans? If the waitress asked, she must know . . .

The four women stood, each pulling their hair back and tucking it into their shirts, behind their necks. Setting one perfect shot glass with chocolate liquor and a thick layer of cream floating on top on the floor at each woman's feet, the server stood back and grinned.

"Haven't seen this in ages," she added.

"Haven't seen this ever," marveled Lars, eyes solely for Jordan.

Emma had four eyes on her. Bending down at Miki's feet, her knees hit the rough wood floor, eyes now level with his bulging cock. It strained through the tight jeans he wore, her own clit swollen with untapped release and years of restraint that begged to be discarded.

Before she kneeled, she tucked her hands behind the small of her back, then opened her mouth nice and wide.

"Oh, my," he groaned.

Bending over, she fit her teeth around the shot glass. It had been years since she'd done this, but her mouth still had it. Lifting up, she tipped the glass high in the air, the blast of cream and liquor slamming the back of her throat. One good swallow and she lowered herself, set the empty shot glass on the floor, and stood.

Look, Ma! No hands!

Miki clapped, a slow, appreciative process that showed his strong forearms and made the muscles in his chest press against his shirt. He leaned down to kiss her, sweeping his tongue across hers, tasting the drink.

"Creamy. Delicious. But I prefer the other definition of a blowjob."

"What about me?" David's voice caught her off guard from behind. His first touch seared her, two hands planted on her shoulders, then the press of his chest as he dropped to his knees on the floor, too. "Don't I get a blowjob . . . performance?" With a flick of his wrist he got the waitress to bring another shot, the layer of cream so suggestive it made Emma's body flood with nothing but the need to go have sex. Now.

Now now now.

Miki just cocked an eyebrow and said nothing. The alcohol had loosened her, and this time she slowly unbuttoned her outer shirt, revealing a navy blue cami underneath. "It's getting hot in here," she added.

"Too hot for me," Jordan said, standing with Lars. "We're getting some . . . air." She grabbed her shot glass and downed it, winking as they disappeared through the crowd.

"Emma's the blowjob champion back home," Melissa said airily, drinking hers with tiny sips.

"I can see that," Miki mumbled, shifting in his seat.

Turning to David, she repeated her efforts, hitting her

mark with each step, leaving the empty shot glass on the floor and standing, again, without using her hands. This time, though, David remained on his knees, his hands sliding up the sides of her calves and thighs, settling on her ass.

"That was the best blowjob I've ever seen."

Whatever thin resolve Emma had left melted away in that moment.

"I can show you far better," she whispered, bending down. "But not here," she murmured, nipping his ear with her teeth.

In all her years as a teen and young adult, it had never occurred to her that she could just flirt with a man to have sex with him. She had programmed herself for intimacy. Meaning. Her entire identity was wrapped up in being sincere and profound and all these rules that seemed like utter bunk now that a complete stranger's hot, eager hands were touching parts of her that had only ever been touched by one young, clumsy man who had betrayed her so deeply three weeks ago.

That version of her seemed muted and distant. Wanting. A hollow version of what she could be.

This Emma? This one was ready to taste life. Touch life. Tease it and tongue it and explore who she was through thrills and risks and conquest.

YOLO, right?

"We have a room across the street," David said.

"So do we," Emma replied. A glance at Melissa, who was currently wrapped in a kiss with Mike. And where was Heather?

"Heather went off with Luke," David explained, reading her mind. "If your room is across the way, there are no worries."

He tapped Mike's arm. The guy pulled away from Melissa, whose mouth was red and raw from the kiss, eyes hazy and primal. David looked at her and said, "We're in Room 344 in the same hotel as yours."

"Is that an invitation?" Melissa asked, looking at Miki, David, Mike, and Emma.

What? I didn't sign on for an orgy!

"No," David said firmly, suddenly serious. "I'm letting you know in case you want to watch out for your friend. Don't you all stick together?"

Emma was touched; he seemed genuinely concerned that she should feel safe leaving with them. His warm eyes reflected a combination of arousal and responsibility.

"You have sisters, don't you?" she asked.

He tilted his head in surprise, hands planted on hips, leaning on one leg in a sexy stance that made her want to touch him all the more. "Four. All younger."

Melissa pulled out her phone and held it in the air. "We all have an app that tracks each other."

He laughed. "Are you sheep?"

"Just careful." With that, Mike pulled Melissa away from the table and murmured something in her ear that made her burst into throaty laughter.

"Shall we?" Miki asked, suddenly behind her. "A nightcap in our room would be divine."

What he had done to her in the airplane bathroom

had been divine. Being with them was sublime. What the three of them might do together, alone, in a hotel room would be . . . well, there wasn't a word for it.

Not a single, damn one.

The walk to the hotel across the street felt like she was moving in slow motion, savoring each breath, each flicker of taillights, the way the wrought-iron balconies called out to her, sophisticated and filled with people seeking insight and pleasure.

New Orleans had already branded itself in her heart as a place to find her real self. And now, flanked by two men who both wanted her, needed her, pursued her at all costs, Emma released herself into an existence she wouldn't have recognized three weeks ago.

Pure experience.

"Here we are," Miki whispered, sliding the card key into the door slot and gently ushering her into a room far nicer than the one she shared with her friends. Two king beds. A large, stocked bar. A cherry table with damask-upholstered chairs near the balcony, giving a wonderful view of the street through open French doors. The sound of smooth jazz floated up through the air, and Emma re-laxed into a state she knew other people sank into but that she had never quite achieved herself.

This was more than the alcohol, more than the men, and certainly more than the past six years. Being in touch with all she was before Ryan and the Emma she'd been, coupled with the opportunity to forge a new identity with each breath right now, each innuendo and glance from Miki and David, gave her a new perspective.

She became her body. The mind faded completely. Every other person was an entity she could connect with through touch. The light fixture in the room was the most beautiful assemblage of colored glass and metal she had ever laid eyes on. The clink of ice cubes in a glass as David made a drink was like a melody that came straight from his heart to hers.

This was bliss.

The old Emma was so tortured and demented and pained in comparison.

Maybe Ryan was right.

As that thought—one of her last—ripped through her consciousness, David called out to her, "What can I make you?"

Bzzz. Her phone vibrated in her purse. He waved her to answer it.

A text from Jordan. *Have you checked Facebook?*

Two taps of her screen and—

You have got to be fucking kidding me.

Ryan, shirtless, with his face between what looked like a pile of cantaloupes. Naked cantaloupes. Melons with nipples.

Though she felt gut-punched, it wasn't the picture that got to her. The caption was the kicker: *I'm a man let out of a six-year prison term.*

Red flashed through her, dashing away all traces of the relaxed contentment she'd just experienced.

Fuck, she texted Jordan. Tears threatened the edges of her eyes, the boozy mix of shots and a broken heart about as appealing as a root canal.

Fuck him, Jordan texted back. *Go for it, Emma. Just live.*

Emma looked up and found two very interested men watching her. Years of rules—mostly self-created and imposed—lifted, her own internal desire the only compass she would use right now. Miki wanted her. David wanted her.

Emma wanted herself. *Who, exactly, was that?* Was it the woman Ryan had just "escaped"? Or someone more, someone expansive and aware and sensual and alive?

"Everything okay?" David asked, his voice hushed and concerned. And then—*bzzzz.*

His own phone hummed with a text. "Shit. It's morning in Ireland. I have to get that." As he stepped out into the hallway, Miki came and sat next to her, pressing the bed's enormous mattress down at the edge and sending her off kilter. Bed. Luscious man. All the time in the world.

When he caressed her jaw—his eyes dark and mysterious—the ache in her belly intensified, accompanied by a brightness. Her body fueled by the unknown, now unfurling before her, second by second, stroke by stroke. As that same hand slid over the soft skin of her throat and she shuddered, she knew which Emma she was choosing.

YOLO.

Bold and ready, she leaned in to taste him, knowing it would be better than their furtive kisses on the plane, the slide of her palm against the bedspread's silky cotton like touching freedom. Miki's fingers gripped her ribs as he pulled her to him, the catch of his breath as her hand found his thigh making her smile through the kiss.

"What's so funny?" he murmured against her mouth. "Does what you find make you giggle?" He moved her hand over his rock-hard cock.

"Quite the opposite," she rasped. "I smiled knowing I made you this way." One small squeeze and she had him, eyes closed and throat taut with need, his face open and vulnerable in a way that made her study him. So *this* was what a man looked like when she had the power of his arousal in her hands. Literally.

Sex with Ryan had been so scripted, often in the shadows or complete darkness, something where pleasure was an afterthought, something she sneaked in between the choreographed moments designed to complete the act so they could cuddle. Making love with Ryan wasn't about raw need—or, at least, not hers—but about being intimate with the least disruption. About checking something off their respective to-do lists and being naked together.

Miki was all improv, fire and heat and making it up as they went along. His hand went to the hem of her camisole and peeled it off, her shoulders swaying and twisting with it, leaving her black bra and breasts shining in the bright light of the room.

"So beautiful," he whispered, taking her in. Without hesitation, his hands reached behind her, sure and steady, and unclasped her bra, the two ends dragging down the skin of her spine like fingernails.

Warm palms cupped her cleavage into a rack that would be the pride of any serving wench, and Miki's smile shifted to a serious countenance as he pulled her over onto her side, her own hands jumping to life.

I can't believe I'm doing this, she thought, mouth coming up for air from his kisses, eyes wide and searching the room. A groan of appreciation from her throat spilled out as he sucked one nipple, pulling so far her clit jumped and her abs tightened, the connection intense and overwhelming. Frantic to press him into her, she dispensed with his button and fly, reaching in to grasp his rod, the warm, soft flesh calling for her mouth.

A soothing, musical sound, the kind of winding tune that makes you mellow and pure, floated through her mind, carried in on the wind through the open window as Miki's hands guided her pants down to her ankles. Kicking them off, she stroked him slowly, the two entwined and exploring, hands, mouths, and skin caught up in the rush of uncharted territory. His skin was so smooth, the thatch of hair at his belly leading to a deliciously hard and long sight, and the feel of his hands parting her thighs, then slick with her juices, made her more reverent of what bodies could do to one another.

"You are so lush, so sweet," he sighed as he pressed her, languid and hot, onto her back, then used his fingers to guide her legs open as his head dipped down.

"Oh, oh!" she cried out before his mouth had even touched her, eyes closed and hair a tangly mess on the bed, holding her breath with hope that he would actually—

It felt better than she'd ever imagined. Ryan had tried, once or twice, but when a guy actually gags after giving a

part of your naked body some attention, the arousal quo-
tient tends to drop to negative one hundred.

Miki loved her body—she felt it in his touch, his eyes,
and in how his breath changed when he moved against
her. That tongue wanted to be on her, those fingers savored their paths, and as Emma felt a craving build up
inside her, she realized her orgasm was at the ready, her
second this day, and her second, ever, from a man.

This man.

Just when she thought she could no longer stand his
tongue's fevered thrusts interspersed with wider, softer
licks, he slid a finger inside her. Clamping down, she rode
his tongue, her hips consumed with a mind of their own,
modesty thrown aside. The Emma who wouldn't speak
up in bed, who would send telepathic messages in hopes
that her mental pleas would be answered—and who was
eternally unheard—now moved like a woman unleashed.

"What do you like best?" Miki asked, pulling back
and looking at her with smoky, smiling eyes. He leaned
back down and used the tip of his tongue to move in tiny,
butterfly motions vertically on her clit. "This?"

She groaned.

"Or this?" Two fingers entered her as he put his entire
mouth, relaxed and soft, on her slit and, positioning the
tongue just under it, suckled gently on it, like a nipple.

"All of it," she gasped. "All of it."

And then the fingers in her hooked and reached up,
finding that spot, that same spot he'd touched so perfectly on the plane, her hips arching for his mouth and
fingers. The rhythm caught so fast it seemed impossible,

blinding white light blocking out the world as she cried out, her body pooling with warm wetness. His face and hand followed her gyrations as she released herself with total, mindless abandon, her limbs loose and her body pulsing as every nerve ending cried out in unison.

"Oh, my," she groaned, the most intense of the climaxes over, her body ragged and exhausted as Miki moved up, hips over hers. He straddled her, that fabulous cock at attention, as he reached for his pants and pulled out a condom.

In me, she thought. I want you in me. The thought slammed her like a sonic boom, looping over and over, her hands and hips and breasts and pussy all in concert in their insatiable need for Miki inside her, for their sweaty bodies to be linked together, to feel him fill her and pound and thrust her out of her body and mind with an orgasm that would raise the roof.

He dispensed with the formalities as she watched him, eyes roaming over his body as if carving the memory in stone: chiseling and shaping a perfect marble statue of her fantasies. Arms on either side of her, he lifted himself over her, a pensive grin lifting one side of his mouth.

"You really enjoy this, don't you?" she asked.

His face went cloudy. "Don't you?"

"Of course!" He teased her clit with the tip of himself, rubbing up and down, making her own hips curl up to meet him.

"Then why do you ask?"

"It's more an observation," she said in a hushed tone as he eased the first inch into her, making her breath hitch.

"You're not like any man I've ever"—another inch"—"been with."

"You mean the only"—more inches—"man, Emma." The words scraped against her soul, though the tone was kind.

"Yes."

"I want to share so much with you." His voice went low and deep as he plunged completely into her, their bellies pressed together, her breasts flattened and heart pumping hard as she found herself enveloped by this man she'd only just met, yet committing the most intimate of acts with.

And loving it.

Every sigh, each push, all the gliding of her fingers across his back over his muscled ass as he pumped into her, using hips that moved with a slow, deep concentration that was all about her—it was like traveling to a distant world and finding your dreams had come to life. Emma had read about sex like this—instant attraction, heat beyond compare, a sensuality between strangers that overpowered everything.

But to live it? She'd always trained herself to believe that the quiet, content physical life she shared with her ex was enough. Would be enough. Would sustain her year in and year out because that's what everyone did. Sex wasn't all fire and sparks and gasps and fevered fucking.

It was steady and reliable. Like a good Ford F10. Awesome when you got one new, and then eventually part of the landscape, something you knew was there when you needed it.

Miki was a Tesla. A Ferrari. A Lamborghini.

Being fucked by a sports car was so much better than being driven to church in a Ford F10.

"Touch yourself," he whispered from above, shoulders dropping so he could snatch a kiss. His hips halted their relentless strokes and Emma gaped at him.

"Touch myself . . . where?" Each breath caught her off guard. Yearning for even more orgasms, her body began to argue against their pause, screaming for attention.

"Wherever you like. Wherever it feels good. Like on the plane." As if he had done it a thousand times, Miki bent down to nip her breast.

She had heard about this; friends whispered that their boyfriends touched them during sex, or masturbated with a dildo, but she . . . no. She had been too shy to ask for this from Ryan, and too inhibited to buy a sex toy. What if someone found the receipt in her online account? Or, worse, her mother found it when she came home on break?

Eager fingers slipped into the tight space between them, her index and middle fingers long enough to touch right where she needed them most. Miki smiled down on her, the look they shared more caring and tender than she'd thought possible. Years of disparaging casual sex and it turned out it could be like this?

The swell of orgasm rose quickly as Miki hammered into her, then pulled back, his tip teasing her opening as her own fingers drove her over the edge. His tempo increased, his body tensed, and her legs wrapped tighter around him, ankles hooking together and helping her to lift up, meeting his thrusts.

"Oh, baby," he groaned.

"Fuck me," she begged, the words out so fast she shocked herself.

"You like it," he replied, but she didn't *like* it.

She fucking *adored* it. Miki stopped talking and shifted into a taut wall of muscle as a low keening formed in her throat, the rocking of their hips and the flick and massage of her wet fingers on her clit tipping her over, Miki's hoarse voice calling her name as she stretched her head back, hands frozen in place on her clit as her entire body went stiff, legs quaking with a climax so powerful she couldn't move.

Three extremely rough thrusts and Miki shouted her name, "Emma!" spilling over into the streets of New Orleans like laughter, a branding of sorts, as if he'd announced her, claimed her, and taken her.

With one word.

"Emma," he said again, his husky voice stealing all the air she could find, her own voice long gone, body strummed and thrumming as she twitched and cried out nonsense. The state of bliss their coupling had given her was a landscape without words or context. She was just . . .

"Emma," he said a third time, tender and appreciative as he collapsed, rolling off her and pulling out, leaving her to stare at the ceiling, breathing hard as if she'd run a marathon. Her scent was on her hands, the taste of him in her mouth, and while she was still tipsy from so many shots, she was wildly sober, too.

Free, as well.

A soft, polite knock, and then David strolled in. David!

She'd forgotten about him. A laugh burbled up at the sight of him discovering them, both naked, on twisted sheets, covered in postcoital sweat.

"I see I haven't missed a thing," he said pleasantly, reaching for his belt buckle and beginning to undress.

What?

"You missed the most amazing woman in the world," Miki countered, running one hand through Emma's jet-black hair.

"Bet you say that to all the girls," David teased. He peeled off his shirt to display the most amazing chest Emma had ever seen—and one of her hands currently rested on the previous owner of that title.

"You would know," was all Miki said.

Before Emma could ask what that meant, David was completely nude, absolutely not self-conscious, and utterly in possession of a sense of entitlement that allowed him to simply climb into bed on the side of Emma not occupied by Miki.

"Um, hi?" she ventured.

David's eyes took in Emma as if he were measuring a piece of art. "Thank goodness you've got actual flesh on you."

"You normally sleep with zombies?"

He grinned. "Close enough. The last two women we've been with had a flock of vultures following after them."

Her weight. "My ex-fiancé told me I was too fat." Why not spill it? What did she have to hide? Already naked with two men in a bed, it's not like she needed to be modest. Right?

"Your ex is a fooking idiot." David's harsh comment made her take a deep sigh, letting the air come out slowly.

"And he's the only guy she's ever slept with," Miki added, an angry tone in his voice.

"Until you," David pointed out.

"Until me." Miki nodded and pulled the covers over them, as if it were perfectly normal for the two men to be in bed, chatting away, with a naked Emma. A naked, sticky Emma who had just come and come and come and who found her nipples tightening, thighs at the ready as a very sleek, nude David made certain that they were touching from shoulder to toes.

And lips. The kiss came so brazenly, with so many assumptions that Emma's protests—had there been any— would have centered around the fact that he didn't ask. Not the actual kiss. When she'd first met Miki she was impressed by his sophistication and intelligence.

David?

She was most impressed with that thing he'd just done with his tongue. And how his hand traveled from her collarbone down to her breast, over her navel and down to her hip, as if he'd just read a Lonely Planet Guide to Emma and was riding the subway from memory.

And *zing*! There's one of the stations.

Time to go down.

"What was his name?" he asked, his eyes more the color of brandy than brown, eyes that said he was ready for whatever she wanted.

"Whose?"

"The fooking idiot's."

"Oh. Ryan."

David groaned. "One of my own countrymen? That's just sad."

"My friend Jordan says Irish guys are the worst lovers." Miki snorted and started to laugh, the snicker a whisper that covered Emma's breasts in goose bumps.

"That's just wrong," David demanded. "You need to—"

"How about you prove Jordan wrong?" Emma's words were an arrow that seemed to strike David in the cock. Now that was an attractive bull's-eye.

"You bet your sweet ass I will," he growled.

With two of them, Emma was unsure how this worked. She would have thought she'd feel weirded out by having two naked men in bed with her, but it seemed perfectly natural for David to take her mouth with his and to use his hand to cup her ass, while Miki just sat and, um . . . watched.

Neither man seemed possessive; David hadn't yelled or shouted or fought with Miki when he'd come in and found them there. Instead, he'd just stripped down and climbed in, and now David had slid one finger inside her, his way of mastering her body no less arousing than Miki's, yet completely different. Her body responded more rapidly, her need bursting quicker, and David seemed to want to take things faster.

Where Miki had been gentle and appeared to understand how new she was to—hell, everything sexual— David wanted to own. Command. Take and take and take, within the context of giving and giving well. His hands visited her breasts, her neck, her pussy and clit as if he'd been there thousands of times and was reasserting himself to make sure it was clear that he was there to give, because he was going to be back, soon, to take.

Miki climbed out of bed, the movement from the corner of her eye the last distraction she registered as David plunged into her mouth and used masterful fingers to make yet another complex web of orgasms unfold and unfurl. How could there be so many when she had convinced herself this just wasn't part of making love?

David's lips bruised hers with their insistence, his fingers bringing her to climax as she called out his name against his jaw, her nose inhaling the mix of sweat, musk, and acrid cologne, an aroma she would remember years from now, she knew—indelibly linked to the sheer pleasure of being taken by her second man in one night.

And then he held a condom before her. "Do the honors?" he asked.

Only one set of orgasms from David's attentions? Perhaps he intended to give her more. The abrupt way he'd stopped his ministrations made her uncertain and shaky, both inside and out. Rolling the rubber over him was one of the few ways she found power over him as he stretched next to her, face impassive, except for the gritting of teeth as she pulled her hand slowly up from the base to stroke him.

And then he pulled two pillows up, fluffing them at the head of the bed. "Your Ryan ever make love to you in any position but missionary?"

The words jarred her. "What? Um . . ."

"I'll take that as a no. Fooking idiot," he declared,

pulling her up for a deep kiss. "Have you ever been on all fours?"

A zing of tortured joy shot through her. She'd always thought that was so debasing. That she should be able to kiss the person who was inside her. "Um, no?" she answered, her voice rising at the end. What kind of question was he asking, exactly?

"Would you like to try something new, Emma?" Miki reappeared now, his body damp, smelling of lemon and soap. The ends of his hair were wet and she guessed he'd showered.

"What would that be?" Two men. *Two men are naked with me, and so help me, this is fucking fantastic. What more can they do to me?*

She was about to find out.

David moved her body for her, guiding her on knees and hands, elbows resting on the pillows. Miki slid under her, giving her a quick kiss as David braced his knees braced on either side of hers, his hands plying the flesh of her breasts, her belly, her thighs, all of which were at the mercy of gravity.

This time, self-conscious thoughts plagued her.

Again, as if reading her mind, both men said the exact right thing.

"My God, what man wouldn't want to take you every way he can and make you come and come and come, Emma. You luscious beast." The old Emma would have been offended at being called a "beast" in bed, but the rolling of the words off David's tongue, the clear sensuality and appreciation in his voice, and the way his hands admired her body, made the experience completely different.

She felt the emotion in him. Miki, too, who added, "You're so fun and warm and wonderful." Another kiss from him, and then he whispered, "And would you like to try this?" sliding his hips under her face.

As if she weren't boring, or fat, or prissy, or uptight, or OCD, or any of the other ridiculous versions of herself that Ryan—and she—had planted in her, Emma reached down and took Miki's cock in her mouth just as David splayed her before him and entered, the glorious feeling of the angle enough to make her clamp on first entry, a visceral, guttural moan pouring out of her around Miki's hard rod. With one hand, David reached under her hips and found her clitoris, which felt so swollen it had become a new limb, the touch of his fingers like a virtuoso playing her. She was the instrument.

And the chorus.

And the audience.

And the *everything*. Between her mouth working Miki into a frenzy, and David gliding in and out of her slowly from behind while pulling yet another series of orgasms out of her with those divine fingers, she wasn't quite sure when that paradigm shift happened—when she'd let go of her former self—but it had something to do with David's hoarse cry and her request for more, just as Miki shot his own climax straight into her, hissing her name over and over, like a mantra.

"God, Emma, you're so tight. And so lush, and so—" David's last words disappeared in a groan so strong she tightened around him, using her ass and vagina to trap him, the feeling going deep inside her like a tightening coil.

Miki lay beneath her and David froze behind her as he orgasmed, and Emma just turned into a floating nerve center of pure ecstasy, thrashing her ass back up against David, wanting, as she shouted, "More, David. Oh, God, give me more!" Wild and free, she craved what they offered, and in the taking learned that just giving wasn't ever going to be good enough.

Being good hadn't been good enough, either.

Taking? That was turning out to be far, far more than she'd ever bargained for.

Stubble pressed into the middle of her back and slid upward as David's cheek pressed into her, stopping at her shoulder blade, the scratchy sensation tantalizing and oh, so good. He slumped on her, his full weight pushing her down on Miki, who laughed, kissed one of her nipples, and extracted himself.

"Emma, my dear, that was extraordinary." David's voice had a muted quality. Her body bowed as he leaned in and she found herself on her elbows, her own cheek burrowed in the cool cotton pillow, her ass open and wide for all to see as David slid out of her.

Smack. The little spank made her yelp with glee. She rolled onto her side and stared up at David's naked ass as he walked to the bathroom. Miki was stretched out on the bed and twisted to reach for something on the nightstand.

"Here." He held out a glass of water.

She snorted and took it. "Hydrate, hydrate, hydrate." Still tipsy, she took the water and drank it greedily.

Miki took the empty glass and set it back down, then patted the mattress beside him. "Come here," he beckoned. Nestling in, she snuggled, marveling at how natural this all felt. In the morning, she knew, she would feel a ton of embarrassment and probably regret, but right now?

This was fucking awesome.

David returned and took a place on the other side of her. "Stay, Emma?" he asked, brushing one hand through her long, tangled hair.

Eyelids drooping, she yawned, thighs sticky and body thoroughly spent. "I just want my friends to . . ."

"They know where you are," Miki soothed.

"You're both safe to be with, right?" Sleep sounded soooo good right now.

"Of course," one of them whispered. Someone kissed her head. She spooned with a round, muscled ass and wondered whose it was as she faded out.

Boring? she thought. Fat? Fuck you, Ryan. You have no idea who I really am.

You fooking idiot.

Her fingers sought out the bare flesh where her engagement ring used to be. A brief moment of panic, then the memory of the fortune-teller. What had she said? Emma's mind filled with cotton as she struggled to remember, the feel of four warm palms drowning out her worries as she faded, completely, surrendering to slumber.

Four

***

"ROOM SERVICE!" THE *rap rap rap* of knuckles on the hotel door felt like a gemstone hammer scraping down a chalkboard. Room service? Who orders that? She and her friends didn't have enough money to—

Nude skin. Not hers. Hairy man's arm. One, two, three—four of them? Huh? Where was she?

"Room service!" the voice outside the door announced with more urgency. A woman's voice. A familiar one.

David—that was his name, right? The Irish dude—stood, grabbed a towel from the bathroom and wrapped it around hips so sculpted she wanted to lick them. Had she? The details from last night were fuzzy. Like her tongue.

After opening the door, a woman marched in carrying a tray. "You ordered?" she asked.

Wait. That wasn't the wait staff. As the woman put the tray down on the chair, she turned and looked at Emma, eyes bulging.

"OMIGOD EMMA YOU REALLY DID IT!" Melissa screamed, pulling out her phone and snapping pic after pic of her in bed with Miki.

"Stop taking pictures, you fooking idiot!" Emma screeched.

"Fooking what?" Melissa began the telltale tapping on her screen.

"I don't understand," Miki said, sitting up in bed, planting a kiss on Emma's shoulder. "You know the wait staff?"

"That's her friend, Mick. The ditzy blonde from last night."

"Not ditzy!" Melissa punched David in the shoulder, making him drop the towel. Her friend gaped at David's half-mast as Emma shook her head.

"You hijacked the room service person so you could come in here and snap pictures of me to sext?"

"I have plenty of my own sexting pics, thanks," Melissa scoffed. "No—we need ammunition against Ryan."

"You're going too fast," Emma groaned. Her head felt like someone had placed it between their thighs and squeezed. Shit—had one of the guys done that last night? Anything could have happened.

"Jordan texted you last night, right? You saw all those pics he posted."

"All those pics?" Emma sat up. The world hurt. How could sunlight be so cruel? David turned back to the bed, crawled in next to her and began massaging her neck.

Melissa cocked one eyebrow and took her eyes off her phone. "You didn't see them all?"

"Just the one with the boobs."

"Oh, Em. He . . . he's gone wild." Melissa tapped her screen a few times and then handed Emma the phone.

Miki and David crowded around her. It was like having the world witness her utter humiliation.

Actually, it wasn't *like* that.

It *was* that.

Ryan with naked women. Ryan naked with beer bottles. Ryan surrounded by topless, young women twerking. Ryan with a penis drawn on his chest in Sharpie.

Status after status: "*So glad to be free . . . Freedom's just another word for getting laid . . .*"

Like that.

David pointed and hooted. "That's Ryan? I was right."

"Fooking idiot," she said in unison with him.

"Emma, you deserve so much more." Miki frowned and shook his head, eyes sympathetic.

"Oh, God," Emma choked. "He tagged my brother and half my cousins on these. My mom is going to have a panic attack. She thought Ryan was so perfect."

Melissa took the phone back and said, "Say cheese!" the non sequitur throwing Emma for a loop.

David and Miki turned the three of them into an Emma sandwich as she clutched the sheets to hide her breasts. Melissa's phone *click-click-clicked* and then, *tap. Tap tap tap.*

"Don't! Nooooooo," Emma said, crawling over the men's legs to get to Melissa.

"Too late," her friend crowed. "Ryan just got a taste of his own medicine."

"Douche," Miki muttered. Returning to the warmth of her men, Emma settled in between them, their bodies helping to shake off the chill of Melissa's news.

"You realize my grandmother is one of my Facebook friends. She's going to . . . well, she won't need her fiber supplements when she sees that."

"Yer soooo sexy," Melissa droned.

"Maybe," David said, snuggling up to Emma, one long, hairy leg rubbing her thigh, "he'll realize what he's lost."

Emma reflexively reached for the bare skin where her ring used to be.

"Maybe."

"Anyhow, Emma needs to come back to our room." Melissa snatched a piece of bacon from the tray. "Mmmmm. I used to be vegan until we came on this trip."

"What changed your mind?" Miki asked, clearly amused.

"Um, New Orleans! And bacon. Yum."

That made about as much sense as half the crap that came out of Melissa's mouth. Emma shooed her friend out and prepared for the Walk of Shame, finding various garments and putting them on.

"So, guys . . ." she said, her head pounding. Orgasms on the motherfucking plane. How many shots at the jazz club? Ryan's asshole statuses and pics. And fucking two guys at once.

That little detail.

Now that she was dressed, if crookedly so, the awkward part had arrived. David wrapped his arms around her and gave her a chaste kiss on the cheek. Miki copied him. Both were buck naked, standing at attention.

"Um, I don't know how this works," she confessed. "This is my first one-night stand."

"No, it isn't," David argued.

"I think I'd know if I'd done this before." She rolled her eyes and took one more step toward the door.

A hand caught her wrist. Dark, passion-filled eyes met hers. Two pairs of them.

"I meant," added David, "that this doesn't need to be a one-night stand."

"I definitely don't want just that," Miki confessed.

Bzzzz. Her phone vibrated in her pocket. Saved by the text. Real life was crashing into this surreal wonderland of New Orleans, and the dissonance was too much for her. Real social media, real Facebook, real Ryan, and now—her mom?

She liked her wonderland so much more.

"Oh," she said to Miki, the response weak and silly yet all she could manage as she slipped out the door into the hallway.

Head spinning, she checked her phone.

R U NUETER her mom texted. Jane Barton was just beginning to master the finer details of texting and was a walking autocorrect joke.

Neuter?

NUTS.

No. Why? Wandering down the hallway, she realized she had no idea where she was going, and that her cami was on inside-out.

UR broccoli just showed me the pickle.

Sigh. In Jane textspeak, Emma was fairly sure she

meant, *Your brother just showed me the picture*, but Emma took the chance to evade.

Was it a dill pickle?

U NO WAT I MEANDER, her mom texted back.

Mom, just call me, Emma texted.

Cannot bc UR father is going down on me.

EWWWWWWWW! MOM!

DOWNTOWN. Dad is going downtown and hell to pack.

Translating that one made her head hurt more than all the alcohol and fucking two men in one night. One bed. At one time (almost).

The picture is a joke, Mom, she texted back.

Joke?

Yes, a joke.

Trying to get Ryan jelly belly?

Jealous?

Yes.

Um, sure, Mom. Whatever you say.

Whew.

The truth would kill her mother, so Emma kept her mouth shut. Or her fingers quiet. Whatever.

LUV U hummingbird.

Hummingbird? WTF. That wasn't some nickname. What did she intend to type?

I love you, too, Mom.

WAIT. Who R they?

Pretty close, actually.

Who R who?

The meningitis in that pickle?

Just some guys we met.

R THEY NICE?

Emma started laughing, the kind of giggles that take twenty minutes to run their course. Before the laughter overtook her, she quickly typed out:

They are so much nicer than Ryan.

Emma found her room then and was greeted by six very eager eyes staring at her like she'd just announced her new job in porn as a fluffer for James Deen.

SHOWERED, SOBER, AND ready for more, Emma sat at a table that night flanked by Miki and David, her three friends, as well as Lars, Mike, and Luke.

Everyone was talking about Ryan.

Emma had most certainly not spent two grand on a week of debauchery in New Orleans only to find herself talking about him nonstop with the two men she'd fucked last night, but that is what fate had brought her, apparently.

"You bastard," Jordan said in a low, dangerous voice that made Emma's ovaries coil in terror.

"What are you reading?" Melissa asked, watching Jordan on the phone.

Heather snuck her face over Jordan's shoulder and inhaled sharply.

"Check out Ryan's page again," Heather said, mouth set in an angry snarl. Her eyes flickered over Emma's face and changed to something close to pity.

Resigned, Emma tapped and found the page.

"*I see your two and raise you one*" was all his status said, with a picture of Ryan in a strip club, flanked by three nearly nude women.

As she read and looked on in horror, a new comment appeared.

Anyone can buy the appearance that three women find you attractive, Ryan. Congrats on having enough cash to flash.

It was Jordan.

Sonofabitch, Emma thought.

Then she noticed a message waiting for her in her in-box. Ryan. *What the hell—might as well read it.*

Emma, honey, I don't know what you're trying to prove, but nothing will make me jealous. You're obviously just finding some guys to get naked with you for a stunt, and good for you. It's cute. But be careful. You're sensitive and I would hate to see you do something you regret. Your friend, Ryan.

What are we, in fourth grade? Your friend, Ryan—as if they hadn't been engaged to be married three weeks ago?

"Fuck you," she hissed, practically flinging the phone. "Bastard messaged me."

"What did he say?" Miki growled. Seeing red, Emma couldn't even answer, instead handing the phone to Miki, who read the message aloud.

The bite was less intense when someone else read it, and especially in that smooth, accented voice. Made it seem trivial. Silly, even.

"Fooking idiot," Melissa barked.

"Now you're talking," David added.

"You realize he is projecting," Miki explained, putting his arm around Emma. Showered and dressed in business casual khakis and a gray polo, Miki looked like he could be in a Ralph Lauren ad. "He is the one who had to stage his photo. Yours," he breathed into her ear, "is all too real."

Jordan's eyebrows shot to her hairline and Heather shifted in her seat. "So she was telling the truth," Heather whispered to Jordan.

"You thought I wasn't?" Emma asked.

Both friends had the decency to look shame-faced.

"What you need, Emma, is a trump card," Miki said. "Something so big he will be shocked and cowed."

"Like what?" Jordan's eyes went wide with new admiration for Miki.

"Getting married."

The other eight heads at the table swiveled, hard, to look at him.

"What?" Emma squeaked.

"Not really married. But post a picture of you getting married. In a gown."

"Like a Las Vegas quickie!" Melissa clapped her hands and bounced up and down in her seat.

"Mmmm, a quickie," David said, nuzzling Emma's neck.

"That's just a staged picture, though," Miki said. "You need something more to wipe the smug look off his face."

"Like what?" Jordan asked. Emma watched the two as if at a tennis match, enjoying David's increasingly amorous attention.

"Like a marriage license!" Melissa chimed in.

Now the other eight heads were pointed at her. "You can't do that," Emma scoffed.

"Why not?" Melissa chirped. "Go get a fake one and take a pic and post it on Facebook. Ryan would shit his pants and never live it down."

"He needs someone to pop that ego of his," Lars agreed.

"If you posted a marriage license three weeks after he dumped you, that would be hilarious," Jordan said, nodding slowly, the idea sinking in. "And after the way he trash talked you—"

"When?" This was new to Emma.

A very uncharacteristically uncomfortable Jordan turned a shade of pink. "We were at Shooter's during happy hour and he was there with a bunch of football players, and he was . . ." She frowned.

"He was . . . ?" Emma's voice went up at the end, just like the lump in her throat.

"He said you were going to be this sad little wallflower who would spend Spring Break saving orphans or reorganizing your computer desktop. That 'boredom' should be renamed 'Emmadom.' That kind of crap." Jordon shot her a sympathetic look and mouthed the word *"Sorry."*

"Emmadom?" Emma's mouth tasted metallic, like blood and salt, the tears threatening to rise up and drown her.

Melissa and Jordan shared a look that made Emma bark out, "Spill it!"

"I was there, too," Melissa confessed. "He said the next guy who fucked you would probably find that blow-up dolls have more personality."

"And warmth," Jordan muttered.

"He's an asshole," Melissa rushed in, her words tripping over themselves. "And was drunk and with those stupid football players. I'm sure he—"

"A blow-up doll?" Emma hissed.

"How crass," Miki rasped, his eyes rejecting the idea, soothing and reassuring as he gave Emma a look of ça-maraderie and passion, somehow fusing the two. "Any man who would reject you is a fool. I would fake marry you any time."

At war inside, Emma's tears and laughter fought for supremacy. Laughter won out. "So let's have a fake wedding!" she snorted, smiling, the cloud beginning to lift.

"Better yet," David said, giving Emma a quick, public kiss and a not-so-public caress on the inside of her thighs that left her chest heaving and her heart racing, "how about two?" He and Miki exchanged an unreadable look.

"Double the fun," Emma cracked. "But do tell me where we can find a fake marriage license in New Orleans."

"You can find anything here," Heather said flatly. "Last night I saw Drew Brees doing things I'm pretty sure are illegal even in Bangkok. If you can find that, you can find two fake marriage licenses."

Emma was warming to the idea, but had her doubts. "Ryan didn't want to marry me, so why would a marriage license freak him out?"

"Guys who dump women can't stand to see some other guy get them right away. Shakes their confidence," Jordan said in a voice that might as well have said *Duh*.

"It's more than that," Miki added. "No man likes to think he's made a mistake and let another man fish in his waters."

"So now I'm a fish?" Emma snickered.

Miki frowned. "Did the euphemism not make sense in English?"

"He means Ryan's such a pussy that when he sees you sleeping around with other guys," David interjected, "he'll wish he could have his hot Emma back. But he's too fooking stupid to understand that he never can."

"Why?" Emma asked, fascinated.

"Because women become who they really are when men invite them to open up," he explained, a dazzling smile aimed straight at her, turning his face from contemplative to suggestive.

"Why the hell are we talking about Ryan?" Jordan asked.

"Melissa, engage your Google-fu," Heather ordered.

"Google what?" Miki asked, mildly amused. "This is a new Americanism."

"Juju. Google mastery. Prowess."

"Ah. You want her to search to find some good, fake marriage licenses."

"Yes."

Twenty minutes later, a pitcher or three of margaritas, and more grilled ribs than Emma knew she could contain, the group had determined that finding a fake marriage license was going to be tough. No one had access to color printers or anything online resembling something they could doctor.

Again, David and Miki exchanged a strange look. "Let's get the real thing, then," Miki ventured, his voice thick and halting.

"A real license?" Emma gagged.

"Not to really get married. Not that I don't like you," Miki added, eyes smiling. "We get one, take a picture of it, have some pictures of you in a veil and some rings and the charade is done."

"Then we tear up the license."

"Of course, Emma," Jordan barked. "No one is suggesting you legally marry two guys you fucked last night." The mean girl was coming out in her.

It seemed to turn everyone at the table on. Some dominatrix quality in Jordan made Emma want to add, "Yes, mistress," in answer to everything.

"Just go to the local town hall and draw up a license," David said in an even, amused voice. "Consider it a souvenir."

"Wouldn't a bunch of beads be a little less innocuous?" she teased.

A squeeze of her breast, with just enough pain to be suggestive, was her answer. "Worth a thousand strands."

"I want to see Ryan's face when you post this on Facebook," Melissa urged.

Everyone watched her. Emma felt cornered. What was the worst that could happen?

"Fine. Let's go get one."

"Or two!" Melissa cheered.

"Let's start with one," Emma protested, "and see where that takes us."

Five

GETTING A MARRIAGE license in New Orleans turned out to be a distressingly simple affair for people who were not residents. They needed a birth certificate and a Social Security number. That was it.

"And a divorce decree if you were married before, or a death certificate if you were widowed," the clerk at the Parish of Orleans, New Orleans's version of a town hall, explained.

Emma was numb. Hilariously numb as she looked at Miki and asked, "You been married before?"

"No. You?" He seemed thoroughly amused by the entire enterprise as the clerk handed him a form to fill out.

"I've never been *licked* by a man before. You think I've been married?"

"I don't know how to respond to that."

Emma had her birth certificate because she was paranoid and brought it in case the TSA pulled her into a booth and strip-searched her. Miki and David both had theirs because, they said, it was easier to carry with their passports in case they were ever questioned. Both had SSNs, also, because they both worked for U.S.-based organizations.

It was almost too simple.

Her friends had come with her, Melissa on her phone now, digging around on Facebook. "Looks like Erin Middleton found her inner joy at Daytona!" she crowed. "And forgot her sunscreen. Ouch. Did you know that nipples could peel?"

Emma shuddered, her hand shaking as she completed the marriage license form. Maybe she needed more from those margarita pitchers, because her hands weren't shaking simply from the idea of sunburnt nips.

This was the form she was supposed to complete with Ryan in a year and a half.

Fooking bastard. Shithead. Asshat. Motherfuckingsonofabitch. Her cursing vocabulary was woefully underdeveloped as she brewed invectives against him in her mind, pen nearly ripping the paper as she angrily finished the form.

Miki was a sport, wasn't he? That impossibly smooth, perfect hand held the pen with confidence, his handwriting barely legible in that unique, European script she found entrancing.

David stared at his phone with a piqued expression.

"You okay?" Miki asked him after he handed his paperwork to the clerk.

"Yeah. Stupid work shit. The director won't let me out of the afternoon session."

Miki's face fell and he looked at Emma with regret. What did that mean? "I know," she overheard him say, "it's not like we're here to party the way they are."

Ah. She certainly understood that. Being a responsible adult with duties and places to report to as part of an important position was her goal in life. Working in Biglaw and, eventually, earning her place as a judge—or even on the Supreme Court . . .

"Miss Barton? You need to sign here," the clerk explained. Miki needed to produce his passport. That was pretty much it. A few more formalities and they had, in their possession, a copy of a perfectly valid, nonexecuted marriage license. It didn't mean they were married.

But they could be, if they wanted, within three days.

"Ryan is going to—" Melissa gasped and giggled as Jordan rolled her eyes.

"Shit a brick," Heather added.

The group made their way through the main doors and outside into the mild spring day, Heather and David lighting up as soon as the sun hit their skin.

Melissa turned the paper face out and had Emma and Miki crowd in front of the building's sign. *Click.* A picture of them, smiling. *Click.* A picture of the license.

"Here goes! Get ready for a million texts and calls from your mom."

"You're seriously uploading that?" Emma whispered.

Jordan pulled her arm, dragging her toward a nearby

bar. "You need more alcohol. You look like a nervous bride." The crowd headed toward the open-air, terraced bar, Melissa in the lead. She grabbed two tables, squished them together, and flagged down a waiter.

"Hold on!" David protested, flicking his cigarette into the ground and smashing it. You're littering! Emma thought, her old self reemerging.

Hot, possessive hands on her shoulders. "If Miki gets to marry you, so do I!" he declared.

"You do have to be fair," Jordan intoned, nodding gravely.

"If you're sleeping with two guys at the same time, there needs to be balance," Melissa agreed.

Heather just snickered.

Emma looked at Miki, who shot her an *Aw, shucks* grin. Her friends wouldn't meet her eyes. David's eyes bore into hers as the waiter delivered the first round of drinks. Blowjobs. He grabbed one, sucked it down, slammed the shot on the iron table, and pulled her into his arms with a kiss that tasted like cloves, smoke, and chocolate liquor.

Breathless when he pulled away, Emma could only stare, clit alive and glowing, body pumped and ready for what those hands, those hips, that mouth could do to her.

"I'll be back!" David promised. "We have this stupid work panel, but I'll see you again."

"We will," Miki added.

And then they were gone, leaving four stunned women with nothing but a table full of blowjobs.

THERE WERE ONLY so many haunted mansion tours, midnight chocolate buffets, and pitchers of margaritas, sangrias, and mimosas one woman could consume in three days before boredom set in. Emma was that woman and she was craving a man.

Or two.

Miki and David—and their friends Lars, Luke, and Mike—had disappeared without a trace, and as Emma awoke on their fourth morning in New Orleans, head pounding from too much alcohol, clit throbbing from too little attention, she found herself ready to get mind-blowingly drunk and go find some other guy (or two) to take out her frustration on.

That, or another Café du Monde café au lait and beignet.

It was hard to choose.

Wearing only a silk T-shirt and undies, she rested in bed, Melissa snoring lightly next to her. Not the kind of warm body she wanted to wake up next to.

Her phone was no solace. No contact from Miki or David, though she had plenty of activity on it—127 ignored texts, thirty-three ignored voice mails, and a Facebook page that had become so popular she was pretty sure every acquaintance since preschool was trying to friend her now.

The marriage license joke had worked.

Ryan's own Facebook had gone quiet, with no new pictures of naked chicks on the beach.

But he had managed to send her two tirades.

The content of both messages boiled down to one theme: she was just trying to make him jealous to win him back.

Fooking idiot.

This was quite fun, actually. Being free and open and not pining away for him. Perfect Emma would still be perfect Emma when she went home. She'd still go to Harvard in the fall, still volunteer at the hospital, still have perfect grades, still be . . . Emma.

Here, though? Perfect Emma was on ice. In hibernation. Taking a break.

Because man, did she need one. It was so hard being that perfect.

Some might even say it was impossible.

"Emma!" shouted a voice outside the window. "I've come to claim you for my bride!"

Was that David? Who the hell else could it be—that voice was unmistakable.

"And with my trusty steed!"

Rushing to the balcony, she looked down to find David riding Miki, whose face was turned up, tongue out in a poor imitation of a horse.

Laughter gripped her and half the passersby on the street. Plenty of other balconies soon filled with hungover college girls like her, all in various stages of *awwwww*, giving Emma thumbs-ups or jealous looks.

"Will you pretend to marry me?" David shouted, now off poor Miki and down on one knee, holding a cellophane-covered red thing.

A candy ring.

Melissa was by her side, braless and wearing a cami that hid nothing. Emma looked down.

"Oh, my God, Mel—where are your pants?" Light bounced off something in her shaved pussy. Was that a—

"Pants or no pants, I'm not missing this!" With rapid speed Melissa took pic after pic of David and Miki.

"I don't need to know you this intimately!" Emma hissed, grabbing a blanket and draping it around Melissa's hips.

Two guys from the street who apparently had been enjoying the show made booing sounds when she covered Melissa up.

"Show's over!" Emma she said to them with a tight smile and a wave as they walked off.

David grabbed a fire ladder Emma hadn't noticed before, extended it and climbed up to their balcony with breakneck speed. She was in his arms and on his mouth in seconds.

"I'm taking the stairs," Miki shouted up, laughing hard.

By the time he joined them, Melissa was gone and David had Emma undressed and bent over a chair, pounding her so hard she was breathless, all the blood draining from her head and legs and flooding her core, her clit screaming *more more more* as David's slick cock entered and pulled out, the thrusts exquisite, her need over these past couple of days so great she was ready to come any second.

And then Miki's mouth was, somehow, on her clit, the two men moving her so she could be savored by both David's aggression and Miki's mastery; the perfect combination for orgasms that shattered her, making her scream and wrench and groan and wiggle and curl and unfurl as she exploded and reintegrated, shattered and rebuilt, imploded and finally went limp.

Slumped over the chair, half burying Miki with her thighs, she panted heavily, wishing David could just stay in her forever, a tinge of regret and longing as he pulled out and she heard the bathroom sink turn on.

Speaking of turned on, poor Miki hadn't been given a chance to—

David came back into the room, reaching for his jeans. "We haven't much time. This is a break from our workshops, and we have come seeking one thing."

"Two, actually," Miki growled.

"Okay, yes—two. The first was just done. Did we accomplish our goal, my sweet Emma?"

"If fucking me until my eyeballs exploded was the goal, then yes."

"GOAL!" Miki shouted, like an Italian football announcer.

"What's the second?"

"I want to pretend to marry you, too," David said, pretending to pout. "What did the fooking idiot say when he saw the marriage license?"

Oh, yeah. Ryan. For a while, she'd forgotten he existed. Emma pulled her phone out and showed David the two messages.

He read the first aloud, that fine Irish accent giving more poignancy to Ryan's words than they deserved.

"Emma, are you crazy? Unless someone there has mad Photoshop skills, that looks like a real marriage license, and is that the same guy from that staged picture of you in a threesome? If you're trying to embarrass me, it's working. Your mom is having an absolute fit. Please call her and get her off my back. Please call me."

"You think?" Miki shook his head. "He sees what he gave up, Emma." He stroked her thigh as she slid on some pants, the hunger evident in the way his fingers gripped her.

"Oh, this second one is a doozy," David snickered.

"Emma, now people from school are flooding my Facebook and telling me I was an idiot for breaking up with you. Maybe they're right. Please call."

"Not an idiot," David said, "a fooking idiot."

"A motherfuckingsonofabitch," Emma muttered. First Ryan tries to guilt her. Then—only because *other people* told him he was an idiot—he thinks about getting back together. Oh, no. Hell, no.

Hell to the fucking no.

"Attagirl," David added. Miki was impatient for his turn, and Emma wanted to give it to him. A quick blowjob—and not the kind that tasted like chocolate— should do the trick.

"Let's freak him out with a second marriage," David said, winking.

Miki, to her surprise, climbed off the chair and gave her a quick, Emma-scented kiss. "Sounds good."

"What about your workshop?" she asked.

David tapped rapidly on his screen, then held up one finger. "Hold on." He and Miki stared at the screen with a patience Emma found maddening.

"Yes!" they said in unison.

"We're out for the next two hours," David explained, grabbing Emma's hand. "Just enough time to cause more mayhem."

Two hours later Melissa was snapping pics of her and David with their marriage license at a table at yet another outdoor patio along the street. A different clerk had been at the desk, and David managed the process so well Emma found herself wondering why it took more time to pay a campus parking ticket than it did to get a marriage license.

Melissa uploaded, tagged, and grinned wildly. "Let's go party in honor of the newly not-married couple!"

David winced, exchanged an unreadable look with Miki, and the two groaned. "We have to get back to work."

"Work, shmerk. We only have one more day here. We leave day after next," Emma whined. It clearly caught the guys by surprise, and Emma wasn't certain whether it was her whining or their departure.

"We leave that day, too. When's your flight?"

"Ten A.M."

"Ours is at seven A.M. Damn. So today and tomorrow are it?" Miki asked, clearly chagrined.

"Yes." She held her breath. Her dorm room seemed so far away. Not just physically or geographically, but like a different life she'd shed just days ago. That she would plan and study, get ready for finals, finish up her extracurriculars, begin graduation party plans, send invitations, unwind the wedding plans, and check little boxes off to-do lists, which she had always been relieved to finish. As if being a good person meant having all the to-do's she'd invented for herself done and out of the way. Life was a series of *transactions* for Old Emma.

New Emma?

For her, life was one big *experience*.

"Look, we can't do anything about tonight," David said. "Work shit has us booked. But tomorrow—tomorrow, we party. Wait for us and we'll be here around nine, okay?" His smack on her ass promised so many things.

"Wait!" Emma called out. "What about Miki?"

Looking forlorn and dejected, Miki turned to David. "What about me? You got what you needed. So did Emma."

"You are first in line, right. Emma?" David assured him.

"Both of you give me one final night in bed and we'll make sure everyone's happy," she promised.

The guys groaned. As they rushed to grab a cab, Miki shouted back: "Best service project trip ever!"

Emma had to agree. The Unboring of Emma Barton service trip was, thus far, a rousing success.

Six

THE CONCIERGE, the same smooth, older blond woman from her first night there, held a cordless phone in one hand as Emma opened her hotel door. Disappointed it wasn't David and Miki, she nonetheless let politeness kick in and smiled at the woman.

"Yes?"

"You have a very concerned man who says he is your fiancé, calling to speak with you, Miss Barton."

Fiancé. Haha. David and Miki were hilarious.

"Thank you." The concierge stepped back to give her some privacy.

"Very funny, guys," she said into the phone. "Now, get over here so we can get our drink on and—"

"Emma? What the hell are you doing?"

She stopped cold.

"Ryan?"

"You're ignoring everyone's calls and texts, you post

pictures of marriage licenses with two different guys, and no one knows what the hell is going on. Are you being drugged? Have you been kidnapped? I keep assuring Jane that you must be well because you're with friends who would never let you—"

"I am fine, Ryan." Her voice was like a cold noodle. "I assure you. Remember? I'm *boring*."

Silence. Then, "Is that what this is about?" Smug laughter poured out of the phone, but his voice was higher and more frantic than usual. "You're taking these fake photos and—"

"Nothing fake about those photos."

If silence could have levels of quiet, then what passed for the next thirty seconds was the deepest level of shocked silence known to mankind. Finally, he choked out, "You slept with two guys at once?"

"I had fun." The grin that spread across her face was impossible to control, the cheerfulness in her voice a sly dig.

"Emma, you wouldn't have sex with me unless we'd both showered and brushed our teeth before. I find it hard to believe that you would—"

"Do you have any idea how good it feels to have a guy lick your clit while another man does you from behind, Ryan?" she said in a sultry, empowered voice.

"Do I . . . what?" His voice shot up high, choked.

"Or to have an actual orgasm with a man? Or two?"

"It's not my fault you faked it," he sputtered. "Two? You're really having threesomes now, Emma?"

"I'm having fun. Tell my mom I'm fine, and you just

go off and bury your head in more melons, Ryan. Don't be afraid to live your own life."

"No! No! That's not what I—" Anguish and confusion came through the line, tearing her in half. But not in the same way it would have a few days ago.

"And by the way—thank you." She meant it, deeply, a rush of gratitude pouring into her limbs, her mind, her heart. "Thank you for dumping me, Ryan." Her fingers worried the spot of skin where the ring used to be.

"You're *thanking* me?" His tone was beyond incredulous.

"Yes. I would never, ever, in a million years have broken up with you. Ever. I was too duty bound and too loyal. But now you set me free, and oh, Ryan . . ." Her voice dropped off, choked by genuine appreciation. Flashes of David's commanding voice as he pleasured her from behind flew through her mind, blending with Miki's fevered kisses as he stroked her to climax on the plane.

"I never realized what I was missing."

A strangled sound was all she heard.

"So thank you so much. I mean it."

"That's not what I meant, Emma! I never—"

She tapped "End."

"Miss Barton?" the concierge said.

Shit. She had forgotten it was her phone and that she was still there. Handing the phone over, she could barely make eye contact.

"Yes?"

"Brava." And with that one word, the concierge turned

on her heel and left Emma wearing a smile that no fucking idiot could wash away.

AND BACCHANALIA ENSUED.

As promised, David and Miki reappeared, with Luke, Lars, and Mike in tow, at their hotel bar around nine. It was probably nine, at least; Emma wasn't really sure. All the numbers on her phone had blended together into one sweet wall of glow after she'd had shot after shot of whatever Melissa brought her.

Time ceased to matter. Miki and David were time itself, embodied flesh and love and thrust and everything to her. The night passed in flashes of fun and silliness. Stumbling upstairs to her room, she was conscious only of how the three of them were all she wanted in the entire world, to blend and commune and just be.

Tongues and mouths and kisses and sighs punctuated the air, along with thrusts and groans and moans and cries. Their names mingled in this new consciousness; her nakedness, the new norm; the freedom of three bodies entwined in whatever configuration brought the greatest ecstasy, the new rule of law. It was sexual utilitarianism at its finest: the greatest good for the greatest number.

And, by God, it was the greatest kind of good.

Emma's final awareness came as she straddled Miki, impaled by his sheathed rod, on the small settee in her room. Raucous crowds in the streets cheered, an old saxophone player on the corner wended tunes that pierced her heart, and David's hot body behind her used one slick hand to stroke her ass, a finger slipping in where none had ever been, making her gasp and clamp, triggering a hoarse groan from Miki that was so powerfully arousing, Emma wanted to hear it on an endless loop.

"That feels so, oh," she moaned as David slipped the finger past her thick, tight wall of muscle, her anus virgin and untried, the fullness and the illicit sense that what they were doing was so untamed a powerful aphrodisiac.

Old Emma would have been keenly aware of this. New Emma embraced it, sought it out, and a brief, linear thought found its way into her mind as she reached for a pitcher of Long Island iced tea that David had brought up with them, drinking straight from the side of the glass container.

Ménage is the new anal.

David's finger in her ass began to stroke the thin wall of flesh between it and Miki's cock, the slick, twinned sensations so powerful she rode both, trying and failing to get the right rhythm to reach perfection.

You don't have to be perfect anymore, something deep inside her said in a soothing voice.

And then David's finger was gone, replaced by something much larger, more bulbous, more—

"Emma, may I?" he asked from behind her, mouth nipping at her earlobe, tongue teasing the skin just behind the curve of her ear.

This was the moment when her brain was supposed to halt, right? She was supposed to be terrified and to reject the idea of—geez, what was it called when two guys were in two holes at once?

The word escaped her.

Nudging her ass back in encouragement, her body answered for her, even as her mind struggled to decide what to say. David took that as a yes—and it most definitely was, she realized—as he pushed gently against her ass. Alas, it was not mean to happen, for he was too big and she too new to this.

After what seemed like nine hours but was likely only a few minutes, that familiar warmth and chuckle came, and he simply said, "Another time, my dear," and then the glorious finger came, stroking her from the inside as Miki thrust his hips up into her, kissing her so deeply and with a tenderness that made her melt.

Whatever came after was a sea of bliss.

A dark, hot, joyful place of no return.

Seven

"EMMA! GET THE fuck up!" Melissa screeched. "We have twenty minutes to catch a cab! Holy shit!" The covers were stripped off her and lasers masquerading as sunshine burned her eyes out.

"Fuck! What are you doing?" Emma groaned. Opening her eyes, she found not the frantic movement she expected of her three roommates—really? only twenty minutes?—but, instead, three sets of eyes gawking, wide and horrified, with mouths dropped like fish dying.

"You're—what are you—why?" Their mingled voices made Emma look down.

She was naked.

"What? Never seen a naked woman? Hell, I saw Melissa's naked pussy the other day and she has a piercing right on her—"

Melissa pointed at Emma's head, while Jordan and

Heather pointed lower. "Did Emma really just say 'pussy'?" Heather whispered to Jordan.

Emma reached up.

Gauze. She pulled on it. White gauze. The kind brides—

She stood up and ran to the mirror.

Naked as could be, there she stood, breasts full and waist curvy, wearing a bridal veil.

Her hand—the left hand with the exposed flesh where Ryan's engagement ring used to live—now held bright red candy rings on the ring finger.

Rings.

Two of them.

Laughter burbled out of her like a fountain of amusement. Then pain pounded her head. "What the fuck happened last night?" she asked.

Melissa threw a pair of undies and some sweats at her. "We have no idea. You completely disappeared with David and Miki and—here you are."

Emma's mouth felt like there was sand in it. She began sucking on one of the rings. "Mmm. Cherry."

"Cute, but we really will miss our flights, and I don't feel like spending another $150 that I don't have on a change fee," Jordan snapped. "I already have a bar bill that equals a semester of tuition."

Emma laughed.

"You think I'm joking? Wait until you get yours when you check out, chickie babe."

Melissa handed Emma her shoes. "Thank goodness you were so anal—"

"How do you know?" Emma choked out, suddenly remembering parts of the previous night. *God, that felt sooo good.*

Three sets of eyebrows shot up. Melissa snickered and said, "I was about to say, you were so *anal-retentive* about packing last night so we wouldn't be late."

"What did you do with those guys? A little DP action?" Jordan said in a confidante's voice. The attention she paid to Emma felt like a compliment.

"DP?" Emma squeaked. The room spun. Her clit felt raw and ripe all at once.

Three eye rolls.

Bzzzz.

"Don't get that!" all three said as Emma reached for her phone. "We don't have time!"

Emma finished dressing, pulling the veil off with a tinge of regret and stuffing it in her carry-on. She took over the bathroom, ran a washcloth over her face, and combed her hair into a ponytail. A few glasses of water and three ibuprofen later, she was good to go.

Good enough, at least.

Bzzzz.

She giggled. "I'm popular."

"Don't answer it!" they all shouted, dragging carry-ons and suitcases down the hall, in such a rush they didn't bother to ask for a cart.

The race to the street made Emma's stomach churn, and she was glad she'd packed light.

Jordan flagged down a cab with a glare and a whistle,

and then, ensconced in their seats, the four breathed deep sighs of relief.

Bzzz. Emma pulled her phone out, but Melissa snatched it away, turning the ringer off. She opened an app and tapped away on the phone, looking at Emma in awe, then back at the phone screen.

"If you're wondering what happened last night, Emma, here you go." Melissa handed her the phone, and as Emma flipped through page after page of photos that only intensified her sense of gratitude to Ryan, one thought looped through her:

YOLO.

Her eyes burned and belly churned as her exhausted brain and throbbing nether regions tried to make sense of the night. The phone's tiny screen shot poisoned-darts into her eyes. Or, at least, it felt that way, a giant boulder of nausea making its rumbling way down a path into a pit of despair where her stomach used to be.

"Melissa, you dumbass," Jordan said in a near monotone. She grabbed the phone from Emma. "She'll puke in the car if she does anything other than stare straight ahead."

Jordan was right.

Deep breaths, two half-liter bottles of water, and a pill Heather extracted from a mysterious vial of multi-colored caplets that looked like the pharmaceutical equivalent of a bag of Skittles, were able to keep Emma together through the security check points, and as the four settled in their seats, she looked longingly at D3.

No Miki. Why should there be?

Bzzzz.

C3 isn't the same without you, the text read, and she smiled, the nausea fading, her body humming with the memory of last night.

Or, rather, the lack of a memory. Two red candy rings replaced whatever her cerebral cortex was supposed to have recorded, her hippocampus about as functional as her stomach right now.

That's because I'm in A11, she texted back to Miki, leaning her forehead against the cool glass.

"I'm sorry, miss, but you need to turn your cell phone off. We're about to take off." The flight attendant's smile was kind but all business.

Before she turned the phone off, a quick response from Miki—*You haven't seen the last of us*—filled her with a deep sense of longing for the Emma she knew she needed to become. Whoever that was. However that might be.

"Wild child," Melissa said, nudging her hand, flicking the giant sugar rocks, red and shiny. The plane began its taxi down the runway, Emma closing her eyes, her thumb worrying the spot where her engagement ring used to rest, now covered with cheap plastic.

Madame Ysabeau's words intrigued her as she watched New Orleans recede as the plane ascended, becoming miniature, then a pinpoint, then nothing at all as the clouds covered what had been the craziest week of her life.

I see fear in you so full it crowds out all that your heart needs.

Opening her eyes, Emma looked at the candy rings and lifted one, sucking on it.

Ryan's comment—*Emmadom*—intruded, gnatlike and invasive. She chuckled, a dismissive sound that made her suck harder on the sweet cherry candy.

Fooking idiot.

SHAKE ME

By Sara Fawkes

To the readers, who are made of awesome.

One

"I WANT TO get laid."

Melanie nearly choked on her coffee. "Say what?"

"I'm serious." Cassidy set her chai tea on the table. "I'm tired of being the only virgin I know."

"Come on, Cassidy . . ."

"Chad never seems to want to make out. It's frustrating, really. He wants to wait until we're married, and I thought so too, but sometimes . . ." She trailed off, then threw her hands in the air. "Ugh. I just want to see what the big deal is."

Melanie smirked. "That bad, huh?"

"It's not bad, I just . . ." Cassidy sighed. "I just get horny sometimes."

"Oh God." Melanie covered her ears with her palms. "I didn't need to hear that."

Cassidy glared at her friend. Melanie said more than that—and worse!—on a daily basis. The redhead was a

Chatty Cathy about her own love life, and it was high time she returned the favor. "Well, it's true. What I'd give for even a good make-out session, some heavy petting." Her mouth twisted. "But any time I tell Chad that, he gives me the same speech about chastity before marriage. I mean, he'll kiss me, but that's about it."

"Well," Melanie said slowly after a moment's silence, "I suppose if I went nearly twenty years without any kind of sex, I'd be a little bitter too."

They sat in silence for another moment, sipping their drinks, then Cassidy's mouth tipped up in a rueful smile. "It's good to have you back in town."

"Admit it," Melanie said, a smug look on her face, "this place is boring without my presence."

Cassidy laughed and shook her head. The sleepy little coastal town was slow to change, and proud of it. Attempts at modernization tended to be met with reluctance by the locals. Even the coffee shop they were in wasn't immune to the effects. Old-timers who'd been frequenting the joint still came by on a regular basis. Over in one corner, two old men played checkers, while a local ladies club conducted a meeting. Even though the owner was trying for a more modern feel, the clientele still looked like your average Mississippi crowd.

"Well," Cassidy said, "I have you for the week, so hopefully we can catch up more." Melanie was back in Mississippi for Spring Break from college up in Tennessee, and Cassidy planned to spend most of the next week with her.

The little coffee shop was hopping for lunch, people

coming inside from the chilly day for a warm drink. Rain tapped against the roof, echoing through the small space. "If this weather keeps up," Melanie said, stabbing her stirring stick into a leftover pastry, "this is going to be the lamest Mardi Gras ever."

Cassidy sighed. "I wish I was going to New Orleans with you."

"Hey, I invited you along."

"I know and I appreciate that, it's just . . ."

"Yeah, you're busy."

The disappointment in her friend's voice dug at Cassidy's heart. "I'm sorry."

Melanie took a deep breath. "I know. It's just, how often do you get Mardi Gras *and* Spring Break on the same week? If there was ever a time to hit New Orleans and do the party thing, this is it." She smirked. "Of course, your dad would probably follow after you and drag you home the minute you even look at any alcohol."

Cassidy rolled her eyes at the imagery. "Yeah, he can be a bit . . . overprotective."

"Girl, if he was anything but your papa, I'd say he was downright stalkerish."

Cassidy hitched a shoulder. "I'm his only daughter. Makes sense, right?"

Melanie snorted. "You're too practical. Come on, you gotta live a little." She elbowed her friend, a sly smile tugging her lips. "Especially if you're seriously looking into getting laid."

Cassidy felt her face heat up. "I don't want some nameless encounter," she murmured, "I just wish . . ."

"Well, well, well. Sounds like Chastity Cassidy is looking to ditch her nickname."

Cassidy closed her eyes and took a deep breath. *Why now?* "Go away, Travis."

"Not on your life." The boy who had been her biggest tormentor through middle and high school fixed her with a big grin. "This is the most interesting conversation of yours I've ever eavesdropped on."

Blood rushed to her face, and she laid her head down on the table. "Please, please go away," Cassidy begged, knowing it was no use. Why did she let herself have this conversation in public?

"And here I always thought Chastity Cassidy didn't know what the word 'sex' even meant." Travis grabbed a nearby chair and pulled it up to the table backwards, straddling the wooden backrest. He looked back and forth between the two girls expectantly. "Don't stop your conversation on my account," he said, beaming widely.

Cassidy let out a frustrated groan.

The boy wore his usual plaid shirt and white tank underneath, the buttons undone just enough to show off the muscles his clothing hid. His dark blue jeans were tight in just the right places, hugging a backside that had the girls lining up to look. He had that chiseled jawline and rugged good looks that could charm the teeth off a gator, and wasn't afraid to use it to get what he wanted. He was a Southern boy through and through, with his ball cap and cocky smile, just the sort of guy Cassidy tried to avoid.

Yes, Travis Dean was too handsome for his own good, but that wasn't Cassidy's problem with him. The boy had been her self-appointed tormentor through high school, and even after graduation he still dogged her footsteps. She mostly ignored him, especially now that they were both supposed to be adults, but Travis apparently hadn't received that particular memo. He still poked fun at her whenever they saw one another, and considering how small their little Mississippi town was, that happened more often than Cassidy preferred.

Melanie's phone went off and, glaring at the new arrival, she checked it. "Dammit, Cass, I gotta go. I was supposed to pick up Jaime almost an hour ago." Melanie stared glumly at her friend, then her eyes narrowed. "Unless you've changed your mind about going?"

Cassidy opened her mouth to answer, then closed it again with a sigh. "I've got too much going on this weekend." A part of her wished otherwise, especially now that she was caught in such a quagmire. Between the spring pageant the church was hosting and the food drive she herself had organized, her weekend was booked.

New Orleans during Mardi Gras was too dangerous anyway, she reminded herself. She'd been to the city before and had loved the architecture of the French Quarter, but she'd shied away from the bigger celebrations. Too many stories of debauchery and lewd behavior for her tastes. The pictures she saw of the parades, the various floats and spectacles, did sometimes make her want to see it in person, but this year, at least, she couldn't. She had her whole life ahead her; things like this could wait.

Melanie looked from Travis to Cassidy. "If you want me to stay, I can."

Cassidy shook her head, motioning her friend away. "No, it's all right. I'll have you all next week, I won't begrudge you one weekend. Anyway, I was just leaving too."

As her friend waved and hurried out to her car, Cassidy stood up with as much pride as she could muster. "If you'll excuse me," she said in a frosty tone, barely glancing at Travis as she gathered her purse and sweater.

"Don't worry, sugar." He sprang to his feet, still grinning. "I can at least play the gentleman and escort you to your car."

Gentleman. She rolled her eyes. Travis had never been a gentleman in his life. She of all people would know.

"What do you want, Travis?" she said as they exited the small café. "Besides to be a pain in my backside."

"You know, there was a time you would've said I was a pain in the ass."

Cassidy pursed her lips. "People grow up," she said in a clipped tone, eyeing him sideways. "Some people, at least."

Travis clapped his hands to his heart. "Oh, Princess, you wound me."

He'd always been good at goading her. Cassidy could feel her temper rising, and tamped it down. "Travis Dean, a bayou gator couldn't bite any sense into you."

"Now there's the Cassidy I used to know."

Trying to ignore him, she made a beeline for her car. Travis had been tormenting her for as long as she could remember, but it hadn't always been this way. Their families had been neighbors, and there was a time growing up when they'd been friends. Once, she'd gotten herself into as much trouble as him, but as she reached adolescence, her mother started teaching her how to be a lady. The change had been an uphill battle, as Cassidy remembered it, but by the time her mother passed away her freshman year, she was a different girl. Her life wasn't as full of adventure as her youthful exploits, but she'd learned to take pride in keeping up appearances.

Travis, meanwhile, had never matured beyond a little boy. Oh sure, he'd grown up to be one of the sexiest men in the area, but he was still as immature as ever. He had himself a harem of groupies who followed him around like dopey-eyed fawns, but he still made time to poke at Cassidy. It was a habit she'd always hoped he'd grow out of, but that didn't seem to be the case.

"Aren't you the least bit curious why I was looking for you?" he asked as she fished through her purse for the keys.

"Not in the slightest."

"I have a picture you might like to see."

This time she did snort. "I'm sure you do but I'm not interested in your . . . naughty bits."

He let out a loud laugh and Cassidy flushed. Now, why on earth had she said that?

"Hm, so Chastity Cassidy thinks about my 'naughty bits'?"

He was leaning against her car door, less than a step away. It was close enough that she could tell he smelled really good. His tank top dipped low, the line of sun-kissed muscles catching Cassidy's eye. Her train of thought suddenly making her uncomfortable, she tried to open the door, which wouldn't budge with his weight against it. "Get off my car," she said primly, staring pointedly at the hollow of his throat, not allowing her eyes to dip any lower again.

He stepped forward. "Or you'll do what?" he said, leaning in close.

Goose bumps broke out over her skin as Cassidy sucked in a breath. It was on the tip of her tongue to tell him where to shove it, but no words would come out of her mouth. His proximity was doing weird things to her body, and mustering the courage for battle, she looked up into his face.

Big mistake. *He really has grown handsome.*

Now, where the heck had that thought come from?

"Well, I'll be damned," Travis drawled as the silence dragged on, "Cassidy Dupre is speechless. I didn't think I'd ever see the day."

Angry words boiled up, but Cassidy shoved them back down. It didn't matter, she could wait him out. There were some calls she had to make anyway. Lifting her chin, she gave him another chilly look. "Good day, Mr. Dean."

Crossing his arms, he just leaned more heavily against the car door. "You sure you don't want to see the picture I found?"

The thought of getting in through the passenger side was looking more and more appealing, but she had the feeling her tormentor would follow her around the car. "What do you want?" she said finally, exasperated.

Grinning, he pulled his phone from his pocket. "You remember my little sister Deedee? She loves all that social media bullshit, and usually I ignore it, but this one caught my attention."

Cassidy remembered Travis's sister as a girl who'd sometimes tagged along on her brother's adventures. When Cassidy had stopped playing with the neighborhood kids, Deedee disappeared from her life. Bracing herself for whatever trick he was pulling, she glared at him for several seconds before glancing at the phone. "I don't see what this has to do with . . ." She trailed off, blinking at the happy couple staring back at her from the screen. "What the hell?" The curse slipped freely off her tongue and she snatched the phone from his hands.

Deedee was easy to identify, even after all these years. The bleached blonde younger girl was making a goofy face for the camera, but it was the boy who she was hanging from that got Cassidy's attention. She swiped the image sideways, revealing another photo of the duo, kissing for the camera this time. Fingers trembling in shock, Cassidy dug her own phone out of her purse. Scrolling through the texts and phone calls, she realized with a sick feeling that she hadn't heard from Chad since the previous day. No texts, no phone calls, nothing. "When did you find this?"

"Three hours ago."

Three hours? "But . . ."

"She took off two days ago," Travis supplied when Cassidy said nothing for several seconds. "My parents figured she'd gone to a Mardi Gras celebration somewhere, but they didn't bother asking specifics. This was the first I'd heard from her since she left, and I figured you might know something. You are dating Captain Incredible, right?"

It was a nickname Chad had picked up in middle school. Everything he touched was gold. He excelled at sports and had been student body president and summa cum laude of her graduating class, beating her out of the honor by only a hundredth of a point. It was how they got to know one another, actually. They were highest in their class academically, and it just made sense that they would end up together. He was as good a boyfriend as a girl could have, remembering every special occasion or anniversary, always the romantic. If he'd been a little more chaste than Cassidy sometimes preferred, it was only by mutual agreement, despite her earlier protests to Melanie.

And yet, now he was caught on camera being kissed by a girl with a cigarette and a beer bottle poised in one hand as she took a selfie with her phone.

Shoving the offending cell phone into Travis's chest, Cassidy quickly dialed Chad's number and held it up to her ear. It went straight to voice mail, and she gripped the phone hard, waiting for the automated message to play through.

"Hey sweetheart," she said, trying to keep her voice light, "I haven't heard from you in a while, give me a call when you get this."

"No answer, huh?" Travis said as Cassidy ended the call. "Convenient."

"Whatever you might say, I'm sure this is a misunderstanding. I trust him." Despite her words, inside she was reeling. Her brain couldn't come up with a single tolerable excuse for the picture of Deedee kissing his cheek.

"The location was tagged on the picture," Travis continued as Cassidy pulled up the texting screen on her phone. "New Orleans."

Her fingers tightened around the phone as Cassidy drew a blank on what to write in the text.

Hi, I was just told you were in New Orleans with some blonde chick. Hello, are you really as big a douche as I've just been led to believe?

"You must think this is hilarious," she murmured, surprised by how emotionless her voice sounded.

"Actually, I was wondering if you wanted to look for them with me."

She looked up, expecting to see a smirk, but his face was curiously serious. Whatever barbs she'd expected from Travis weren't coming; he was watching her silently, waiting for an answer. It was unnerving seeing him so still; as long as she'd known him, she couldn't remember when the notorious prankster was ever this serious. "Lord help you, Travis Dean, if this is some prank . . ."

"Despite what you think of me, Cass, I'm not asshole enough to stomp on a broken heart."

His words stopped her short. Swallowing, she looked away, her emotions too jumbled to think straight over this new development. *Travis Dean, being nice to me?*

When had hell frozen over?

"Come on, I'll drive."

It wasn't until she was already in the small pickup driving down the road that Cassidy realized she'd just voluntarily gotten into his truck. She must have been more shell-shocked than she realized to willingly get into the same vehicle as Travis Dean. Melanie, she knew without a doubt, would have turned right around and picked her up, happy to take her friend to Mardi Gras. Thinking about that, however, Cassidy wouldn't have wanted to ruin her fun with drama and she didn't want Melanie to know she was teaming up with her archnemesis. When they were kids, he'd sabotaged Melanie's hair gel with crazy glue, so she had her own reasons for disliking Travis.

No doubt people had seen her leave with the handsome Cajun boy, but for once she didn't care how the rumor mill portrayed her. At the moment she had more important matters to attend to—for one, a potentially philandering soon-to-be-ex boyfriend. Thoughts on revenge superseded any other consideration, except how people might react if she were to turn murderess on Chad's cheating backside.

Now there was a novel idea.

Two

CASSIDY DUPRE WAS sitting beside him in his truck, staring quietly out the window. *In his truck.*

He was a nervous wreck.

Travis gripped the steering wheel, the worn vinyl slippery. His hands were sweating and his foot kept tapping with nervous energy. For a man used to constant action, the silence was nearly intolerable. But he kept his mouth shut, afraid to scare off the one girl who meant more to him than any other in the world. God, he was such an idiot. Yet here she was, giving him the golden opportunity he was scared shitless he'd mess up.

Cassidy. He snuck a sideways glance at her. She hadn't moved a muscle, staring out the passenger window at the pine trees whipping past. His dream girl sat barely two feet away, the same girl he'd been tormenting now for years. She had on a red dress and a yellow cardigan, bold colors that were as vibrant as the girl he remembered from his childhood. Her blonde hair was curled and tied back with a matching red bow, the same ponytail he'd chased after until puberty hit them both like a freight train.

Once upon a time they'd been inseparable. He'd loved her fiercely from the moment he laid eyes on her. All she wanted to do was have fun, and Travis he had been her willing companion. Oh, the chaos they'd created. They got caught doing pranks more times than he could count, and she'd insisted on sharing the punishments despite her parents' best efforts to keep her out of trouble. He'd never cared about detention, but Cassidy's parents had argued to get her out. She always managed to sabotage their efforts, and they two of them ended up spending hours together after class, figuring out ways to get into even more trouble.

Then middle school came around, and almost overnight Cassidy's mother attempted to civilize her, restricting her time away from the house, insisting that Cassidy wear skirts instead of jeans and cover her bare feet with heeled shoes. Still, Cassidy managed to sneak away some days, rebelled by hiding her shoes to go around barefoot. She didn't care if her dresses got muddy or whether the boys could see her panties when she climbed trees.

When her mother was diagnosed with cancer just before freshman year, everything changed. Cassidy wholeheartedly embraced the lifestyle she'd fought against, and the wild girl who'd been his constant companion fell away. By the time her mother passed away only a few months after the diagnosis, Cassidy was almost beyond his recognition. In a way, he understood her desire to please her dying mom, but the sight of the strange closed-off girl in his freshman classes prompted him into action.

Travis started doing things to get a rise out of her, like putting bugs in her hair or calling her names—anything to break through the growing ice he saw forming around her like a shell. The more she withdrew, the harder he pushed. Not all of it had to do only with Cassidy. He became very good at organizing events like locker room raids where they stole all the girl's clothes, and good at practical jokes he pulled on teachers and in class. The girls also began to notice him much more, which he didn't mind at all.

Sometimes the old Cassidy would emerge, much to his chagrin. Sophomore year, after a particularly nasty prank involving sanitary pads on her locker door, she brought a tray of homemade brownies to class. Smiling sweetly after presenting them to the class, she watched as they were quickly scarfed up. None of the boys noticed that neither the girls nor the teacher were touching them, and found out why less than an hour later, when they all rushed to the bathroom.

Laxative brownies. He was never been able to duplicate that prank, although he'd tried. Word had spread too well around their little Mississippi town, and nobody was gullible enough to accept food from him. That was one story they'd be telling for years, he was sure.

Time had marched on, and he'd despaired of ever getting the girl he knew back. The further they'd grown apart, the more he admired her and she despised him.

He knew he deserved it, but despite everything, he loved the lady she'd become. It hurt to see her glares or, worse, when she ignored him outright, but that didn't stop his tongue from digging his grave deeper any chance he got.

The girl he'd grown up with was still inside there, itching to get out—he had to believe it. And now she was in his truck. He didn't like what Deedee had done but he couldn't argue with the results.

Trying to get rid of some nervous energy before he said something he'd regret, Travis fiddled with the radio dial. "You like country?"

When she didn't answer, he took her silence for assent and settled on a local station. It was on the tip of his tongue to apologize for his sister's behavior, but that was a can of worms he didn't want to open. He didn't want her associating the situation with him, or thinking it was his fault. Because it wasn't. Sure, he wanted to make himself the hero of this whole thing—that was why he'd approached her in the first place—but unlike his pranks, he had no game plan going into this. So he kept silent, twisting his hands over the wheel, tapping his foot against the pedal.

"If you're trying to annoy me with that tapping," Cassidy said, "you're doing a good job."

"Sorry." He forced his foot to stop moving, which only served to magnify his internal tension. His parents had given him ADHD meds growing up, and now that he was on his own, he was trying to live without them. He could have used them right then, though—trapped in his truck with the girl of his dreams, unable to speak or move for two hours. The situation was hell, but at least he was with Cassidy.

The drive from the Mississippi coast was quick, and they reached New Orleans close to seven o'clock. The sun was a distant memory in the dark skies, winter still ending the days far too early. Travis switched on his phone GPS, realizing they needed a plan for their impromptu trip. "Should, ah, we look for a hotel or something?"

"I don't intend on staying the night."

Her clipped tone made him more nervous. He was used to his small coastal town, which was difficult to get lost in, but New Orleans was a maze to him. The notorious Louisiana city was huge, the drivers not nearly as friendly as the ones back home. Unable to merge over, he missed his exit as the GPS recalculated the route.

"Oh, gimme that." Cassidy took the phone out of Travis's hands, which he relinquished with no small amount of relief. "Take the next exit then turn right."

"Yes, ma'am!"

"How do you intend on finding your sister anyway?" she asked as they began navigating the downtown streets.

"My parents don't really care too much what we get up to as long as it's not illegal, but I don't like the attention my little sister gets. She, ah, developed early, and was boy-crazy in middle school. So, I put a tracking app on her phone."

"Tracking app?"

Her voice was disbelieving, but in for a penny. "The little program has saved her bacon more than a few times. Made me bash a few skulls together too when I found her with older guys, but that's my job. I'm sure you can tell that she and I aren't on the best of terms, but at least Deedee didn't drop out of high school like our cousins."

"You're a good brother."

Her words almost made him drive off the road. He glanced over at her, but she was staring straight ahead, face unreadable. "Well, I'll be damned. Cassidy Dupre actually said something nice to me."

Travis could have kicked himself the moment the words left his mouth. *Stupid, stupid!* He watched her lips compress into a thin line and felt like banging his head against the steering wheel.

"Just drive," she muttered, and his heart sank.

He really was his own worst enemy.

CASSIDY SLID OUT of the truck, looking up and down the dark road. "So," she said slowly, her eyes darting around in the darkness. "Wanna tell me how this is going to work?"

"It's simple, actually." Travis pulled his phone out of his pocket, brought up the app, and tossed the phone onto the passenger seat for Cassidy. "It loads up the map program. Pretty simple, the dot is where she is. Follow it and see if your guy is with her, then confront."

Cassidy played with the map a bit, orientating herself with the area while the app did its search in the background. "What if she doesn't have her phone on her?" she asked as Travis came around the front of the truck.

He gave her a droll look. "This is my sister we're talking about. She can't survive five minutes without the damned thing."

Cassidy fell silent, staring at the phone and then at the street signs around them. They were on the outskirts of the French Quarter, but away from Bourbon Street, there was practically no one about. It had taken them forever to find parking. They'd driven in circles before finally pulling into an open lot along the Mississippi River levy. It didn't look like a legitimate parking lot, but cars were lined up on the dirt anyway, so at least their truck wasn't alone.

"Come on," she said, starting down the sidewalk toward the lit cathedral nearby. They'd passed it twice, and she at least knew the way there.

"Can I have my phone back?" Travis asked, trotting along after her.

She shook her head, not slowing her pace. "I don't need for you to drag this out like some kind of sick game. The sooner we find them, the sooner I can go home and forget any of this ever happened."

And the sooner I can get away from you.

It was strange. The thought went through her mind, but the words were devoid of any emotion. In fact, she felt badly for even thinking them, considering Travis was only trying to help her.

"What are you going to do when we find them?"

She didn't answer immediately, unsure what to say. Finally, she sighed. "I don't know. All of my plans seem to devolve into me beating the crap out of someone."

Travis's eyebrows went up at this candid confession. "I

can help with that, at least," he said, cracking his knuckles.

"Thank you, but no," Cassidy replied, her voice stiff. "Violence never solves anything."

"It does make you feel better, though."

She didn't add anything to this as they took the street beside the cathedral and drew nearer to Bourbon Street. Even from two blocks away, it was impossible not to identify the street simply by the sheer number of people there. Cassidy's steps faltered as they drew closer. "I didn't realize it would be so crowded."

"This is nothing, wait until after nine o'clock. Just stay close to me and try to avoid the falling beads." He bumped her with his shoulder, then plucked the phone from her limp hands. "And I'll take that."

IT WAS LIKE there was an invisible line along the edges of Bourbon; they crossed it and immediately were surrounded by people having a ball. The energy of the place was incredible. Travis couldn't help but smile, excitement coursing through his veins. He'd been to Mardi Gras celebrations all his life—the holiday was celebrated everywhere in the Southern states—but he couldn't remember anywhere being this intense.

Cassidy, however, seemed to freeze as the crowd streamed around them. Travis moved in beside her, laying a hand on the small of her back, and she stiffened under his touch.

"Easy there, grasshopper. Let's take your initiation nice and slow."

She shot him a dirty look, and then her eyes grew wide as saucers as a nearby girl, yelling at someone above them, yanked her shirt and bra up, showing perfect tits. Never one to miss an opportunity, Travis enjoyed the view with a big grin as several strands of beads rained down. The girl, quick to rearrange herself, missed a few, which fell to the ground. In fact, there were beads all along the crevices of the street, but nobody bothered to pick them up. That just wasn't done.

Cassidy elbowed him as the girl walked off, looking for another balcony to flash. "We have a job to do," she hissed, and Travis tipped an invisible hat to her.

"Yes, ma'am!"

The phone app, despite what he'd said to Cassidy, wasn't an exact science. The dot bounced about on the map, indicating Deedee was on the move. Given how close some of the clubs were to one another, sometimes it was difficult to tell which one the signal came from. It took them two tries, going into the wrong bars and failing in their search, before they finally found their target.

Travis was the first to notice his sister and her new beau, and despite knowing what was going to happen, his heart sank. *Dammit.* Seeing his little sister dancing with a guy wasn't as bad as knowing how the sight would affect Cassidy. Even with his back turned, Travis could tell who it was. Chad Somerfeld was the classic golden boy: shaggy blond hair, good looks, the kind of guy who'd be captain of any athletic team and drive an expensive car. In fact, Travis would have thought him a douche in high school except that he was so damned *nice* to everyone.

Easy to hate him now, of course.

Best to just get it over with.

He leaned down toward Cassidy's ear, then made the mistake of breathing in. Her subtle scent filled his senses, and the hard-on he'd been fighting all evening stirred in his pants. *Not now,* he furiously reprimanded himself. "Eagle spotted," he murmured. "Ten o'clock."

Travis watched as her head swiveled around, and knew she saw the two of them when her jaw went slack. Having no idea what she was going to do, he braced himself for battle. But Cassidy didn't move a muscle. After nearly a full minute of stillness, he risked giving her shoulder a small shake. "Earth to Dupre, are we go for liftoff?"

She jumped at his touch and turned wide blue eyes to his. She wasn't crying, which was something of a relief to Travis, but there was a dazed look of shock on her face. When she still didn't say anything, he began to get worried. The sudden desire to protect her shivered through him, and he asked, "Should I go over there and beat him to a pulp for you?"

Cassidy looked back at the two dancing figures, and Travis followed her gaze. Deedee was gyrating her backside against Chad's crotch, and as they watched, she moved down his body to crouch low to the ground and then slowly slid back up. Wincing with distaste, Travis looked away. Little sisters should *never* be allowed to do things like that.

Chad, for the most part, looked stunned by what was happening, but clearly enjoyed the teasing. Travis's gaze zeroed in on where his hands were placed, around

Deedee's waist, as if unsure what to do. His brotherly protective instincts kicked in then. *If he moves them even an inch lower, he's toast.*

"I gotta go."

Travis frowned as Cassidy shoved past him, bolting toward the door. He glanced back, making sure Chad's conduct was still within brotherly limits, then followed her. The crush of bodies made moving around difficult in the packed club, and he was mindful not to lose her in the crowd.

She stopped just outside the door, staring into the street. Travis wasn't sure what he'd expected, but this quiet wasn't it. He'd expected some kind of confrontation, and he peered down at her face, confused. "Should I go in there and hit him?" he asked when she continued her dogged silence. "Drag my sister out of the bar? Pants him in the middle of the dance floor?" When she still didn't answer, he moved around to face her, willing her to look up at him. Her silence was almost painful, making him desperate to know what she was thinking. "Cassidy, baby, tell me what you want, and I'll do it."

"What I want," Cassidy said, looking coolly up at him, "is to get drunk."

Well, hell. "I can definitely help you there."

Three

CASSIDY HAD NEVER tried a Horny Gator before, but right at that moment it was the most delicious concoction on the planet.

"Careful, don't suck it down so fast."

She snatched it away from Travis's reach, stumbling sideways a step. "Mine."

"Not trying to take it from you, sugar." His eyes danced in merriment. "You're drunk."

"I don't drink," she said in a prim voice, then pointed up at him. "Except for maybe right now." Cassidy paused to think, something that proved very difficult at that moment. It was a weird sensation. "So if I'm drunk, it's only because I don't have the practice yet."

"Whatever you say, Princess."

Travis's grin was getting on Cassidy's nerves, so she rolled her eyes and walked back outside, head held high. Taking a long sip from the alligator-shaped cup in her hand, she looked down both ends of the street. "I'm bored."

For the first time in far too long, she felt free. Maybe it was the alcohol coursing through her veins, but she didn't care about anything anymore. She wanted to do everything, but she didn't know where to start. Anytime her thoughts turned to Chad, or her responsibilities back home, her mind shied away, leaving her a jittery mess. Boredom didn't quite cut it, but she didn't know how to describe it otherwise.

"Baby, you're in New Orleans. Let's go find you something to do, then."

Cassidy whirled around and poked his chest, startling Travis. "Don't call me baby," she said, then paused and cocked her head sideways. It seemed natural to put her hand on his chest and feel the muscles beneath the thin layers of fabric. That was something she'd wanted to do for a long time, but right now it was so much easier to admit that fact. He was also right there, so why not touch?

Travis froze under her hand, muscles stiff. Cassidy could feel his heart beating quickly beneath her palm . . . or was that her heart? It was confusing suddenly, and she frowned, unsure what to do next. She looked up into his face and saw him staring down at her, wide-eyed. She blinked, then pointed a finger at him. "Has anyone ever told you that you're really cute?"

The surprised laugh her comment brought was interrupted as someone wearing a massive amount of beads around her neck shoved between them. The interruption broke Cassidy's train of thought, but her eyebrows went up when she noticed the girl's back was naked. Cassidy squinted after her. "She doesn't have a shirt on."

"Well, anything goes on Bourbon for Mardi Gras."

Cassidy pouted. "I want some beads," she muttered, glaring after the other girl.

Travis cleared his throat. "Around here there's one surefire way to get some."

Dropping her empty drink into a nearby trash bin, Cassidy tugged at the thin fabric of her bra. She looked over to see Travis staring at her hands, his mouth slightly ajar. He shut it when he noticed her gaze but seemed unable to tear his eyes from her hands. Something wicked bubbled up inside Cassidy, and she squeezed the soft mounds, rubbing her thumbs over her hidden nipples. The simple act made her shiver as her nether regions clenched, her body trembling.

Travis looked poleaxed, his eyes bright on the dark street. Cassidy's gaze fell to his lips, fascinated by how incredibly sexy they were. All of him was sexy, come to think of it. Travis's dark hair flopped down across his brow, and not really thinking about it, she reached up to brush it back. The strands were soft as silk, and she had the sudden urge to run her hands through his hair just to see if it was as soft all over. One of his hands came up to grasp her arm, but he wasn't pushing her away. This only made her bolder, and her eyes again fell to his lips.

What would he taste like?

Somebody stumbled into her from behind, knocking her sideways into the trash can. Pain shot up from her hip and the spell was broken, her hand landing in something wet and sticky. "Oh, *gross*."

"Gee, thanks," Travis said drolly as she wiped her hand on his shirt. "Admit it: you're just trying to cop another feel."

"I need more drinks," Cassidy said, ignoring his question as her mind flitted to a new thought.

"Here, take mine." He handed the white plastic foam cup to her. "Be careful with this one, though, Hurricanes are one of the most, uh, potent drinks . . . Oh boy."

Cassidy sucked it down, a happy sound coming from her throat. "That's really good," she exclaimed, taking another sip of the delicious, almost punchlike drink. "Is it alcoholic?"

"Ah . . ."

Before he could get out anything more, she turned away, having already forgotten the question. "What's in here?" she asked, stepping inside the dimly lit doorway. There was only a counter in the entryway, with a man and a stunning half-naked girl manning a cash register. The man stepped in front of Cassidy, grinning as his eyes swept over her. "Sorry, little mama," he said, clearly amused by her presence, "it's pay to play here. And you'll need to ditch the drink."

An entry fee? Cassidy screwed up her face. None of the other clubs so far had charged for entry. She was just about to tell him that when Travis intervened. "Here, this should cover it."

This better be worth it, Cassidy thought as the man

stepped aside. His eyes followed her as she dropped the empty cup in the trash and headed past him, eager to see what was so special about this place.

Only to be pulled up short as she realized where they were. "This . . . this is . . ." she stammered, staring at the woman dancing on stage.

"You wanted to come in here." Travis's hand dropped to her lower back, steering her deeper into the dimly lit club. "Why don't we see what we find?"

Jaw slack with shock, Cassidy stared around the room. It was probably the same size as most of the bars along the strip, but lacked the overwhelming crowds. Heavy music played near one end where a woman dressed only in a thong slid down a pole upside down, large heels pointing up at the ceiling. Some of the alcoholic fog surrounding her wore off, and she frowned. "I really shouldn't—" she started, and then fell silent as a topless girl holding a tray of drinks walked past. Her breasts were almost too large for such a petite frame, but it was the wink and smile the girl gave Cassidy that rendered her momentarily speechless.

Travis chuckled. "First time in a strip club?"

I really shouldn't be here. But her feet felt rooted to the spot. Stunned, she stared around the large room, taking it all in. Nearby, one girl, seated on the lap of a businessman, laughed loudly and leaned in so her bare breasts were almost in the man's face. Up on stage, the music changed as a bouncer helped the last dancer off, her clear heels ridiculously high, and a new performer started her act.

"Come on, let's find a seat."

Travis didn't seem fazed by her silence or the entire situation, and she glared up at him. "You planned this."

"Whoa now, you're the one that chose this place. I'm just playing babysitter for the night."

Another girl needed to squeeze past, and Travis stepped close to Cassidy to let her by. Cassidy's stomach did curious flip-flops at his proximity, but when the girl paused to eye Travis, something ugly welled up inside her. Back off, bitch, she thought as a smile tipped one side of the girl's mouth. "Come on," she muttered, grabbing Travis's hand and half dragging him to a nearby table.

"What, you jealous?"

Travis was grinning ear-to-ear when they sat down, clearly pleased by Cassidy's reaction. Some of the humor managed to seep in around the edges, and she gave a bemused smile as she realized she was really in a strip club. Cassidy Dupre, surrounded by strippers.

The whole situation struck her as suddenly funny, and she giggled. Laying her head sideways on Travis's shoulder, she murmured, "When did I turn into such an uptight bitch?"

She hadn't meant to say it out loud, but she felt Travis stiffen beneath her. "You had a tough go for a while," he said after a long moment, bumping her head with his chin in an almost commiserating gesture. "After your mom died, you kind of went overboard trying to become what she intended."

"Yeah." He'd always been good about getting straight to the heart of the matter. Cassidy wasn't sure if it was the alcohol scrambling her brains, but leaning up against Travis Dean felt *right*. A rueful smile tugged at her lips. "I've missed hanging out with you."

"Same here, Princess."

The old nickname, more a curse while they went through high school, seemed oddly right on his lips now. Nuzzling his shoulder, she moved her head up until her nose brushed the skin of his neck. Beneath her cheek, she felt him go rigid, and a curious rush of adrenaline filled her. The beautiful Travis Dean was seated next to her in a strip club, where apparently anything was allowed.

Why not play a little?

THE FIRST TIME Travis felt her lips graze his neck, he nearly leapt out of his skin. When one of Cassidy's hands finger-crawled across his chest, he almost couldn't breathe. "What are you doing?" he asked, his voice high and tight.

"Playing."

Travis's muscles clenched at the word, and when her wandering fingers grazed a nipple, he bit back a groan. He looked down at her, but she seemed preoccupied by her new task. Unsure whether to push her away or grab her tight, he did nothing, bearing the delicious agony of her touch. His cock strained against his pants, desperate for some contact with the girl beside him.

Apparently Cassidy didn't appreciate his restraint, because she gave a small mewl of annoyance and stood up. He was ready to follow her wherever—he just needed a moment to get his raging boner under control—but then her hands went around his neck as she straddled his lap. All the air whooshed from Travis's lungs as she settled around him, the thin material of her skirt flaring over his thighs. Unable to control himself, his hands went to her buttocks, pulling her against him, and it was Cassidy's turn to gasp.

"Someone seems really happy to see me," she murmured, wiggling her hips over him as her hands locked behind his neck.

Cassidy's breasts were right in line with his face, and he couldn't tear his gaze away. A thin line of cleavage peeked out from above the sweater, and as if answering his silent plea, she unbuttoned the yellow cardigan and pulled it off her shoulders, letting it slide whisper-soft to the ground. Travis's fingers dug into her hips as she laughed.

"If I'd known it was this easy to shut you up," she said softly, leaning in close, "maybe I'd have done it years ago."

Her words made him tremble, need coursing through him. Licking his lips, he closed his eyes and tried to get ahold of himself, only to find her face inches from his when he opened them again. Cassidy laid her hands on either side of his head, eyes searching his face curiously. "You really are so beautiful," she breathed.

Girls had been telling him the same thing for years, but somehow coming from the girl before him, it was different. The words energized him, making him feel like he was on top of the world while at the same time scaring the hell out of him. Words wouldn't come and, speechless, he could only stare up at her as she ran her thumb down his nose and over his lips. Capturing the soft pad between his teeth, he saw her sharp intake of breath and it enflamed him more than ever.

He was ready to come in his jeans from her touch alone.

Wonder and trepidation crept into her eyes as his hand smoothed up her back, bowing her toward him. Her breasts pressed against his chest, just below his chin, and he nuzzled the soft skin there. The hand that was still clutching one butt cheek surreptitiously snuck under the line of her skirt, gliding over surprisingly lacy panties.

Was there nothing about this girl that wasn't sexy to him?

Above him, her lips parted, a shaky breath shuddering out of her lungs. Even with the din of the music, he could read every breath she took, every emotion and thought that crossed her face. Her eyes were fixed on his lips, her breathing coming in pants, but she didn't seem prepared to take that one last step. So Travis took it for her, leaning in that tiny space and capturing her lips with his.

He kissed Cassidy Dupre, the girl who'd stolen his heart when she put a snake down the back of his jeans at age five.

It was everything he could have dreamed of, and more.

Cassidy moaned against him, her arms tightening around his neck. Sliding his fingers beneath the elastic of her panties, he let them wander between her legs, pressing intimately against her soft wet core as his tongue darted in her mouth. She jerked in his arms, fingers clawing at his scalp. Grinning, he repeated the action, and Cassidy went wild in his arms. There was no finesse to her response, and the raw need she exhibited made his blood burn with a similar fire.

"Travis, please," she whispered, pressing herself down against his raging hard-on. She ran her hands over his torso, across his chest, palming his nipples. He hissed in a breath at the touch, pressing up inside her opening and reveling in its tightness as she closed around his first knuckle. The thought of that liquid heat around his cock was a powerful aphrodisiac, and he didn't protest when Cassidy's hands went to his belt, pulling at the leather and jean clasps.

A hand clapped down on his shoulder. Startled out of the moment, he looked up and back to see a bouncer staring down at him with grim amusement. Cassidy didn't seem to notice the interruption, moving her mouth down to his exposed neck to suck and nibble the skin there.

"Sorry, buddy," the bouncer said in a low voice. "You want to do any more of that, you'll have to get a room."

Still gyrating on his lap, Cassidy made an annoyed sound, and Travis shared an amused, if somewhat pained, look with the bouncer.

"Sorry kid," the bouncer said, then winked. "Have fun tonight."

Travis blew out a breath, then reluctantly removed his hand from between Cassidy's thighs, fanned her skirt so it provided cover, and stood up. She still clung to his body, her knees tight around his waist, and he bit back a groan. God, he wanted to fuck her so bad, but now wasn't the time or place. He might have already gone too far letting her walk into a strip club, or even just kissing her like that.

As much as he craved her right then, he also didn't want to take her drunk like this. He wanted a sober Cassidy, one who was free of the alcohol's effects. If he took her now, he'd be taking advantage of her, and that wouldn't work at all. She could wake up truly hating him, and that wasn't something he was prepared to deal with. More than likely, she would be mortified if she remembered any of this, but so far there was no real damage done, and he intended to keep it that way.

Even if he had to protect her from himself.

"Come on," he murmured, "let's go see what else this town has to offer."

Cassidy gave a frustrated snort, but as his grip loosened so did hers, and she slid down his body. He didn't need any added reminder of her lush curves, the way she fit him perfectly; his dick was hard as a flagpole, but there was nothing he could do about it right now. Cassidy, meanwhile, had the annoyed pout of a child that hadn't gotten what she wanted. It was adorable, and amused the hell out of Travis. Who could have known Chastity Cassidy was such a wildcat once you got past her inhibitions?

That would be me. He still remembered the reckless abandon with which she threw herself into tasks, usually pranks and dares. The uncontrollable young girl had grown into a woman who kept herself locked up tight, but still held that same wildness. The thought of what she'd be like in bed taunted him and made it hard to stay responsible.

Travis Dean and "responsible" in the same sentence. His friends would laugh their asses off.

Four

"So I THOUGHT you were going to clobber your boyfriend when you saw him. What gives?"

Cassidy wrinkled her nose in distaste and frowned up at Travis. "Why are you asking me this now?"

He shrugged. "Because I was waiting for the right time that never came, and I'm curious as hell."

"Meh." Maybe if she wanted to be honest with herself, it had been her confused response to seeing Chad with Deedee that drove her away. She'd expected anger, hurt, rage at seeing her longtime beau in the arms of another girl.

Instead, she'd felt nothing, and she wasn't sure how to feel about that.

At the moment, she wasn't in the mood to focus on anything as deep as wayward boyfriends. She shoved the empty plastic cup into Travis's chest. "I need another drink."

"Baby, you've had a Horny Gator, half my Hurricane, and just finished off your second Hand Grenade."

"Didn't I tell you not to call me that?" It was easier to be pissed off at Travis than contemplate her situation with Chad.

"Might be time to cut you off," Travis said, moving fast to keep up with her. "You keep this up, you're going to puke your guts out later."

"First time for everything." She squinted up at the balconies above them, her mind sliding to a new subject. "How do people get up there anyway?" she wondered aloud. "Are they hotel rooms?"

Travis grabbed her hand and pulled her into one of the nearby clubs. "Come on, I'll show you."

Loud dance music beat from the speakers near the entrance as dancers gyrated and bounced madly in the center. Travis stayed along the far wall, moving determinedly toward the back of the bar. Cassidy stumbled along behind him, lip turning up in distaste at the way her soles stuck to sections of the floor. They bypassed the bathroom, and then Travis stopped before a narrow staircase. "Ladies first."

She started up the stairs, then jumped as a hand grabbed her ass. Spinning, she glared at Travis's unrepentant grin. "Go on," he said, and followed her up. Cassidy swatted at his hands as he tried to goose her again, but it didn't deter him. Instead of anger, laughter bubbled up in her at his attempts, and she was giggling by the time they got up the steps. She couldn't remember the last time she'd had this much fun.

"Over here." He steered her through the people milling about the upper floor and toward a set of nearby double doors. The crowd was much thicker here, but Cassidy could see it was indeed a balcony. Travis pushed his way through, eventually finding a tiny open spot along the metal railing, and managed to find her a spot in front. "Behold, Bourbon Street."

Cassidy stared down at the sea of moving bodies. From above, the mass of people on the street was insane. Up there, they definitely drew a lot of attention from folks on the ground. Several people on the balcony called down to the crowd, while others threw beads down to the street as girls did the requisite flashing.

"Is that the only way to get beads around here?"

"Definitely the quickest."

Cassidy peeked back at Travis. He was staring out along the street, his face placid as he surveyed the revelers below. The familiarity of his profile gave her a pang of nostalgia. Travis Dean hadn't changed much since childhood; he could easily be identified in old pictures by his grin and mop of dark hair. Sure, he'd grown taller and filled out, but to her, he still looked like the next door boy who'd followed her on every backwoods adventure.

The boy hasn't changed, but what happened to that girl?

The question was too deep and depressing for her current state of mind, so she filed it away for future contemplation. Travis didn't seem to be paying much attention to her, so Cassidy leaned over and pressed her backside against him. His hands immediately went to her waist, holding her there but not pulling, and she slowly rotated her hips. A wicked smile crossed her lips as she felt the hard bulge in his jeans. Travis Dean wanted her, and the thought was a heady mix of confusion and lust.

"Hey up there!"

Pausing her hips, Cassidy frowned down over the railing. One of the men below held a string of beads above his head. "I'll give you these if you show me your tits," he called up to her, shaking them as added incentive.

His crude request and the absurdity of the situation made her want to laugh. Nobody ever asked things like that of her; it was surreal to hear the question directed her way. His accent definitely wasn't Southern, but sounded more like Boston or the Northeast somewhere.

The fact that she was even contemplating doing it did elicit a laugh. For so long, Cassidy had kept herself buttoned down, sticking to the rules and what others expected of her. Nobody but Travis had ever dared ask any more of her, wanted her to break out of her shell. "How do I know I can trust you?" she called down, not sure how else to respond.

"Come on, live a little!"

She covered her mouth, fascinated and conflicted, then looked back at Travis. He had obviously seen the exchange and was watching her, his raised eyebrows practically daring her. He was grinning widely, as amused by the situation as she was, but he still leaned in and said, "You don't have to do it, you know."

"Obviously." But she was tempted, badly too. It was unnecessary and ridiculous and there were all sorts of other reasons why she shouldn't do it, but it was the silent challenge she saw in Travis's eyes that clinched it. He didn't think she'd do it, and that, more than anything, spurred her on. She turned back around, her fingers going to the neckline of her outfit. The material of her dress was fairly stretchy, and her cardigan had gotten lost somewhere along the way.

Oh, to hell with it. Grasping both sides of the wide-neck dress as well as the bra cups just beneath, she closed her eyes and yanked them down.

The cool night air made her nipples tighten almost immediately. Cheers erupted below her, and suddenly nervous about the attention, she hastily covered herself back up. Her face was flaming but she caught a brief glimpse of Travis's wide eyes and gave herself a mental pat on the back. It wasn't often she got one over on him, and he looked like he'd been hit by a truck.

She turned her attention back down below for her reward. Sure enough, the man, a wide grin on his face, tossed the strand up to her waiting hands. Cassidy laughed out loud when she saw that the large pale shapes on the necklace were twin breasts, interspersed with gold and purple beads. Grinning, she settled it over her head and then turned around. "What do you think?"

Travis looked impressed. "Not a bad start."

"So, what else is there to do?"

His grin widened. "How do you feel about mechanical bulls?"

"OOH, I REALLY don't feel good."

"I'm telling you, drink the water. Small sips, but I have another bottle when you're done."

Cassidy moaned again, leaning heavily against Travis, and the sound of her discomfort made him feel terrible. They were standing outside the Western bar near the end of the strip, the streets as crowded as ever. Cassidy had been having fun line dancing and watching people ride the mechanical bull until she'd decided to hop on and take a ride herself.

Big mistake.

Between one moment and the next, she went from party animal to groaning discomfort, and Travis blamed himself. Even though he surreptitiously cut her off two hours ago, he'd kept a careful eye on her as they hopped from bar to bar. He should have known better than to let her drink so much alcohol; he doubted she'd ever had more than a sip before tonight, yet he hadn't thought to find her food or water until she started complaining.

He wasn't sure what he'd been expecting, but the teasing minx was more than he'd bargained for. After their make-out session in the strip club, he'd tried to keep his hands off her, but hadn't counted on Cassidy's single-minded attempts at seduction. When she danced, he couldn't keep his eyes off her; she would touch him and it was like a jolt of electricity. He could see in her eyes that she knew what she was doing, and it made acting like a gentleman very difficult. His main goal was to protect her and let her have as much fun as possible. He'd even foregone alcohol for most of the night to keep a cool head, hoping to steer her clear of things she might regret the next day.

That part hadn't gone quite so well.

The neckline of her dress hung lower, stretched out by her actions over the last hour. After flashing on the balcony, she threw herself into the fray, going for broke and amassing quite the collection of neckwear. Now, an impressive number of beads hung around her neck, hiding the edge of the white bra visible above the red hem. At one point she'd proudly proclaimed the mass of beads covering her breasts was her "treasure chest," and smugly watched as Travis almost collapsed from laughter. But having had her fun flitting from club to club, chatting randomly with an assortment of strangers, it tore him up that he hadn't taken better care of her.

"I'm going to be sick."

Travis quickly steered her down a side street and behind a Dumpster. Her retching made him feel terrible, but he stood guard, rubbing her back until she was done. He weighed their options on what to do next, but there weren't too many. He doubted there were any affordable hotel rooms available within walking distance, and he didn't want to risk getting pulled over at a road block. No doubt the cops were out in force looking for drunks, and he wasn't sure they'd take kindly to him carrying Cassidy around.

"I think I'm done for the night." Cassidy stood up, wobbling on her feet. Travis picked her up in his arms, and she laid her head on his shoulder.

Really, there was only one option. He just hoped he remembered the way there.

Royal Street was practically dead this late at night, especially in comparison to Bourbon. The small shop front was closed up, but his destination was the alleyway gate. The entrance was a facade, masking a sizable residence behind the shop. The narrow brick walkway behind the gate opened up into a large courtyard that he still remembered playing in as a child.

Setting Cassidy on her feet but keeping an arm wrapped around her shoulders, he knocked on the narrow wooden gate. It was a long shot, at best, that anyone would hear. Most folks living in the French Quarter kept their windows closed during the winter, especially during Spring Break or Mardi Gras. So he was surprised when he'd barely lowered his hand and the gate swung open. An older woman in a flamboyant night dress stepped forward, head raised in a grand fashion.

Travis waggled his fingers. "Hi, Grandma."

Madame Ysabeau stared down her nose at the unexpected arrival. He opened his mouth to explain their presence when her eyes got that faraway look Travis remembered back from his childhood. She sighed and stepped back. "Come on in, then," she said finally, swinging the gate wide. "I have some tea brewing for you." She peered down at Cassidy. "Doesn't seem you'll be needing it tonight."

"Did Mom call you?" he asked as he helped Cassidy up the steps. He hadn't told anyone he was going to the city, let alone to look for his sister, but Deedee hadn't been discreet with her posted pictures. His parents weren't the most modern, but they did try to keep up with friends and family on social media.

"No, I foresaw your arrival."

Given what he knew about his grandmother, he took

her words at face value. The novelties shop in front catered both to the tourists who flocked to the Quarter looking for ghost stories and the occult, as well as local voodoo practitioners looking for supplies. His mother's family had owned and run the shop for generations, until she married a Mississippi boy and moved away from New Orleans. It had been quite a while since he'd made the trek to see his grandmother, although she semiregularly came across the border for family functions.

Travis followed his grandmother up the stairs and into the house, and was immediately hit by the scent of patchouli incense. It was a smell he associated with this place, and made him feel at home.

The older woman had always had a bohemian flare, and her home was no different. There wasn't a single open space on the wall and only narrow walkways around the furniture, but somehow it managed to keep a homey vibe without feeling too cluttered. The decorations were as wild as her paisley robes, with contrasting colors that stood out even in the dim light.

"Your lady friend may stay in here," she said, indicating the old room he'd slept in as a child. "Now if you'll excuse me, I need my beauty sleep."

"Thank you," Travis murmured, and she nodded, then he steered Cassidy toward the queen bed in the far corner. His grandmother's room was on the opposite end of the hall, and he could hear the boards creaking long after her footsteps faded. The room was full of furniture and various artifacts; a single bulb above the bed gave scant light, but enough to maneuver, at least.

Cassidy groaned as he sat her on the bed. He removed her shoes before tucking her under the covers. Her grip on his arm didn't relent, however, and he paused when she mumbled, "Don't go."

It didn't occur to him until that moment that his grandmother hadn't given him a place to sleep. He gave a rueful smile, then pulled off his shirt and carefully slid into the bed behind Cassidy. She snuggled back against him, and he gathered her in his arms, breathing in her scent. It wasn't easy, but he kept his hands from roaming over her sleeping figure. There was no way, however, he could prevent the boner that came from hugging her soft form. He ran his fingers along the side of her face, the skin like velvet, and Cassidy gave a contented sigh.

God, he loved this girl. Her sudden turnaround that evening was the best and the worst thing. It reminded him of everything about her he'd always loved, but he knew it could all disappear once she woke up.

Still, there was no place he'd rather be at that moment than in bed beside her. Worrying over what would happen the next morning wouldn't change anything at this point, so he allowed himself to savor the moment. If they woke up and were back where they'd been before, more enemies than friends, then tonight would have to be enough.

Nuzzling her neck, he scooted beneath the covers, pulling her back against him before closing his eyes for sleep.

Five

SOMETHING UNFAMILIAR AND hard lay across Cassidy's ribs, but she was warm and comfortable in her present position so she paid it little mind. It wasn't until something against her back shifted that she finally came awake enough to comprehend the strange surroundings. An unfamiliar, earthy smell tickled her nose, and when she moved her hand up to investigate the pressure across her ribs, she discovered a hairy arm.

Okay. This is weird.

It occurred to her that she should probably feel more that someone was in bed with her, but she couldn't seem to dredge up the energy to care. Besides, they weren't doing anything; soft snores came from the pillow behind her, and the hand wasn't covering anything scandalous. In fact, part of her wanted to just go back to sleep, wrapped in the warm cocoon of blankets and body heat.

Moving carefully, she twisted herself around to look at her companion.

Muted light streamed in through a nearby window, barely enough to see by, but Cassidy had always had good night vision. The moon lit the lines of Travis's face, the faint glow enough for her to recognize him. She stared down at the sleeping boy, waiting for the shock and horror at being in bed with another man to engulf her, but the feelings never materialized. All she felt was an easy curiosity, and she reached out and traced her fingertips along his hairline, moving aside the soft hair from his temples. Her hand moved down his jawline, light stubble scraping her fingers as her exploration curved around his chin and down his throat.

She remembered everything that had happened the previous night, enough to know that, given the circumstances, she should be ashamed with herself. Yet the funny thing was, she had no regrets. Well, she thought ruefully, the vomiting part could have been skipped, and the multiple flashing episodes could be chalked up to her first experience with alcohol. But try as she might, she couldn't make herself feel sorry for everything that had happened.

She had no idea what time it was, but dawn hadn't yet begun to light the skies. The invincible feeling she'd had most of the evening since having her first drink was gone, replaced by a curious introspection. It had been an interesting night of firsts, from the strip club and the flashing, to the alcohol and general merrymaking. Now she was lying beside a half-naked boy in a strange bedroom, and all she could think about was what would happen if she leaned in and kissed him.

She couldn't blame the alcohol on these feelings, not now—maybe not even ever. Somehow, knowing it was Travis made it feel as if whatever would happen was destined to happen.

Cocking her head to one side, Cassidy smoothed her hand lightly up his arm, enjoying the line of muscle and smooth skin. The snoring had stopped, and she knew that if Travis wasn't awake already, he would be very soon. She couldn't bring herself to stop touching him, however. In the dim light she maneuvered more by touch than by sight, running her fingers across his lower lip. His head shifted ever so slightly, turning to follow her touch, and Cassidy shivered. Swallowing, she leaned her head forward until it was only an inch or so from his face.

Tiny pinpricks of light reflected in his eyes, telling her Travis was indeed awake, but he didn't move. Bolder because of his stillness, she brought her hand up his chest, only slightly surprised to find he wasn't wearing a shirt. His skin was hot to the touch, smooth and tight, and his ragged intake of breath when she skimmed her palm over his nipple made butterflies break out in her belly.

He moved slowly, levering himself up and over her. She drew her knees up to straddle his hips, and trembled as he settled himself above her. He made a small tilt with his hips, pressing his hard length against her core, and it was Cassidy's turn to gasp. All rational thought fled her mind as her body ignited. It was hard to believe something she'd always been taught was wrong could feel so *right*.

"Tell me to stop, Cassidy baby, and I will."

His words, said in almost a painful whisper, rocketed through her. "Travis . . ."

"I need you so bad it hurts," he murmured, running the back of his fingers down her cheek. "I want to touch every inch of you, feel every part of you against me, fuck you so hard you scream as you come." His forehead came down atop hers as he rasped, "God, Cassidy, I need you so much . . ."

It was so simple, really, giving in. A tiny tilt of the head, a little press upward, and her lips brushed his. She kissed him softly, the touch little more than a caress, but the tension that had been holding him stiff above her dissolved. Travis grabbed her head and took her mouth, sucking and nibbling her lips in a way that set Cassidy's body ablaze. She moaned into his mouth, overcome by the sensations as her fingers dug into his sides.

"Cassidy," he whispered against her mouth, as if her name was a blessing, a prayer. What his lips and hands were doing to her, however, was positively sinful. But she couldn't care less. A tide of desire swept her away as one of his hands crept between their bodies, fingers sliding beneath the skirt and under her panties. When he glided between her folds, teasing her throbbing opening, she shuddered and gave herself over to the sensation.

Travis wasted no time in getting her naked, pulling her dress up and over her head in one swift motion. His mouth immediately fell to her neck, sucking and licking the skin at the base of her neck, then down her chest to one breast. He moved aside the small material of her bra, exposing her nipple, and pulled it roughly into his mouth. Cassidy gave a loud gasp, craning up off the bed as the roaring in her head became a raging inferno that threatened to consumer her. "Travis," she moaned, her hands fisting in his hair.

The finger that had been teasing her mercilessly, causing her hips to shudder and thrust, pushed between the folds and up inside her. Her cry was swallowed by Travis's mouth, his body keeping her from coming up off the mattress.

"Fuck, you're tight," he whispered, and Cassidy gave another small cry as he bumped up against something inside that sent sparks showering through her.

"Oh, you like that?" He did it again, and Cassidy went wild, her fingernails dragging along his back. His chuckle called out her inner rebel, and she moved her own hand down until she was cupping his hard length, still encased in his jeans. Travis cursed again, pushing into her hand.

"Get them off," she whispered harshly, and pulling his hand away from her, he quickly complied, undoing the belt and shoving them down his legs. Cassidy immediately found him again, wrapping her fingers around him and pulling.

"God, baby," he bit out, shuddering. "I'm going to come on you if you keep that up."

Despite his words, she gave another tug, loving the way he glided in her hand even through the silk boxers. "Promise?"

"Hell, you really are the perfect woman."

His underwear was the next thing to go, and as he settled himself fully against her, Cassidy began to comprehend the enormity of the situation. Or, well, at least an enormity of some sort. If she felt tight with one of his fingers inside her . . . "Are you going to fit?"

She was mortified the minute the words left her mouth, but Travis didn't laugh, just pressed his lips to her forehead. "We'll go slow," he promised, and then took her mouth again in another searing kiss. His hands tugged at her panties, and she lifted her hips off the bed to help him in removing them.

He slid his finger inside her again, then another, stretching her tight as his thumb played with the small bud of her clit. The double sensation made her cry catch in her throat as Travis's attention went back to her breasts. He rubbed the nipple with his thumb, squeezing the mound, before dipping his head and flicking her nipple repeatedly with the tip of his tongue. Panting, Cassidy clawed at him, desperate for more but unsure what.

Plastic crinkled as Travis tore open a condom packet with his teeth and one hand, then moved his free hand down between their bodies. She gave a mewl of protest when he removed his fingers from inside her, before something thick moved in their place. Her hips tilted up, desperate for more, but Travis held himself back.

"Cassidy, look at me." When her eyes met his in the darkness, he asked, "Are you sure you want this?"

Groaning in frustration, she grabbed his ears so they were eye-to-eye. "Travis Dean," she muttered, "fuck me."

In the darkness, a smile spread across his features. "Yes, ma'am."

He ripped, more than removed, her panties from her body. Cassidy didn't care in the slightest, the roughness and mild stinging nothing in comparison to her throbbing agony of desire. One arm hooked beneath her knee, lifting and spreading her thighs, he began to press inside.

Cassidy gave a small whimper at the stretching, but true to his word, Travis took his time. His teeth grazed her neck down to her breast, momentarily distracting her. Not fully sheathed, he drew himself out a bit then pressed in again, and the tiny bit of friction had Cassidy seeing stars. He did it again, pushing in deeper each time, until he was fully inside her. Kisses rained across her neck and chest as Cassidy shifted beneath him, rolling her hips.

Travis drew in a shaky breath, so she did it again. The stretching wasn't painful, not really, but she wasn't sure how far to push it. Leaning up, she dragged her teeth down the side of his neck, and he shuddered above her.

"You keep doing that," he murmured, "and I won't be able to stop myself."

She bit him, and his body jolted. "Who's asking you to stop?" she replied, raking her nails up along his sides.

Growling, Travis jerked his hips back, then slammed himself deep inside her. Cassidy's back arched, her hands clawing at the headboard for purchase. She cried out his name again when he repeated the movement, hips rolling as he worked himself in and out of her body. When his hands clamped down around her upper arms, pinning her to the bed, she reveled in the helplessness of his grip.

It was the hottest thing she'd ever experienced, and she couldn't get enough.

Her legs wrapped around his narrow waist as he pumped furiously inside her, his mouth locked to her neck. With each stroke, Cassidy could feel something building, although she wasn't sure what. She just knew that the pleasure was becoming unbearable, almost too much for her to handle.

"Oh God, Cass, I'm going to . . ." He pumped hard into her three times, thrusting deep, and everything inside Cassidy shattered. She gave a small cry, her body trembling and shuddering as Travis stiffened above her, the air leaving his lungs in a harsh groan. Her nails dug into his biceps as he lowered his head to lay a soft kiss to her collarbone.

They stayed like that for a moment, catching their breaths. Cassidy could have stayed like that forever, Travis's weight pushing her down onto the bed, but he pulled carefully out of her and rolled sideways. Her body was boneless, as if she'd just done a hard workout. She squeezed her legs together, definitely noticing the strange pressure deep inside, as Travis gathered her in his arms.

"I think I might like sex," she mused quietly, and his chest shook with laughter.

"Get some sleep, and maybe we can go again later."

It felt incredibly natural to snuggle inside his arms, burrowing under the warm covers and using his bicep as a pillow. A smile tugged at her lips, and she laid a kiss on his knuckle as he squeezed her tight, then let her eyes fall shut as slumber took her.

THIS WAS HEAVEN, and he didn't feel worthy.

Cassidy's breathing had long since slowed with sleep, but Travis was wide-awake. Whatever post-sex euphoria he'd experienced had long since died away, but he couldn't get over the fact that he held the girl of his dreams in his arms. He lifted a strand of her hair and rubbed it between his thumb and index finger. This couldn't be real, and yet here she was, naked and asleep beside him, her clothing strewn about the room.

Taking her virginity hadn't seemed to faze her, but it had been nerve-wracking for him. Intense need for her had warred with his desire to make it special, but the minute he was inside her, he'd been ready to explode. Their coupling had been hot and fast and dirty, and she was a wildcat. The scratch marks on his back still stung when they rubbed against the sheets, a constant reminder of her eagerness.

He'd never loved a girl more, and never been more scared in his life of what the morning would bring.

Focus on the present. For now, he had her in his arms and he could appreciate that. Laying his head down on the pillow, he nuzzled the back of her head and pulled her close again. She shifted slightly, then stilled, and Travis finally closed his eyes, one thumb casually stroking the soft skin of her breast.

Six

THE MASSIVE HEADACHE that woke Cassidy was not fun. Shutting her eyes tight, she nevertheless arched backwards, stretching beneath the sheets. It felt strange to be naked in bed; the sheets were decent if a tad threadbare, but she rarely slept in the nude. At least she was alone to figure out what to do next, but found it difficult to care around the hammer pounding away inside her skull.

Groaning, she pulled the covers over her head, wanting only to dissolve into the bed. From somewhere outside the room the sweet smell of food hung in the air, and her stomach rumbled in appreciation. Peeking out of the covers, she tried to find a clock, anything that would tell her what time it was. Boxes were stacked neatly against the far corner, and the shelves beside them held a variety of items Cassidy couldn't identify. She squinted, and then groaned as her headache grew worse. *So, this is a hangover.*

She remembered every minute of the previous night, and was still struggling to figure out whether that was a good thing. It would be so easy to blame the alcohol for everything that happened, but she knew she had Travis to thank for taking care of her. He'd allowed her to have fun, steering her away from bad situations and finding her a place to stay when the night abruptly ended. As strange as it seemed, Travis Dean had been– dare she say it?—a gentleman through the evening,

Right up until she'd awoken horny and jumped his bones.

It was a toss-up, really, as to which was worse, the pounding in her head or the whole waking-up-naked-in-a-strange-bed thing.

Oh yeah, definitely that second part.

Laying atop the small table beside the bed was a single long-stemmed flower. She stared at the yellow carnation for a long minute before reaching over, picking it up and bringing it to her nose. A tiny smile tugged at her lips as she touched the soft petals, the presence of the bright flower warming her heart.

Cassidy could still feel the aftereffects of their earlier lovemaking, a dull ache deep inside her. It wasn't uncomfortable, but served as a reminder of what had happened between the two of them. She had no idea what to do next. For so long, she'd had a certain path lined out for her life. It wasn't until now that she realized just how *generic* it sounded, how boring her life had become. At some point she'd become stuck in a rut she hadn't seen, living her life on autopilot.

Even her relationship with Chad had been that way. Watching him dance at that club, Cassidy had waited for the anger, the disappointment, some kind of strong emotion. Instead, she'd felt nothing, no real desire to force any confrontation. That lack of response had sent her reeling, wondering if something was wrong with her.

Cassidy's mind flickered back to earlier that morning, Travis's face flashing through her mind, and she swallowed. She'd sure felt something last night, but Chad definitely hadn't been involved.

What a mess.

"Ugh," she moaned, gathering the sheets around her and sitting up. Her dress was lying at the foot of the bed, and she picked it up, along with her bra. Dragging her legs over the side, she threw her clothes on then shivered as her feet stepped onto the old wood boards. Her shoes were set neatly beside the door, but she had to search long and hard before she found her panties behind a small end table next to the bed. The band on one leg looked stretch out, but there was no way she was going without underwear in a strange house.

She had no idea where Travis had gone, but maybe it was for the best that she woke up alone. She doubted he'd leave her to fend for herself, but a heads-up on where she was or what to expect would have been nice. Grabbing the flower off the table, she poked at the bead pile on the ground with her foot before leaving them and peeking out the door.

The layout of the main area of the house reminded Cassidy of a hotel. The hallway curved around in an Lshape, with about five doors dotting the outer edges. The railing overlooked an open area downstairs, and two sets of stairs on either end of the hall led straight down toward the kitchen. An older woman in a billowing dress bustled around, humming softly to herself.

"You can come down, child," she called, not even looking up toward Cassidy. "I don't bite."

So much for sneaking. Cassidy picked up her shoes and padded softly along the narrow walkway. The old wood floors creaked with each step, especially as she went down the stairs. "Good morning, ma'am," she said politely, unsure what else to do.

"Travis went shopping for food," the woman said brusquely, still flitting about the kitchen. She reached a wizened hand into a flour bag and grabbed a handful, spreading it out over the countertop. "Gives us some time to chat about your intentions with my boy."

Oh dear. Cassidy felt her face heat up. The older woman looked at her, then snorted. "No, I didn't hear you last night," she said, "although I've no doubt about what happened." She waggled bushy eyebrows at Cassidy, to her total mortification. "You may not believe it, but I was young once myself."

"Ah." Cassidy wished the ground would open up and swallow her. "Travis and I, um, we grew up together." She held out her hand. "My name is Cassidy. I take it you're his grandmother?"

"Oh, I know who you are." The old woman shook her hand, her grip tough. Her sudden laugh sounded closer to a cackle. "That boy's been pining after you near 'bout his whole life."

Cassidy stared at the old woman. *Pining?* "He spent all of high school making my life miserable," she said, before thinking better of it.

"Well, of course he did. He's a boy, and they's idiots at that age. You like your eggs scrambled?"

The Cajun woman had a strong presence, and not just because of her loud outfits. A bit dumbfounded by the disjointed conversation, Cassidy just nodded her head and scanned the kitchen. The room looked old and well used, with painted white cabinets and thick tile that went up the walls several feet. Above them, a large skylight let in the morning light, illuminating the room better than any lamps could. Herbs of various sorts hung in bundles near the stove, and as Cassidy watched, the older lady broke off a couple sprigs to add to her recipe.

"So, what are you going to do about your man problem?"

"My . . . what?"

"Finding your beau in the arms of another woman? Nasty business, that. Shame it was my kin too."

Cassidy fiddled with the flower in her hand nervously. "How do you know about . . ."

"I am Madame Ysabeau." She gave Cassidy an arch look. "I know these things."

Cassidy blinked at her, then drew in a deep breath. "Whatever Travis told you—"

"Nay, *chéri*, that boy wouldn't betray your confidence,

not even to his grandmam." She gave her a piercing look, long enough that Cassidy grew uncomfortable under the scrutiny. "You made a mistake, you move on. Get yourself a boy who will cherish you."

The whole conversation was odd, but, stuck as she was in the present situation, Cassidy decided to go along with it. "I thought I had that with Chad," she murmured, setting the flower down before she destroyed it. "We seemed compatible; he was cute, and our families were already friends. It was so easy."

"Since when is anything worthwhile easy?"

Point taken. "I was vulnerable and needed someone when he came into my life." Cassidy sighed. "He showed up at the door holding a bouquet of carnations, my favorite flowers, not long after my mother died. Silly me, I took it as a sign we belonged together."

There was a crash behind them, and Cassidy jumped and whirled around. Travis stood beneath the second floor walkway, just staring at her. A grocery bag was on the ground at his feet, items strewn about on the floor.

Madame Ysabeau peered around Cassidy. "Oh no, child," she said, a note of regret in her voice, "please tell me that weren't my marmalade?"

Travis cast a quick look between his grandmother and Cassidy before stepping carefully into the kitchen. "Good morning," he murmured, setting the other bag of groceries on the counter and turning around to pick up the mess he'd made.

He's nervous. Travis barely looked at her, which of course made her stare unabashedly at him as he moved around the kitchen. He was carefully avoiding her, as though he expected her to lash out at him.

That was a meeting she'd been thankful to put off since waking up, but now she realized a discussion was due. Only, she had no idea what to say. The area between her thighs still felt deliciously raw, a potent reminder of what had happened between them only hours ago. A lifetime of conditioning and proper etiquette clearly stated what her response should be, and yet she couldn't dredge up the conviction to voice those concerns.

Well, that and his grandmother was right there listening. Some things just weren't discussed around the elderly, no matter how "enlightened" they might seem.

"I appreciate you letting us stay . . ." she started, only to have Travis begin speaking at the same time.

"I was wondering if you wanted . . ."

They both trailed off, looking at one another. When nobody spoke, Travis's grandmother threw up her hands. "Well, spit it out, boy."

He gave his grandmother a pained look, as if regretting he was having the conversation in her presence. "If you want to stay through the weekend," he said to Cassidy, "the parades are pretty spectacular."

She looked at Madame Ysabeau, who shrugged. "If you've never been to a New Orleans parade," she said, pronouncing it *Nawlins*, "these are the best you'll see."

Cassidy nervously played with the phone in her purse, suddenly uncertain. Now that it was daylight and most of the alcohol had left her system, reality threatened to intrude on her little Mardi Gras fun. She hadn't checked her phone since the evening before, and there were several functions at home that she was supposed to be helping with. But, dammit, for the first time in far too long she was having fun, cutting loose, being irresponsible.

Heaven help her, but it felt *good*.

"Yeah," she said, nodding, "a parade or two sounds fun." That sounded fantastic, actually. She had grown up with the Mardi Gras parades in her hometown, but they didn't hold a candle to the ones here.

Cassidy moved in close to Travis as the older woman busied herself once more in the kitchen. "How much did you tell your grandmother about Chad?"

"Nothing, why?"

"Your parents, maybe?"

"They don't know what's going on yet." He bumped his shoulder against hers, lowering his head and voice conspiratorially. "But she does make a decent living off being a fortune- teller, if that explains things . . ."

Cassidy peered at Travis, wondering if this was a joke, but he looked serious. "Ah." She cast a troubled look at the older woman, who was whistling a jaunty blues tune, and then put it out of her mind. The particulars of how his grandmother knew didn't matter anyway; everyone would know soon enough that she and Chad weren't together anymore. She imagined there would be disappointment, shock, and gossip running rampant about their split as soon as word got out, but she was tired of considering what other people might think. She had the urge to be selfish and have fun, if only for a single weekend.

Picking up the flower again, she measured a few finger

lengths down from the bloom, then bent the stem until it broke free. Travis's eyes followed her hands as she put it over her ear, securing it there with a bobby pin from her purse. "What do you think?" she asked, lifting her head up proudly.

Slowly, a smile lifted his lips. "Perfection."

His reply warmed her heart, and she returned his smile as an idea popped into her mind. "Do you think you can get me on a float?"

TRAVIS WOULD HAVE done anything to fulfill Cassidy's wish, but it turned out his grandmother had connections in town. More than anything he could have done, they got them just below the bright stage of a parade float, rolling slowly down Poydras Street.

"This is fantastic!" Cassidy yelled out over the music blaring from above them, her grin practically splitting her face. "I never thought I would ever do this!"

Travis knew he owed his grandmother big-time for getting them into the Endymion parade. They were on the lower tier of a big float, tossing out strands of beads and the occasional T-shirt, and having an absolute blast. Cassidy hadn't stopped smiling since they were introduced hastily to the group and ushered onto the float.

It was almost magical how easily everything came together. After Cassidy's request earlier that morning, his grandmother had made a couple quick calls, then told them where to meet the folks later that afternoon. To pass the time, Travis had paid for a tour of the nearby cemeteries for Cassidy's benefit. She'd found it entertaining, and making her happy gave him pleasure.

They'd also stepped out of the Quarter to get her some new clothes, since neither of them had thought to pack. Cassidy seemed more excited by this than any grave tours, balling up her dress in the bag and sporting jeans and a long sleeve shirt. He loved the way they hugged her ass, and the prissy way she swatted at his hand anytime he laid his hand there. He hadn't intended to get himself anything to wear—he didn't stink yet, anyway—but Cassidy had convinced him to ditch the plaid for a black button-up shirt. She insisted he looked good, and then proved as much by making out with him in the dressing room.

If Cassidy hadn't been quite so loud with her pleasure, perhaps they could have gone further. As it was, he quite enjoyed kissing her thoroughly.

At the appointed time, they'd arrived at the address his grandmother had given them and were ushered onto a waiting float. Their only costume was a matching set of masks, tiny ones that only covered their eyes and foreheads, and then the parade started.

"I'm out of beads," Cassidy said. "Give me one of yours."

Bossy little thing. He was perfectly content, however, handing her two thick rolls of beads and watching her do her thing. It was more fun for him, anyhow. She grinned at him, and his heart did a weird flip-flop as she turned and began throwing the beads to the crowd.

Oh yeah, he was a goner, but strangely, he didn't mind.

The parade lasted the better part of three hours, and by the end of it they were both spent. Travis helped Cassidy off the float, and before he could step away she wrapped her arms around his neck. "That was incredible!"

It was his turn to grin like a loon, and he spun her around. "Did you save any of those beads for yourself?"

"Not a chance." She beamed at him, waggling her eyebrows. "I can get my own."

She could too. He squeezed her tight, reveling in the feel of her body against his. When he looked down at her, Cassidy's lips were parted, her face flush with excitement.

Nothing could have kept him from kissing her in that moment.

She responded immediately, twining her arms around his neck and arching against him. Travis deepened the kiss, smiling against her lips when he heard her soft sigh. He doubted she even noticed the crowd forming around them. Keeping one hand firm on her lower back, he dipped her over backwards, maintaining the kiss. Cassidy's arms tightened around his neck, her leg rising into the air, and as they came back upright there was applause around them.

Her face was flushed, from the kiss or the applause. Thanking the people they'd ridden in the float with, Travis put his arm around her shoulder as they walked off. "So, what's the plan tonight?" he asked as they started back toward the French Quarter. "More Bourbon Street fun?"

At his words, Cassidy groaned. "Not a repeat of last night, please. I thought my head was going to explode this morning."

Travis grinned. "Dinner sound like a plan?"

"Why, Travis Dean, are you asking me out on a date?"

He just smirked, but didn't confirm or deny anything. "I know just the place too. Come on."

The French Quarter had several fine-dining restaurants, but he wasn't interested in any of them. "Fried chicken?" Cassidy asked a little while later, looking dubiously at the sign when they arrived.

"You'll thank me for this, I promise."

She looked doubtful, but accepted the small box of chicken he handed to her. He watched as she took her first bite, her eyebrows popping high in surprise. "My grandmother used to bring me here all the time," he said as she tore into the delicious chicken. "Save room for the biscuits, they're even better than the meat."

"You sure know how to spoil a girl."

"Hey, you should see this seafood place I know just north of the city. You'll think you'd died and gone to heaven when you try their gumbo."

After dinner, they meandered through the dark French Quarter hand in hand. Travis had his phone out and was furiously searching the Internet. Cassidy peered over his arm. "What are you looking for?"

"It's a surprise," he said, quirking an eyebrow at her, and she rolled her eyes. As the moments passed, however, he realized his plan was going to need less finger work and more footwork. They passed by a particularly grand entrance, and he stopped, removing his arm from around her shoulders. "Wait right here for one second."

Cassidy frowned at him, and he held up his hands in a placating gesture. "I promise I'll be right back."

She didn't look too happy at being ditched, but stayed

in place as he ducked inside the hotel they'd just passed. As much as he loved his family, he wasn't interested in staying with his grandmother another night with the girl he loved. The morning after had been awkward enough without her there, and he didn't want a repeat.

The lobby didn't seem too busy, but he knew that didn't necessarily mean they weren't booked. In fact, trying to find a room in the Quarter was a long shot at best, but he needed to try. "I was wondering if you had any rooms available," he asked the clerk at the counter.

"I'm sorry sir, we're sold out."

He figured as much. At least she sounded apologetic about it. "Is there a waiting list or anything I can join?"

"You *bastard*!"

It was the smack of skin on skin that got his attention as a dark-haired woman stormed past. She was dressed smartly in an expensive designer gown of some kind, no doubt for one of the balls happening around the city. An older man, dressed to the nines in a tuxedo, his shirt and bow tie askew, followed after her. "Dear heart, that wasn't what it looked like."

"Oh, so you weren't sucking face with my assistant?"

The man's guilty look said it all, and with a groan of frustration the woman turned and stormed out of the hotel. "Honey," the man called, hurrying after her.

Travis turned back to the clerk, who looked as interested in the scene as he'd been. "What about their room?" he asked, jerking his thumb toward the retreating couple and flashing his most winning smile.

Seven

THE HOTEL WAS old, but that didn't make it any less grand.

While it was no Ritz, the room had an old world charm that Cassidy found interesting. This wasn't a small or generic cookie-cutter room; it had character, from the balcony overlooking the street below, to the large tub in the bathroom held up by four clawed feet. She wasn't sure how he'd managed to find this place, but there was nothing for her to complain about.

She opened the door leading out onto the wrought-iron balcony and leaned down to look at the folks below. While the street this hotel sat on wasn't nearly as bois-terous as Bourbon, there was still a crowd wandering around the French Quarter, even after dark. Part of her wished she'd brought along some of the beads she'd ac-quired the previous night, especially when she saw the expectant looks on the faces of people below. They all expected her to toss them down, just like most people on various balconies across the Quarter did. Cassidy had no doubt she could inspire a few people to flash her with the proper incentive, but just waved down at them instead.

Hands grasped the railing on either side of her, and then Travis settled himself against her back. His face nuzzled her hair, and she sighed softly, rolling her head sideways to offer him her neck. Teeth grazed the skin there, and she shivered.

She'd never understood the romantic appeal of getting a hotel room, but she was starting to get an inkling. There was no doubt in her mind what they both intended to happen, but she wasn't about to make it easy. Still, it felt good to be held like this, to be desired this fiercely. She'd never felt this level of passion with Chad, hadn't even realized it was possible.

Chad. Her mind didn't want to linger on the relationship she'd been in for the last several years. There was a huge difference between the two men in her life, and not just in personality. Even in the brief time they'd been together, she knew that being in Travis's arms felt a million times better. Chad had never been possessive, never acted jealous or like he needed her. Cassidy's history with the two boys was so radically different, but her relationship with Chad seemed so shallow in hindsight.

"I was wondering," Travis murmured, his lips whisper-soft against her ear, "if you wanted to try out that tub?"

Tucking away the introspection for later, Cassidy looked back at him, her eyebrows raised. "'Try out'?" she echoed.

He grinned, his hand moving down to cup her backside. "Or we could fuck out here. Bet folks would appreciate the show."

His vulgar words sent a shiver down her spine. The thought of him bending her over the railing and taking her . . . The imagery had her trembling with sudden need, and she let out a shaky breath.

He took her hand and pulled her back inside the hotel room. Cassidy turned and pushed softly against his chest, subtly taking charge. Travis walked backwards, and when his legs hit the bed, he sat down heavily, staring up at her.

There was a sense of power in standing over him that Cassidy relished. Pushing against his chest again, she put one knee on the bed and straddled him, running her hands over the muscles of his chest. Travis's deep breath and shudder told her she was doing something right, but she had other ideas in mind. She pulled her shirt off in one smooth motion, tossing it carelessly over the side of the bed. His hands immediately moved up to her ribs, thumbs caressing the bottom of her still-covered breasts. Need made her hands tremble as she tugged at both his pants and belt, then she leaned down until she was pressed against his chest. She pulled herself down his torso, scraping her sensitive nipples along his skin until she reached what she wanted to play with.

Travis wound one hand in her hair as she passed the heel of her hand down his hard length, then she pulled aside the boxers to get a real look at him. Cassidy had never been this close, and she took the time to savor it. She ran her hand up Travis's dick, marveling at the smooth feel of the skin. Her thumb went over the tip and heard Travis let out a strangled groan.

Like that, do you? Emboldened, she repeated the gesture, and smiled as his hips bowed off the bed, pressing him further into her hand. At the same time, the hand in Cassidy's hair tightened, pulling her down toward him. She followed his lead, leaning down and flicking her tongue over the tip. Travis gasped, his whole body jolting at the tiny contact. She put her hand around the base and leaned in close, pulling the top half into her mouth, rolling her tongue around the edge of the bulbous head.

"Fuck!" Both of Travis's hands tangled in her hair as she pulled her head back, running her tongue along the smooth underside, then pulled him deep inside her mouth once more. He cursed again, the word a needy groan that ignited Cassidy's own lust. Removing her hand from around him, she tilted her head up and pulled him deep.

It was awkward, especially since she'd never done it before, but Travis didn't protest. Everything was new to her, but she reveled in the power she had to give this man pleasure. She reached underneath and gently massaged his balls, and his hips nearly came off the bed. Her core was already throbbing, her belly fluttering with need, but she was having too much fun teasing Travis. She pressed her thumb against the base, rubbing down and massaging just above his balls, and was rewarded by a panting groan.

Releasing her mouth from him, Cassidy crawled up Travis's body. He pulled her into a searing kiss that took her breath away, then shoved her sideways. She laughed in surprise as she rolled onto her belly, Travis leaping atop her like a panther.

"My turn to play," he said in a deadly whisper, looping his arm under her hips and pulling her up onto her knees. Cassidy grabbed the headboard as his teeth and lips made a trail down her backbone and he pulled her pants from around her hips. She kicked off the jeans but he didn't wait for her to fully remove her panties before fingers opened her folds and a wet tongue licked her opening. She cried out, surging forward, but Travis followed, his mouth an unrelenting force of pleasure. All laughter was gone, replaced by a delicious tension that threatened to break her. When his thumb entered her roughly, its way helped along by her own juices, she cried out, the pillow muffling her sounds.

"I want to hear you scream."

Travis inserted two fingers inside her, curving around to play with a spot that made her whole body shudder. His hand went around the back of her neck, pushing her shoulders into the bed as he finger-fucked her, his thumb massaging her clit.

"Ah, Travis!" Everything inside Cassidy's body surged to a single point, rising up to some narrow precipice, then with a cry she came, her body splintering into a million pieces. She muffled her cries in the pillow as his fingers left her, grabbing the lobes of her ass. There was no preamble; he positioned himself behind her, probing her entrance only a second before pushing himself inside. The sudden pressure took her breath away, but he wouldn't be denied entry.

"Fuck," he murmured as she clenched and fluttered around him, her orgasm still sending shock waves through her body. "You feel so goddamn good."

His hands gripped her hips as he moved inside her, slow at first but rapidly gaining strength. Still on her knees, Cassidy cried out, the new position rubbing and hitting parts of her body that only continued the ecstasy. Almost sobbing from the overwhelming pleasure, her fists balled in the sheets as Travis slammed in and out of her.

He pushed her sideways again, grabbing one leg and bringing it to his opposite shoulder. Wasting no time, he pushed inside her, keeping her body sideways as he fucked her hard, and Cassidy felt another pressure building inside her.

"I want to feel you come around me," he growled, twisting his hips and lifting her leg.

Cassidy could barely catch her breath, scrabbling for purchase, then another orgasm was ripped from her and she gave a piercing cry. "Travis!"

His name on her lips seemed to change something in the man, whose grunts grew louder. Leaning down over her, he captured Cassidy's lips with his, bending her leg so her knee was beside her head. "God, baby," he whispered, voice strained, then with a shuddering cry he came, laying his head on her shoulder.

The heavy sound of their breathing permeated the silence as both struggled to catch their breath. Travis let go of Cassidy's leg and collapsed beside her, keeping his hand on her thigh. "I didn't think it could get better," he finally said, his voice strained.

For her part, Cassidy could only manage a small whimper, all her strength having vanished. The bed was completely tossed about, but he was still able to find a corner of the comforter to pull over her as he rolled out. She appreciated the small courtesy.

"Let me get cleaned up, then I'll draw you a bath."

He kissed her forehead, lingering overlong, before padding off toward the bathroom. Still struggling to catch her breath, she listened as the water ran.

Who was this strange man who'd somehow taken the place of her tormentor? Travis Dean had been little more than a thorn in her side since freshman year, yet now he was in her bed, drawing her baths, and doing things to her body that surely weren't in the Bible. The previous night could have been chalked up to the alcohol, but here she was, completely sober and still doing the exact same thing.

Lord knew, though, it felt good to break loose like this, and she had to give Travis far more credit for helping her with everything.

Her former tormentor appeared again through the bathroom door and sat down on the bed beside her. He helped her remove the rest of her clothes, then gathered her in his arms.

"Your chariot awaits, madam," he said with a cheeky grin, and Cassidy laid her head on his shoulder as he walked her into the bathroom.

IF ANYONE HAD told Travis he'd ever be taking a bath with the girl of his dreams, he would have wanted whatever they'd been smoking. So having her in his arms, lying back against his chest, felt like an undeserved blessing. He couldn't stop touching her, sliding his hands down the back of her arms, across her belly and to the swell of her breasts. She seemed perfectly content to just lay back against him, cocooned in the warm water, but her soft sighs told him she enjoyed his explorations.

"So now tell me," Cassidy said, lazily running a thin bar of soap along her arm, "there isn't some other girl in your life I'll have to beat up when we get back, is there?"

Startled by the line of questioning, Travis laughed. "Nope," he said, shaking his head and grinning. "Although if you really want to fight over me, I'm sure I can find someone to oblige you."

She smacked his knee, spraying water into the air. He almost splashed her back but stopped himself, enjoying their current situation too much. Resting his chin atop her head, he asked, "What will you do about Captain Incredible?"

Perhaps it was too bold a question, but she didn't tense up when he asked it. She stayed silent a moment, obviously thinking, and Travis let her take all the time in the world. Finally, she said, "I don't know. We're through, that much I'm sure of."

"On behalf of myself and my family, I'm sorry for what my sister did."

"It's not your fault." She rubbed his knee absently. "I just wished I'd had some warning it was going to happen."

Travis mentally cursed himself for even bringing it up. Why had he said anything anyway? *Way to ruin the moment, dumbass.* To try and get her mind off her crappy choice in men, he traced lines around her belly, thumbing her nipples then moving his hands lower under the water. Cassidy pressed back against him, spreading her legs to allow him better access.

"Put your feet over the sides of the tub."

He felt her shiver, but she did as he said, lifting first one leg, then the other. Her head lolled onto his shoulder as he sank down in the water, teasing her with one hand while positioning himself essentially beneath her. Needy pants and gritted moans echoed off the tile bathroom as Travis pulled her up onto his lap, then slid the head of his cock between her exposed lips.

Cassidy's breathing hitched, her hips jerking when his hand massaged her clit. Even with the water, he could tell she was ready for him; the small bud was swollen, begging for attention. Grasping her waist, he braced his feet against the end of the tub and tilted his hips, easing inside of her.

She was already a tight fit, but from this angle she squeezed him almost unbearably well. It was Travis's turn to gasp, wanting only to sheathe inside her but forcing himself to take it slow. Cassidy's moans were louder, her hands gripping his thighs for balance. Careful to make sure she wouldn't slip out of his grip, he grabbed one of her hands and brought it down to her spread open pussy. "Feel that," he said, voice harsh with need as he tilted his hips back a fraction, then pressed deeper inside.

A throaty cry flew from Cassidy's lips, and she flexed her legs, lifting herself up and then back down over

Travis. He hissed out a breath through his teeth as they found a rhythm, the water in the tub sloshing with their movements. Their cries bounced around the small room as Travis pumped furiously inside her body. Cassidy was helpless against his onslaught, and with a startled cry she came again, trembling in his arms.

Fuck. It felt so good to be inside her, feeling her muscles contracting around him, so warm and soft and tight. His orgasm was coming on fast, however, and he didn't have a condom handy. He pumped into her one last time, then pulled out and gave a long groan as he came hard, semen pumping high on her belly. It took him a moment to catch his breath as he surveyed the damage. Seeing the thin white fluid on Cassidy's belly made a spark of possession course through him, as if he was marking her as his.

Cassidy lolled her head sideways and peeked at him with one eye. "You're going to clean that up, right?" she asked, the question more of a demand.

He laughed and laid a kiss on her temple. "Whatever the lady says."

Cassidy pulled her legs back into the water, settling her body below the surface as Travis washed her with a cloth. Stepping carefully out of the bathtub, he reached down and picked her up, moving out of the bathroom and setting her on the bed. He covered her with the comforter, and she moved sleepily beneath the sheets as he climbed in beside her.

Gathering her in his arms, Travis closed his eyes and reveled in the feel of her body against his. The last two days had been long, and sleep tugged at the edges of his consciousness. He allowed himself to doze, his arms wrapped securely around the girl of his dreams.

It wasn't until she pulled herself out of his arms sometime later that he woke again. Cassidy scooted lower under the covers, her mouth moving down Travis's torso, until she took him fully inside her mouth.

He fell backwards against the pillows, his hands moving to her head as it rose and fell over his cock. The girl was a natural; within seconds she had him completely hard and begging for more. She sucked him deep, working the tip with the back of her throat as she massaged his balls with one hand. Pulling back, she teased him with her tongue before pulling him deep again, bobbing with an inexorable tempo he couldn't resist.

"Oh fuck, Cassidy," he grit out, fists clumping in the sheets. "I'm coming, baby, I'm coming!"

He half expected her to pull away and not let him come in her gorgeous mouth. He wasn't going to push her to do it, but when she didn't release him, only sucking him deeper, it was the last straw. With a loud shout he came, shuddering beneath her as she swallowed him down to the last drop.

"God," he breathed when she crawled back up into his arms, "you're so fucking amazing."

She smiled sleepily, kissing his neck then curling up beside him like a warm, wet blanket. "I am, aren't I?"

He squeezed her tight, all the strength leeched from his body over that orgasm. One last kiss to the top of her head, then he fell over into slumber, dreaming of his blonde-haired angel with a sly, crafty smile.

Eight

CASSIDY STARED AT her phone for a long moment, trying to decide whether to power it up or leave it off.

Since finding Chad in the arms of Travis's sister, she'd left her phone off, ignoring any texts or voice mails she might have received. It felt wonderful to be free of the stifling responsibilities, but as Sunday rolled around, the old familiar tension crept over her. This minivacation, or whatever it was, had to end sometime, and then she'd have to face the music.

Familiar footfalls padded out of the bathroom, and she stuffed the phone under her pillow, rolling over onto her back as Travis entered the room. Her eyes moved over his naked torso and she smiled in appreciation. He'd put his black silk boxers back on, but was otherwise naked. *Damn, he's sexy. I could stand to wake up like this more often.*

He's mine.

"You all right?" he asked, sitting down on her side of the bed.

"It's nothing," she replied, clearing the frown from her brow. Where had that thought come from? It was absurd, getting possessive of Travis Dean. He'd had a certifiable harem all through high school; his sense of commitment was as ephemeral as the wind. Plus, it could never work between them, they were too different.

But despite the logic, it hurt to think that as soon as they left New Orleans they might be back to the way they were. That she might see him again in somebody else's arms hurt like crazy, but she didn't know how to bring up anything beyond the now. She had allowed herself to focus on the present for the last two days, and contemplating her suddenly uncertain future scared her.

"Hey, what's wrong?"

Cassidy didn't answer, just leaned in and hugged him tight. Vocalizing her feelings then would ruin the moment, bringing an end to the perfect experience. She wasn't ready to let this go, so she decided to distract herself, running her hand down and over his boxers.

"Ah, I see."

She said nothing as he bore her back to the bed and settled against her body. Cassidy could feel the heat of him through the thin comforter, and gave a contented sigh. This felt right for some reason, too perfect.

The thought of it ending hurt more than she cared to admit.

"I was going to suggest we head out and get some

breakfast," he said, leaning down to kiss her neck, "but I wouldn't mind starting with dessert first."

Cassidy's heartbeat sped up as his lips trailed down her neck and breasts, her belly tightening with anticipation. She'd never been the kind to roam naked, but Travis made her feel sexy, so she hadn't yet dressed from the bath the night before. He lifted her legs over his shoulders and settled himself between her thighs. Cassidy gripped the headboard tight, suddenly overwhelmed by the intimate display as he spread her folds and pressed his tongue inside her.

There was an almost lazy indulgence in his ministrations, as if her pleasure was meant as a reward for them both. It was new and exciting all at once, the position more intimate than anything she'd experienced before. He'd tease her one minute and then go back to exploring. When she was a quivering mess, ready to do *anything* for release, he crawled up over her and stole her mouth in a searing kiss. She welcomed him with a sigh, shuddering as he moved between her legs and stabbed deep.

Their lovemaking this time was lazy and natural, but Cassidy didn't mind. She ran her hands over his body, silently memorizing the lines of his muscles and the curves of his butt. He tasted and felt all man, and she took pleasure in knowing that, for now at least, he was all hers.

"HAVE YOU EVER had a beignet?"

"A what?"

Travis grinned. "You're going to love this place, then."

The open air Café du Monde was packed on Sunday afternoons, but they still managed to snag one of the smaller tables. Cassidy let Travis order for them as she watched the variety of people file past on the street. A white carriage, pulled by a thick palomino horse, ambled past, the family inside taking pictures of the architecture and nearby street acts. Behind them a band was playing some marching music, upbeat tempos that couldn't help but pull a smile to her lips. Artists lined the iron fence of St. Louis Cathedral, selling their various paintings to tourists and residents alike.

"Here, try this."

The waitress set down two plates on the table, each holding what at first appeared to be huge white mounds of confectioners' sugar and little else. Cassidy poked at the mass, frowning, and managed to unearth a squarish roll of some sort. "Geez, want a little bread with your sugar?"

"Just try it, Cassidy."

Shooting him a smirk, she bit into the warm pastry. It was delicious, but she said nothing, chewing it thoughtfully as if trying to decide on her response. "Tastes like a doughnut to me," she said, careful to keep her face neutral, and was delighted when Travis's eyes widened.

"Now, those there are fighting words," he said, and she bit her lip to keep from giggling. "See now, anyone from New Orleans would tell you that—"

"Cassidy!"

The sugar turned to ash in her mouth when she heard her name called. She turned around to see Melanie sitting nearby with her cousin Jaime and several friends. The other girls' eyes were as big as saucers. Her mouth ajar, Melanie raced over to Cassidy's table. "Oh my God, where have you been? Your dad's been freaking out all weekend trying to find you!"

Unsure what to say in the face of her friend's urgency, she pasted a smile on her face and spread her hands wide. "Surprise!"

Melanie threw her arms around Cassidy, hugging her fiercely. "Holy crap, your dad is so going to kill you. He told me this morning that he was about to call the cops and file a missing person's report!"

"Seriously?" Maybe she should have turned on her phone sooner, or at least sent her father a quick text. It had only been two days, but James Dupre was protective of his only daughter. Cassidy was used to fielding calls from him several times a day, and she knew she should have known better than to step off the grid.

"Chad called me too, wanted to know where you were." Melanie's eyes darted over to Travis, then back to Cassidy. "Anyone want to fill me in on what's happened since I last saw you?" she said carefully after a short pause.

"I'd like to know the same thing."

At the sound of Chad's voice, Cassidy's stomach twisted. Her hands balled into fists but she stayed in her seat as the blond man appeared behind her friend. Melanie must have seen her expression because she darted a confused look between the two. "We found him here this morning and so asked him to join us," she said hesitantly. "Bad call?"

"Where's Deedee?"

Travis's voice was harsh as he asked, and Chad frowned. "She left," he said simply. He sized up the dark-haired Cajun, but if he recognized him, he didn't indicate it. "Went home this morning before I even woke up."

A slight tightening of his lips was the only indication to Cassidy that the news actually hurt him. She had grown adept at reading her placid ex-boyfriend's moods, and could tell the younger girl's disappearing act weighed heavily on Chad.

Travis abruptly stood up, his chair skidding loudly against the concrete. He was staring at Chad as if ready to leap over the table and go after him, and without thinking about it, Cassidy laid a hand on his arm. Everyone's eyes went to that touch, but she refrained from snatching her hand away.

Disappointment flickered across Travis's features as he looked between Cassidy and Chad. "I'll leave you two to hash it out," he finally muttered. Throwing some cash on the tabletop and giving everyone a wide berth, he stalked off, shoulders hunched and hands shoved into his pockets.

"Cassidy, can we talk?"

Anger bubbled up at Chad's mild voice, the emotion threatening to choke her, but she tamped it down. As much as she wanted to go after Travis, now wasn't the right time. She rose stiffly from her seat, ignoring Melanie as she moved past to walk with Chad. When it was all over, she'd have to do damage control with her best friend—she'd seen the hurt in her eyes that she had come to New Orleans with Travis and not her—but for right now, she could only focus on one argument at a time.

Chad didn't seem any more eager to talk than she did, following her outside. Behind the open-air café there was a small rotunda where a three-piece band was playing a slow dirge. Their path wound up the stairs behind the makeshift stage, up onto the Mississippi River levy that ran the course of the street. The river was wide enough to let huge barges up the river, and nearby a big cruise liner sat along the shore, ready for passengers. Seagulls called out above them as Cassidy stopped beside the large cannon, not really interested in drawing this out.

"What do you want?" she asked bluntly, no longer caring about making a scene. At his frown, she fisted her hands around her purse handle, not in the mood for games. "I saw you with Travis's sister."

She waited for him to make excuses, to try and explain away what she saw, but he only took a deep breath. "Ah."

It was the wrong answer.

Taking a step forward, Cassidy smacked her palm across his cheek, snapping his head sideways. Her lips compressed into a thin line, she watched as his hand went to his face. Myriad emotions flit across his face before he finally settled on acceptance. "I suppose I deserve that."

"You run out on me with a girl who's still in high school, without giving me the courtesy to at least mention that, oh by the way, we're over. I have to hear about it from her *brother*."

"Well, you seemed to have a lot on your plate at the time. I didn't want to add more—"

Her second slap rocked his head around the other way but still didn't get more of a rise out of him than a rueful twist of the lips. "I deserved that one too."

What had she ever seen in this boy? Here they were, talking about the end of a relationship that had spanned nearly all of high school and beyond, and the most emotion he could dredge up was humor? "Just tell me why," she said in an icy voice.

"At the risk of another slap, perhaps I can show you instead?" He took a deep breath, as if getting ready to face a lion. "I want you to kiss me."

In your dreams. There was no way she'd lock lips with this snake, never in a million years.

"Cassy, please. I'm not trying to pull anything, I just need to show why I did what I did."

She glared at him, trying to decide if he was serious. Then again, everything Chad Somerfeld did was serious. If he said a kiss at this point would prove anything, he was in earnest. Whether it would actually prove anything was what she doubted.

"Just relax and pretend this was two days ago, when nothing had happened yet."

Easier said than done, but dropping into the role was easier than she thought. They'd been at this now for over five years, after all. Blocking out the texted picture and the image of him on the dance floor with the other girl, Cassidy stepped forward and kissed him.

She wasn't sure what this was supposed to prove, but stiffened when his arms went around her. His lips were chill from the air, limp and lifeless compared to the kisses Travis had given her. Suddenly uncomfortable, she stepped away, and he let her go.

"Now," he said reasonably, as if teaching a class, "tell me what you felt, and be truthful."

Cassidy stared at the black iron cannon beside them, her hands twisting around her purse. For a long moment she wasn't sure what to say. Finally, she sighed, releasing her frustration. "Nothing. I felt nothing."

Had it always been like this? She'd thought herself in love with Chad, but until that weekend she'd had nothing with which to compare their interactions. They'd been together since freshman year, always exclusive. It had been so easy to grow complacent, to fall into the status quo.

Spending the last two days with Travis, however, had opened her eyes. The Cajun was everything that Chad wasn't: a smartass, sarcastic, and emotional. He made her heart beat faster just by walking into a room, and made her body sing with a single touch. Looking at Chad, meanwhile, was like looking in a mirror. They were so much alike, but now the things that had attracted her made her cringe. She didn't want to be cold or emotionless, analytical in every situation. Travis felt deeply and wasn't afraid to let those feelings show, and Cassidy admired him for it.

"I'd always known Deedee liked me, but I'd put her down as harmless. Then two days ago she approached me, said she'd just turned eighteen and wanted only one thing: a kiss from me. I swear to you, Cassy, I told her no, but she kept on asking. And, I'm sorry to say, it was flattering."

"So you kissed her," she said, not caring to hear everything psychoanalyzed.

Chad sighed. "Yes, I kissed her and it was . . ." He trailed off as if searching for the words. "It felt as if I'd just been introduced to a whole new world. Infinite possibilities lay before me and . . . I won't lie, I went a little crazy for a while trying to figure it all out."

Cassidy thought about her night on Bourbon Street and its aftermath. "It happens to the best of us," she said softly.

"She really is an interesting girl. Do you know she plays the violin? Classically, not just the fiddle. And she has the second-highest GPA in her graduating class." He looked almost confused, as if the dichotomy didn't make any sense to his perfect world.

"So are you in love with her?"

The question seemed to shock him. "I've only really known her less than a week, there's no way . . . I mean, a feeling as complicated as love can't possibly materialize out of thin air."

"We were together nonstop for five years and the feeling never materialized," she pointed out. "Maybe it really is an instant thing." Cassidy sighed. "I still remember the first time I really noticed you, when you visited my house after my mother died. You brought me a bouquet of my favorite flowers, and I took it as some kind of sign."

He looked away sheepishly. "My mother suggested I go over there to try and get you out of your shell. I do have a confession though; the flowers weren't actually from me."

Cassidy blinked. "They weren't?"

He shook his head. "They were already there when I

arrived, and you opened the door as I picked them up. I'm sorry now that I pawned them off as mine."

Cassidy's heart squeezed painfully and her hand went up to the flower she'd pinned in her hair once again that morning. Her smile was fleeting; all she wanted to do now was cry. "All boys are stupid like that, I suppose."

Except one.

"Now, if you'll excuse me—" he started, but Cassidy put out a hand to stop him.

"Oh, there is one more thing."

Balling up her fist, she drew back and let it fly straight at Chad's face. He staggered back and fell onto his backside, staring up at her in shock. She would have been lying if she said it hadn't felt good, although her knuckles were going to be bruised for a while.

He cursed loudly, the first real emotion she could remember seeing out of him. "You broke my nose!"

"You lied to me about the flowers and strung me along for five years. I think I'm entitled to a little anger. You also denied me sex." She drew herself up, staring down her nose at him. "That, is unforgivable." Turning around, she moved quickly down the stairs, leaving the boy in the dust.

Melanie was still waiting for her, but Cassidy wasn't looking for her friend just yet. "Did you see which way Travis went?"

"Travis?" She wrinkled her nose. "I thought you two were mortal enemies or something."

"Melanie, please, I need to find him."

The hurt crept back into her friend's eyes, even though

she tried to hide it. "He kind of followed you when you went off with Chad, then I saw him walking down St. Ann Street back into the Quarter."

"Thank you." As much as she wanted to take off running, she still drew her best friend into a hug. "I'm sorry if I hurt your feelings, and I really want to tell you everything that's happened since I last saw you, but right now I have to go find a man."

"Hey, if you see an extra one, send him my way."

Cassidy smiled. "I'll be back, promise."

Nine

TRAVIS ANSWERED THE hotel door on the second knock, but he wasn't interested in looking at her. Cassidy stood quietly by the door, waiting for him to acknowledge her, but it seemed to be a losing battle. He'd already gathered up their stuff, even bagging up the mass of beads she'd accumulated their first night on Bourbon.

"So. You and the Captain are getting back together, I take it?"

Cassidy frowned. "What gave you that idea?"

He didn't answer, just gave a derisive snort, and she suddenly realized what happened. "You saw the kiss, didn't you?" Of course he would think that, especially if he left at that moment and didn't see all that had come after. "Travis—"

"I don't get it," he exploded, throwing his hands into the air. "The boy cheated on you and you're taking him back? You deserve so much better than that."

His protective response warmed her, but she kept her own emotions in check. "I can make my own decisions."

"Yeah, that's turned out well for you, hasn't it? Why didn't you just tell me I was a phase, a little vacation before going back to your golden boy there?"

Seeing him mad at her like this made her heart squeeze painfully. "Well, why didn't you tell me it was you who left me those flowers?"

He paused, frowning at her. "Flowers?"

Cassidy swallowed, suddenly nervous. "After my mother died. You left those flowers on my porch, didn't you?"

He looked away, and she had her answer. "Travis, this might sound stupid, but it was more the presence of those flowers and less the boy who I thought gave them to me that helped."

Travis still wouldn't look at her, and Cassidy continued somewhat desperately, "I'd shut myself down for weeks, wouldn't leave the house or anything. You knew this; my father told me you used to come over to see me but he'd have to turn you away. Those flowers did something I couldn't even do myself; they helped to get me out of the house.

"Afterwards, I realized how miserable I'd become, refusing to even leave the house, and, well, I guess I shut down my emotions too. Chad was so easy; he didn't demand anything except loyalty, and I'd convinced myself that was enough—I convinced myself that was love. Then you go and show me that picture, and upend my world again."

"I love you, Cassidy."

His words stole the breath from her lungs. Travis dragged his gaze to hers, eyes tortured. "I've loved you every minute of every day since the moment I met you. I worshipped you up close, and then when you withdrew into yourself, I worshipped you from afar. The teasing, the pranks, it was all me trying to get through to that girl again, the one I couldn't forget."

Cassidy took one step forward, then another, until she was standing in front of Travis. He stared down at her, his throat working, a muscle ticking in his jaw. She laid one hand on his arm, and could feel the tension nearly vibrating off him. "I think I broke Chad's nose." Whatever he'd been expecting, that wasn't it. Confusion twisted his face, and Cassidy poked him in the chest. "If you'd stuck around past that fiasco of a kiss, you would have seen what happened next."

"I did see you slap him," he said, one corner of his mouth tipping up ever so slightly.

"Twice, actually." She said it proudly, and his small smile deepened. "The asshole deserved it, and I think he's in love with your little sister."

The smile fell from his lips. "I'm going to fucking kill him."

A big smile broke out over Cassidy's face, and she threw her arms around Travis. He paused for a short moment, and then hugged her tight. "I would have liked to see you sock him," he murmured against her hair.

"I love you too, you know."

He stiffened, and she squeezed him tighter. "There's no way you could have gone half as far with me, even drunk, if I'd ever really hated you." She looked up at him, desperate to make him understand her sudden change of heart. "You're everything I need, and everything I now know I want. Plus," she added, drawing a finger down his chest, "you're really hot too."

A slow smile spread again across his face. "So," he murmured, stroking her cheek with his thumb, "we're friends again?"

"With benefits, hopefully." At his surprised laugh, she fixed him with a superior look. "I like sex. You have a problem with that?"

"No, ma'am."

Cassidy squealed as he swept her off her feet, then sighed against his lips as he kissed the ever-living daylights out of her.

"If I ever see you kiss another man," he growled, "heads will roll."

"Yours are the only lips I want, anyhow," she said softly, wrapping her arms around his neck.

"So, you like sex." He chuckled. "Guess I can't call you 'Chastity Cassidy' anymore."

She swatted at his arm. "Not if you want to keep *getting* any sex, sir."

Travis waggled his eyebrows at her. "You know, we have this room for about . . ." He checked his watch. " . . . another hour. You up for something?"

Cassidy looked pointedly at the bathroom, then back at Travis. The smile on his face widened to a full-fledged grin.

"Whatever the lady wants." Capturing her lips in another sizzling kiss, he carried her into the bathroom and the waiting tub, kicking the door shut behind him.

About the Author

SARA FAWKES is an avid traveler whose dream job includes seeing the world on two wheels and living off her writing. She resides in California and, when she isn't writing, loves to rebuild old cars/motorcycles and pester her very own Dude. You can find her online at Facebook or Twitter.

Visit www.AuthorTracker.com for exclusive information on your favorite HarperCollins authors.

SHOW ME

By Cathryn Fox

To Valerie, a brilliant physics student who is as beautiful on the inside as she is on the outside. Thanks for helping me with this one!

One

FOLLOWING HER GROUP of girlfriends through the busy French Quarter, Eva Parker lengthened her already long strides in order to keep pace. Nighttime had fallen over New Orleans and a mosaic of stars shimmered against the black canvas as drunken college kids spilled out onto the sidewalks, slowing her steps even more. She pushed through the crowd, not about to let anyone or anything stand in her way tonight. Because before the night was over, one way or another, Eva Parker, geek girl extraordinaire, planned to get laid. Oh yeah, this trip was all about pretending to be something she wasn't so she could finally experience a man's lips on her flesh, his hands on her body, his cock between her legs . . .

Equal amounts of excitement and nervousness knotted her stomach as she thought about stripping bare and putting herself in some random guy's hands. Of course if she had the choice, she'd rather not have a simple casual fling with someone she didn't know, considering there really was only one college boy she wanted—Mr. Bad Boy himself—but she'd long ago given up on him seeing her as anything more than his best friend's nerdy kid sister.

As she pushed that disheartening thought aside, and took in the hotties all around her, another bout of anxiety hit like a sucker punch. But she'd be damned if she was going to let a little apprehension stand in the way her of losing her virginity. She was a sophomore, for God's sake. Not only was her innocence and lack of experience embarrassing, she was dying to have orgasmic sex, the kind she'd longingly listened to her friends describe in blissful detail for the last year. Which was why she'd flown from her college town to the Big Easy during Spring Break. Here, where no one knew her as the too nerdy physics student, one who hot guys ignored, she could be anything or anyone she wanted, and finally seduce a man into her bed.

She turned quickly, nearly losing sight of her petite, agile friends as they cut a corner, and silently cursed under her breath when her long legs failed to keep up.

Her groans of annoyance turned into an unexpected moan of pleasure when a smoking hot guy bumped up against her, warming her body and punching her hormones into hyper drive.

"'Scuse me, *chére*," the guy said in a sexy Cajun accent that had her above average IQ dipping below the median and her pussy moistening with want. When sultry eyes met hers, she sucked in a quick breath to jump-start her brain, giving the hot guy standing before her a quick once-over.

A local. Sweet. The perfect guy to give her what she wanted before she returned to school, to the nerdy, rather lackluster life she led. Her head dipped, taking pleasure in his rock hard body and sun-kissed skin before her glance moved back to his face to admire chiseled features and full lips made for kissing. Her. Everywhere. Now.

Okay, Eva. This is your chance. Don't blow it.

Or rather, blow it!

Taller than average, she stood eye-to-eye with the dark-skinned hottie, her mind racing, desperate for something sexy to say, or at least something that sounded interesting and didn't involve her deep love of science. But as her brain stalled, some hot little number sidled up to him, went up on her toes, pressed her humongous breasts into his chest and whispered in his ear. He gave a deep laugh full of heat and promise, and when he wrapped his arm around the girl's waist to lead her away, Eva exhaled a heavy sigh, cursing herself for choking on her words with the first hot guy she came across.

What the heck happened to being anyone or anything she wanted?

Damn. Damn. Damn.

With her mind racing, Eva ran to catch up to her friends, thinking back to what that crazy fortune-teller from this morning had told her—she wasn't going to have sex with some random guy this week—or ever. It wasn't like she'd wanted to go see the clairvoyant or gave credence to anything she'd said, anyway. Eva believed in physics not psychics, and had only gone because her friends insisted on it.

Now, determined to prove to her friends that Madame Ysabeau was nothing but a fraud, and that she *would* have sex with a random guy, she glanced at the cute boys walking by her. Too bad they were completely oblivious to her presence.

Her best friend, Allison, reached out and snatched her hand. She gave a little tug and said, "Come on. Hurry up before all the hot ones are taken."

Eva quickened her pace, well, as much as she could with so many bodies slamming up against her, and followed Allison into a dimly lit dance club called Bourbon Heat. At least the name of the establishment sounded promising, considering what she had in mind tonight—bourbon and heat—and not necessarily in that order.

Mimicking her confident friend, Eva tugged down the neckline of her blouse and jutted her cleavage out, well, what little of it there was. She tried for sexy as she entered the busy club, only to get knocked back when a group of loud party girls rushing outside dragged her right along with them. She let out a little yelp and lost Allison's hand in the commotion as she stumbled toward the door. Once she was able to right herself, she slipped to the side, braced herself on the cool interior wall and took a rejuvenating breath. Even though she was out of her element, preferring labs over dance clubs, she was determined to follow through with her plan. No one here knew her for a too tall, nerdy science geek who thought watching particles collide in an accelerator was sexy. And since the particles in *her* accelerator were all charged up tonight, her object was to collide . . . several times, if possible . . . with a hot guy.

Straightening her shoulders and gathering her bravado, she scanned the club, and while her cursed height did little to attract guys, it came in handy when searching for her friends. She spotted the trio gathered around the bar, a group of hot guys flocking to them like dim-witted moths to a lightbulb.

God, why couldn't she be more like her outgoing roommates, able to walk into a room, any room, and have guys eating out of her palm? She studied the tight knit group of girls who'd all been friends since kindergarten, taking a moment to consider their small, voluptuous bodies, their short shorts, and the way their breasts bounced in their too tight tube tops, before she gave herself a once-over.

She exhaled another heavy sigh. Okay, so she didn't have to be the top physics student at her school to know why guys gravitated toward her friends and avoided her. She was a gazelle in a room full of bambies and had a brain made for science, not fun and flirtation. And since the last thing she wanted to do was accentuate her already too long legs, she avoided those cute little short shorts at all costs. Then there was her cleavage to consider. Honestly, without the use of duct tape, she'd never be able to keep up a tube top, let alone look sexy in one. Which was why she was in an unflattering white shirt that resembled a lab coat and stuck to her flesh like a second skin in the moist, southern heat.

With so many strikes against her, how the hell was she ever going to get a guy into her bed?

As she mulled that over, she came to the logical conclusion that she needed help and fast. She needed someone to show her the ropes, to teach her how to walk, talk, and dress for seduction. Someone who knew women, and knew what guys looked for when picking one from the crowd.

She continued to toss that idea around inside her head, and when her glance landed on the one guy she'd always wanted—the one guy she'd given up on noticing her—she found the answers to all her problems. Hot, hard, and popular, Luke Hackett sat on a bar stool with his elbows propped on the long oaken bar top behind him, his dark, wolfish glance sweeping the dance floor like a predator stalking its prey. Her stomach fluttered as she watched Mr. Bad Boy himself, because he was perfect in every sense of the word. Perfect face. Perfect body. Perfect . . . *everything*.

But not only was he perfect on the outside, he was perfect on the inside. Having known Luke since she was a kid, she knew there was more to her older brother's best friend than met the eye. He might come across as wild and dangerous on the outside, but there was a quiet, reflective, sensitive side to him, and when it came to her, he'd always been patient and caring.

Her heart skipped a beat when she thought about how he'd watched out for her when they were young. She smiled as she remembered the time he'd helped her learn to ride a bike. Her brother was too busy jumping dirt piles on his BMX to give her lessons, but Luke had put aside his own fun to spend hours with her, even bandaging her bloody knee when she fell and skinned it. Then there was the time he'd taken her to the empty school parking lot to teach her how to drive when her folks had given up hope that she'd ever learn. He'd been so understanding when she had trouble with the clutch, letting her practice over and over again until she got it right. And she couldn't forget all the times he'd listen to her ramble on about her school projects when the rest of her family had tuned out. She laughed quietly thinking about how she always found him at the dining room table with her when she was up late working on a physics report. They'd shared numerous late night pizzas over homework back then, and even though he sucked at grammar, he always insisted he read over her reports before she turned them in. Maybe it was because he wanted to hang around for an extra slice, or maybe he really just wanted to help. Either way, how could a girl not love a guy like that?

She swallowed hard and tamped down the tsunami in her stomach, knowing better than to let her emotions get ahold of her where her Luke was concerned. He was into bambies, like every other guy she knew, and while he'd always looked out for her, she was certain he'd never seen her as anything more than an unattractive brainiac. Which, when she really thought about it, meant he would be the perfect teacher; if he could help transform her into the kind of girl *he* wanted between the sheets, she could become the kind of girl every guy wanted.

Hope surged inside her, and her smile widened. Oh

yeah, he was just the guy she needed to help her out. Not only did he know women, but as a fourth year business student at the college in their hometown—the same college she was attending—majoring in both marketing and finance, he knew all about packaging and selling a product, and could most definitely teach her how to package and sell herself.

Now, what would it take to convince him to help her with this naughty project?

MOUTH AGAPE, LUKE Hackett raked his fingers through his mussed hair and stared at his best friend's kid sister. "You want me to do what?"

"You heard me," Eva said, squeezing her body between him and the guy sitting on the bar stool to his left.

The bartender stopped by and Eva ordered a fruity drink before turning back to him. Luke took that opportunity to spin on the padded seat to face her and widened his knees to make room for her in the tight space. When the guy beside him bumped up against her back, he drew her closer in a protective manner and rested his hands on his knees as she settled between his thighs. Her hot body molded so perfectly with his, fitting so nicely between his legs, that there wasn't a damn thing he could to do stop his traitorous cock from rising to the occasion.

He cursed under his breath and called on every ounce of strength he possessed to get his shit together before he gyrated against the girl who'd been getting under his skin for as long as he could remember.

"What I heard," he began, "or at least what I think I heard, was that you want me to teach you how to sell yourself."

"That's right," she said, her chin held high. "I want you to teach me how to be the perfect package before the week is over. The kind of girl who has guys eating out of the palm of her hand."

He stiffened, his fingers clamping around his knees as he pictured Eva working the room in a pair of short shorts, like every other girl in the club. Not that he was opposed to the sexy look. It was just that the thought of other guys eyeing her long legs filled him with a dangerous kind of rage. "You've got to be kidding me?"

Dark lashes blinked over innocent eyes. "I've never been more serious in my life."

His heart thumped in his chest as he considered what she was asking of him. No way. No fucking way was he going to go there. Not with her. Not with Eva.

"Eva—" he began, but she cut him off.

"If you don't want to do it . . ." She paused when the bartender came back with her drink, then glanced around the bar. She pointed her finger. " . . . then maybe I'll ask Jacob."

Fire burned in his gut when he followed her gaze and found her staring at Jacob, one of his two roommates—the other one being her brother Brad. Thank God Brad was temporarily tied up in New York interviewing for a few marketing positions—positions that Luke himself would love to be applying for, instead of settling into a boring job at his father's firm—and wouldn't be here until later in the week. If her brother knew he was even having this conversation, Brad would kick his ass all the way back home.

He watched Jacob whisper something into a girl's ear, and while he'd do just about anything for his pal, the fact that Jacob's goal was to fuck his way through every female dorm across campus before graduation this spring meant he wasn't someone he wanted Eva hanging around.

"Forget it. You're not asking Jacob for anything," he growled, unnerved, but not surprised by how much it bothered him to picture her hanging out with his roommate, or any other another guy, for that matter.

The truth was, he'd been crazy about Eva for as long as he could remember, but she'd also been off limits for just as long. When they were all just kids, Brad, being the protective older brother, had enlisted his help in looking out for his little sister. And since looking out for her didn't involve sleeping with her, it meant she was hands off. The last thing he wanted was to be disloyal to his friend, a guy who was more like a brother than a pal, actually. Brad had been there for him after his mother died during his teen years and his father buried himself in his work in order to cope with the loss. Brad and Eva's family had practically taken him in and treated him like he was one of their own, feeding him when his own father stayed late at the office and giving him a place to sleep when his dad didn't bother to come home at all.

Luke felt a responsibility to them all, and didn't want to betray a brother who didn't like the idea of his sister being with any guy, let alone his very best friend.

He took a much needed pull from his beer bottle and slammed it back down with more force than necessary. Desperate to find something, anything, to do with his hands before he wrapped them around her body and ravished her right there against the bar—because yes, a part of him wanted to take her up on her offer, wanted to be the guy eating out of her hands—he worked his nail over the paper label. "Brad would kick my ass if I agreed to this."

"Brad's not here," she challenged, swirling her straw around the strawberry concoction in her glass before placing it on the bar top.

"But," he countered, "he'll be here mid-week."

"He never has to know," Eva said.

Luke jammed his thumb into his chest. "Brad might not know, but I'll know."

"Okay, so if you don't want me to ask Jacob, and you won't do it, then I'll have to find someone else. I wonder who I should ask . . ." She tapped her chin, and when she scanned the club it occurred to him that she knew him too well, knew that no matter what, he'd always be there for her and always help her with whatever she needed.

Shit.

He scrubbed his hand over his face and spoke slowly. "What exactly is it you want me to do, Eva?"

She waved her hand over a clingy shirt showcasing small, perky breasts that would undoubtedly fit perfectly in his palms—not to mention his mouth—and mid-thigh shorts that teased and tortured his suddenly overactive imagination.

"Just look at me," she said, disgust in her tone.

Look? Hell, he'd been looking ever since she'd transformed from a gangly teen to a tall gorgeous girl who no longer asked him for piggyback rides—thank God! And even though he knew it was a bad idea, he looked again. And what he saw rocked his world. But since she was off limits, he wasn't going to do a damn thing about it. No, that wasn't entirely true. He'd definitely been doing something about it. And what he'd been doing for the last four years of college was fucking every girl he'd come in contact with in an effort to get her out from under his skin.

"I have no idea how to dress sexy."

Ah, Jesus . . .

"You want me to teach you how to dress?"

"That would be part of the package, yes," she said. "And I want you to teach me how to hold an interesting conversation with a hot guy."

He snorted, and shot a glance around the room. "I hate to break it to you, Eva, but there isn't a guy in this place looking for an interesting conversation."

"Then teach me how to talk sexy, or at least talk about something guys are interested in." She crinkled that cute little nose of hers. "Cleary it's not physics."

"I like it when you talk physics."

She gave him a look that suggested he was insane. "No one but my professors like it when I talk physics." He was about to protest, to tell her how much he loved her brilliant mind, when she cut him off. "I promise I'll make it worth your while."

"Oh really?" he asked, his mind taking him down an X-rated path it had no right going. "And how do you plan to do that?"

With those almost too big blue eyes of hers, she looked at him in a way that always set his heart racing. "How about that old Pokémon card of mine you've always wanted."

Luke grinned. "We're not kids anymore, Eva."

"Okay, then why don't you tell me? What do I have that you want?"

Everything . . .

"Nothing."

She frowned and looked around the bar. Her eyes lit when they moved back to his. "How about a date with Allison?"

Luke scanned the room and gave a slow shake of his head when his glance landed on her cute best friend. "I can get my own dates." She shifted between his legs and he could almost feel the heat of her pussy reaching out to him. Stifling a groan, he moved restlessly and asked though clenched teeth, "Is there some guy in particular you want? Is that why you're doing this?"

"No," she answered. "I . . . I just . . . I'm still a . . ."

Ah, fuck . . .

She was a virgin.

Her eyes met his and his heart pinched at the desperate look that moved over her face. "Will you help me?"

Help her? Hell, he'd like nothing better than to sink his cock all the way inside her and fu—

"Luke?"

Christ, when she looked at him like that, how could he say no? But then again, how could he possibly say yes?

"I just want to be . . . normal."

"Normal?"

"I want to have sex," she blurted out bluntly. "And the only way for me to do that is to figure out how to be hot."

"You are hot," he murmured under his breath. When she angled her head and gave him a curious look, he squared his shoulders. "I mean . . ." he backtracked, desperate to snatch his words back. The last thing he wanted was for her to know what he really thought of her, or that he thought of her at all. A lot.

"Come on, Luke." She threw her hands up in the air and shook her head. As her long brown curls flowed over her shoulders, the sweet tang of her citrus shampoo wafted before his nose. Raw lust erupted inside him as he resisted the urge to breathe her in. "We both know I'm not."

Was she serious? Did she have no idea how fucking sexy she was, or that she was still a virgin because most guys his age were too fucking stupid to understand that smart was sexy? But he knew. Oh yeah, he knew all right. But not only was she brilliant, she was thoughtful and generous and didn't need revealing clothes or sexy talk to make her the perfect package. She already was the perfect package. He sucked in a breath to clear his lust-addled brain before he threw caution to the wind and bent her over the bar and proved to her just how desirable she really was—even when she dressed like a nerdy scientist who cared little about fashion, and maybe even more because of that.

"Luke?" she said, and when she blinked at him, he understood just how desperate she was, how important this was to her. *Christ* . . . He could feel something inside him give, soften, because if it was this important to her, then it was damn well important to him too. He exhaled slowly, hardly able to believe he was going to teach his best friend's kid sister how to fuck a guy before the week was over.

Shit. Shit. Shit.

He briefly squeezed his eyes shut. "Why me?"

"Because you know women, and . . . well . . . you know what turns a guy on."

She went quiet for a moment, thoughtful, and he probed, "And?"

"And because I know you, Luke, and I trust that you won't screw this up for me. You've always watched out for me so I know I'll be in good hands."

Good hands?

Christ she had no idea what he wanted to do to her with his hands. How many nights he'd tossed and turned visualizing her beside him, beneath him, on top of him, his hands and mouth on her beautiful lithe body, her loose curls spilling down her back as he drove his cock all the way inside her.

"I don't think—"

A look of desperation came over her face. "Wait," she blurted out before he could finish.

"What?"

"I know how to make it worth your while. I have something to offer in exchange."

He clenched his teeth. "Eva—"

"You're taking English this term right?"

He grimaced, thinking about the major term paper he had to write when the week was over. "Yeah, why?"

"Because I don't expect you to give up your own week of fun for nothing."

Of course she didn't, which was one of the things he loved most about her. And while he'd happily forgo his own pleasure for her, he wasn't about to tell her that. "What are you getting at?"

"I'll proofread all your papers this term. We both know grammar isn't your thing."

A low tortured groan caught in his throat, and he knew he was going to do what she was asking, even without getting something in exchange. "Fine," he said, letting her believe her offer of help was the reason he was agreeing, even though it wasn't. No, he was only conceding because at least this way he could see to it that she didn't end up in bed with some random asshole, even though that seemed to be her game plan. "But I have a condition."

"What?"

He put his mouth close to her ear and said, "If I'm going to train you for another guy, I get to pick him."

"No frigging way!" Allison blurted out, her sleepy eyes widening as she jackknifed in her bed.

"What?" Samantha asked, coming in from the adjoining hotel room. With her blonde curls in a tumbling mess, she stretched her arms over her head and yawned, her short nighty riding up her tanned thighs. "What's going on?"

"Apparently last night Luke Hackett agreed to teach our Eva here how to be a stud magnet."

"What?" Samantha said, stopping dead in her tracks. "Luke Hackett. As in *the* Luke Hackett, your brother's best friend and the hottest fucking guy at college?"

"Yeah, that's the one," Eva said, towel drying her long wet hair as her glance ping-ponged back and forth between her two friends.

Then Andie, Eva's third friend, came in from the

bathroom and pointed her toothbrush at her. "Ah, did I hear what I think I just heard?"

"Oh yeah," Allison said, answering for Eva from her unmade bed. "Our innocent Eva is putting herself in the most capable, most sought after hands on campus." She writhed on the sheets and said, "Oh what I could do with those hands."

Andie squealed and dropped down next to Eva, nudging her with an elbow. "Well done, girlfriend. You're here one day and end up with the hottest guy in town."

"About time, too," Samantha murmured.

Eva was about to ask what Samantha meant when Allison went up on her elbows and said, "But Brad is going to kill him. You know that, right?"

"Brad never has to know," Eva said with a shrug that came off as more nonchalant than she felt. "Besides, it's not like that. He's just going to teach me how to market myself. He's not going to sleep with me."

"So he's going to prime you for another guy?" Andie frowned. "I don't get it. If the idea is to get laid, why doesn't *he* just fuck you?"

"He's not into me, he's just helping me," she explained, a nervous feeling mushrooming in her stomach at the thought.

Her three friends exchanged a look that confused Eva. "Yeah, let me know how that goes," Samantha said, smirking.

At a knock on the door, she glanced at her watch. Though she'd asked Luke if they could get an early start this morning and only had one week to find a guy and get him into bed, she was sure it couldn't be him. He was probably still sleeping off last night's party.

The girls dispersed, each picking out their outfit for the day as she padded to the door. When she opened it and found that it was Luke casually leaning against the door frame, a sexy bad boy grin on his face as he looked her up and down, her throat tightened and her pulse kicked up a notch. God, everything about him set her on fire, but telling herself that emotions should play no part in her lessons on seduction, she swallowed down the want.

Trying to appear unaffected, she fussed with the top button on her starched blouse, then jammed her hands into the pockets of her khaki shorts. "You're here early."

Dark eyes met hers. "Isn't that what you wanted?"

Oh, God, if he only knew what I wanted . . .

"Hey Luke," Allison said from the other side of the room.

He tossed her friend a smile that had the needy little spot between Eva's legs pulsing, then turned his focus back to her. "I thought we'd grab breakfast."

"Breakfast?"

The corner of his mouth turned up. "You do eat breakfast, don't you?"

"Yeah, but I thought . . ."

"What, that I was simply going to show you how to dress like a sex kitten and toss you to the wolves? You're not ready for that, *chére*."

She thought about her run-in with that sexy Cajun yesterday and how she'd struggled for something to say, something to keep his interest. Luke was right. She wasn't ready for that just yet, and when she caught a glimpse of herself in the hallway mirror, taking in her flat top and knobby knees peeking out from her long, unflattering shorts, she knew he had his work cut out for him. "Yeah, I guess you're right."

"So let's go."

She slipped into her flats, and leaving her hair to air dry despite the fact that it would frizz in this weather, waved to her friends and followed Luke outside. The warm morning air dampened her recently showered skin, and she shaded the rays from her eyes as he led her onto the sun-drenched sidewalk.

"Where are we going?"

"I found this great café down the street."

Catching her by surprise, Luke grabbed her hand, and she kept pace as he led her along the quiet walkway, the partygoers from last night nowhere to be found at this early hour.

Madame Ysabeau, however, was wide-awake and standing on the sidewalk next to her storefront window, almost like she was expecting her and Luke to walk by. Long, wiry gray hair, which looked like it hadn't seen a brush in ages, hung around her weathered face, and when knowledgeable green eyes locked on Eva's, Eva got the distinct impression the woman was remembering her prediction from the day before. But there was more to it than that. She almost seemed to be daring Eva to prove her wrong. Which was exactly what Eva planned to do. Still, she couldn't help but feel a little creeped out by the woman, and she moved closer to Luke as they approached the fortune-teller, her hand tightening in his grasp.

"Everything okay?" he asked, his gaze leaving Eva's to slide over Madame Ysabeau, who'd suddenly turned her attention to him, a smile reaching her piercing, birdlike eyes as she took in their locked hands.

"Yeah," Eva said, the strong scent of patchouli curling around her. After they moved past, she glanced up at Luke, curiosity getting the better of her. "Do you believe in psychics?"

"No. Do you?"

She shook her head.

"Why do you ask?"

"No reason."

The fact that Luke didn't believe in the supernatural renewed her belief that she *would* indeed have sex during Spring Break.

He cocked his head like he was about to probe, but when they reached the café and delicious smells of freshly baked bread filled the street, Luke let the subject drop and pulled opened the glass door. He touched the small of her back intimately, warming her blood as he led her inside the quaint air-conditioned café, guided her to a small corner table, then sat across from her.

As they made themselves comfortable, a few more people trickled in. A nervous feeling grew inside her when Luke leaned back in his chair, his gaze settling on hers.

"What?" she asked, wondering if she had toothpaste on her face or had left something unzipped.

He opened his mouth like he wanted to speak, then shut it again. She was about to ask if he was having second thoughts about tutoring her to be sexy when the waitress came by.

He leaned toward her then and winked. "Lesson number one. Pay close attention." Pushing back in his seat, he turned his focus on the pretty brunette, glancing at her name tag before saying, "Hey Janette."

Notepad in hand, Janette tossed Luke a flirty smile that made Eva feel ridiculously jealous, partly because she could never pull off such a sexy, come-hither look, and partly because Janette was aiming it Luke's way.

"What can I get for you?" she said as she blinked thick dark lashes over even darker eyes.

"I'm not sure. Do you have any suggestions for me? Something that you think I might like?" Luke asked.

She giggled and twirled her hair around her index finger. "I have all kinds of suggestions for you," she answered, then drew her bottom lip between her teeth.

"I'm listening."

Grinning like they'd just shared some secret code, the waitress began rambling off the breakfast specials. Luke turned his coffee cup upright, his eyes never leaving Janette's. He sat there hanging on her every word, like the breakfast specials were the most exciting thing he'd ever heard.

When the waitress finished, he shot Eva a quick glance. "Combo three?"

She nodded, and Janette leaned forward, toying with

the neckline on her low cut uniform as she filled Luke's cup with coffee, barely sparing Eva a glance when she poured hers.

Once she was gone, Luke gave Eva a lopsided grin, leaned back in his seat and looked at her like he was waiting for something. But what, she had no idea.

"Well?" he asked.

"Well, what?"

"Didn't you just see what went on here?"

"We ordered breakfast?"

He laughed and said, "That was Flirting 101."

"You're going to have to be more specific."

"The eye contact, the touching of the body, the leaning toward one another. The little innuendos. Those are all signals to let the other person know you're interested."

She took a sip of her coffee, thought things through for a moment, then asked, "So she flirted with you, even though you were sitting here with me." She waved her hand back and forth between them. "How did she know we weren't a couple?" As soon as the words left her mouth she already knew the answer. A guy like Luke would never really *be* with a girl like her. She shook her head. "No wait, I get it. I was never a part of the equation."

"No, you don't get it. It has everything to do with you. You were definitely part of the equation because girls want what other girls have."

"So it didn't matter to her that you might be taken?"

"Oh, it mattered all right. It's the allure of the forbidden fruit. It makes you want it all that much more."

She shook her head. "Don't people have any morals?"

He arched a brow. "This coming from the girl who wants me to turn her into a sex kitten so she can get laid."

"Yeah, but I don't want to have sex with another girl's guy."

He gave a slow nod of his head. "You're not like other girls."

She nodded and threw her hands up in the air. "I know, which is why I need your help."

Luke's brow furrowed and he went quiet for a moment, reflective, and she wondered what he was thinking. He shook his head like he was trying to clear it, and with his easy demeanor back in place, looked around the café as she followed his glance. Then he leaned toward her and pitched his voice low. "See that girl over there, the one in the white skirt and low cut tank."

"Yeah," she said, lowering her voice to match his.

"Watch her for a bit."

Eva leaned back in her chair and sipped coffee as she studied the girl, watching the way she flipped through the pages of her magazine, sipped her smoothie, and toyed with her straw, paying little or no attention to anyone around her.

After a long while Eva turned back to Luke and frowned. "I don't get it. What am I supposed to be looking at?"

Before Luke could answer, Janette returned with their food.

The waitress gave Luke a brilliant smile then walked away with a little too much sway in her hips, as far as Eva was concerned. Still, she watched the way Janette moved, hoping to learn from it, before turning her attention back to Luke.

"Look again," he said, "and watch the way she's toying with her straw, running her hands up and down it, and letting it linger in her mouth."

She turned to study the girl again, paying closer attention to the straw this time.

Luke arched a brow. "You know what she's doing, right?"

"Drinking her smoothie and reading her magazine."

He smiled. "Look two tables to her left."

She took in the group of guys watching the girl, their tongues practically hanging from their mouths.

"Oh," Eva said. "Oh," she said again, her eyes going wide.

"She's playing with them. Believe me, she's not just drinking a smoothie; she's mimicking a blowjob and driving those guys nuts."

Eva felt heat move through her body as she visualized herself on her knees, running her tongue along a guy's cock in much the same manner, except it wasn't just some random guy she was imagining herself with. It was Luke. A strange sound crawled out of her throat as she reached for her coffee.

"I'll be right back," Luke said, and as she watched him go, her eyes latched on his tight ass and she enjoyed the view until he rounded the corner. God, he had such a perfect body. It was no wonder he had a harem of women to pick from. Once he disappeared, she tossed a piece of bacon into her mouth and reached into her purse, searching for a distraction. Needing something she was familiar with, something to help tamp down the heat rising in her, she pulled out her iPhone and clicked on the lecture notes she'd downloaded last week.

She was so lost in her notes, she didn't even hear Luke's approach. "What are you doing?"

She jumped. "Reading."

"About what?"

"Nuclear fusion."

"Fusion?" he asked as he placed a strawberry smoothie in front of her. He reclaimed his chair and leaned back, arms folded and gaze fixed. "Care to explain?"

Unable to help herself, she rushed out, "Well, fusion is when particles come together and give off energy in the form of heat. It's fascinating stuff."

His brow furrowed. "So fusion is when two things that are meant to be together bond?" He grabbed the salt shaker and put it in the middle of the table. "Like sodium and chloride. Separate, chloride is dangerous, but when combined with something it's meant to bond with, like sodium, it forms NACL." He grinned and shook the shaker. "Or rather, salt."

She stared at him, eyes wide. "How do you know that?"

He laughed out loud and said, "Because, Eva, I've been listening to you talk about science for years now."

It was true, he had, and right now he wasn't supposed to be listening to her, she was supposed to be learning from him.

Eva sagged in her seat, planted her elbows on the table, and dropped her face into her palms. "Shit," she mumbled. "I just went into serious nerd mode, didn't I?"

She shook her head and peeked at Luke, expecting to see his eyes glazed over, but when she saw real interest on his face, it reminded her of all the times he'd been there for her, all the times he'd stayed up late and quizzed her when she was preparing for a big test. But now was not the time to be thinking about that, or how much she really liked him. "Am I a lost cause?"

"Not a lost cause at all." He pulled her hands from her face, and for a moment she thought she spotted heat in his eyes. But she had to be mistaken. Guys like Luke didn't lust after girls like her. At least not yet. He angled his head. "I'm sure there are plenty of guys out there who like it when you talk nerdy."

"You mean dirty."

"No, I mean nerdy." He pushed her smoothie toward her. "Now why don't you try that straw trick for me?"

JESUS CHRIST, DID she have to be such a quick learner?

Luke nearly swallowed his tongue as he watched her work her lips over the straw. Perched on the edge of her seat, with her hair in a frizzy mess and her face makeup-free, Eva exuded naiveté and sweetness, and while he loved that about her, he couldn't deny that he wasn't immune to the sex kitten act. His cock ached, and he shifted to alleviate the pain. That's when he noticed every guy in the place watching Eva.

"Eva," he croaked out. "We need to go."

"Why?" She blinked up at him, and when she swiped her tongue over her strawberry drenched lips, he damn near climbed over the table to help himself to a taste. "What's wrong?"

"You're drawing attention."

"Really?" She shot a glance around the café and her eyes lit. "So it's working."

Luke shifted his chair, trying his damnedest to block her from all the staring assholes. "Oh, it's working all right, which is why we need to get out of here."

"I don't understand. Wasn't that the point of the drink? To get guys to notice me?"

Shit, she had him on that one. He fisted his hands and clenched his jaw hard enough to grind bone, trying not to come off like a jealous lover. But fuck, he hated the way those guys were looking at her, and if he didn't get out of there now, he was pretty sure he was going to punch someone in the face. "Yeah, but you're not ready yet."

She glanced at her clothes. "Oh, right. You mean because of what I'm wearing."

"Yeah," he said, for lack of anything else.

"And because we haven't worked on how to talk sexy yet."

"Yeah, that too."

She nodded, and said, "Maybe we should go shopping first and work on the sexy talk once I get the outfit nailed."

Nailed?

Jesus, why did she have to say that? Now all he could think about was him nailing her, right here, up against the wall in the café, oblivious to everyone but the girl who was pushing his buttons and making him forget why getting involved with her was a bad idea.

Working to scrub that hot image from his brain, he said, "Sounds like a plan."

"Okay." She pushed her food and drink aside and climbed to her feet.

He sat there looking at her, taking in her long lithe body, the subtle curves beneath her blouse and shorts, and the way her uncombed hair hung around her shoulders, making her appear warm and sexy, like she'd just climbed out of bed. The pink flush on her cheeks added to her softness, giving such warmth to her sensuous girl-next-door look that it had his heart tightening and his body craving her all that much more.

Ah Jesus . . .

And just as want began to override common sense, urging him to take her to his bed, give her what she really wanted, he glanced at the door, ready to bail, to call an end to these lessons before he did something he would only regret later. But when she smiled at him and said, "I really appreciate you helping me, Luke. You're a good guy," he knew he was done for. So totally fucking done for.

"Come on," he said, pushing out of his chair. "Let's go find something appropriate for clubbing tonight."

"You mean inappropriate, don't you," she said, grinning. "Something that drives guys like you crazy."

Yeah, because you're not driving me crazy enough as it is.

TWENTY MINUTES LATER they entered a store a few miles from the Quarter. Eva thumbed through a rack of dresses as he followed behind. "What do you think of this one?" she asked, holding it against her.

He took in the knee-length dress and said, "It's perfect for you, but not for who you want to be."

She frowned and put it back on the rack. "You're right. Maybe you should pick something out for me, then."

As much as he hated the idea of her in something sexy, parading her body around the clubs for all to see, he grabbed a pair of frayed shorts and a top that exposed her midriff. "Try these."

She paused for a moment. "These short—"

"Trust me, Eva. Just try them on."

When she turned toward the change room, he followed, but there wasn't a damn thing he could do to stop his gaze from dropping to her ass, and the sexy way her lush cheeks toyed with his aching dick as she walked. She stepped into the change room and turned back to him, her finger toying with the top button on her blouse as she said, "Don't go anywhere."

"I'm not going anywhere, Eva," he mumbled

"I'll need you to look me over." She crinkled her nose. "You know, to see if these clothes make me look sexy."

"Yeah," he managed to get out, biting the inside of his mouth before he told her she already was sexy, as he gripped the curtain to close it.

He listened to the rustling sounds of her undressing and dressing and fought down his rising lust. But his efforts proved futile. His cock thickened with need as he envisioned himself in there with her, running his hands and tongue over her body until she cried out his name.

His name! Not the name of some random guy who cared nothing about her.

Fuck!

"These shorts are kind of cute," she said.

Okay, there was something very sexy, and oddly intimate, about her talking to him from behind a curtain while she was changing. He listened to the hiss of the zipper, then she went quiet.

"What's wrong?" he asked, bracing one hand on the wall beside the closed curtain.

"I don't know, Luke . . ."

The uncertainty he heard in her voice had him saying, "Let me see."

A moment passed, then when the curtain finally opened and he found the long-legged beauty standing there, his heart missed a beat. A fever broke out on his skin and he inched closer, lust rushing through him.

"Jesus," was all he managed to say as his body urged him to crush up against her, to kiss her hard and deep as he ripped those clothes from her so he could get her naked and give her everything she'd ever wanted. He took a heavy breath, briefly pinched his eyes shut and dragged his hands through his hair.

Clearly mistaking his reactions, she jerked back. "I know. They make my legs look freakishly long, don't they?" She made a move to turn around. "I'll get changed."

An unexpected rush of emotions rolled through him when he caught the stricken look on her face. . "Eva, wait." He cupped her elbow and pulled her close, hating that she was so unsure of herself. When her body collided with his, he trembled. Christ, he wanted her so badly, on so many levels, it was all he could do not to plant his mouth on hers and show her what he really thought of her. As his blood flowed hot and heavy, he called on every ounce of strength he possessed and held her against him, positioning her in front of the mirror. "Look at yourself."

She fidgeted in front of the mirror and his dick responded. "I'm looking."

He bit down a growl as hunger clawed at him. Jesus, she was so fucking hot, and yet she had no idea.

"Your legs aren't freakishly long, they're gorgeous," he said, fighting the urge to tell her how much he would love to climb in between them and feel them wrapped around his back. He cleared his throat. "And since I happen to be a leg guy, I know what I'm talking about."

Just then a middle-age sales lady came by. "Those shorts look great on you," she said, her bangles jangling as she pressed her hands together. "But wait. You need shoes. What size do you wear?"

"Ten," Eva said, looking a bit embarrassed. "Freakishly big feet to go with my freakishly long legs."

The sales clerk disappeared for a second and came back with a smoking hot pair of shoes, along with a short jean skirt and another midriff top. "I thought these would look good on you too." She handed the pile to Eva, who looked a little skeptical as she dangled the shoes from her fingers.

"We just got those shoes in," the sales lady said. "And I know they're going to fly off the shelves. By tonight every girl in town will be in a pair of them."

Heat ripped through Luke, hunger rising sure and swift, because the thought of her in those strappy red shoes, the too-high heels emphasizing her long, sexy legs, was more than he could take. No way, no how, would he be able to keep his hands to himself if she went clubbing in shoes that screamed *Fuck me!* He took a moment to imagine her in them—and nothing else. As he indulged his wayward thoughts, moisture broke out on his flesh and his traitorous cock grew another inch.

"What do you think, Luke?"

As reality came rushing back in a whoosh, lifting the mist from his lust fogged brain, he knew he had to put a stop to this. She hadn't even put the shoes on yet, and his cock was already throbbing like mad. Jesus, if she could do that to him, he could only imaging how other guys would react when they saw her in them.

Hoping to dissuade her, he leaned toward her and whispered, "You don't want to be like every other girl."

"Yes I do," she said, and slipped into the shoes, which brought her to his six-foot height. "That's the whole point of this." Eva turned sideways in the mirror to examine herself, and as her warm scent drifted past his nostrils, his mouth watered. "If my legs didn't look long before, they sure do now." She nibbled her lip. "Maybe you're right, Luke. Maybe they're not so freakish and I should emphasize them."

"The shorts are enough," he croaked out as he worked to keep his shit together. "You don't need the shoes too."

"Really, you don't think they look good?" She paraded

back and forth in front of the mirror, mimicking the way the waitress had walked earlier.

"I never said that," he murmured, his body growing tight with need.

When the sales lady disappeared to help another customer, Eva took the shoes off. "Maybe you're right." She gave herself a once-over in the mirror, the sexy shoes dangling from her fingers. "So what do you think?" She crinkled her nose and smoothed her hand over the top, which exposed the silky smooth skin of her midriff and short shorts that barely covered the soft swell of her ass. "Does this outfit say sex?"

"It doesn't say it, Eva. It screams it."

And speaking of screaming, if she dared to put those damn shoes on again, he'd have no choice but to back her up into that changing room, strip her naked, and fuck her until she screamed—his name—over and over again.

"You mean to tell me Luke picked these out for you," Allison said, waving a finger up and down Eva's body as she pointed to the short shorts and midriff top she was wearing.

"Yeah. Do you like it?"

"Like it? I love it." Allison smacked her lips and added, "You're going to knock them dead, girl."

Eva grinned, thinking about how sexy and desirable Luke had made her feel today at the shop, insisting her legs were sexy, not freakishly long. A smile touched her mouth, but she quickly tamped down the things he made her feel, not wanting her emotions to get the best of her. Even though he'd been kind and complimentary, he was training her for another guy, and she'd be wise to remember that. Still, as she ran her hands over her shorts, she couldn't help but imagine that she was getting ready to meet him, to spend a few hours dancing and laughing at the club before they made their way back to his place for a night of hot sex. She swallowed and brushed hair off her face as she tried to quiet her racing heart.

When she noticed Allison eyeing her, Eva slipped into her flat shoes and gave herself a once-over in the bathroom mirror.

Allison finished applying her lipstick, and looked at Eva's choice in footwear. When she frowned, Eva stiffened. "What?"

"Maybe you'd like to borrow a pair of my shoes?"

Eva turned sideways in the mirror. "You don't think the flats work?"

"No. Try these." Allison grabbed a pair of hot pink shoes from the entranceway, even though they both knew they'd never fit.

"If I squeeze my feet into those, I won't be able to walk tomorrow," Eva said, her mind drifting back to the strappy heels she'd tried on at the store and the way they made her feel so wickedly sexy. She took an extra moment imagining herself parading around in them, accentuating her long legs—for Luke.

"What?" Allison asked when Eva went quiet.

"Well," she began, "I did try a really nice pair on today. At first I thought they made my legs look too long, but I actually think Luke liked them."

Allison grinned and cocked her head. "Did he, now?"

"Yeah. He said he was a leg man and knew what he was talking about."

"Come on," Allison said, grabbing her purse off the bathroom counter.

"Where are we going?"

Her best friend's grin turned wicked. "To get you those shoes."

Three

WHAT THE FUCK have I done?

One look at Eva and Luke knew he was a dead man. So fucking dead that once her brother found out what he was doing, he'd have to pull him from his grave just to kill him all over again.

Along with every other guy in the club, Luke gawked at the tall, gorgeous brunette in the frayed shorts and fuck-me shoes as she walked through the front door with her girlfriend. A head taller than everyone else, she stood out in the crowd, prancing through the horde like a newborn deer finding its legs. And holy hell, did she ever find her legs.

Luke tucked his phone back into his front pocket, deciding to check his messages from Brad later as he swallowed the saliva pooling on his tongue. His body stiffened, one part in particular, when Eva said something to Allison before coming his way.

Caught off guard by the brilliant smile she aimed at him, not to mention the sexy sway to her slim hips, he shifted on his seat as she slipped in beside him to rest one of her elbows on the oak bar top.

"Sorry I'm late. I decided to go back and get the shoes."

"Yeah, I noticed," he said, pushing his words past a tongue gone thick.

She stretched one leg out, but there was a hint of uncertainty in her voice when she asked, "Do you think they're all right? I know you said the shorts were enough. I worry the look—"

Before he could reassure her and tell her that her look was all kinds of right, some tree-climbing ape sidled up next to Eva. He leaned in close, and Luke fisted his hands, fighting the urge to punch the guy in the throat.

"What are you drinking tonight?" the primate asked, his knuckles practically dragging on the ground.

"Oh," Eva said, turning in the guy's direction. "I . . . uh . . . I'm not sure yet."

The asshole's lecherous grin widened as Eva toyed with the frayed hem on her shorts, following Luke's morning lesson on Flirting 101 to a T.

Well done, Luke. Well done.

"Why don't you let me help you decide, then?" He inched back to give Eva a once-over, and said, "You look like a lemon gin kind of girl."

What the . . . ? Okay, fuck this.

Luke climbed to his feet and grabbed Eva's hand. "Come on. Let's dance."

He dragged her away caveman-style, and when they

reached the dance floor, pulled her into his arms. As people danced around them, her body crushed against his, and his mind filled with lusty images. A groan crawled out of his throat, the loud music doing little to drown it out.

She swiped her tongue over her bottom lip and shot him a confused glance. "What was that all about?"

He tried not to look at her moist mouth, tried not to think about how all he had to do was dip his head if he wanted to steal a taste when he grunted out, "Lemon gin is panty remover, Eva."

"Oh," she said, and then her eyes lit with excitement. "Oh, that's good then, right?" She jerked her thumb behind her. "It means that guy—"

He put his mouth close to her ear so he didn't have to talk over the music. "No, it's not good." Her hips aligned with his, her pussy brushing his cock in mind-fucking ways. "Jesus, Eva. You have to be a little choosier about who you sleep with. That guy wasn't even the same species as us." He inched back to see her. "Christ, it's a wonder he could walk on two legs."

A strange look came over her face, then she began with, "Anthropology really isn't my field of study, but if you're talking about bridging the gap between humans and apes, then what I know about the missing link is that—"

"He wasn't good enough for you," Luke said, cutting off her dissertation on evolution. "Let's just leave it at that."

She shot a glance over her shoulder. "He didn't seem so bad."

"The condition was that I get to pick the guy, and

he wasn't the right one for you, okay?" She opened her mouth like she wanted to protest, but he shook his head and said, "You put yourself in my hands, so you have to trust me on this."

Eva sucked in a tight breath, and something came over her face, something that looked like desire as he gripped her tighter, holding her to him. Jesus Christ, he hoped he was reading her wrong, because if she wanted him as much as he wanted her, it would surely be the death of him.

"Okay, fine," she said. "I guess it's still too early for me to hook up, and you've yet to give me a lesson on talking sexy, anyway." She gave an eye roll. "I probably would have screwed things up the second I opened my mouth." As though moving of their own accord, Luke's hands slid lower down her back and she relaxed into him. "Perhaps now is a good time for you to teach me how to talk to a guy?"

Hyperaware of the way her hot body was pressing against his, he shifted slightly to hide the bulge in his pants. When a bevy of hot bodies brushed up against them and the music became slower, she put her arms around his neck. As they stood eye-to-eye, he tried not to think about how sexy she was in those shoes, or how he was dying to see if she tasted as sweet as she smelled.

He swallowed. "Eva."

She arched a brow. "Yeah?"

"I like the shoes. You look gorgeous. I should have told you that already."

She smiled, and her eyes were so warm and honest his heart pinched. "Thanks."

Knowing how much she wanted to feel desirable . . . *normal* . . . he continued, "I can tell you right now, every guy in this place thinks you're hot."

Her glance moved over the guys dancing nearby. "You think so?"

"I know so." Heat broke out over his skin as he pulled her impossibly close, wanting her attention on him, even though he knew it wasn't in his best interest. "You know what they're thinking, *chére*?"

She grinned at him. "No, why don't you tell me."

"They're thinking how much they want to take you home, peel these sexy clothes off your hot body, and touch you all over."

Her breathing changed, became a little more erratic. "They are?"

"Uh-huh." When a couple brushed up against them, he and Eva both turned in time to see the two grind against one another on the dance floor. The guy cupped the girl's ass, lifted her against his hips and dry humped her right beside them, mimicking the kind of hot sex he'd like to be having with Eva.

Eyes alive with curiosity, he could feel Eva's heart pounding against his chest as she watched them. Even though he knew he should put a measure of distance between himself and the girl who was making him bat-shit crazy before she felt the thickening of his cock, his hand dipped lower, resting on the sexy swell of her ass. He pitched his voice low and purposely put his mouth near her ear.

"Tell me something," he whispered, and when his

breath washed over her neck, he felt her shiver, a clear indication that she wasn't immune to their closeness either.

Fuck.

"What do you want to know?" she murmured, her voice a slow, soft seduction that tortured his cock and practically rendered him senseless.

Walk away, Luke. Just shut your mouth and walk away.

"What do you want, Eva?"

"I want to lose my virginity," she admitted honestly. "I thought you understood that."

He inched back, his eyes moving over her flushed cheeks. "But you must want more than that. Haven't you thought about what you want, how you'd like to be touched?"

What the fuck am I doing?

She nodded, a sheepish look on her face. "I guess."

"Tell me. Tell me how you want to be touched." Tension rose in him as he dragged his thumb over her pouty bottom lip. "How you want to be kissed." His hand slid down her neck and brushed the outer edge of her pert breast. "*Where* you want to be kissed."

"Luke . . ."

While his one working brain cell urged him to cool it, his body, savage with the need to feel her wrapped around him, had other ideas. Making no attempt at discretion, he pushed against her, the heat arcing between them enough to set the room ablaze. "Tell me, Eva," he urged.

A small gasp caught in her throat, as a flurry of emotions moved across her eyes. His heart thundered as something potent passed between them, something he feared could very well be the end of his restraint. Christ, if he knew what was good for him, he'd shut his fucking mouth and put an end to this. But then again, when was the last time he'd ever done anything that was good for him?

Her breasts pressed into his chest, and the way her hard nipples pushed against him made him delirious with want. "Eva," he said again, his voice sounding harsh even to himself.

She wet her lips. "I've never really been kissed," she admitted. "Not really."

He angled his head, his glance moving over her face. "You're fucking kidding me?" He ran his thumb over her lips.

She nodded, her eyes wide. "Not unless you count seventh grade during a game of spin the bottle."

Jesus Christ, he'd had no idea how innocent and inexperienced she really was, yet here he was training her for the big bad wolf, who would only eat her alive and take what he didn't deserve.

Get your shit together and end this now, dude.

"So where would you like to be kissed?"

"I . . . I just . . ."

The way she looked at him turned him into a hot fucking mess. Jesus, he wanted to sink his cock into her in the worst way.

"Here?" he asked, running his fingertips along her neck, because he just couldn't seem to stop himself. There was something about Eva, something that made him feel crazed and out of control. When she didn't answer, he continued. "And what about here?" He brushed his thumb over her nipple, and she briefly closed her eyes. "I'm sure you must want to know what it feels like to be kissed here."

She gave a telltale moan, and when she moved against him it was all the encouragement he needed. He pushed a knee between her legs and used his other hands to shape her curves, knowing there was nothing impersonal in the way he was touching her. Her heat seeped under his skin and he damn near exploded. "How about here, Eva? Have you thought about what it would be like to be kissed here?" Despite those around him, he moved his leg in a circular motion, rubbing her clit against the seam in her shorts, and when she opened her mouth, he knew he was well past the point of no return.

"Oh, God, Luke . . ."

He needed her and he needed her now. He dipped his head and wet his mouth, ready to take her.

"Luke?" she said, and as his name lingered on the tip of her tongue, his mouth closed over hers. Maybe, just maybe, if he had one tiny taste it would get her out of his system. With pressure building in his body, and knowing he was too far gone to pull back, he teased her lips open and adjusted his stance to better position himself. His body pulsed hot at that first sweet taste of her mouth, and as her warmth fired his blood from a simmer into an inferno, he knew: when it came to Eva, a simple kiss would never be enough for him.

Their tongues joined and tangled and he sucked her bottom lip as he fisted her curls, wanting to take her home so he could lick, touch, and kiss her in all the places she needed it. Pleasure raced through him as her palms moved over his body with aroused eagerness. Cock aching, and entirely lost in the moment, he deepened the kiss, unable to get enough of her.

Their moans mingled, and his body shook with the things he wanted to do to her . . . *for her.* He held her tighter, crushing her softness to his hardness as they both became lost in the sensations. After a good, thorough kiss, he abandoned her mouth and pressed his lips to her neck. She whimpered, and when she gyrated shamelessly against him, he knew he was going to take her. Right here. Right now. Hard and fast.

"How about sharing the love, pal?"

The sound of a guy's slurred voice in his ear had Luke breaking away. He stepped back and sucked in a sharp breath as reality inched its way back into his lust-ridden brain. Ignoring the drunk guy holding two beer mugs, Luke stood there staring at Eva for a long moment. Her cheeks were flushed as she nibbled her kiss-swollen lips.

"Eva . . ." He shook his head and raked his hand through his hair.

She shot him a confused glance. "What . . . why did you . . . ?"

As he worked to rein himself in, he struggled for words, to explain why he'd just ravished her on the dance floor when he was supposed to be training her for another, but before he could think of something plausible, something that didn't give away his feelings for her, she came to his rescue.

"Wait! I get it," she began, and Luke wanted to kick his own ass when he caught the glimmer of dejection in her eyes. Dammit, the last thing he wanted was to make her feel like she wasn't hot. "Guys want what other guys have." She waved her hand back and forth between them. "The allure of the forbidden fruit and all. By making guys think I'm with you, they'll want me even more." She grinned, and added, "And all those things you were saying, it was about teaching me how to talk sexy, right? How to engage a guy in conversation?"

"Yeah, right," he agreed, knowing better than to tell her the kiss had nothing do with the allure of the forbidden truth and everything to do with him wanting her. *Shit.*

"Wow, you really are good at this marketing stuff. I bet the advertising firms are lining up for you." Her eyes lit with respect, and his heart beat faster at her compliment. Even though the kiss had nothing to do with marketing herself, the truth was, he prided himself on being good at what he did. Too bad his father was a workaholic who believed in finance and numbers and frowned upon the creative side of business.

Luke's thoughts came crashing back to the present when Eva turned her attention to the big bad wolf staring at her like she was Little Red. Luke stepped between them, possession gripping him by the throat as he put his mouth close to her ear. "He's not the guy for you."

"How do you know? You didn't even give him a chance."

"He's drunk."

She threw her hands up in the air. "It's Spring Break in New Orleans, Luke. Who isn't drunk?"

"I'm not," he said. He grabbed her hand. "Come on. Let's go sit at the bar. It will give us a good view of the room."

He ushered her to the bar, found them two stools, and asked the bartender for a beer, and a daiquiri for Eva, the same fruity drink he'd seen her with the day before.

She perched on the stool and pinched her lips in thought as she glanced around the club. "Okay, so if not him, then how about that guy over there?"

The bartender brought their drinks, and Eva nibbled on her straw as Luke followed her gaze to a douche bag wearing a Hawaiian T-shirt and surfer shorts.

"No."

"Okay, so what's wrong with him?" she asked.

"I know him. He's an asshole. Try again."

"Okay, then," she began, as she slipped the straw into her mouth and twirled it around her tongue.

Fuck.

"Ooh, how about that guy?" She took a long pull from her straw and said, "He looks like a local, and he's looking my way."

"Stay away from the locals."

"Hmmm, so no assholes and no locals."

She twirled the straw around her tongue again, and his blood ran thick. If she kept that up he was never going to be able to walk out of this place without her noticing his erection. He took the straw from the drink and set it on the bar top next to his untouched beer. "Stop doing that."

"But I thought—"

He bit back a tortured moan and said, "Just stop, okay?"

He spotted her friend Allison watching, a curious look on her face as her glance bounced back and forth between them.

Eva drank the rest of her daiquiri and ordered another as she continued to pick out possible candidates. But for every guy she picked out, Luke had a reason to reject him. Three daiquiris later she threw her hands up in the air.

"Okay, Luke, so why don't *you* tell me which guy you think I should go home with."

He slammed his mouth shut before he could tell her *him*, and when her cell phone chirped he was thankful for the distraction, needing a moment of reprieve to get his shit together.

She pulled it from her back pocket and checked the display. Luke sat quietly, listening to her side of the conversation, and when she frowned, he said, "What?"

"It's Andie. She's in the bathroom at a place called Howl at the Moon and she's sick." Eva scanned the room, and when she caught Allison, gestured her over.

Allison stumbled toward them, clearly having had one too many drinks, and giggled, pointing an accusing finger at Luke. "You're into her," she mumbled.

"Allison," Eva said, clearly missing the comment. "Samantha called. She said Andie is sick and she needs our help to get her back to the room." She grabbed her friend's hand and wobbled in her too high heels when she slipped off the stool.

"Whoa," Luke said, capturing both of them.

Eva tossed him an apologetic look. "I'm kind of a lightweight when it comes to alcohol."

"That's okay, I'm coming with you."

"You don't have to—"

Cutting off her protest, he wrapped his arms around the two girls and said, "Right now I'm guessing Andie's howling at the toilet, not the moon, and with the amount of drinks you both had, I think you're going to need my help."

Eva paused and looked at him. Her deep, expressive eyes moved over his face in a way that roused the hunger in him again. "Luke," she murmured. "You really are a good guy."

"No I'm not."

"Yeah you are. Maybe tomorrow night, when we go clubbing again, you can help me find someone like you."

"Fuck," he murmured under his breath.

Four

EVA SAT ON the floor outside the bathroom door, Luke beside her, staring at the ceiling as he rested his head against the wall.

"Do you think she's asleep?" Eva asked quietly. Andie had insisted they leave her in the bathroom for the night because she was too sick to go to her bed.

Luke angled his head her way. "Let's give it a little longer and then I'll move her."

Eva shifted on the floor, listening to Allison snore on the bed a few feet away while Samantha slept in the adjoining room, as Luke's thigh brushed up against her. She yawned, the drinks having made her tired, but she didn't want to go to bed just yet. She kind of liked sitting here with Luke, liked this quiet, reflective side that he rarely showed the world.

Exhaling a slow breath, she plucked at a piece of lint

on her short shorts, anxious to get into her comfy yoga pants.

Luke gestured toward the bed. "Why don't you get some sleep?"

"I'm okay. Besides, I'm not going to make you take care of Andie. She's my responsibility."

His smile was slow and warm, like he was remembering something from his past. "You girls all really look out for each other, don't you?"

"Yeah, I'd do anything for them. Just like you and Brad would do anything for each other."

The smile fell from his face, and when he looked back at the ceiling, she took a moment to think more about Luke, the sweet boy who'd always been there for her. But he wasn't just good to her, he was good to her brother too. He'd helped Brad get back on his feet after a rough first year of college. If not for Luke, Brad never would have made it four years and currently be in New York, which made her wonder . . .

"Luke?" she asked. "Why are you here?"

He gave her a strange look. "To help you take care of Andie."

"No, I mean why are you here in New Orleans and not in New York interviewing?"

"Ah," he said. "Because I already have a job lined up."

"You do? Where?"

He frowned. "Corner office. Dad's investment firm."

Okay, that took her by surprise. Luke was creative and outgoing, and she couldn't imagine him locked in some corner office crunching numbers. She made a face and said, "Sorry, but that doesn't sound like you at all."

"Yeah, I know."

When she stifled a yawn, he put his arm around her neck and drew her head to his shoulder. She breathed in his scent and tried not to feel so overwhelmed by his closeness. "Do you have to take it?"

"It's expected."

She thought about that and after a long moment said, "You can't be something you're not, Luke."

He touched her chin, lifting her head until they were eye-to-eye, and when he said, "You're absolutely right," she knew they were no longer talking about him. He brushed a lock of hair from her face, and she suddenly became very aware of him next to her, his body pressing against hers, his heat curling around her and arousing all her senses. "Let me ask you something?"

"What?" she whispered, her breath growing a bit labored.

"Wouldn't you rather be with a guy who likes you for who you are, instead of changing yourself to become someone he wants?"

She shrugged as warmth and desire enveloped her. "What you're missing, Luke, is that guys don't like me for who I am."

"Then maybe you're going after the wrong guys."

"Luke—"

"All I'm saying is that instead of thinking about what a guy wants, you should be thinking about what *you* want. If you're going to give your virginity to someone, it should be because it's someone you like, not because it's someone who likes you. Know what I mean?"

When she looked at him, something passed through his eyes, something that had her lips parting, eager for him to kiss her again. God, maybe she never should have asked him to help her, because the more time she spent with him, the more she wanted him. As his body shifted against hers, she wondered how she could she ever sleep with some random guy without imagining he was Luke.

"What do you want, Eva?" he asked quietly, as she breathed in his warm familiar scent. "What do you want in a guy?"

She went quiet for a long moment, then said, "Truthfully, Luke, I want a guy who is sweet and sensitive and cares about me for who I am. Someone who is interested in hearing what I have to say, even when I slip into nerd mode. A guy who would drop everything to help out a friend." She swallowed, and wondered if he knew she was describing him.

"It sounds like you've given this a lot of thought."

"Maybe, but none of that matters because I'm not here looking for a relationship."

He slid his fingers through her hair, and she was almost certain she heard desire in his tone when he whispered, "It should matter."

"Luke—" was all she could get out as her heart thumped wildly.

"You should have what you want, Eva," he whispered, his voice deeply intimate, highly suggestive.

What I want is for you to kiss me . . .

Perhaps it was the three daiquiris giving her false courage, or perhaps it was the way he was looking at her that had her acting out of character, but either way, she lifted her mouth, her lips parting even more, and before she even knew what was happening, Luke's mouth closed over hers.

The air around them was charged with sexual energy as he drew her closer, taking full possession of her mouth. His tongue slipped inside and she drew it in deeper as she lost herself in the taste of him. Heat bombarded her and her brain shut down, not wanting to think about what was happening, instead wanting only to concentrate on the sweet sensations rushing through her body.

She moaned, and put her hand on his chest, loving the feel of the hard body beneath his shirt. His hand left her hair and slid down her neck as he deepened the kiss. A moment later Luke was on his feet, pulling her up with him.

He pressed her to the wall and grabbed both her hands, pinning them over her head in one of his big palms. Her entire body shook, and if she'd had a free hand, she would have pinched herself, because she was pretty damn sure she'd fallen asleep on the floor next to him and was dreaming—because everything about this situation was straight out of her fantasies.

He caged her body with his, one knee parting her legs as his mouth found hers again. He kissed her hard, like a guy hell-bent on taking what he wanted, and that's when it occurred to her that his breath tasted like mint, not beer, as she'd expected.

His hand slid down her sides, and her thoughts scattered when he brushed the outer edge of her breasts through her shirt. Her nipples hardened and poked against the lace of her bra. Luke growled and dipped his head, licking her through the thin material, and she let loose a ragged moan, her body coming alive beneath his touch. The heat of his mouth felt like fire on her skin, fueling the hunger inside her. She writhed against the wall, pushing her pelvis forward in a not so subtle invitation.

"You are so fucking sexy," he murmured, releasing her hands as he dropped to his knees.

She wrapped her fingers in his hair and just stood there on shaky legs as he gripped her shirt to lift it, exposing her bra. Everything in the way he looked at her body—his eyes so dark and full of lust—made her forget her breasts were too small, her body too tall. In fact, he made her feel like the most wanted, most desirable girl in the world.

He lightly brushed the rough pad of his thumb over one breast, then the other. "Perfect," he murmured, exhaling a shaky breath. "So goddamn perfect," he said, before he pulled the cup down to close his mouth over one nipple.

Eva arched her back, never having felt anything so sweet. He swiped his hot wet tongue over her sensitive flesh, then drew her nipple in for a hard suck.

"Oh, God," she cried out, melting against him. "So good . . ."

Heat moved through her body, pressure building deep inside her as she hungered for so much more. He left her breasts and dipped lower. He drew a deep breath, his nose pressed against her stomach.

"You smell so good." His hands toyed with the button on her shorts as he pressed kisses to her flesh. A whimper escaped her lips when his mouth began a downward path. He pushed her thighs apart, and her heart hammered when he kissed her sex through her shorts.

She shivered, her body spasming, begging him to end the sweet torment and take her where she needed to go.

"Eva . . ." he murmured. "Oh, Jesus, Eva."

She held his mouth to her pussy, and the heat of his breath drove her wild. Her clit swelled and she rolled her hips, wanting to remove the material separating her body from his tongue. She began moving, pressing against him. Her head spun, and even though she was too far gone to think rationally, some small part of her brain registered the sound of footsteps. She angled her head and spotted Allison stumbling toward them. Eva made a small, tortured sound and Luke stiffened.

"Oh," Allison said. "I was just going to the bathroom . . . I didn't mean . . . oh shit, sorry."

Luke sprang to his feet and stepped back, the intimacy between them severed as Allison stood there staring at the two, like she didn't know what to do next. Cold moved through Eva when he ran his hands through his mussed hair and shot a glance around the room, looking everywhere and anywhere except at her.

"I . . . uh . . . I should go."

Eva opened her mouth and closed it again, not sure

what to say because she still wasn't quite sure what had just happened.

Luke briefly met her glance, and her heart missed a beat when she saw him frowning. "Do you need help with Andie first?"

Just then Andie stumbled from the bathroom, moaning something incomprehensible under her breath.

"I got her," Allison said, leading her to her bed.

"I'll catch up with you later, then," was all Luke said before he disappeared out the door, leaving Eva standing there confused, disheveled . . . *aroused*.

"Eva, I'm so sorry," Allison said as she came back down the hall. "I didn't mean to interrupt." She smiled. "But man, he's got it bad for you."

She tried to keep her voice from wavering, her body from trembling when she asked, "What are you talking about?"

"What do you mean what am I talking about? He's into you. Damn near fucked you right here in the hall with me in the other room."

Eva blinked, wondering if it could be true. Even if it was, it had to be because he'd made her into the kind of girl he liked, right?

Allison planted her hands on her hips and arched a challenging brow. "You know, this is your chance to sleep with the guy you've always liked, so if I were you, I'd do something about it."

"Like what?" she asked.

Allison shook her head. "Hasn't he been giving you private lessons?"

"Yeah so?"

"And you'd like for him to be your first, right?"

"Uh-huh," she admitted.

Allison grinned, and before she shut the bathroom door said, "Then maybe it's time to use a few of his lessons against him."

Eva's heart raced as she made her way to her bed and thought more about what her friend was suggesting. Then she thought about some of the things Luke had said to her.

You should have what you want, Eva. You should give your virginity to someone you like.

She stripped out of her clothes and climbed between the sheets, her body still hot and needy from that surprise kiss. If Luke really was into the new Eva, then maybe she really should do something about it, maybe it was time for her to take his advice and go for what she wanted.

She considered all the sexy things he'd taught her over the last couple of days, all the things she could do to seduce him.

But what if she used his tricks on him and he turned her down?

What if he didn't?

WHAT THE HELL did Eva think she was doing?

Stomach tightening, Luke set his beer down and glared at Eva as she gyrated against some asshole on the dance floor. When another guy sidled up to her, caging her half-dressed body between two dueling cocks, his temper flared and he tried to ignore the stab of possession ripping through his gut.

Clenching his jaw hard enough to grind bone, he fisted his hands and forced himself to look the other way. Last night, after he'd practically fucked her in the hallway, he'd made a vow to keep his distance and put an end to this . . . this thing . . . between them. Christ, there was an unwritten code between best friends: you take care of their kid sisters, you don't sleep with them, and you sure as hell don't take their virginity.

Working to keep his hands from trembling, Luke drummed his fingers on the bar top, but unable to help himself, he stole another glance. When he caught her watching him, and spotted the invitation in her baby blues, his thoughts went haywire. He groaned out loud, his cock swelling in his pants because he knew . . . sweet innocent Eva was damn well fucking with him.

He turned away from her again and downed the rest of his beer in one gulp. No way, no how, was he taking the bait, but when he heard her laugh, he couldn't help but swivel on his stool to see her. Dancing in her too-high heels, in her too-revealing clothes, as guys crowded her, she gyrated her body and curled her fingers in her hair in a flirtatious way that tightened his balls.

Fuck.

The music changed, and she fanned her face as she followed some guy to the bar. Luke raked shaky fingers through his hair and gestured for another much needed drink. Sitting only a few seats away, he listened as she ordered a daiquiri, and when the bartender came back with it—masochist that he was—he angled his head to watch her drink it. She briefly caught his glance and stroked her hand up and down the straw. His cock throbbed, aching for her to do that to him. He sucked in a sharp breath and gave his head a hard shake to clear it.

She said something to the asshole she was with, then wrapped her pretty mouth around the straw. As she took a long pull, the guy beside her looked like he was salivating.

Luke's anger spiked and he slammed his bottle on the table, harder than necessary. The sound garnered Eva's attention, and when she looked his way again with a wicked gleam in her eyes, his muscles bunched, everything inside him urging him to go over there and put an end this once and for all.

She swiveled on the stool and stretched one leg out. As she toyed with the strap on her shoe, giving him a good view of her long, sexy leg, one he wanted wrapped around him in the worst way, a storm raged inside him. A rumble crawled out of his throat, and when she slipped off her stool and made her way to the dance floor again, an extra sway to her hips this time, he knew he had to get out of there before he crossed a line and did something he would only regret.

He made a move to go, but then stopped when their eyes met across the room. The want in her gaze proved too powerful for him to deny, and before he realized what he was doing, he stalked across the dance floor. When he reached her, he cupped her elbow and pulled her to him.

"What do you think you're doing?" he asked between gritted teeth as their bodies collided.

"I'm selling myself," she answered. "Just like you taught me."

"Eva—" he began, then stopped himself. What the hell was he supposed to say? *I'm crazy about you, and want to be your first . . . and more importantly, your last.*

She blinked innocent eyes at him and gestured toward the two guys behind her. "So, which one of those guys meets your approval?"

Jesus Christ, how could he let her go home with one of those guys: dipshits who cared only about fucking her fast and hard and wouldn't bother to take the time to touch her, kiss her the way she wanted. No, she needed her first time to be with someone who was going to take it slow and make it good for her.

"Luke?" she asked again.

"Neither one of them," he growled, every muscle in his body tensing.

She looked at him, her eyes full of heat and want. "If not them, then who, Luke?"

The soft way she said his name unleashed something wild inside him. His nostrils flared, and while everything in his gut told him to walk—no, run—the other way, he knew he was fighting a losing battle. He grabbed her hand, tugged her close and purposely put his mouth to her ear.

"Me."

She gave a little gasp when he suddenly hauled her through the crowd, dragging her out to the sidewalk, where he put his arm around her waist and pulled her hard against him. Bodies bumped against theirs, the crowd alive and full of energy as they drank and partied in the streets. The mood intensified everything he was feeling, and had him breaking all the rules where his friend's kid sister was concerned. He cut down an alleyway, needing to get her alone so he could do things to her—things they clearly both wanted.

"Where are we going?" she asked, her voice unusually high, the pleasure lingering beneath the surface exciting him even more.

He stopped to look at her, and while his brain urged him to do the right thing, everything about her called out to him in ways he couldn't even understand.

"To my room."

"Tell me what's going on, Luke." She swiped her tongue over her bottom lip and regarded him with wide, questioning eyes. "Why are we going to your room?"

Hunger consumed him when his glance met hers, and it took effort to fill his lungs. His muscles bunched and his cock thickened, and he knew there was no way they'd make it back to his hotel room without him tasting her first.

"Because I'm going to fuck you, Eva," he said, even though he knew what he was about to do went way beyond sex, or helping her lose her virginity.

She let out a broken gasp, and when her eyes lit, his baser instincts took over.

"Isn't that what you want?" He crowded her with his body and heat arched between them—so volatile and unstable, he was sure they were going to set the alleyway on fire.

He backed her up, caging her against the wall and his chest. Feeling crazed, frantic, he dipped his head, drawing in the scent of her freshly showered skin as he pressed his mouth to hers. Her lips parted, and he moaned out loud, losing himself in the sweet taste of her.

"Tell me, Eva," he said. "Wasn't that why you were teasing me at the club, using everything I taught you against me? Because you want me to fuck you?"

"Yes!" she cried out. Her body moved restlessly against his, making no qualms about what she wanted.

He reached between her legs, his fingers climbing up her short skirt until he reached her damp panties. "But before I do," he said, "I'm going to kiss every inch of you. I'm going to start with these lips . . ." He brushed his thumb over her mouth. ". . . and I'm going to end with *these* lips." he said as he ran his other hand along the wet slit between her legs.

"Oh, God, Luke."

He inched back and met her glance. "You don't have a problem with that do you?"

She shook her head.

"I mean I'm not some random guy . . ."

"Luke, please . . ."

"What?"

She opened her mouth and closed it again, her eyes troubled, like she was afraid she'd say something nerdy, something to break the moment.

His heart pinched, and he softened his voice. "What?"

"I . . . you . . ."

"You know you can say whatever you want to me, right? It's not going to change things and I'm still going to give you what you want."

"What about what you want?" she asked quietly.

"Come on, I'll show you."

He captured her hand and less than five minutes later he opened his hotel room door and hauled her in with him. Her eyes lit, her body visually quaking when the bolt clicked into place, locking the world out and them in.

He took a step toward her, need pumping through his veins as they exchanged a long look. "I need you naked. Now," he said, their breaths mingling. He cupped her head, his body pressing against hers, his raging erection letting her know how hot he was for her. "There are so many things I need to do to you. Things I've been dying to do to you for so long."

Her chest heaved and her skin flushed hotly as she gripped the hem of her short top, ready to remove it. He grinned at her enthusiasm and shook his head to stop her.

She gave him a perplexed look, and he said, "I'll take over from here."

Her eyes came alive, and when her hands fell to her sides, he lowered his head and planted his mouth on hers. He ran his tongue over her lips and her neck, reveling in the softness of her skin as he reached under her top and unhooked her bra.

He touched her skin, trailing his fingers over her flesh as he moved his hands higher, dragging her top up with him. "Lift your arms." When she did, he tugged her shirt off, then slipped her bra off her shoulders.

Dressed in nothing but a short skirt, he stood back to admire her body and the way her pert breasts, so high and perfect, beckoned his mouth. He exhaled slowly. "I want you so much."

"I want you too," she whispered, reaching for him.

He took a step toward her and released the button on her jean skirt. His cock throbbed, urging him to hurry so he could bury himself inside her, but he knew this was her first time, and he really wanted to make it good for her.

She shimmied as he pulled her skirt and panties down, and when they reached her ankles she kicked them away. He stood back up and a slow burn worked its way through his body, forcing him to suck in a sharp breath, to get himself under control before he shot a load off at the mere sight of her.

"Jesus, Eva." He dropped to his knees and buried his face between her breasts, pulling her scent into his lungs. His body convulsed and he feared if he didn't get out of his jeans soon he'd do permanent damage to his rock hard cock.

She ran her hands through his hair, and his brain stalled when she guided his mouth to her nipple. "Luke," she began. "You asked me where I needed to be kissed. It's here," she said. "I need to be kissed here."

Holy Christ!

He closed his mouth over one pebbled nub and she

threw her head back, arching into him. Tension coiled through his body and his muscles bunched as he nibbled and nipped and sucked and licked.

She leaned forward, her hair sweeping over his shoulders as her nails dug into them. He gave another swipe to her nipple then looked up at her. "Where else, baby? Where else do you need to be kissed?"

She moaned and pushed on him, urging him downward. He ran his hand between her thighs, and her body quaked when he lightly brushed her clit. "Tell me, Eva."

"I need you to kiss my . . ."

"Kiss your what?"

A blush colored her cheeks, when she said, "My . . . pussy."

Luke climbed to his feet and confusion moved over her face, but it was quickly replaced with excitement when he picked her up and tossed her onto his bed.

"Open for me," he demanded in a soft tone. "Show me exactly where you need my mouth."

As she widened her legs, she fed the intensity of his arousal. Blinded by lust, he gripped his shirt and tore it off. Eva's eyes went wide when he made quick work of his pants and kicked them away to expose his fully erect cock. She gyrated on the bed and made a sexy bedroom noise as she reached out to him.

Wanting her so much, and having no idea how he was going to take it slow, he stood there, eating her up with his eyes, his cock so hard he was sure he was going to explode on impact. He took a step closer, his mouth watering for a taste, but when she reached out, closing her palm over his shaft, his body shuddered and he almost fucking came in her hand.

He inched back. "Baby, you can't do that. I'm too close."

Pleasure danced in her eyes and he couldn't help but grin.

"You like it don't you? You like doing this to me?"

"Yeah," she said, and when pre-come pearled on his crown and she licked her lips, he let loose a moan.

"Fuck, Eva."

"What?"

"Don't look at my cock and do that."

"I thought guys liked it—"

"Yes, we do, but if you touch me, I'm going to come, and I don't want to come yet."

"You don't? Why not?"

"Because I want to fuck you first."

"Oh." As her eyes lit, he climbed onto the mattress, frightened by how much he wanted her. He settled himself between her legs. Using a light touch, he stroked her skin and spread her legs until she was wide open for him. He groaned when he saw how wet she was.

Muscles trembling, he stroked her pussy. "You are so hot, baby." When she writhed, he leaned in for a taste, something he'd fantasized about doing for far too long now. With his heart pounding, he made a slow pass, and as her sweet flavor exploded on his tongue, her hips came off the bed.

"Oh. My. God," she cried out, fisting his hair. "Oh. My. God. Luke."

"You like that, baby?"

Heat flashed in her eyes, and seeing her this aroused, this hot for him nearly did him in. Even though he could barely think, he forced himself to slow down when all he wanted to do was rip his clothes off and drive into her.

He licked her harder and her skin tightened beneath his mouth. She pitched her hips forward as he continued to kiss her hungrily, moaning as her dampness wet his face.

"Luke . . ."

"Yeah, baby," he said from deep between her legs. "What is it?"

"I . . . I always wanted you to be my first."

He stilled, momentarily stunned to hear her say that, but then he gathered himself and said, "You should always have what you want, Eva."

He turned his attention back to her pussy and ran his tongue over her clit, not wanting to think about what might happen after tonight, where they would go from here, or how many broken bones he was going to have if Brad ever found out. As he teased her hard nub, he slowly dipped a finger inside her and she shivered. Her tight walls gripped him hard and he groaned, pleasure clutching his balls.

His whole body shook. "Jesus, you're so tight."

He pushed his finger in another inch, and she grew slicker. His cock pulsed, frantic with the need to be inside her. He forced himself to slow down but when desperation moved over her eyes, he gave her his entire finger. A wheezing sound escaped her mouth as he put pressure on her clit, teasing it between his thumb and finger. She threw her head back, her hair splaying over his pillow as he indulged in her body.

"That feels . . ." she began, her words falling off as she tossed her head from side to side, her hair a tangled mess around the pillowcase. Her hips began moving, pussy so wet and needy he slipped another finger inside, desperate to make her come.

Moving urgently against his mouth, her hands went to her breast, and when she squeezed her nipples, he damn near lost it.

"Ah, Jesus . . ."

"Luke, I feel . . . I just . . . I don't know . . . I just . . ." She began panting, and writhing, moving her hips up and down as he pumped his fingers in and out of her.

"Yeah, baby, that's it. Ride my fingers," he said, need swamping him as she turned herself loose, taking what she wanted.

She opened her mouth, but no words came when she wet her bottom lip and grabbed a fistful of his hair. A second later her body grew tighter, her muscles rippling, clenching so hard around his fingers he knew if he didn't soon get inside her he was going to go insane.

"Ohmigod!" she cried out, a violent quake moving through her as she creamed on his tongue. "So good, Luke. So good."

Loving her little moans of pleasure, he buried his face between her legs to hydrate himself with her juices, except he somehow knew when it came to Eva, he'd never be able to quench his thirst.

BARELY ABLE TO think let alone breathe after that incredible orgasm, Eva lifted herself up on shaky elbows and looked at the guy with his face buried between her legs. As he lapped at her, she could feel the need in him, the hunger brewing just below the surface. Knowing he liked going down on her aroused her all over again.

"Luke," she said, pulling him toward her. "I want you to fuck me."

"I know. I know," he said, the urgency in his voice curling her toes and turning her on even more.

He grabbed a condom from his pants, then climbed up her body until she was pinned beneath his weight. When dark eyes full of passion and promise met hers, a thin sheen of moisture broke out on her flesh and her stomach tightened. He pushed her hair from her face and stroked her cheeks.

She moved her hips, pushing her body against his cock. "Fuck me, Luke."

He growled and pressed down on her stomach to stop her. "Eva, we need to take this slow. I don't want to hurt you."

Her heart clenched, but she was just as desperate to feel him inside her as he was to get there. "Please, Luke. I've wanted this for so long."

"Eva," he said between clenched teeth, his breathing becoming a little more frantic.

She lifted her hips again, and when his cock pressed against her opening, his muscles tensed. He shut his eyes and fisted her hair, and even though she'd never seen him so intense, like he was waging some internal war, she kept moving her hips, urging him to do it already.

He opened his eyes, and when their gazes locked, he adjusted his body on top of her. "Tell me when it hurts and I'll stop, okay?"

She nodded, even though she had no intention of stopping him.

Her heart raced as he pitched his hips forward, driving himself into her. When his cock met with restraint, his glance moved over her face.

"More," she whispered.

He held her shoulders and began pumping, easy at first, but then he pulled his cock almost all the way out.

"Eva," he questioned, between breaths, agony all over his face.

She bucked forward. "I'm ready," she assured him.

With a quick jerk of his hips, he slammed into her, driving past the barrier in one fluid movement. At that first sharp stab of pain, his mouth found hers and he kissed her deep, swallowing her gasp as he sank all the way into her.

Once he was deep inside, he stilled, a worried look on his face when he asked, "Are you okay?"

"I'm okay," she answered, and ignoring the stinging sensations, she began moving her hips, her nails clawing at his back. She squeezed her pussy muscles and a growl ripped from his lungs. Her stomach fluttered. God, she loved that she could do this to him.

"Wrap your legs around me," he bit out, his voice rougher than before, a little more demanding.

When she did as he requested, he began to pound into her with hot, hard strokes. She whimpered, the combination of pain and pleasure overwhelming her senses, but she didn't want him to stop, didn't want this moment to ever end.

She closed her eyes against the flood of emotions.

"Look at me," Luke said.

Her lids fluttered open, and when she met his glance, her heart missed a beat. She bit back a breathy moan as the world around her spun out of control. He pumped deeper and shifted his body to slip a hand between them.

"Luke," she cried when his fingers found her clit. He stroked her lightly and she moved against him, sure she couldn't come again, but when he applied the right amount of pressure, a climax came out of nowhere and took her by surprise.

Her body pulsed and quaked, and as her cream lubricated them even more, Luke groaned and buried his face in the crook of her neck. "I'm right there, Eva. You've got me right there."

She drew a shaky breath, still unable to believe she was in bed with Luke, or that his cock was buried deep inside her, making her feel so gloriously wanted . . . desired.

"I can't hold on," he bit out.

"I don't want you to," she said. "I want to feel you come inside me."

"Fuck," he cried out as he gripped her hips and stilled his movements. His mouth found hers and he kissed her hard as he let go. When his cock finally stopped pulsing, he dropped down on top of her, sweat coating his body.

She held him tight and listened to his breathing while she tried to wrap her head around what had just happened between them. As the lust cleared from her brain, she wondered where things went from here. The truth was she still wanted Luke, but if he only liked her, only slept with her because he'd turned her into the kind of girl he wanted, then what did that mean for them when Spring Break was over and she returned to geek girl extraordinaire?

As he rolled off her and pulled her close, she worked to get herself under control. While she had no idea what would happen next, one thing was for certain—Madame Ysabeau was right. The fortune-teller had said she wouldn't be sleeping with some random guy this week, and that prediction had come true. Because Luke was far from random.

Five

As MOONLIGHT FILTERED in through the open curtains and partygoers could be heard in the street below, Eva sucked in a sharp breath and turned to Luke. The second her eyes met his, and she noted the way he was staring back, she knew she was in a shitload of trouble.

"I'll . . . uh . . . I'll be right back."

He frowned and her heart lurched. Now that the lust had cleared, was he regretting his decision to sleep with her? "Eva . . ."

"I just have to run to the bathroom for a sec."

"Oh," he said, his glance dropping to the condom still on his cock. "Right."

As he turned to take care of it, Eva climbed from the bed and grabbed her cell phone before locking herself in the bathroom. She sat on the edge of the tub and turned on the tap so Luke couldn't overhear her, then dialed Allison.

As soon as her friend picked up the phone, Eva blurted out, "I'm screwed."

"Well I should hope so," Allison said, laughter in her voice. "You've been gone an awfully long time not to be."

"No, you don't get it. I'm screwed because I really like him, Allison." Eva raked her tangled hair from her forehead, her body still tingling in all the places Luke had touched and kissed her. "I'm just not sure what to do now."

"Ah," Allison said. "Well, I think he really likes you too."

"Yes, but I think it's only because—"

"You didn't see the way he was looking at you in the club, or the way he was about to eat you alive in the hallway. Jesus, he's got it bad for you."

Eva opened her mouth to speak, but Allison cut her off. "And it's not just because you were dressing and talking sexy. Samantha always thought he did, and well, now I'm convinced of it too."

Eva's heart pounded. "Samantha always thought Luke liked me?"

"Yeah, we all kind of did. Think about it, Eva. Think about how he's been acting over the last couple days."

Eva stopped to think things through, things like how in his eyes no guy was ever good enough for her, how he'd practically went down on her in her hotel room when there was nothing sexy about the situation or their conversation, and how he always listened to her, even when she went into geek mode.

Then she remembered something else.

There are so many things I need to do to you. Things I've been dying to do to you for so long.

Sweat broke out on her skin and she nearly slipped off the edge of the tub.

Oh, God! Was it possible? Could her friends be right?

Was Luke into the geeky science major who talked nerdy, or had he only taken her to bed because he'd taught her to become the kind of girl he gravitated toward—and then had his tricks used against him?

Damned if she didn't need to find out.

"EVERYTHING OKAY?" LUKE asked when Eva slipped back in bed beside him.

"Yes."

He brushed her hair from her cheeks as he cursed himself for not going slower. "I hurt you, didn't I?"

Her eyes lit. "Is that why you looked so upset a minute ago?"

"I never want to hurt you." When she went quiet, he touched her cheek. "Eva?"

She gave him a shaky smile when she asked, "I hear it gets better though, you know, the more you do it."

Ignoring his buzzing cell phone on the nightstand, he ran a light finger over her pussy to soothe the sting of penetration. Wanting to put her mind at ease, to let he know he wasn't going to ravish her again, he said, "Don't worry, we won't be doing it again." At least not tonight. She was far too sore for that.

The smile fell from her face, just as her stomach started to grumble.

"Did you have dinner?"

She shook her head. "No, I was so busy getting ready for tonight, I actually forgot."

"How about I order us some room service?"

She went quiet for a moment, then said, "Okay, but then I have to go."

A knot tightened Luke's gut, and he was about to ask her what was wrong when a knock sounded on his door. "Can't be room service," he said, trying to lighten her mood. "I haven't ordered yet."

Eva wrapped the sheet around her body and darted nervous eyes his way when the lock clicked and the door opened.

"Don't you ever answer your damn messages—"

Brad stopped mid-sentence, his glance darting back and forth between Luke and Eva, who scrambled to gather her clothes off the floor, then darted into the bathroom.

"Fuck," Brad said in a dangerously low voice after she disappeared.

Luke grabbed his pants and quickly pulled them on. "Brad, wait. Let me explain. It's not like that."

Brad took a threatening step toward him. "Oh, no? I find you in bed with my sister and you're telling me it's not like that? What exactly is it like then, Luke?"

Just then Eva came out of the bathroom dressed in her short jean skirt and tank top, her hair a mess and her cheeks the soft pink of a woman well-fucked. Luke cringed as he looked at her, knowing her appearance wasn't going to help his case.

Brad looked her over, shock on his face. "What the hell are you wearing?"

Luke held his hands up and stepped in front of Eva. "Listen, it's not what you think."

Brad fisted his hand. "What I think is that you just fucked my sister."

Luke cringed at the crude comment and ran shaky hands through his hair, needing Brad to understand it was so much more than that. "Yes . . . but . . ."

Brad took another step closer. "Jesus Christ, Luke."

"Back off, Brad," Eva said, coming to Luke's defense at his side. "Luke was only helping me."

"Helping you?" He shook his head, incredulous. "Oh Jesus, this night is just getting better and better." He looked over her clothes again. "When the hell did you start dressing like that?"

"I asked Luke to help me sell myself."

Luke closed his eyes. Christ, he knew she was trying to help, but she'd just dug his grave. "It's okay, Eva. I got this," he said.

Ignoring Luke, Brad's eyes nearly popped out of his head as he glared at his sister. "Sell?"

"Not like that," she explained, looking exasperated. "I just wanted to fit in here." She waved her hand toward the window that showcased the city below. "I asked him to help me be more like the girls he gravitates toward. So, you know . . ."

He frowned, confusion clear on his face. "Hell no, I don't know!"

"To get guys to notice me."

"Well, it looks like one guy noticed you, all right, since I just found you in his bed." He glared at Luke, his nostrils flaring. "So what? You dress her up and then can't keep your hands off her?"

"No. It's not like that."

With his eyes and stance radiating danger, Brad asked, "Then why don't you tell me what it is like."

"I'm into her, Brad. I've always been into her."

He looked at Eva, and when her big eyes widened with both shock and confusion, his heart swelled with everything he felt for her. He turned back to Brad in time to see the muscle along his friend's jaw clench, and knew it was finally time to lay it all on the line. He loved Brad like a brother, but he loved Eva too, and now that he knew she was into him as much as he was into her, it changed everything.

"What the fuck are you talking about?" Brad growled.

"I'm sorry, Brad. I really am. But I've been crazy about her for as long as I can remember." He wrapped his arms around Eva's waist and pulled her to him. "I just never acted on it because she was your sister and it felt wrong. I'd never do anything to hurt you, you know that, right? But I couldn't help myself, couldn't hold back any longer. And just so you know, I never would have slept with her if I didn't really care about her, and I didn't do it because of the way she was dressed. I don't care what she wears because she doesn't need to be something she's not. Not for me."

As Brad stood there, like he was trying to absorb what he was hearing, Eva looked up at Luke, confusion all over her face. "But I thought . . ." She paused and looked at the bed. "You said we wouldn't be doing it again."

"Eva," he murmured, and lowered his voice for her ears only. "I only meant tonight. " He gave her a sheepish look and added, "I was kind of rough."

She went up on her toes and whispered into his ear, "I like it rough."

Luke felt heat move through him, then straightened, remembering her brother was in the room.

Eva glanced at the outfit that was so not her. "So you really care about me? You like me the way I am, and don't want me to be someone I'm not?"

He gripped her shoulders. "Baby, don't you get it? You're the sodium to my chloride."

Her smile warmed his heart, and she wrapped her arms around him. "So does that mean you want to . . . *bond* . . . again?"

"Over and over again," he assured her. "I want you in my life, Eva."

She laughed, her eyes beautiful and bright as she went up on her toes to kiss his mouth.

"One condition," she said.

He laughed with her. "Oh, so now *you* have a condition."

"Since I no longer plan to be something I'm not. I don't want you to be either."

He knew she was talking about his future with his father, the career path he planned to take. He exhaled slowly, having learned so much from her in such a short time. "You're right. My father and I are definitely going to have a talk."

Brad's voice boomed. "What the hell are you two talking about?"

Luke looked at Brad and shrugged. "When it's meant to be, it's meant to be."

Shaking his head, Brad wagged a finger back and forth between the two of them. "Are you seriously telling me that what's between you two isn't just about sex?"

"That's right," he said. "I'm in love with you sister."

Brad's mouth dropped open and he stared at Luke for a long time before something inside him seemed to give. "Fuck, you're serious, aren't you?"

"Yes," Luke said. "I'm serious. In fact I've never been more serious in my life. I love her, Brad. I have for a very long time now."

Brad scrubbed his hand over his chin as his glance went to the mussed bedsheets. "Shit, I need to go bleach my eyes and then get a drink to help me wrap my brain around all this."

"Lock the door on your way out," Luke said. "And if you still want to kick the shit out of me later, just let me know."

Brad gave a resigned sigh and scratched his neck. "Yeah, I probably should . . . you know . . . just on principle."

"Yeah, I know."

After Brad left, Luke pulled Eva close, and when she looked up at him with desire in her eyes, his heart nearly stopped. "I'm crazy about you Eva. You're beautiful, smart, and sexy just the way you are." He planted a kiss on her mouth and continued, "But you know what I love most about you?"

She shook her head, and looked at him with desire in her eyes. "No, why don't you tell me?"

"I love it when you talk nerdy to me."

When she laughed, he gathered her into his arms, dropped her onto the bed, and climbed on top of her.

"You know," she said, running her finger along the scruff on his jaw as he lifted her skirt. "There is a name for it when people are aroused by intelligence."

"Oh yeah, what's that?"

"Sapiosexual . . ." she began, and then launched into a lecture about the behavior of attraction.

As she continued to talk, he tapped her legs with his fingers and she automatically widened them for him. Since he currently wanted to concentrate on the sexual side of sapiosexual, he slipped between her thighs, and when his hungry mouth found her sweet spot, her nerdy words were lost on a moan.

SHOCK ME

By Lauren Hawkeye

Prologue

Callie

"IF YOU ARE brave, you will obtain your heart's desire."

The words blended so sinuously with the seductive heat of the New Orleans evening that it took me a moment to comprehend what the woman leaning in the doorway had said.

Long, frizzy gray hair hung in tangles around her face, and her skin was paper thin and white. Startlingly bright green eyes peered out of the wrinkles, catching my attention, even though I didn't much care for idle chatter.

"Come. Come here." She held out her hand, her fingers curled with what looked like a severe case of rheumatoid arthritis.

I hesitated. I'd come out for a walk so I could snag some time alone in the middle of a crazy, party-filled week. I wasn't in the mood to talk to anyone at all, let alone a woman I didn't know who smelled strongly of patchouli.

But I was always nice, and I had a hard time saying no. Plus something about the woman's . . . aura, I guess . . . was drawing me in.

Not that I believed in things like that.

Tentatively I took her hand. When she flipped it over and began to scrutinize my palm I shifted my weight from one foot to the other. Squinting up at a sign illuminated by a nearby streetlight, I was able to make out the words MADAME YSABEAU—PALMISTRY AND TAROT on a faded burgundy awning above the door.

"Hmm, hmm," the woman muttered, poking her finger into my palm. I winced—her nails were long and sharp.

Though not as sharp as her stare, which she pinned me with once she had finished reading my palm . . . or whatever it was she was doing.

"You feel differently inside than you appear to others." Returning her gaze to my palm, she nodded and hummed low in her throat. *"Oui?"*

Startled, I stared at her, the skin she was so avidly examining growing damp with perspiration.

How the hell had she known that?

"Um . . . yes. I suppose so." No, I *knew* so. I'd always felt . . . oh, I didn't even know how to say it.

My parents had always had a very clear idea of who I was and what I would do with my life. Though I'd never felt that I fit into a mold very comfortably, it hadn't been optional.

It still wasn't.

"Yes," she nodded enthusiastically, narrowing her eyes and tilting her head back and forth like some exotic bird. The rare Ysabeau Patchouli Finch. "You yearn. You must be daring, and you will get what it is you desire."

I sucked in a deep breath, my mind immediately flashing to what—*who*—it was that I'd wanted for a very, very long time. Madame Ysabeau smiled, knowing she'd caught me in her web.

"You wish to know more?" She didn't bother to hide her cunning. Shaking my head to snap out of it, I tried to hide my grimace.

No, no more palm readings for me . . . or tarot, or crystal balls, or any other kind of woowoo. I was far too practical for that.

"Thank you so much for the . . . ahh . . . advice." I didn't want to insult the woman, but even though she'd drawn me in for a moment with her words, I wasn't buying any of it.

If things like this worked, I'd have already purchased a love potion.

"Deny it if you like, child. Fate will catch you." The woman cackled—there was really no other way to describe it—then, drawing a string of bright green Mardi Gras beads up over her head, she tossed them around my neck. I flinched, halfway afraid she was going to flash me her boobs along with them, but instead she settled back against the curtain of brightly colored beads in the doorway and looked at me expectantly.

Belatedly, I realized that she was waiting to be paid.

Steam built up inside of me—I hadn't *asked* to have my palm read. I was a college student and not exactly rolling in cash. But I supposed that I also hadn't stopped her, because confrontation was just not my style. So I swallowed back my true feelings, tugged a wrinkled twenty dollar bill from the pocket of my shorts and handed it to her.

She snatched at it, then pushed away from the wall with a grace belying her years and swept behind the long fall of beads in the doorway. Once she'd gone, the air around me seemed to clear, and I was left blinking on the street in front of the small magic shop, feeling like a dumbass.

She played you but good, Gilmore. Irritated as hell with my inability to say what I really meant, I scowled, stuffed my hands in my pockets, and looked up at the darkening sky. I contemplated finishing my walk despite the threatening storm. I knew that once I returned I would be drawn into the wild party being thrown by the organizers of this trip to NOLA for Spring Break.

We were all supposed to wear masks and beads, even though it wasn't Mardi Gras—*when in Rome*, and all that. I wasn't big on parties, or crowds of people for that matter, and I'd only come on the trip in the first place because of Ryder.

My friend Ryder. The guy I'd had a crush on *forever*, the one who didn't seem to get it, no matter how many hints I tossed his way.

I'd almost worked up the nerve to tell him how I felt a couple of months earlier. But Hannah, someone who was supposed to be my friend, had moved in before I could.

She'd told me after that she couldn't help but act on her feelings, even though she knew about mine, because I was so sweet and nice that she knew I'd let her have him.

And I hadn't said a word, had just smiled and nodded. It's what I always did.

She and Ryder had broken up just before this Spring Break trip. And I was still angry enough with her, with *myself*, to want to shed some of my good girl, nice person image.

But since arriving here, I'd talked myself back out of my plans to seduce Ryder. I would shock him to the core if I did, and while part of me relished the thought, the other part knew that he just might be freaked out by the thought of his sweet, nice best friend taking the reins and trying to jump into his bed.

Groaning to myself, I turned back in the direction of my hotel, my frustration a hot burn that wasn't soothed at all by the steaming air of the French Quarter. All around me were people my age drinking, dancing, rubbing against one another—having *fun* on their spring breaks.

Why did I always feel the need to hold back? Why couldn't I be like everybody else?

I knew I'd hoped that somehow, amongst all of the mayhem that was Bourbon Street, I'd find it in my shy, practical self to finally make a move on him. And yet here I was, hiding from the party, from people, from *life*.

"Oh, baby. Yes. Now." In a tight alley between two buildings a couple clung to one another, his mouth sliding down her throat, her hands working on his belt buckle. Though I averted my eyes and hurried past, a strain of melancholia like nothing I'd ever felt before worked itself into a tight knot in my gut.

They were *right there*, in public, so wrapped up in one another that they didn't seem to care who saw.

What would it be like to be that free? That bold?

If you are brave, you will obtain your heart's desire.

Unbidden, an image began to swirl through my head. I watched the daydream pass through my mind—me, wearing the half mask that I'd packed for the party, leading a masked Ryder by the hand to my room. Undressing him. Touching him the way I'd dreamt of doing so many times.

If I was hidden behind a mask, would I be able to find the courage?

Could I do it?

Swallowing hard as I approached the front door of my hotel, I cast one look back over my shoulder at the couple in the alley. They were cast in shadow now, only the flickers of light from the French Quarter keeping them visible to my eyes, but the passion in their movements gave me a mental shove.

If I couldn't find the courage to do this while I was in New Orleans, then I knew damn well that I never would.

The flight of butterflies that had been nesting quietly in my belly flew in a million different directions at once as, suddenly giddy, I made up my mind. I pressed my hand flat against the glass of the front door, my palm smudging the clear surface, as I sucked in a deep breath and forced myself onward.

I might have been a stereotypical good girl for my entire life, studious, respectable, and sweet.

But this good girl was going to take a chance at what she wanted for once.

Watch out, Ryder Hawkins. I felt my lips curve into an almost maniacal smile as I made my way through the busy lobby and across to the elevator. I paused when I passed the larger of the two bars that the bottom floor of the hotel offered.

Callie Gilmore is about to go bad.

After one or two shots of liquid courage.

One

Callie

BACK IN MY hotel room, my fingers trembled as I settled the mask over the upper half of my face.

Claustrophobia settled in for one long minute as I adjusted to the sensation of the hard plastic against my skin, and I was glad that my roommate Annie was already out, because she would have wanted to know why I was so nervous. The party that Annie was undoubtedly at was already in full swing, spread out across three different hotel rooms, overflowing with music, people, and booze.

Normally I'd have to be dragged kicking and screaming to a gathering like that, and Ryder was the one usually doing the dragging.

But I was just a little tipsy, and more than a bit excited by what I was planning to do. So when I looked into the mirror, saw the way my pale blue eyes looked almost exotic through the cutouts in my mask, I felt anticipation rather than the usual social anxiety.

I was dressed in black shorts that showed off my legs, which were a little curvier than I liked, and a black camisole to match. I'd actually added some makeup, outlining my eyes with charcoal smoke and painting my lips deep pink.

Looking at my reflection, I could almost believe that I was someone else. Someone who liked parties, someone who could seduce a man she wanted and be confident that they would want her back.

"Do it, Gilmore." Swallowing against a suddenly dry throat, I wrenched myself away from my mirror. Looking out from behind the mask felt . . . different. Like I was seeing the world a new way.

Actually, I *was* seeing the world a new way, I realized as I stumbled a bit, then caught myself. The two margaritas I'd had as I sat downstairs in the bar and tried to shore up my courage had possibly been one too many.

I could still walk. I could still think clearly—mostly. I'd just have to be careful.

Especially in the cute black sandals with the little heel that were still a far cry from the sneakers I wore most days.

The music hit me like a slap in the face when I opened the door to leave my room. I felt my heart leap into my throat as I forced myself to push my way into the throngs of people, all of whom were drinking, laughing, talking.

Kissing. Touching.

The masks lent a surreal atmosphere to the entire scene. As I walked down the hall, I realized that no one knew who I was any more than I did them. Oh, some were easy enough to tell, of course, like the girl with the blue hair from my chem lab.

But for most—if I didn't look too closely, I wouldn't know. And knowing that applied to me too, snapped the last rubber band of my resistance.

But I also found that I didn't want to look too hard to discover anyone's identity. Wasn't that the point of the masks, after all? There was something sexy in the mystery.

In this mask, I was free. I could be whoever I wanted, do whatever I wanted, because tonight I was leaving Callie Gilmore the good girl behind.

Wandering through the first room, I accepted a sealed bottle of water from a girl that I thought I vaguely recognized from a coffee shop on campus. I'd had enough alcohol already—if I managed to seduce Ryder, I wanted to be able to remember it.

Sipping my water, I looked around for Ryder. When we parted ways after dinner, he'd had plans to meet up with his brother, whom I'd never met. He was riding his motorcycle into town for a few days. People were everywhere—people I knew, yet didn't, people whose inhibitions seemed to have been stripped away when they put on their masks. Everywhere I looked, people were touching—a quarterback-sized guy and a petite girl, two sorority types, and a group of three.

There was kissing. Hands covering breasts. Fingers

searching between legs. Lust was thick in the air, and I wasn't immune to its sweet smell.

This wasn't simply the result of too much alcohol or of coeds just looking for a good time.

Everyone seemed to be feeling the way I was—wild. Free.

"Do you like to watch?" The voice was male and husky, and even though the words were spoken so close to my ear that I could feel the warmth of the speaker's breath on my tender flesh, it was hard to hear them clearly over the throbbing beat of the music, something wild and Cajun.

I should have startled—would have, under normal circumstances—but here, now, it seemed right.

Turning my head to look over my shoulder, I found a plain black mask that couldn't hide the rawboned appeal of the face beneath it, or the intensity of the blue eyes that pinned me with their stare.

Hair the color of black licorice stood up in messy spikes—hair that I'd dreamt of running my fingers through so very many times.

"The mask suits you." His grin held a tinge of wicked-ness that I'd never seen Ryder show, and a delicious tingle went through me as I realized that the masks must be affecting him too.

But wait . . . his hair. His hair wasn't that long, was it? Hadn't he gotten it cut right before we'd left?

Then his lips skimmed down the curve of my neck, the barest hint of pressure, and I lost my train of thought. I'd decided that I didn't want to look that closely, hadn't I? Didn't want to know.

So instead I shivered and savored the sensation when the moist kiss ended in the tender spot where my neck and shoulder met.

"What are you doing?" I whispered, which was somehow louder than yelling over the music. He grinned at me, that sinful curve of his lips, and again I was struck with how different the expression was from his norm.

I'd had feelings for Ryder since I met him—who wouldn't? He was smart, handsome, considerate—everything I wanted in a partner. I knew we'd make a perfect match, even if the chemistry between us didn't sizzle like all the movies said it should.

But I'd never picked up on this . . . this *bad boy* quality from him before. It upped that hint of heat that I usually detected, set the air around us to *smolder*.

I'd never felt this level of heat with him, and it made me burn.

Cocking an eyebrow at my question, he wrapped his arms around me from behind. A shiver ran down my spine when he turned me to face the threesome that were now so intimate they would all be lovers if they weren't clothed.

Feeling his breath against my ear again made my thighs tremble.

"You didn't answer." His hand slid beneath the hem of my shirt, palm spread flat on the curve of my belly. "Do you like to watch?"

The movement of the bodies all around us was mesmerizing. But I'd waited too long for this moment, and it was finally within my grasp.

He'd even made the first move. Now I just had to be brave enough to step into the game.

And here, with his fingers strumming over the flesh of my abdomen, so tantalizingly close to the undersides of my breasts, I found that it wasn't nearly as hard as I had imagined.

I wanted to relax a little bit of the rigid hold that I had on myself. No one would care—no one put these expectations on me but myself. Just this one time, just for one night, I was going to reach out for what I wanted. And what I wanted was this man whose touch ignited my arousal like nothing I'd ever been able to imagine.

No matter how much I'd wanted him, we'd never even kissed, though it had come close after one of the frat parties that he dragged me to.

The kiss had been aborted by one of the drunken frat boys hosting the party, and there hadn't been any close calls since. But the fact that he once found me attractive enough to almost kiss—even if he'd had a few beers in him at the time—made me think that maybe here, in the crazy city of New Orleans, during a wild Spring Break, it could happen again.

If only I was brave enough.

Turning, I brushed a tentative kiss over the line of his jaw. Stubble rasped my lips, and there was something about it that niggled at my brain too. But it didn't matter.

Nothing mattered except for the electric chemistry that was sizzling in the air around us.

"I like watching," I finally answered him, shifting so I faced his profile. His hands slid over my skin as I moved, and those fingers came to rest on the small of my back. He teased the waistline of my shorts, and though the touch itself was fairly innocent, it set me on fire.

"But I think I'd like to participate even more." I held my breath, hoping that he understood what I meant—I wasn't asking him to haul me over to one of the groups around us and join in.

But a dark light flashed in his eyes. The fingers on my back pressed, released, pressed again.

Without a word he took my hand. I followed silently, my pulse beginning to hammer in my veins.

This was it. This was really happening.

I let him lead, following him down the hall to his room. The room I'd been in just that afternoon when I waited for him to shower so that we could go to dinner.

As I watched him slide the key card in the door, my mind whirled. The people who'd laughed over sandwiches earlier that evening seemed like strangers now, replaced by the two of us, sexual beings with lust on our minds.

I followed him into the room. Closing the door behind me, I stood for a moment in the soft darkness, letting my eyes adjust to the lack of light.

In a few minutes Ryder was going to stop seeing me as just a friend. I was keyed up, anxious, and unsure of what to do.

I shivered.

"You are the sweetest thing." Hands that I couldn't quite see in the dark landed on my waist, sliding up over my rib cage, then up farther to tickle the sides of my breasts. I gasped, my nipples contracting, rubbing against my bra.

"Kiss me." The words were a plea, but I wanted—*needed*—that sensation.

He pulled back, and though I couldn't see him clearly, I got the sense that he was considering, which left me a moment to think about how this kiss that I'd dreamt of would be.

I'd always imagined that Ryder would be a considerate lover, would ask me what I liked, what I wanted.

I was so wrong.

He approached so fast that I didn't even know he'd moved until his mouth was on mine, bruising in its intensity, his tongue sliding over the seam of my lips, then demanding entry.

I gasped, the air stolen by his lips. There was nothing considerate about the kiss—he simply *took* what he wanted, the lines of his body telling me that he hadn't asked because he knew I'd like it.

"You taste good, sweetheart." He pulled away far too soon for my liking, leaving me struggling for breath. "But these masks are in the way."

I felt his fingers dance over my temples before I tilted my head back out of the way.

"No. Please." I was being ridiculous—Ryder knew damn well what I looked like, not to mention it was dark. But I was afraid that once the buzz from the margaritas was gone, I would lose my courage without my mask.

It was like my Tinker Bell wand. I needed its magic pixie dust.

He didn't miss a beat, chuckling softly and letting his fingers trail down my neck.

"Kinky. I like it." He teased me with another of those heart-stopping kisses. When he pulled away, I acted without thinking, not wanting to give myself time to chicken out. Fisting my hands in the hem of my tank top, I pulled it up and over my head. Beneath my simple black clothes I wore a lace bra and bikini panties constructed of soft pink lace.

They were feminine, and I thought they were sexy, in an innocent kind of way. Not that he could see them in the dark, but they were like my mask—armor to make me feel strong.

"I like a girl who knows what she wants." The words were so incongruous with the Ryder I knew that I couldn't help but grin. This felt a bit like role playing—him the bad, bad boy and me the seductress.

It was naughty. I loved it.

"Lie down." Placing both hands on his chest, I pushed until, with a low laugh, he let himself be pushed down onto the mattress of one of the two beds in the room. He groaned slightly when I let my hands linger on his rock solid pecs, and if I squinted I could just see the outline of him, propping himself up on his elbows.

"Give me a second, babe." His voice was low, husky with need, and just hearing it was like fingers playing over my skin. My nipples tightened with arousal and excitement.

That need was for me.

I heard the sound of a zipper being pulled down, of his shirt being pulled over his head.

"Come here." It wasn't a request, and hearing Ryder—

mild-mannered Ryder—speak like that made heat pool in the cleft between my legs. In that moment I couldn't have said what was hotter, him being bossy or me finding the courage to climb onto the bed.

The Mardi Gras beads that I'd impulsively kept on at the last minute dipped between my breasts, cool against my feverish skin as I went on instinct and straddled his long, hard male body.

"Get right to the point, don't you?" A grumble of satisfaction rumbled from his chest as he reached out for my hips, anchoring me in place. I shuddered as I realized that I had what I'd wanted for so very long—Ryder, between my spread thighs and at my mercy.

Maybe Madame Ysabeau hadn't been full of crap after all.

"I want this." Worrying my lower lip between my teeth, I sat back on my heels, which had the added effect of bringing the heated space between my legs into contact with something . . . hard.

Something very hard, and very big.

Sucking in a startled breath, I shifted slightly, sliding down the length of his now very obvious erection.

He groaned in response, propping himself up on his elbows.

"Mmm." My heart sang when, rather than living up to my fears, he made a noise of pure pleasure and dug his fingers into my hips. Pressing his pelvis up against my own, he slid his hands up my torso to cup my breasts, boldly rubbing his thumbs over my nipples, which tightened and pressed against the lace of my bra.

"Oh." I heard the wonder in my own voice as I bowed my back, arching into the touch. This felt even better than anything I'd dreamed of. Oh, I'd imagined . . . I'd hoped . . . but I'd never actually believed it would come true.

When he released one breast I whimpered, but then those fingers—God, how had I never guessed that he'd be so sure with his hands?—trailed over the soft plane of my belly, then lower.

I couldn't stop from crying out when he dipped his fingers just inside the elastic at the waist of my panties.

This was . . . oh my God. I knew Ryder better than I knew almost anyone, and he knew me. But even though I'd nursed feelings for him for so long, I'd never guessed that the chemistry between us would . . . sizzle . . . the second we were skin on skin.

And oh, but I was enjoying that skin. It was hard to see his torso in the darkness of the room, but I could feel the hard planes, the ripples of his abs, the jut of his hip bones, everywhere my fingers danced. He smelled different than he usually did, no trace of the cologne he liked to wear—just soap and man, and it turned me on more than the expensive scent ever had.

With a surge of bravery I'd never known I had, I took hold of his hand, where he was teasing the flesh right above my mound. My heart in my throat, still a bit afraid that he was going to turn on the lights and ask me what the hell was going on, I urged his hand lower, then lower still.

We both groaned when he slid a finger through my

folds. I was shockingly wet, and might have been embarrassed if he hadn't growled with satisfaction, then slid that finger right inside of me.

Shutting my eyes and leaning back to better enjoy the sensation, I let my mind go blissfully blank, a rare occurrence for me.

I didn't know if I was ever going to get to do this again, but this one time, this one night, I was going to show Ryder how I felt. And while I did, I was damn well going to enjoy the ride.

Liam

IT WASN'T RARE for me to have a woman on top of me, but this one was more intriguing than most, a delightful combination of need and nerves. An amazing woman, one with curves in the all the right places, one who smelled so very much like cupcakes that my mouth watered with the need to take a bite.

She'd looked so damn sexy at the party, watching the exhibitionists with such obvious curiosity and lust that it had made me instantly hard. I have a bit of a hedonistic nature, and I'd wanted her, so I approached her.

But nothing had prepared me for the sweetness of her mouth, of the way my blood roared through my veins when she shoved me back on the bed. In fact, I wasn't entirely sure that I wasn't dreaming.

But when the woman took my hand and slid it into

her panties, into the tightest, wettest paradise I could ever have imagined, I realized that this was too damn good to be a dream.

"Yes." She sighed above me, leaning back and widening her legs, the better to let me in. Always eager to please a lady, I added a second finger, sliding back and forth in her slick channel until I found the small bundle of nerves deep inside that I knew would make her real hot, real fast.

"Oh my God!" Her inner walls clamped down around my fingers, and I groaned, eager to replace my hand with my cock. This woman, whoever the hell she was, was hot and tight, and in that moment I wanted nothing more than to be inside of her.

Propping myself up on one hand, I began to work my fingers in and out of her hot little pussy, sliding my thumb over her clit and making her gasp.

More. I wanted more. I wanted to feel her grinding down against my cock.

Reaching for her breasts, my fingers brushed over a long string of beads—Mardi Gras beads, probably. Grinning with wicked intent, I slid them over her head, then looped them around her wrists in a figure eight, leaving a short leash that I could hold onto.

When I pulled on it, she had to lean forward, which brought her close enough that I could see the pale outline of those gorgeous, perfect tits, even in the dark. Could find one delicious strawberry nipple with my lips, could nip at it with my teeth until she clamped around my hand like a vise and began to whimper.

"That's it, baby." I coaxed her, delighting in her response to my touch. The chicks that I tended to attract were nothing like this sweetly innocent yet giving creature on top of me. Oh sure, they might be more practiced, more skilled, but none of them ever trembled from a kiss.

It wasn't something I'd ever realized I wanted, but right that moment I couldn't imagine having anything else.

Man, but she smelled so good. Felt so good. I wished I could see her.

I was no virgin, and this kind of chemistry—the kind that sizzled and set the air on fire—well, I'd never come across it.

Never, until now.

"Kiss me." She pushed into my hand, greedy for my touch, and I almost lost it. Almost rolled her beneath me, parted those sweet thighs with my knees and thrust inside of her.

There was heaven to be found in the oblivion of a one night stand, even if the peace never lasted. But rather than chasing my own orgasm, I found that I didn't want this to end, not yet.

But she'd asked for a kiss, and I wanted another taste of the lips that I knew were so sweet.

Moving my hands from their other tasks, I cupped her waist. Damn it, but it was dark in here. I wanted to see her, this woman who smelled like sugar and moved like sin.

She moaned when I slid my hands up her rib cage, over the sides of her breasts, then over to play in the hollow of her collarbone. Cupping the long line of her throat, I continued moving, the touches feather light, until my hands were tangled in her hair.

Then I pressed my lips to hers. I meant it to be soft and sweet, just a taste.

But when she went wild in my arms, I wasn't sure that one small taste was ever going to be enough.

Surprising me yet again, she parted her lips, her tongue sliding between my teeth, and changed the light flirtation of the kiss to something else. Something dark. Something sexy.

Something that called to every part of me.

Parting my lips as hers demanded, I gave as good as I got, lips pressing, tongue exploring, teeth nipping. Holy mother, this woman who smelled like cupcakes kissed so dirty that a new rush of blood surged into my already impossibly hard cock, making me groan in pain.

Had to be inside her. Where had I packed the fucking condoms?

"Wait . . ." I struggled to pull back, to free my lips long enough to explain. The woman clasped my cheeks in her hands, her wrists still bound in the string of beads, her touch tender, as though she'd been waiting for this moment for a long time.

But she hadn't been waiting for me—we'd just met. Still, I still felt my pulse stutter a bit at the unexpected intimacy. And that alone should have sent me running—I didn't do intimacy. I lived for good times before I got back on my bike and continued on to wherever else I felt like going. Since I was lucky enough to have the trust fund that my dad had set up for me and my brother before he'd died, I didn't have to answer to anyone or do anything I didn't want to.

But before I could reflect on that overly much, her fingers traced over my cheeks, the tips brushing over the harsh rasp of my two day stubble, and the woman in my arms stiffened, pulling away.

"Sorry. That's probably kinda rough on your skin. Haven't shaved for a couple of days." I apologized, then opened my mouth to finally spit out the words that I really didn't want to. But the woman scrambled backward, right off my lap, severing contact.

I missed the feeling of her skin immediately.

"You shaved right before you went out with the guys tonight." The voice that had been sighing into my mouth only moments before was now tight with disbelief.

"Aah . . ." I rubbed the back of my hand over the line of my jaw, wincing at the roughness I found there. "What?"

"The stubble . . . the hair . . ." My mask was torn away. The mattress dipped as the woman slid off of it. I heard the click of the knob on the bedside lamp before golden light bathed the room.

"Oh my God. You're not Ryder."

"Ah . . . no. I'm his brother." As the dark fled and our features came clear, we both sucked in a breath and stared at the other, though for different reasons.

She was staring at me with horror, plain on her face, because I wasn't my brother.

I was staring at her because she was the most beautiful girl I'd ever seen in my life. Well, that wasn't exactly true—most others would call her cute rather than pretty, maybe even plain, with her long golden hair hanging in a straight sheet down her back and little makeup on that creamy skin.

But it was as if she'd been torn straight from the pages of my wildest fantasies. She was my dream girl come to life.

Two minutes ago I'd had my hands on her.

Now it looked like I'd never get my hands on her again, because she wanted my brother.

Fuck me.

"You . . . you . . . *how*?" Pink stained those creamy cheeks, and perversely, I wondered what I could do with my hands, my cock, to make her flush like that all over. "Ryder went out tonight to meet up with you."

"Yeah. His cell seems to have died and I couldn't get through. I couldn't find them, so I came here and checked in. If he'd known he'd get lucky, though, I'm sure he'd have stayed." I cringed inwardly even as the words left my mouth. Shit, no wonder everyone in the world thought I was a cocky bastard, if that's what came out of my mouth. "Sorry. Bad joke."

The mortification on her face made me wince.

"Um . . . we've been mistaken for twins before. If that makes you feel better." It didn't help the awkwardness of the situation, even though it was true enough. My younger brother was an inch taller, his features a bit finer, but our coloring, our builds, were similar enough.

Easy to confuse, especially if you were expecting the big bro you'd never met to be somewhere else.

"I'm sorry." Apologies didn't come easily to me—I

wasn't very good with words. "I didn't know you thought . . . I wanted . . ."

I'd thought she was just looking for a good time, like I was, like so many people who came to New Orleans for Spring Break were.

And I wanted to get my hands on her again, because I wasn't nearly through.

From across the room the lock on the door beeped, signaling that someone in the hall had slid a key card in. I swore at my little brother for his timing.

The girl squealed and covered her breasts with her hands. The sweet gesture, combined with the sweet but still oh-so-sexy pink lace scrap that she was wearing . . .

I wanted her. I wanted her bad.

"I've always wanted to do a college boy on Spring Break." A distinctly feminine voice purred, accented with the syrup sweetness that told me whoever was out there was a local.

The seductive comment was followed by the all too familiar chuckle of my brother—aka the college boy.

I groaned. This was about to get weird.

"Cover yourself up." Lunging across the bed, I wrapped a sheet around the girl. This brought my hands into contact with her soft skin again, which made my erection surge. Not something I wanted my brother to see, but for the first time in my life I cared more about the woman I was with than anything else.

I didn't miss the way her nipples pebbled at the touch either, but that was something I'd have to convince her to explore later.

"Heads up, Ryder! Nakedness in here!" I shouted, but my words were too late. Ryder stumbled through the door of the room, his mask askew, his hair messy and a smear of bright pink lipstick on the side of his mouth.

"Liam." He stopped short when he saw me on the bed. "You didn't call— Oh fuck. My eyes." Throwing his arms over his face, he turned away, not that I could blame him.

The strangeness of the situation had made my erection recede slightly, but it was still standing at half-mast. Not something a guy wanted to see from his brother.

"Jesus, Liam, I'm going to have to sandpaper my corneas to get rid of that image." As if already trying, he rubbed his hands over his eyes.

"What is it?" The girl behind him pushed her way into the room. Unlike Ryder, *she* had no problem looking my naked frame up and down. "Ooh. Big."

Normally I would have cast her a cocky glance and told her that I could give her lots of things that my brother couldn't. Tonight, all I could feel was the red hot embarrassment of the woman standing next to me.

The Cajun hottie with Ryder pulled her gaze from my cock and looked the girl—*my* girl—over. Running a tongue over lips moist with red gloss, she ran a hand down Ryder's arm seductively.

"And who is she? Naughty Ryder, you didn't tell me we were having a *ménage à quatre*." The woman didn't seem at all nonplussed by the idea—and actually, on any night but tonight, I would have been right there along with her.

"*Ménage à quatre?*" Ryder slowly lowered his hands, his brow furrowed. "What are you talking about, Emma?"

Looking across the room, his eyes widened and his mouth fell open when he saw the blonde—*my* blonde.

"Callie?" Ryder's voice was incredulous as he looked from Callie—so that was her name—to me, then back again. I could almost hear the wheels in that big brain of his start to spin as he took in my complete nakedness, and Callie's flushed face and messy hair.

And he didn't miss the alluring bits of pink lace that peeked out from the white bedsheet either, I noted—he shifted a bit as he quickly looked her up and down, and I knew that he liked what he saw every bit as much as I did.

Unfounded jealousy flared up inside of me. Or maybe it wasn't unfounded. After all, Callie had clearly been intent on seducing my brother, not me.

Though from the look of the now pissy bombshell with Ryder, he might have had other plans.

"My name is Eula, not Emma." Irritation crackled in the depths of Eula-Emma's eyes. She placed her hands on her hips and looked both Ryder and myself up and down one more time. Rather than making comments about my big body parts, this time she didn't look like she saw anything in either of us that impressed her.

"I don't fuck guys who are too stupid to remember my name." Ouch. I flinched on Ryder's behalf, though he didn't look like he much cared, the way he kept darting glances at Callie. "You can't remember two syllables, how are you going to remember where a woman's clit is, hmm?" And with that she was gone, leaving a very awkward triangle in a room full of thick, dense silence.

Callie spoke first, her voice so halting and full of embarrassment that I wished wasn't there. It was a far cry from the breathy sighs she'd been making only minutes earlier.

"I— Ryder, I—" She looked from me to my brother, then back to me, her confusion plain. "I didn't know."

Hell, *I* was confused by the intensity of what had just happened between us, and I wasn't the one who'd come in here with other ideas.

"Liam?" Brow furrowed, Ryder turned to me, then winced again. "For the love of God man, put some clothes on. Then will someone please tell me what the fuck is going on?" Leaning backward, he peered out into the hall, in the direction that Eula-Emma had left.

Callie inhaled as sharply as he did, and there was no mistaking the emotion behind the sound.

Pain.

Good God, she didn't just have the hots for my brother. She was seriously into him. No wonder she was so upset.

Feeling protective, an emotion that wasn't entirely comfortable on me, I reached to put an arm around her, to hug her or maybe rub her arm or something—to offer comfort, I guessed.

But she jerked back like my touch had burnt her. Her face bright red, she held out her wrists to me; silently, I unwound the beads from around them.

Ryder watched as I did, a muscle in his jaw quivering.

Wrapping the sheet around her like a tent, Callie shuffled around the room, pulling on her shorts, then her shirt, with jerky movements. Once she was dressed, she hurried to the door to slide her feet into her sandals, her movements a combination of haste and dignity.

"Your cell phone was dead. He wasn't supposed to be here," she snapped at Ryder. I had to admire her spine, even under the circumstances.

He looked equally annoyed as he pulled his cell from his pocket, checked it, and huffed out an exasperated breath. "Well, sue me for having a dead cell phone. How the hell was I to know that you were going to pick him up?"

The accusation in his words was clear, but I didn't understand why he had his panties in such a twist about it.

Unless . . . oh please no.

Callie was clearly into my brother. But I prayed to whatever big guy was up there that my bro wasn't into my newly discovered dream girl too.

"You're not one to judge, not when you brought that . . . that *trollop* back from the bar!" Shoes now on, she stood rigidly and poked my brother in the chest. It was clear to see the familiarity between them, which made unease settle in my gut.

While I kinda enjoyed watching my brother sputter for words, more than anything I wanted him to say that he wasn't into my dream girl. Instead he grabbed the finger that she was pointing at him and narrowed his eyes.

"Why do you care who I bring home from the bar, Callie Anne Gilmore?" His voice was full of confusion.

What an idiot. I wanted to smack him upside the head when I saw the dismay on the girl's face.

"You—You—" Shoving his hands away from her, I watched, fascinated, as anger swallowed Callie's clear hurt. "For a smart guy, sometimes you are incredibly dumb." Raking fingers through her messy hair, Callie let her hands fall to her hips, clearly fuming as Ryder looked at her, bewilderment on his face.

"What the fuck?" he said, stepping toward her.

She stepped back, holding her hands up with a clear *don't touch me* message.

"And I didn't know he was your brother. I thought he was you!" She gasped as soon as she'd spoken, clapping a hand over her mouth. Ryder looked like she'd knocked him on the head.

"Shit," Callie whispered seconds before she bolted from the room, eyes wide with terror over what she'd just said. Ryder called out for her once, then closed the door with his heel, turned and ran his hands through his hair.

Pinning me with a stare I hadn't seen since we were kids and he'd somehow deduced that I'd gotten to first base with our babysitter Marsha, he picked up a pair of boxers from the duffel bag lying by the door and tossed them at me. Normally I would have thrown them right back at him, but Callie had looked plenty sexy as she'd stomped away, and though my mind knew it wasn't a great time, my cock had other ideas.

Standing, I slid into the underwear, then crossed my arms over my chest and faced my brother.

"Friend of yours?"

He scowled, then turned to glare at me. "Want to tell me what the fuck is going on?"

Two

Liam

"Guess we ruined your shot at getting lucky, huh?" Swinging myself out of bed, I stalked naked to where Ryder's duffel bag lay on the floor. He scowled when I nabbed a clean pair of sweatpants and tugged them up over my hips.

"Those are yours now," he said, pretending to gag at the fact that I'd pulled them on without underwear. "We'll sew your name into them."

"I could just take them back off," I offered as I moved to the small minifridge and extracted two of the cans of beer that I'd stored in it earlier. "I know you're a prude, but I'm fine letting it all hang out."

"Dude. Not the best time for jokes." Ryder heaved a major sigh and caught the can of beer that I tossed his way. His brow was furrowed, and I felt a sinking sensation in my gut.

I couldn't go after a girl that my brother was into. Even if he was going to have a hard time convincing her of that fact after tonight's debacle.

"How the fuck did—that—happen, anyway?" Ryder was pinching the bridge of his nose in his fingers when I turned, can of beer in hand. "Callie's not the kind to pick up a stranger."

"She didn't think she was picking up a stranger." My voice was quiet. It bothered me more than I cared to admit that while I'd been marveling at the chemistry between us, she'd thought I was someone else.

The expression on my brother's face was very nearly comical. I would have laughed if I hadn't felt so off my game.

"No." Ryder squinted at me as if I had two heads. "Not Callie. She's . . . she's not that kind of girl."

"It seems she is." And thank the big man for it. If she wasn't, I never would have had a chance to taste those sinful lips.

"Huh." Ryder looked shell-shocked. "I didn't think she had that kind of thing in her."

He didn't mention whether he liked the idea or not.

"So." I cracked open the top of my beer and took a long drink, swiping the back of my hand over my mouth. I decided to just say it. "Did I cock block you tonight? Clearly she's into you. Are you into her?"

Ryder choked on his beer. I thumped him helpfully on the back as he sputtered, then he glared at me.

"Into Callie? No. No!" Looking frustrated, he raked his hand through his hair, which was, like mine, sticking up on end. It was a simple thing, that gesture, but it reminded me of why I was here in the first place.

It had been almost a year since I'd seen my brother in person. After our dad died, I'd taken off on my bike, and had been traveling ever since. When he texted to tell me he was going to be in New Orleans, I knew that I couldn't pass up the chance to lessen the rift between us that time had left. And yet here I was, wanting Callie more than I'd ever wanted any woman, and yet knowing that if Ryder said the word, I'd turn and walk away.

But . . . he hadn't said he wanted her. Still, I wasn't convinced.

"So . . . you're not, like, staking any claim on her?" I sipped my beer casually, but studied my brother's every move.

He tensed and shot me a look full of irritation, but well as I had once known him, I couldn't tell if he wanted me to back off or if he was just pissed off at the way the evening had gone in general. He was drinking beer with me, after all, rather than sampling the delights that Eula-Emma had to offer.

"She's not a prize hog, Liam."

Aah. That was the problem. I was putting the moves on his friend.

"She's not your type." He looked at me pointedly, then leaned back on the bed with a sigh. "And you still haven't told me what happened."

I decided to ignore the comment about my type. He

was right; a sweet girl like Callie wasn't who I would normally go after. But fate had thrown us together, and the connection had been electric.

"You didn't answer me. You're not looking to follow her move with one of your own?" I asked. Ryder narrowed his eyes and looked like he was going to pursue the question, to insist I tell him what happened. I didn't want to—it felt private, so I deflected.

If someone had told me just yesterday that all of this was going to happen, I would have said that I'd walk away and leave my brother and Callie to each other. Women were unique, they were fun, and I enjoyed the companionship and physical release of everyone that I hooked up with.

But there was something about this girl—I'd had a taste, and I didn't want to share.

Ryder huffed out a breath. I couldn't read the expression on his face.

Had I been away for that long, or was he hiding something from me?

"She's my best friend. I'm not into her like that." His words were hesitant. "But . . . she's not like the girls you usually get with, Liam. You can't treat her like that."

Meaning, I couldn't have fun with her—and she would have fun too, I had my pride—but I couldn't just up and leave her once I'd gotten between her thighs.

I couldn't blame Liam for thinking that was what I would do. It was what I always did. But something about Callie . . .

I wasn't about to give her a ring or anything, but I knew that one taste was never going to be enough.

"No offense, bro, but what happens between us is none of your business." I cocked an eyebrow and smirked, which only seemed to piss him off.

And then he burst out laughing, which surprised me. He chugged the rest of his beer, crushed the can, then tossed it in my direction. It bounced off my chest.

"What the fuck, man?" Picking up the crushed metal, I threw it back. He grinned sadistically.

"You've never had a problem with a woman in your life. But from the way she ran out of here—and knowing Callie Gilmore—you're in for a hell of a time of it."

Callie

I'D GONE STRAIGHT from Ryder's room to the smaller of the two hotel bars. Most of the partiers were still out in the French Quarter, or at least in the bigger bar at the front of the hotel, so I was able to settle myself at a table in the back and drink in peace.

What on earth had I just done?

I couldn't stop the shudder from rolling through me as I replayed the events of the last hour.

I'd seduced a stranger. The guy I'd been *trying* to hit on had brought another girl home instead.

And even through the hurt, the knowledge that Ryder

clearly wasn't interested in me the way I was interested in him . . .

It hurt. I couldn't deny that. But more than that, I couldn't stop thinking about the way Liam's hands had felt on me, the way he'd touched me like he couldn't get enough.

The desire overpowered the anger and confusion.

Clearly, I was crazy.

Shaking my head at myself, I took a large sip of my martini, which was something fruity and girly and, best of all, strong. Only hours ago I'd been convinced that I was in love with Ryder, and now I was lusting after his brother. The brother I'd only ever heard mentioned in passing, the one who was a complete stranger to me.

Clearly I wasn't really a good girl at all, not with the slutty direction my thoughts had taken.

Taking another sip, I mulled over my choices.

I could run away and never talk to Ryder again.

I could blame my behavior on the margaritas, and ask him to never mention it to me ever again.

Or I could stop caring what he thought, since clearly he wasn't into me that way. Then I could go have hot sex with his brother, who clearly *was*.

I was hopeless.

Reaching into my pocket, I extracted my wallet, withdrew some cash to pay for my drink. I was going to try to shut off the stream of images that was running through my head.

I would get some sleep and figure out what to do in the morning.

Maybe it would be hilarious by then.

Somehow I doubted it.

I was so wrapped up in my pity party that I didn't notice him until his hand wrapped around my wrist.

"Callie."

My heart shot into my throat—for a split second I didn't know which man it was. My spirits dipped when I realized that it wasn't Ryder, then soared when I saw Liam.

And I was pissed at myself all over again for it.

He knows you thought he was his brother! I lectured myself as I felt my body tense. I should have wanted to run away, but instead . . .

I wanted to lean into the touch.

My traitorous body parts tightened at the memory of just how his touch had felt on other, more intimate areas, the nipples pressing against the thin cotton of my tank top. I watched, wide-eyed, as Liam's gaze dipped down to them.

He couldn't quite hold back a smirk.

"You're clearly not the nice brother." I pulled, trying to jerk my hand away, but he held firm. When his thumb rubbed over the inside of my wrist, my knees weakened of their own accord. I wanted to be mad at him, to give him hell for taking things as far as he had with me.

But he hadn't known my connection to Ryder. And it was difficult to hold onto my anger when his touch made my pulse hum.

"Nope," he agreed, pulling out a chair for me and helpfully pressing on my shoulders until I sat in it. "I've never claimed to be."

I fought against the urge, but I really, *really* wanted to lean into his touch and purr.

He sat down beside me, and my pulse leapt.

Both brothers had stayed away long enough for me to drown my sorrows, and I couldn't help but think that they had been holed up in their room, laughing at me. That was wrong, though, and I knew it. Ryder wouldn't laugh at me. He was surely confused, though, and probably had his "I'm just not that into you" speech all planned out. So I'd figured he would be the one coming to look for me. Instead, the brother with the rough edges sat beside me, and his proximity told me one undeniable truth:

The connection I'd felt—it hadn't been because I thought he was Ryder. No, it was purely *Liam*.

"Why are you here?"

"I think you know why." That voice of his was low as he spoke, continuing to rub his thumb in hypnotic circles over my skin.

"That wasn't . . . I'm not . . ." I felt my pulse skitter through my veins. Oh, this was really, really wrong. But something about this man made me want to be very, very bad. "I care about your brother. This is really embarrassing."

"Well, you could look at it that way." His touch trailed up the inside of my forearm. Against my will, my breath caught in my throat. "Or you could consider this. Instead of worrying that my blind-ass little brother doesn't want you, why don't you think about the fact that his very wise older brother does?"

The question hit me like a bolt of lightning, and I stared.

"What the hell kind of question is that?" I tugged, trying to free myself, but something more than his touch kept me in place.

His eyes met mine, and I knew that he understood what I felt without me having to say it. There was something between us, something electric and inexplicable.

Something far more potent than anything I'd ever felt for Ryder.

He sat back in his chair and watched calmly as I looked him over. Now that we were in a room that wasn't pitch-black, I could see the family resemblance—both men were tall, with thick waves of chestnut hair. The bone structure in the face was similar, though Liam looked like he might have broken his nose at some point.

Ryder's eyes were bright blue, and Liam's edged closer to gray. While Ryder's body was lean and taut, Liam was just . . . bigger. A bit shorter, but harder, with dark swirls of tattoos dancing over golden skin stretched tightly over ropy muscle, the tattoos visible now that he'd changed into a short-sleeved shirt.

His hands were scarred, and he looked just as capable of throwing a punch as he did playing my body. It made me think about his bike, no doubt parked outside, some beast of a machine that rode between his thighs.

The thought made me blush. Damn it, I couldn't even be around him without thinking dirty things.

But wasn't that why I'd come to New Orleans in the

first place? Wasn't that why I'd ended up nearly naked in Ryder's room?

I don't want to be a good girl anymore.

He must have seen it on my face, because he leaned in, leaned close until I could smell that delicious scent of soap and man that I'd first gotten a taste of when I was astride him.

"You're not my type either, you know." Brushing a thumb over my lower lip, he seemed to savor my shiver—man, it felt like he was reading my mind. "I go for wild girls who know how to have a good time, not sweet young things like you."

I moistened my suddenly dry lips with my tongue.

"But I don't think you're as good of a girl as you want the world to believe." Turning, he slid his lips over the lobe of my ear, and fire shot straight down my spine. "Good girls don't take masked strangers to bed, do they?"

My throat was dry; I couldn't speak. But Liam pulled back, cutting off contact, pinning me with that intense stare that was so ridiculously sexy.

"Answer me," he demanded, and though I should have been pissed at his bossiness, I instead found myself thrilling to it.

"No . . . no I . . . I mean they . . . don't."

"Good girl." Liam smirked, then leaned in until his lips were just a whisper away from my own. A ribbon of hot need tangled in my gut.

Good Lord, what was happening to me? This was so much more than anything I'd ever felt with Ryder. But what kind of girl did that make me, tossing aside my feelings for one brother to chase after the other?

Except it didn't feel like I was chasing him. Rather, I felt like I was being hunted, in the most delicious possible way.

"You have to tell me, Callie." Liam stayed just out of reach, and it was infuriating. The need to overcome propriety, to reach out and take what I wanted, just for once in my life, was overwhelming.

I couldn't. Could I?

"I have to know that this is what you really want. I'm not going to be chasing after a chick who has a schoolgirl crush on my little brother."

God, he was infuriating. And sexy, even when he was being an ass.

He was *daring* me, calling me out on the desires that I thought I had buried deep within. And while I knew that it wasn't fair to compare the two men, I suspected that if Ryder could see the thoughts running through my head, he'd try to herd me back into the role he was familiar with, rather than encourage me to do what I wanted.

And this was what I wanted. One wild night in New Orleans with a sexy bad boy who inexplicably wanted me as well.

But I had to form the words.

"Y-Yes." My throat was so dry it hurt. "I . . . I want . . . you."

My face burned; I was sure that Liam could feel the heat from where he was sitting. But if he did, it only convinced him that I was telling the truth.

I saw him nod once, short and decisive, and then I was in his arms. I squeaked as he held me tight with one arm, wrestling a twenty dollar bill from his pocket with the other. Neatly, he dropped it onto the table, scooping up the one I'd left and tucking it back into my pocket.

I could have cared less about the cash, but the feel of his fingers, working at my hip . . . the memory of how they felt inside of me . . .

Yes, I'd made up my mind. I wanted to be bad, and this was the man I wanted to teach me how.

But bad didn't mean helpless. When it became clear that Liam intended to carry me wherever it was we were going, I pushed against his chest.

"I can walk, you know." I had no idea what my classmates would think if they saw sweet, dependable Callie Gilmore crushed against the chest of a barbarian biker.

Liam looked down at me, where my face rested against his bicep. His eyes were thoughtful, but as I'd already come to realize in the short time I'd known him, he used cockiness as a way to hide what he was really feeling.

"Afraid of what people will think if they see us together?" With a wicked grin he changed direction. Now instead of moving to the exit of the bar, we were heading for the back.

"Closing in ten," the bartender called out to us. Liam nodded.

"Noted. Make sure no one comes into the back, will you?"

The bartender looked at the pair of us, me flushed and

pushing at Liam's arms, Liam making God-knew-what face.

The man winked, then began to whistle as he wiped down the glossy wooden surface. He paid no attention whatsoever as Liam lugged me to the back of the bar and into a small alcove that held a single massive table, meant for large parties, I assumed.

When he slowly lowered me down onto that table and I saw the intention written over his face, I felt my breath catch in my throat.

"Not here!" I hissed, pushing at him. Undeterred, he hooked a finger in the belt loop of my shorts and pulled me across the slick surface, closer to him. "The bartender can hear."

Taking one of my wrists in each hand, he brought them together, effectively shackling me. Bending over, he brushed his lips over my mouth, and I was reminded of the wet, hot, filthy kiss we'd shared when we were upstairs and naked.

"Well, I'll beg your pardon, Miss Gilmore, if I've misunderstood. But I was under the impression that you wanted to do something wild. To lose control."

He tugged on my wrists, and heat flooded through me. I'd never considered being bound—never considered much of any of this, really, which only made it more exciting.

"I'm waiting, Callie." Liam regarded me with those dark gray eyes, and the patience there told me that he could wait all day until I gave him the answer he was looking for.

Rather than frightening me, it told me that I was safe.

No matter how much he wanted me—and I still couldn't quite believe that this big bad male creature did—nothing was going to happen unless I gave the go ahead.

And I wanted it to happen. Right here, right now. I wanted to taste something wild, even just so my tombstone someday would read something other than: HERE LIES CALLIE GILMORE. SHE WAS A GOOD GIRL.

It was past the time for hesitation. Swallowing thickly, I reached out and cupped Liam's cheek in my palm. "I want you too."

I was stunned when he turned and pressed a kiss into my palm. His expression was tender, as though I'd given him a gift, not agreed to have wild, kinky sex on a table in a bar in New Orleans.

He kissed my hand one more time, and I felt . . . treasured.

Then his expression darkened, became something wicked. I felt my pulse began to pound in the base of my throat.

"Turn over," he told me, pulling me until my hips were at the edge of the table. "Bend over the table, hands flat. And whatever you do, don't move."

Liam

IF I'D HAD any doubts that Callie was still thinking about my brother, they vanished the second I told her to turn over. I grinned to myself, my mind fleeing to all kinds of filthy places.

Callie might've looked like sweetness and light on the outside, but inside?

I suspected there was one very kinky woman, just waiting to escape.

"Liam." Her voice was quiet, yet still cut through the suddenly still air of the bar. I knew that the bartender could hear us—hell, he had probably stopped working and was listening with his dick in his hand.

I didn't care what he heard, so long as it gave Callie more excitement. I still didn't know why, but something about this woman made me want to wipe all traces of every other man she'd ever thought of from her mind.

There would be time to think about how into her I already was later. Right now I had a woman hot and willing underneath me. I'd be a damned fool not to do something about it.

After all, she knew who I was now. And she was still here.

"Don't talk," I told her, my hands sliding beneath the hem of her shirt. I moved over her torso, pausing to enjoy the soft swell of her belly before moving up to stroke the undersides of her breasts. "You don't have to ask for anything, because I'm going to give you everything you need. So you don't say a word, unless it's my name."

"Oh." The single soft sound was full of wonder, and made me feel ten feet tall.

I wanted to go slow, to savor this woman, but I'd promised her something wild.

Let it never be said that I couldn't give a woman what she wanted.

"I said, don't talk." Tugging until the silky fabric of her shirt was at her neck, I slid a hand inside her bra, playing my fingers over the nipple that drew tighter under my touch. I squeezed gently, following it up with a sharp pinch that had her muffling a cry against her forearm.

"Good girl." With sure hands I tugged on the pink lace until her breast fell free, then paid the same attention to the other side. I filled my hands with those glorious tits, in half a mind to turn her back around so I could see them, could lick my way down the valley between them.

But this . . . this was more impersonal. It would add to Callie's experience.

And it would also allow me to keep a grasp on what was left of my self-control.

Beneath me, Callie squirmed. I imagined the table beneath her was cold, warming slowly under the heat of her skin.

"Hold still." Slowly, I let my hands slide back down her sides, palming the sensitive sides of her breasts, the stripes of her rib cage, the slender span of her waist.

When I dipped my fingers beneath her waistband, she pushed back against me. Grinning to myself, I smacked a hand across the full globe of her ass.

She cried out, though it was clear she tried to muffle it. I hadn't hurt her—she was still wearing her shorts.

But it seemed like my good girl might be open to a good spanking.

When she looked over her shoulder with a shy glance full of nerves, I felt my cock swell. Shaking my head,

I fisted my hand in the long coils of her pale hair and turned her back around.

With sure fingers I undid the button at her waist, then slowly lowered the zipper. I felt her inhalation as I slipped the shorts down over her hips, then hooked my fingers in the elastic of her bikini panties and pushed them down too.

From far away I could hear the clinking of glasses against wood, the rush of steam as the bartender emptied the pressure washer. But my world had narrowed to this incredibly sexy woman who was offering herself to me.

My erection hardening to the point of pain, I ran a finger down the length of her spine. When I trailed it through the cleft of her ass, she shuddered.

"Please." She shifted again, her hips rocking from side to side in a way that made my eyes roll back in my head. "I—I need—"

I needed it too. With hurried movements, I pulled a condom out from my pants pocket. Sliding it across the table until it was under her face, I pressed it against her lips.

"Hold this."

Her eyes widened at the command, but she did as I asked, taking the foil packet between her lips, holding it as I used both hands to undo my belt, the snap at the waist of my torn jeans, the zipper of my fly.

She whimpered in her throat, pressing back against me. Unable to resist, I slid two rough fingers past the elastic of her panties to invade the wet heat that waited there.

One dip, then two, and my fingers were moving again, sliding around to slip into the crevice of her ass. She shivered as my hand explored the darkness, crying out when I pressed a firm digit against the tight ring of muscle that was hidden deep inside.

In another of those lightning quick moves that I couldn't predict from her, she reached behind her back, worked her fingers into the open fly of my pants and grasped my erection in eager fingers. I gasped as she traced her fingers over the veins, the hot smoothness.

The triumphant flush that spread over the gentle slope of her shoulders was my undoing. I could feel there was a fever raging between us, one that I knew only a hard, fast fuck could ease.

"Bite." Waiting until she clamped her teeth into the edge of the packet, I pulled, the foil rending in two. Taking my hands off her body just long enough to smooth the ring of latex down my cock, I flipped her over, grinning with anticipation.

"Oh!" she cried out as I dragged her ass to the edge of the table. I watched as her gaze darted in the direction of the bartender, but when I pressed the head of my cock to her slick heat, she closed her eyes in surrender.

With a low growl deep in my throat, I cupped the sweet handfuls of her ass, lifting her so that her legs could wrap my waist. When she was twined around me like a vine, her gorgeous tits jiggling in a way that made my mouth water, I hooked a finger in the crotch of her panties, ripping them to the side. With a hand unsteady from need, I slid the head of my cock back and forth through the wet heat of her pussy lips, then did it again because it felt so damn good.

Then I surged forward, hilting inside of her in one hard stroke that made her cry out again and left me groaning.

Her pussy was like a vise, swollen from her arousal—arousal that I had brought out of her—and it gripped me like a velvet fist.

Her eyes widened when she looked up at my face, but I wanted to make damn sure she knew which brother it was she was with.

Lowering my face until our breath mingled, I pressed my forehead to hers.

"Say my name."

Her eyes widened; her lips parted.

I halted my movement, fully inside of her, stretching her. She tried to rise up, to get me to move, but I held her in place with a palm to her hip.

"Say it, Callie. Or you don't get any more of my cock." I wouldn't have thought twice about talking to the kind of girl I was normally with that way, but now I found myself getting off on the shocked expression that crossed Callie's sweet face.

We stayed like that for a long moment, frozen in place, my cock aching with the need to slam into her.

Her emotions played out over her face. In the end, lust won.

"Liam," She whispered. I rewarded her with the thrust of my hips, and damn, but she felt good.

"Louder."

She shook her head, and I again stilled, which made her grind her teeth in frustration.

I grinned. She was fun.

"Louder," I coaxed, enjoying the tease. "Come on, sweetheart."

Glaring at me—ooh, I liked that streak of fire—she grabbed hold of my forearms and arched up into me.

"*Liam.*"

And then I began to move, goaded past all control. Our arms and legs tangled, flesh slapped, and pressure began to build at the base of my spine as I thrust my cock into her again and again, and I rotated my hips, the better to let her feel the friction of the coarse hair that surrounded my cock on her clit.

Her legs clenched more tightly around my waist, her breath coming in pants. Fuck, but she was responsive. It was gorgeous.

In that moment, I would have given her anything she asked for. She was giving me all of herself, holding nothing back, and in return just asking for a little pleasure.

Holding her hips firmly, I rotated my hips again.

She cried out as a shudder passed through her, her entire body clenching as the orgasm washed over her. The tightness of her grip on me was more than I could handle, and my own release ripped through me. I thrust once, twice, groaning as I let myself be swallowed by the slick heat of her body.

When I was finally able to open my eyes, I found her staring at me with cornflower blue eyes full of wonder.

No one had looked at me like that . . . ever.

I didn't know what I'd just gotten myself into with this sweet thing, but I suddenly knew that I wasn't anywhere close to being ready to let her go.

Three

Callie

I'D JUST HAD sex in public with my best friend's brother.

Once that thought finally worked its way through my orgasm-fogged brain, I squeaked and tried to sit up, tried to pull my shirt up to cover my naked breasts.

Holy shit.

The rough and tumble man standing between my thighs grinned at the mouselike sound, cupping my breasts in his hands and rubbing his thumbs over the nipples before tucking them back into my bra and under my shirt himself.

He studied my face for a long moment before he slowly pulled out of me. I winced at the sensation—I was going to be tender.

But oh, it would be in the best possible way.

"You all right then, sweetheart?" Removing the condom and folding it into a paper napkin, he tucked himself back into his pants, then helped me rearrange my clothing.

I opened my mouth, then closed it again. I had so many thoughts, but couldn't imagine that a stranger would want to hear them.

Technically, he's not a stranger anymore, Callie.

"Yes." I finally found my voice, though to me it felt strange, rather like it had been broken down and put back together.

I wasn't lying. What the two of us had just done—my mind was blown.

I hadn't known that a connection between two people could be that intense.

But I was already aching over the loss that I knew was going to come.

Ryder had mentioned his brother to me before, but he'd also said they weren't really close anymore. His brother—*Liam*—had spent the time since their dad died roaring around the country on his bike, doing odd work here and there, when he needed to.

That kind of lifestyle wasn't for me.

And yet knowing that this was *it* left me feeling hollow inside.

"What's wrong?" Liam's eyes narrowed and I flushed—I was sure that my feelings had just played out over my face. I'd never been very good at hiding them.

But what was I supposed to say?

I started tonight thinking I wanted to seduce your brother. Turns out I think you're actually the man for me.

Please will you visit next time you come roaring by my school?

Yeah. Right.

"We'd better get going." Now that my senses weren't overcome with lust, the sounds from the front of the bar began to filter back in.

With them came embarrassment.

That bartender just heard me come.

"Do you know what one of the sexiest things in the world is?" Liam asked, clasping me around the waist and helping me down from the table.

"What?" I eyed him warily. I wasn't ashamed of what we'd done—I'd wanted it. Hell, I already wanted it again.

But I wasn't sure how to act, what to do. How to be the girl who did wild things.

Leaning in close, he let his lips slide over mine. Despite the fact that he'd just made me come, I shivered.

"When a woman trusts you enough to do something crazy." He smiled against my lips, then kissed the tip of my nose.

I gaped up at him. Had those sweet words really just come from the mouth of the badass biker?

"I have a few smooth moves up my sleeve, sweetheart. I've just been waiting for the right woman to use them." He winked at me, then without warning scooped me up in his arms again, the way he had when he carried me to the back of the bar.

"I—" I shut my mouth, overcome.

The right woman? That was crazy. We'd known each other for *hours*.

But did I have to analyze everything to death? Did I have to know that we were going to work out in the end to enjoy the here and now?

Hell, no.

I felt the blush spreading from the tips of my toes as Liam carried me out through the main area of the bar. I wanted to bury my face in his chest and hide from the suggestive grin of the bartender as Liam worked some cash out from his pocket and tossed it down the length of the bar.

"Thanks, man."

"My pleasure." The bartender winked at me, and I couldn't help it, I laughed.

So what that he'd heard us? I hoped he'd liked it.

"Now what?" I asked hesitantly as Liam carried me to the front door. I cringed as I spoke—I didn't want to be one of those needy girls.

But I wasn't done. I wanted more. And I wasn't going to be afraid to ask for it.

"Now . . ." Liam kicked through the door and grinned down at me with that panty-melting smile. "I take you upstairs and we do it all again."

"Ahem."

Oh, shit. I knew that voice. Clawing at Liam's chest until he shifted, I met Ryder's wide-eyed stare.

His eyes raked over me, taking in my tangled hair, my sex-flushed face.

Guilt tried to wash over me, but I refused to let it. Ryder and I were friends. What I did with his brother was none of his business.

Still . . . it was all around weird.

"Putting you down, sweetheart." Liam lowered me until my feet hit the ground, looking from me to Ryder, then back to me.

"I want to move my bike off the street before the partying gets too wild." Liam nodded decisively. My heart thudded, wondering if this was it, if he was taking off.

Instead he cupped the back of my head in his hand and pulled me in for a kiss. Not just a peck either, but a hot, open-mouthed flash of heat that left me weak in the knees.

"When I'm done, I'm going to be knocking on your door." His eyes told me exactly what he'd be knocking on my door for too.

God, I hoped Annie didn't come back to the room tonight.

Then he was gone, leaving me alone to talk my way through the weirdness with my friend.

We stood in the hotel lobby, awkwardness permeating the air around us.

"I didn't know—"

"I didn't mean—"

We both broke off into laughter. It helped to break the ice, though it was still an uncomfortable moment.

Inhaling deeply, I shoved my hands into the pockets of my shorts, then forced myself to look Ryder in the eye.

"I didn't know he was your brother. I thought he was you." I did my best not to cringe. "I . . . aah . . . I've had feelings for you for a while. A long while. At least . . . I thought I did."

Ryder raised an eyebrow and chuckled, though the laughter sounded a little bit sad.

"Damning with faint praise, Gilmore." He stuffed his hands into his pockets too, and rocked back onto his heels. "I had no idea. I really didn't."

"Well. I hope it won't be weird that you don't feel the same way that I do. That I did," I corrected myself automatically, wondering at myself as soon as the words were out of my mouth.

If it had taken so little to strip me of my romantic feelings for him, then maybe I hadn't really felt that deeply after all.

"Well . . ." Ryder inhaled deeply, then looked me in the eye. "I can't say . . . I mean . . . I kind of wonder now. What would have happened if I'd had a chance."

My eyebrows almost disappeared into my hairline as I stared at him with disbelief.

"Shut the fuck up, Hawkins. It's so not fair to—"

My words were cut off when the younger Hawkins brother grabbed me by my upper arms, lifted me up and kissed me.

And kissed me.

And . . . hmm.

Slowly, we both pulled back, eyeing one another.

And then we both burst out laughing. I didn't go so far as to wipe my hand over my mouth. But it was close.

"That was like . . ." Frown lines appeared on his brow as he struggled to find the words.

"Like kissing your best friend?" I grinned at him, feeling more lighthearted than I had the entire trip.

He laughed, raking his fingers through his hair, then looking in the direction his brother had gone.

"Not quite. But even if it had been what we thought it would be, I think it's a bit too late." He smiled, but there was a hint of disappointment in it.

I too looked toward where Liam had gone. I couldn't deny it, so I simply nodded.

"You know, Liam's not . . . he's not like us, Callie." Ryder's eyes narrowed. "He's happiest when he's on the move. And you're in school. I know it's your choice, but I just . . . I don't want you to get hurt."

Cocking my head to the side, I stared up at my best friend. My heart swelled with love—just not the kind of love that I'd once thought it was.

"It is my decision," I agreed, a smile spreading slowly over my face.

But this time I wasn't going to analyze it to death, wasn't going to decide why it wouldn't work even before it had started.

Ryder must have seen the change on my face, because he shook his head, apparently resigned.

The side of his mouth curled up in a crooked half smile.

"Come on, I'll walk you up to your room." He offered me his arm, and all hints of awkwardness had fled by the time I took it. "I think you have a date."

Four

Callie

I LEFT MY door ajar as I waited for Liam, hurriedly running a comb through my snarled hair and removing the smeared traces of my lipstick.

Even with the bright color gone, when I looked at myself, the allure that I'd seen when I wore the mask was still there.

I felt . . . different. I thought of Madame Ysabeau's words . . .

If you are brave, you will obtain your heart's desire.

She hadn't been wrong. But it turned out that my heart's desire wasn't Ryder—it wasn't any man. It was the confidence to be exactly who and what I wanted to be.

And though I still had a long way to go to achieve that, I thought I'd taken a pretty damn big step tonight.

With a small smile turning up the corners of my lips,

I sat on the edge of the bed, eyes on the door. When Liam slid through the small crack I'd left open, his large frame casting a long shadow on the floor, my pulse began to beat double time.

I swallowed thickly as he shut the door with his heel, then prowled across the room toward me.

I stood as he approached. He stopped just out of reach, and I groaned with frustration.

"You and Ryder get things sorted?" Tucking his hands into his pockets, he rocked back on his heels, the movement making his shadow dance.

I didn't want to talk about Ryder. I wanted Liam to touch me.

Even though I'd only known him for a few hours, I knew when Liam asked a question, he expected an answer.

Swallowing against my dry throat, I nodded.

"Yes." I smiled wryly, though I wasn't sure how much of my expression he could see in the dim light. "Turns out I'm not as into him as I thought I was."

Liam made a noise of satisfaction, then reached for me. His hands moved down to cup the cheeks of my ass, to toy at the tender spot where the cleft between them began, and I couldn't hold back a slight moan.

"Lucky me." Lowering his head, Liam nipped at my ear. "You want this." I shivered. I couldn't pretend that I didn't know what he was referring to. "Say it." He nipped again, his teeth sinking into the tender flesh, and heat surged through me.

"I . . . I want this." My voice was hoarse and it was hard

to force the words out, but when Liam circled around to press against me from behind, when I suddenly had his hands sliding slickly over the sleek expanse of my torso, I was lost.

I tilted my head back in surrender as he leaned forward to sample the skin at the base of my throat, to run his tongue over the pulse that beat thickly beneath the sensitive skin. I did no more than inhale the scent of his hair, that smell so uniquely him, it set my skin ablaze.

"Say my name." God, I should have been turned off by his bossiness, but instead it made me hotter.

It told me that he wanted me to know it was him I was with. He expected me to remember that he was the one with his hands on me. Like he wanted to brand me, to make me his.

I loved it.

"*Liam.*"

Turning me, Liam slipped his hand beneath the hem of my top, then stroked upward with light, feathery touches until he found my nipple. The tender skin there became humped with gooseflesh as his fingers rotated, just ever so slightly, and I whimpered as the sensation rioted through me. Curving my arms backward, I clasped him around the neck, held on tight, and allowed my head to loll back against his shoulder and my eyes to drift close, the better to feel . . . well, everything.

He moved so quickly that I was startled when cool air bit at the flesh between my legs. He'd distracted me with the attention to my breasts and managed to pull my shorts down, where they pooled at my feet. His fingers were trailing lower and lower, deeper and deeper, sliding into my panties until they found the throbbing nub of my clit.

My hips jerked back, my ass pressing into the ridge of his erection. I ground back into him and he growled.

"Brat." Turning me again, he pushed me down on the bed, then lifted each of my legs in turn, hooking then over his arms.

Opening me. Leaving me vulnerable, despite the scrap of fabric that still covered me.

After placing a wet, full mouthed kiss just above my mound, a kiss that had me crying out loud, he caught the elastic at the side of my bikini briefs in his teeth and tugged, inching the minuscule amount of fabric down until my flesh was bare.

Oh my God. He'd just pulled my panties down with his *teeth*. Fuck, that was hot, and had I been capable of speech at the moment, I would have told him exactly how wet it made me. But my tongue had gone thick and dry in my mouth when I saw him undoing his pants with one hand, the harsh rasp of the zip muffled by the thick air. The heat of his naked hardness, of the skin that stuck to mine with the early dew of sexy sweat, had me squirming, anxious for more.

The squirming only helped him to cover the aching flesh of my cleft with full, rough swipes of his tongue. Over and over he stroked, his mouth teasing me while his hands urged his own pants down and off.

"Hold on." He shifted my weight from side to side, not letting go but managing to strip both of our shirts off. Sliding a hand beneath my back, he opened the clasp of my bra, pulled my bra down, and in one swift move twisted it so that my hands were wrapped in the lace, bound in front of me.

Without being able to hold onto him—to hold onto anything—I was at his mercy. He could do whatever he wanted with me.

It was the most exciting thing I'd ever experienced. How had I never known that what I really wanted was a bad boy?

"Please." I barely recognized my own voice, it was so full of heat, of need. I wanted him inside of me, and I wanted it now. Unable to wait any longer, I rocked my hips against his mouth, a move far more brazen than anything I'd ever done before.

He chuckled, the vibration playing over my heated skin.

"You want it?" God, why was his coarseness so exciting?

"You know damn well I do." I cursed when he pulled his hips back, breaking contact.

Bending over me, he sucked my lower lip into his mouth. I writhed on the bed, wanting more, more, more . . . more of whatever he would give me.

"Beg me." I felt his lips curve against my own, and if I hadn't been so distracted, I might have bitten him. But my entire being was consumed with one thought.

Cock in cunt. I needed it like I needed my next breath.

"Please." I wiggled on the sheets, reaching for him. Fisting my hands in his hair as best I could since they were still bound, I urged him closer, urged him to slide into my heat.

Instead of sliding his cock inside me, he inserted two fingers. I cried out when he pushed until his fist bumped against my labia, then used the pads of his fingers to rub inside of me like he was searching for something.

"Holy shit." My back arched when he brushed over a bundle of nerves that were nearly as sensitive as my clit, but in a different way. "Oh my God."

White heat overtook me as I squirmed against that ruthless touch. It was . . . uncomfortable. And made me feel like I needed to use the bathroom. But it felt so good too.

"No. I don't—I can't—" He barely had time to chuckle when a supernova exploded inside of me, so different from anything I'd ever felt before.

The heat in my body reached a fever pitch as the orgasm slammed through me, a slap in the face that had me reeling. When I would have collapsed, weak and wrecked, onto the floor, hiccupping with the aftershocks that quivered through my muscles, Liam instead slid his fingers out, turning me over so the rough fabric of the comforter scraped at the tender skin of my belly.

I heard the familiar crinkle of a foil wrapper. Then his weight pressed against me from behind, the head of his cock sliding through the crevice that divided my ass.

My cunt throbbed, desperate for what was about to come.

My body welcomed the familiar thrust of his cock easily as I flexed my bound fingers, desperate for something to hold onto. But there was nothing, nothing to cling to but him, as he began to rock back and forth, riding me hard, allowing the sweet friction to wash over me in waves.

The feel of him thrusting up behind me, inside me, had dark pleasure coiling again at the base of my belly. Eyes squeezed tightly shut, I allowed myself to simply be moved, to be guided through the most erotic scene that I had ever had the pleasure of taking part in.

"That's a good girl. Take it all." Despite his words, I felt like anything but a *good* girl.

And being bad sat so much more comfortably with me than being good ever had.

I felt his thighs tense behind me, telling me he was close. I was approaching the edge again too, the pleasure coiling tight and fast.

I whimpered when he suddenly withdrew. I heard his labored breathing, and then felt liquid heat stream onto my lower back, scalding the skin that was pulled tight.

Oh my God. Did he—had he just—

He'd marked me with his pleasure. And I loved it.

Reaching behind me, I cupped my fist over his and squeezed. Together we pumped the last moments of pleasure from his pulsing cock, letting them drip down onto me.

Before I could even catch my breath, his fingers found the now empty space between my legs and zeroed in unerringly on my clit. He pinched the hard nub of flesh, rubbing up and down each side, then pinched again. My arousal stuttered before slamming back into in an orgasm so fierce I was pretty sure I screamed, though it might have just been in my head.

Once my tremors subsided, I collapsed, sweaty and sticky, on the bedspread.

Like he was unable to support his own weight on sex-weakened legs, he fell onto the bed, collapsing beside me. I knew that if I opened my eyes all I would see was him, that he would demand my attention, if only to show me again how much he wanted me. So I kept my long lashes feathered down over my own eyes, hiding the emotions that lay there, emotions that even the most intense sex of my life couldn't dull.

Meeting Liam had been an awakening in so very many ways. And I wasn't yet ready to say good-bye.

On top of me, Liam shifted his weight. I moaned—I didn't want to break the contact yet.

Didn't want him to leave.

But then he was gathering me in his arms for the third time that day, lifting me as if I weighed nothing at all.

"Let's get you cleaned up." His voice was tender, and he pressed a kiss to the top of my head.

I blinked, startled.

Say what?

I was startled enough to be silent as he pulled something from the pocket of his jeans, then brought me to the bathroom. A guy like him—a guy that even his own brother had warned me about—shouldn't he be hitching up his pants and running off into the night?

Instead he was holding me tenderly, setting me down gently.

I'd wanted his body, had wondered at the strong connection pulling us together. But now ...

Now my heart trembled.

"Look at you," he whispered, turning me to face the mirror. "Look how gorgeous you are."

I hissed in a breath at the sight of my sex-touched skin in the mirror. Flushed a bright pink from the rasp of Liam's whiskers, among other things, it startled me to see how lax my limbs looked—loose and satisfied, as if I didn't have a care in the world.

I did, of course—I cared whether he left or stayed—but my body apparently didn't know that.

Liam apparently didn't either, for he appeared behind me in the mirror, his hands splayed against the skin of my naked waist. His skin was far darker than my own pale white, tanned from the elbows down, from hours of riding on his bike, I guessed.

Looking at us like that, a tangle of arms and legs and eyes and skin, made me want him all over again.

"Into the bath." Nudging me forward, he seated me on the closed lid of the toilet as he started the water. I didn't listen, remaining where I was so I could see him, could watch the ripples in his muscles as he bent to turn the handle on the large chrome pipe.

Water gushed out of the wide opening; a fine spray misting the skin of my breasts through a gap in the curtain. Carefully—so I didn't slip on the slick stone floor, I guessed—he lifted me, setting me into the slippery basin, the warm water pooling around my ankles. The heat against my well-used flesh caused my skin to prickle with a chill; the raised pattern soon melted away into the heat, leaving my skin smooth again.

Liam watched me greedily, lust evident in his eyes. His mouth turned up in a lopsided grin that was steaming up and fogging my mind more than the heat from the water.

Unannounced, he slid his deliciously naked body into the tub behind me, a wet slop spilling over the edge as his mass joined mine and displaced the liquid.

I stilled, unsure if I could become aroused yet again—it was so unlike me. But when Liam's hands, bearing a bar of lightly scented, hand-milled creamy white soap, began to knead at the tense muscles of my neck and back, I found myself acquiescing with a sigh, all my reservations over the unexpected intimacy of the moment melting away, into the liquid heat of the bath.

"Have to take care of my dirty girl." His words made me smile, and I closed my eyes, allowing him to pamper me, his gentle caresses and attentions feeling strangely right.

The lingering streaks of sweat rained down my torso, mixing with the soap and the wet, and his fingers seemed suddenly to be everywhere, rubbing away the salt and leaving behind flushed skin and heightened sensitivity. His long fingers fastened on the rosy peg of a nipple, rolling it between fingers until I gasped and arched my back, trying to force more flesh into his palm. Instead he slid a palm, slick with sweat, over the flat of my belly and down, where it burrowed through the channel lined with my curls and found the inflamed, well-used nub of my clit. When he began to work his finger over the bundle of nerves, I tried to maneuver myself onto his lap, onto his cock, where I intended to ride him hard and fast until orgasm blinded us both again and my mind went finally, blissfully blank.

"No."

I knew the tone well already. Bossy Liam was back. Whimpering both at the fact that I had been denied the fuck I so desperately wanted and at the certainty of pleasures to come, I allowed my limbs to become loose and limp, for Liam to arrange as he pleased.

I could get used to this—to being cherished. To being taken care of.

Getting used to it was a bad idea.

When he braced my wrists on the far edge of the steaming basin and urged me to shift my weight there, I felt a delicious thrill. My protest was halfhearted as he bent me fully at the waist, exposing the roundness of my ass.

Nerves shot through me when I felt the first flicker of his tongue, exploring the cleft that divided my behind. I stiffened—this was . . . dirty. I didn't know if I liked it.

I shook that thought right out of my head. I did like it, liked it a lot, I just knew that good girls weren't supposed to.

Well, I wasn't a good girl anymore.

Using his fingers, Liam separated the mounds of flesh, exposing the tiny hidden pucker that lay between to the cool air and the rising steam. Trying desperately to hold still, to not beg or pull away from the strange sensation,

I nevertheless found myself inching backward, trying to force the meeting of my flesh and Liam's mouth.

"Ever been touched here?" he asked, and I felt the warmth of his breath on my skin.

I shook my head frantically, unable to form words.

"Want to be?" He was giving me a choice—I could say no.

I didn't want to.

"Do it." My voice was a plea. "Please, Liam. Please."

When the touch finally came, I let out my breath on a sigh and felt a wave of pleasure dart down the line of my ass, all the way to my pussy, which was aching with need.

The need only became greater when he used his clever hands to toy with that entrance. Oh, this was foreign, and dirty, and *amazing*. Wetting his fingers on the slickness that seeped out of my heat, he slid first one questing digit into my waiting cunt, and then two, all the while using his tongue to lap at and press against my other, tighter entrance. When he crooked his fingers inside of me, and the rough pads again found the soft bump that resided high on my inner walls, I jerked, the instant, liquid orgasm that he pulled from me startling in its suddenness.

Before the trembling stopped, he rose to his knees, grabbed another condom from the bathroom counter and ripped it open. I realized that the condom was what he'd taken from his jeans as he covered his cock with the latex skin.

A finger replaced the hot rasp of his tongue, pushing hard enough against my pucker to break through the tight barrier. At the same time he settled the swollen tip of his immensely engorged cock at the mouth of my cunt and thrust, filling me so completely that it was almost painful. My muscles stretched and adjusted quickly enough, though, and soon I was immersed in pleasure, hanging on for dear life as his hips quickened, pressing my pelvis flat against the side of the tub and then retreating, again and again. And all the while his slowly rotating finger anchored me from above, driving me crazy. It all layered until I felt the crest nearing, felt myself careening toward the peak, and I heard the quickening of breath behind me that told me he was doing the same.

But instead of thrusting me, and himself, over that ledge into oblivion, he withdrew, his cock sliding out of me abruptly. The wild protest died on my lips when I was dragged backward and roughly turned, water splashing every which way.

The wicked grin he gave me as he filled me again made my pulse stutter, and I wrapped my legs around his waist.

Foreheads pressed together, his hands on my hips, he urged me to move. My skittering pulse stopped, then started again, my heart beating double time.

As pleasure again washed over me, I realized that Liam had managed to make me feel more for him in the few hours I'd known him that I'd ever felt for Ryder. It scared me, but I refused to think about it, choosing instead to focus on what I had here and now.

When he emptied himself into me, and our cries echoed out into the dim light of the cavernous tiled bathroom, my mind went blissfully blank and black, and not even the worry that he would leave afterward could intrude.

Liam

HOLY SHIT.

Carefully, I withdrew from the slick heat of Callie's sweet pussy. She whimpered a little, sighing when I pressed a kiss to the top of her head.

I climbed out of the bath, opened a folded towel, then gathered her in my arms, lifting her from the water. I carried her back to the bedroom, which was fully dark now, and pulled back the covers. Lying her down on her stomach, I felt my heart constricting strangely.

I'd known there was something special about this girl from the moment I set eyes on her at the party as she watched people do their intimate dance while pretending that she wasn't looking at all.

But her response to the things I'd asked of her— the sweet wonder in her eyes when I took care of her— combined with the fact that I already wanted her again . . .

No way in hell was I going to let her go.

"Liam?" Her voice was sleepy and sated as she propped herself up on her elbows and looked at me.

"Just relax. I'm not done taking care of you." Returning to the bathroom, I retrieved the hairbrush I'd seen earlier. Settling on the bed beside her, I began to stroke it through her damp hair.

At the first touch of bristles on her scalp, she jolted, wheeling around to stare at me with wide eyes.

"You're brushing my hair?" The incredulity in her voice had me raising an eyebrow at her.

"I could think of another way to use the brush, if you'd prefer." Lifting my arm, I brought the brush, bristle side down, onto the curve of her naked ass, just hard enough to get her attention.

Her mouth fell open, making her look adorable, but I didn't miss the way she arched into the touch, or the way she shuddered when the blow landed on her skin.

"Jesus," she muttered, but she didn't protest, which made me grin. Yes, no matter what the rest of the world thought, this was one kinky girl.

And I was going to keep her.

Returning the brush to her hair, I stroked it through the silky golden strands, keeping my rhythm slow and steady. When I felt all traces of tension seep from her body, satisfaction flooded me.

I liked taking care of a woman after we'd had sex, liked knowing I'd fulfilled all of her needs, even if I wasn't going to stay. But never before had I felt such an urge to bring one woman pleasure.

Placing the brush on the bedside table, I edged her over, then lay down beside her. She stiffened under my hand when I placed it on her hip.

I waited for her to relax again. She didn't.

"What are you thinking of?" Clasping her by her upper arm, I rolled her so she was on her back. Leaning over, I flipped the switch on the small bedside lamp.

She couldn't avoid me in the light, and the way she cast her eyes to the side told me that she was looking for a way around answering the question.

"Callie." Catching her chin in my hands, I turned her back to face me. Unease swam in the depths of those beautiful blue eyes.

"I don't want to tell you," she whispered. "I'll look like a needy idiot."

Bending, I pressed a soft kiss to her lips, then followed the path my lips had taken with a finger.

"After trusting me with your body the way you have tonight, don't you think you can trust me with your thoughts?"

She shook her head, pressing her lips together tightly. I narrowed my eyes, then reached for the hairbrush.

"I'll use this if I have to, Callie, but you're going to tell me what's bothering you." I enjoyed the way a healthy dose of trepidation mixed with lust spread over her face.

She scowled at me, huffed a sigh, tried to look away again. I continued to look down at her, tapping into the patience that got me through strips of never-ending highway on my bike.

Finally, she blurted it out. "Why are you still here?"

I felt as though she'd slapped me and it jolted me backward. "Do you want me to go?" Rubbing my hands over my eyes, I took in her body language.

She was still curling into me—her fingers were clenched in my arm.

No, she didn't want me to go.

She hesitated, and I ran the brush lightly over her ass, making her squeak and shift away.

"No. Of course not. I just . . . what is this? Is it just tonight? Is it just while we're here? I mean . . . I feel . . . there's this connection . . ." She shuddered out a breath, then propped herself up on one hand, bringing her face level to mine. "Everything inside of me is telling me to shut up and not ask questions. But I'm not going to be a good girl and not tell you what I want." She pinned me with that bright blue stare, and I felt my pulse pick up.

"What do you want, sweetheart?" Man, I could get lost in those eyes forever.

"I don't know, not entirely. But I do know that I want to see you again." Her mouth softened, and I couldn't help it—I bent to kiss her. "Is that possible?"

Relief washed through me. I'd been dumped before, but I'd never much cared. But this time—with this girl . . .

I could go find another girl. But I was pretty sure that no one else would ever be as good.

Grinning, I bent down and kissed her again, this time letting my tongue flick over her lips. She sighed and opened beneath me, giving in to my demand.

When I finally pulled back, her lips were swollen, her pupils dilated with arousal. The woman was insatiable.

My kind of girl.

"I was actually thinking that I should spend some more time with Ryder after this weekend is over." Turning the light back off, I snuggled down beside her, wrapping her in my arms.

No, I wasn't going to let this one go.

"Really?" Her voice was wary.

"Really," I agreed, my hand wandering to strum lazily over her nipple. "Since I haven't gotten much of a chance to see him here. I've been distracted."

She laughed lightly, then snuggled into me. "That's all I can ask." I knew what she was saying. Neither of us knew whether this would work for the long term, or what would happen tomorrow.

But we would both give it a chance. And that was enough for now.

About the Author

New York Times bestselling author LAUREN HAWKEYE is a writer, theatre enthusiast, knitting aficionado, and animal lover who lives in the shadows of the great Rocky Mountains of Alberta, Canada. She's published several novels and novellas with Harlequin and under the name Lauren Jameson with NAL.

Visit www.AuthorTracker.com for exclusive information on your favorite HarperCollins authors.

Ready for another *Fling*?

Unleash your kinky side with three tales of erotic romance in an exclusive Mediterranean sex resort during its infamous Fetish Week:

"Take Me" by Sara Fawkes
"Teach Me" by Cathryn Fox
"Tame Me" by Lauren Hawkeye

Keep reading for excerpts from
FLING: A BDSM EROTICA ANTHOLOGY
by bestselling authors Sara Fawkes, Cathryn Fox, and Lauren Hawkeye, available now from Avon Red Impulse wherever ebooks are sold.

TAKE ME

by Sara Fawkes

The minute sexy hotel manager Alexander Stavros spots shy, sweet Kate Swansea at the Mancusi resort, he can tell she's begging for release. This Dom is the perfect man to help her . . . if she's willing to let go of her inhibitions and enjoy the ride.

WHAT HAD SHE gotten herself into?

Kate stared at the scallops-and-shrimp pasta, whose description had made her mouth water only minutes before, but her brain wouldn't allow her to enjoy the sight or taste. Too many questions clamored for attention, and she didn't know the answers to any of them.

Why did I stay here, she wondered for the umpteenth time, giving a quick glance around the room. It all seemed so normal: hotel guests down in the five-star resort's dining room. Sure, the couple in the corner couldn't keep their hands off one another, and the woman two tables over was being fed by the man. But if you squinted, they looked like any other young lovers.

The problem was, Kate didn't know what to expect. The orientation she'd been required to attend, hosted by a Mistress Francesca, who introduced herself as a Domme, had been a real eye-opener as to what sorts of things she might see over the next week. Dressed in neck-to-toe red-and-black leather, Francesca had been more than a little intimidating herself.

"Our goal is to provide a safe environment for those whose tastes are anything but vanilla, where you can explore without any judgment or ridicule. There will be consensual activities that may involve nudity, but do not expect that simply because you are here, you will partici-pate. No means no, ask before you touch."

The Italian woman's accented voice echoed through Kate's head, and the sudden idea of being groped by a stranger killed what appetite she had left. "Can I please get a to-go box?" she asked when she flagged down a passing waiter.

A lot of her anxiety, she realized very quickly, had to do with her own inexperience with all things sexual. There hadn't been many encounters with boys before she met Ted; maybe some light making out and a few nights that didn't leave much of an impression. If she was honest, sex with Ted had never been all that intense, either, but she'd convinced herself that was how she liked it. Maybe that *was* how she liked it, though; perhaps she was the "vanilla" Mistress Francesca had described earlier.

How depressing. This is going to be a long week.

Kate gathered her paper container of leftovers, dug around for a tip, then headed for the lobby. The desire to get up to her room was first and foremost in her mind. The fact that her room was palatial, sporting every amenity she could think of, probably had a big part to do with it. When they'd entered her room for the week, she had to pinch herself twice before believing it was real. While it wasn't the Ritz, the presidential suite had two living rooms, a huge, four-poster bed with canopy, and a bathroom with mirrors taller than she was. It also had a panoramic display of the shoreline, the sight of which had taken her breath away. The floor-to-ceiling windows afforded little privacy but offered an absolutely breathtaking view at which she could stare for days and never grow tired.

Alexander had delivered her and her luggage to the room and graciously shown her around. He had kept it strictly professional, and a big part of Kate had been disappointed when he bowed and closed the double doors to the suite behind him. Hoping for anything more had been a silly fantasy, Kate knew, as the reality of someone that beautiful wanting her was wishful thinking. But if she had to dream, why not dream big?

Exiting the restaurant, Kate headed across the lobby to the hallway leading toward the elevators. Then she heard giggling coming from the outside-pool area. Kate stopped dead at the sound, riveted to the floor by the craziest temptation: to go see what was so funny.

It's not even my business, she admonished herself, clutching the container of food to her body. The warmth of the food through the paper was no distraction from the sound of amusement wafting in on the gentle ocean breeze. *All I want is to be left alone to lick my wounds in peace.*

But what if they were doing . . . *something*?

Myriad ideas flowed through Kate's mind about what could be happening, each thought more salacious than the last. The images going through her head surprised her, but most shocking was her body's reaction to the pictures her imagination produced. She swallowed, her stomach muscles clenching as her belly caught fire in response.

Another laugh, deeper and very male, then a squeal from the woman, and Kate's feet were moving of their own volition toward the sounds. The hall was empty, everyone either in their own rooms or elsewhere in the resort keeping themselves busy. The merriment was in a public place, Kate reasoned; she'd just peek to make sure nothing untoward was happening.

Riiiiiight.

Tiptoeing out the doors, careful not to be noticed, Kate made her way outside toward the sounds of laughter. A hint of twilight still played across the Mediterranean sky, but the lights surrounding the pool had been switched on in preparation for darkness. The cool ocean breeze cut through the remaining warmth of the day, sending a light shiver down Kate's back, but it didn't stop her progress. Drawn to the sounds like a moth to a flame, she rounded the corner and peeked through the pillars and ivy.

A large hot tub full of people, the foamy water lazily swirling around their bodies, sat next to the empty pool. Five different men sat around the edges, surrounding a topless blonde woman in the center. None of them made a move toward the woman as she slowly circled inside the pack. Slim body gliding through the water, the woman moved toward one of the men, her hands reaching under the water. Kate watched, fascinated, as the man's body jerked and he let out a truncated groan.

The woman released her hidden grip and moved to the next man, repeating the unseen gesture with similar results. The black man she was fondling reached out to grab her, but she danced away with a teasing laugh, moving on to her next target. This time, her eyes lit up at what she found beneath the surface, and she gave a saucy smile.

"Well now, aren't you a big boy," she purred, wrapping her arms around his neck and straddling his lap. When he put his hands on her hips, she didn't protest, lowering herself on him as their lips met in a searing kiss.

Kate's jaw dropped as she realized what was going on. The breath in her throat stuttered as the naked blonde woman gyrated her hips, then threw her head back, exposing her breasts. They looked too perfect to be real, but the man beneath her didn't seem to care; he buried his face between them before moving to lick and suck one small nipple.

Desire burned through Kate as she leaned forward

to get a better look. She had never watched porn before, never even had the inclination, so this voyeuristic tendency was new to her. Watching the blonde woman ride the man, listening to the wild cries, Kate could feel her nether regions clench in need. An answering ferocity grew within her, the likes of which Kate had never before experienced. Breathing grew difficult as an ache settled between her legs, the sensitive skin screaming to be touched.

"Would you like to join them?"

A startled cry choked in Kate's throat as she whirled around at the man's voice.

TEACH ME

by Cathryn Fox

There's nothing Luca Mancusi loves more than lingerie. So much so, he's made it his business. Fashion design intern Josie Pelletier is supposed to be negotiating a deal with him, but as talks heat up, he can't wait to teach her the ways of business . . . and BDSM.

"SINCE I'M THE one in charge here, I'll be the one asking the questions."

She shivered, almost violently, and visualized him taking charge of her pleasure, doing whatever he pleased to her.

"I asked a question, Josie, and I want a yes or a no," he said in a tone that clearly indicated his impatience with her. "Do you think it would hit the mark for a lover?"

Suddenly the word *lover* danced along her nerve endings. From his arrogant, take-charge attitude, to the unapologetic grin on his oh-so-sensuous mouth, and the smoldering heat in his gaze, Josie knew she'd better behave and answer his questions with a simple yes or no.

A man like him wouldn't tolerate anything else.

Which was why she lifted her chin high and responded with, "Like I said, until I take a lover, I can't say for certain." She met his glance, wishing he'd bend her over his desk and end this sweet torment once and for all. With her composure vanishing, she moved restlessly against Antonio's finger, encouraging him to plunge it in and out of her.

A bemused expression crossed Antonio's face. He stepped back, and she whimpered in protest when he withdrew his thick finger. "That wasn't a yes or no," Antonio warned her.

"Are you looking to be punished for your disobedience?" Luca asked as he rubbed his temple.

Instead of waiting for an answer, he flicked Antonio a glance, and before she knew it, Antonio had lifted her from her chair and guided her to the desk. In a swift move that had air rushing from her lungs, Antonio spun her around. Then he bent her over the table until her ass was exposed to the two men.

Luca came up behind her as Antonio held her down. The first sweet touch of his hand sliding over her backside had her panting for more, but before he disciplined her, he reached up and unleashed her hair, letting it fall over the desk. She closed her eyes in anticipation and waited for the first hard slap to come.

When it finally did, she gasped out loud, heat slamming into her and raising her passion to new heights. He slapped again, only this time harder, and her clit throbbed, begging for some of that attention. The third whack felt like fire on her skin, and she let out a low, shameless moan of pleasure.

"Are you ready to behave and get back to negotiations, Josie?" Luca asked as he stepped away from her.

"Yes, sir," she murmured.

With that, Antonio lifted her up and turned her until she was facing Luca, who'd moved behind one of the wingback chairs.

She didn't miss the dark, hungry way he was staring at her, and even though she loved the power he had over her, loved how hot it made her feel, for a moment she wondered what it would take for a man like him to lose a degree of that steely control.

"Do you think it would hit the mark for a lover?" he questioned without faltering, a clear indication that she was the only one in the room coming unglued.

Struggling to put on her best professional face, she exhaled slowly, and answered with, "I suppose I would have to take one before I could say for sure."

Luca swiftly crossed the room and pulled her to him. "Are you interested in taking a lover, Josie?"

In a deceptively calm voice, she answered with, "In the interest of our business negotiations, I believe it might be necessary. We've come so far, I wouldn't want to *blow* this deal now." She was being bad, she knew, but she couldn't seem to help herself. These two men were making her crazed, showing her a side of herself that she hadn't known existed until that moment.

Luca's nostrils flared at her use of the word *blow*, and it let her know he was not as unaffected as he'd like her to believe. His hands clenched as he leveled her with a stare. "And where do you think you'd find this lover?"

She glanced behind her to see Antonio, then shifted her focus back to Luca. For a brief time, she thought she saw a flash of possessiveness in his eyes before he blinked it away. "Well, it would take time for me to find someone, and like you said, time is money. It's a little unorthodox, but since you two are already here, it only makes good business sense . . ."

"Are you saying you want one of us to stand in for your lover?"

"No," she said, a slow tremor moving through her, her body so completely and utterly ready to let these men teach her about herself and take her beyond her wildest fantasies. "I'm saying I want both of you to stand in for my lover."

Antonio cupped her elbows and pulled her toward him. When her back flattened against his chest, he gripped her hips tight and pushed against her, his rock-hard cock pressing firmly against the small of her back.

She wiggled against him, and when he placed one hand over her tender ass, she wondered if he was going to take his turn spanking her.

"I believe the lingerie is having the desired effect on your business partner," she said, her voice coming out husky, sensual.

"Oh yeah, she's convinced me," Antonio confirmed before he ran his hands around her waist to cup her breasts.

Sexual energy arced between her and the powerful man studying her darkly. She let her glance drop to his crotch, and when she spotted his mounting desire, she said to Luca, "Now all I have to do is convince you."

"And how will you do that?" Luca asked.

She parted her legs. "By putting myself in your hands so you can test the clothes yourself."

"Get on your knees, Josie. Now."

TAME ME

by Lauren Hawkeye

CEO Marco Kennedy can't help being drawn to Ariel Monroe. When he follows the pop star abroad to the Mancusi resort, she agrees to a deal: he'll win her as a sub through pleasure . . . or he'll disappear from her life. Ariel's game . . . just as long as she doesn't lose her heart too.

"WHAT'S THAT?" Now that she'd agreed to his bargain, he couldn't detect any sense of false protest in her voice. Instead, she sounded curious, and with that curiosity came a hint of anticipation.

It was music to his ears.

"This is the beginning of pleasure for you." Straightening, he stripped off his suit jacket, loosened his tie, then unbuttoned the top three buttons of his starched shirt. He was gratified to see Ariel's stare dip to the skin that was exposed.

"We'll see about that." He couldn't help but grin at the challenge in her words. Though he was certain that she was a natural submissive, he appreciated that she wasn't meek and mild with it.

They could have a lot of fun together. As he studied the mutiny on her face, then the way her eyes dipped when he challenged her, he felt a constriction in his chest.

Could this connection between them be about more than just sex? The little minx affected him like no woman ever had before.

He shook his head to clear it. That was a worry for later. For a start, they would begin with this.

"I want you to strip," he said.

He swallowed his chuckle as her eyes narrowed at him. He could see the argument in her eyes, but after a long moment in which he calmly held her gaze, she shrugged, crossing her arms at the hem of her dress, then lifting it up and over her head.

She was naked beneath, and his cock surged painfully at the sight of her naked flesh.

"Ariel." Though her chin was tilted upwards with bravado, he saw the slight tremble through her limbs that told her she wasn't quite as immune to his scrutiny as she'd like him to believe.

She didn't need to worry. Her body was lush, a wonderland of curves and ivory skin. Her breasts were full and heavy, their nipples posy pink, and his mouth watered for a taste.

The small, neat triangle of golden hair at the juncture of her thighs glistened, telling him that she was already aroused.

"Beautiful." She likely wasn't even aware that she exhaled the breath she'd been holding as he gave her his verbal approval. Oh yes, this woman was submissive, and the fact that she already seemed to seek to please him told him that the connection he felt between them wasn't one-sided.

She started to step out of her shoes, bright red strappy sandals, but he shook his head, halting the movement.

"Leave the shoes on. And come here." She was a walking wet dream, rising naked out of the sexy red shoes, and his nerves began to hum with anticipation as she slowly made her way across the room to where he stood by the bed.

Touching her shoulders lightly, he pulled her close enough that he could feel the heat radiating from her body, could smell the vanilla of her body cream. His erection pulsed, and he winced inwardly. He needed to free his cock soon, before it became painful.

"Now, I believe I mentioned something about a spanking." Beneath his fingers, Ariel stiffened, then tried to step back, but he slid his hands down her shoulders and over her breasts, catching her nipples in his fingers, and she stilled as he expertly manipulated the rosy points.

"Like hell you're going to spank me." But the heat of

her words was lost in the moan as he lowered his head and grazed his teeth over one of her nipples.

"It's going to happen, Ariel." Taking advantage of her distraction, he seated himself on the bed, pulling her onto his lap at the same time. "And you're going to enjoy every minute of it."

She squeaked as he rolled her onto her stomach, her torso resting on the soft, cotton sheets of the bed. The sound was ridiculously cute, he thought as he emptied the heavy velvet bag one-handed, catching the metal spheres in his palm.

"Don't you dare." She squirmed on his lap, and Marco hissed in a breath as his cock strained against the fabric of his pants.

"Be a dear and undo my zipper for me, will you, baby?" She hissed and, looking up over her shoulder, bared her teeth at him. He grinned in response. "The more you protest, the longer the spanking will be."

He watched her blue eyes as they studied his face and saw the truth there. She pursed her lips together as she wiggled backwards, undoing the buckle of his belt, then the snap, then the zipper.

His cock took advantage of the freedom, surging out the top of his briefs. He sighed with relief, smoothing his hand over the curves of Ariel's ass as he admired its heart shape.

His hips bucked upwards involuntarily as he felt something hot and wet close over the tip.

"No," he said.

His nerves screamed as he gently removed Ariel's

siren lips from the head of his cock, groaning inwardly as her mouth released him with a wet, sucking sound. "This is about you."

"You seriously think I'm going to believe that?" Despite her sassy words, Ariel shivered beneath his hands as he stroked his fingers up and over her back, moving her back into the proper position for a spanking again. "This isn't going to do much for me."

He smirked, though she couldn't see it. Oh, she had no idea.